MW01195454

LOVE
AND
MASKS

A Novel

LOVE AND MASKS

A Novel

DAVID WINKLER

RARE BIRD
LOS ANGELES, CALIF.

RARE BIRD

THIS IS A GENUINE RARE BIRD BOOK

Rare Bird Books
6044 North Figueroa Street
Los Angeles, California 90042
rarebirdbooks.com

For more information, address:
Rare Bird Books Subsidiary Rights Department
6044 North Figueroa Street
Los Angeles, California 90042

Set in Minion Pro
Printed in the United States

10 9 8 7 6 5 4 3 2 1

Library of Congress Cataloging-in-Publication Data available upon request

1.

LIV DANCED WITH ABANDON.

Her silhouette pulsed electric blue in the nook she carved out to move unbothered: strategically positioned between a platformed go-go dancer and a stoic bouncer. It was almost midnight, and Liv was celebrating with her friends at High, a nightclub everybody who was anybody or anyone who wanted to be a somebody knew was the most exclusive spot in Hollywood.

Liv let the music and erotically-lit darkness rid her of any cogent thought or worry. Right now, the last thing Liv wanted to do was *think*—especially about *why* she was celebrating. A martini had also been immensely helpful in that regard. Not that Liv drank all that much. For the last few years, she couldn't afford to mix too much alcohol into the chemical cocktail that kept her breast cancer from returning.

Just be fuckin' happy to be alive, she insisted to herself as her body swayed effortlessly to the beat, her arms twisting in the air. Liv was glad she'd finally let Marie and Yasmina convince her to come to High, even if they'd left her to dance alone while they were pulled to a table crowded with men in Prada suits. Liv had no interest in assholes who made a competition of throwing black American Express cards at their bottle service waitresses.

And Liv never minded dancing by herself. Among her favorite memories was dancing alone on the dusty, neon-lit Playa at Burning Man. Liv liked to label herself a "happy introvert," even if her friends teased her for being a hermit. She liked her own company, she liked silence. She didn't need a man or dozens of friends to feel whole, even if it was sometimes frustrating to be basically celibate for three years. Disregarding a fling here and there that hardly amounted to more than heavy petting, of course.

To Liv, the only thing worse than being alone was *feeling alone* when she wasn't.

Tonight was Liv's first time at High and the place wasn't disappointing—the live tree in the middle of the dance floor that seemed to sprout up right from the concrete, the impeccably mixed DJ set, the throngs of beautiful people shouting over the bass to connect.

When Marie and Yasmina begged Liv to accompany them to High before, she had always objected to the obnoxious process required for admittance. At most clubs, women as beautiful as Liv breezed past doormen, but High required an online application: a forum to send in a short bio and a link to her Instagram. She'd been approved within an hour—all doors open when you have over a million followers regularly gawking at you in swimwear and lingerie.

That alone was a miracle, thanks to her decision almost two years back to have her breasts reconstructed during her mastectomy. Blue Shield had balked at that, explaining that it was safer to have reconstruction months after the mastectomy, but Liv had done her homework and knew that a top-notch Beverly Hills plastic surgeon could safely save her skin and nipple. It had cost most of her life savings, but the fact that people nowadays constantly asked if her breasts were "real" was testament to her self-advocation.

Liv didn't quite attain the rank of supermodel. She might have, had she grown taller than five-foot-six. But at thirty-one, she carved out a comfortable lifestyle as a model and influencer through hard work, networking, and a near-magical understanding of how to angle her limbs and torso for the camera. And even if Liv *had* been graced with height genes, modeling had never been Liv's chief ambition. Liv dreamed of singing since she could remember.

But that dream's demise and her pivot to influencing, was pushed from her mind tonight. She was on a cloud after yet another of her quarterly scans showed no signs that her cancer had returned. She wouldn't think about the toll cancer took on her life.

Tonight was a celebration.

DAMON GAUGED THE CROWD below with dread.

Am I being alarmist? he asked himself. Maybe he'd been consuming too much news lately. So what if today the World Health Organization declared the Coronavirus outbreak a pandemic? Nobody Damon knew was sick, and not a single one of his employees at the club had called off work. But two days ago, Italy had placed itself on a nationwide quarantine, the Dow Industrial Average plunged a couple thousand points, and the NBA, MLB, and NFL were suspending all games indefinitely. And really, it seemed that the only reason Covid had come to America's attention was because Tom Hanks and his wife recently tested positive for the virus.

That's America, he rankled. *If someone famous gets sick, there's a problem.*

But how much of one? From his office overlooking the dance floor behind blackened glass, the light of dozens of security monitors flickering shadows on his angular face, Damon couldn't see *anybody* worrying. Down there, it was a typical Wednesday night.

Damon wished he hadn't picked up that book at the airport several months ago. He couldn't remember the exact title—*The Coming Plague, The Next Plague*? He hadn't even finished the thing, having forgotten it on the plane, but what he could recall scared the shit out of him. The writer had predicted everything that was happening, and if the projections continued, everything would shut down for God knows how long. People could die by the millions.

"What's on your mind, man?" asked Jay, his manager, taking his eyes off the monitors he sat in front of. "You don't look happy."

Damon didn't want to scare anyone else. He could be wrong. After all, plenty of news pundits insisted that the virus was merely a flu, maybe like that bird which had fizzled out. Hell, even Asian countries who wore masks as a habit didn't seem to be overreacting or quarantining.

"Nothing," Damon said with a forced smile. "Hey, it's almost midnight, don't forget to shut down the drive. Just keep on the live feed."

"Of course."

Jay knew the deal: at midnight, the club lights dimmed, and Damon didn't allow taping. Sometimes things got *very* sexy in the booths. Damon charged male members a small fortune and in return assured privacy. He even required everyone who entered High to check their phones at the door. Few complained about the policy because it drew in movie stars, recording artists, and famous athletes—every breed of celebrity could cut loose without fear of ending up on TMZ.

And Damon was proud of the rule for another reason: people actually spoke to each other at High, in lieu of beaming for selfies one moment and sulking over lack of "likes" the next. Inside Damon's club, people *connected*.

The thought distracted Damon for a moment—some nagging cognitive dissonance he often tried to shake with good company and fine spirits. Even if people here were momentarily parted from their phones, could nights like these that Damon so often attended really be mistaken for solid human connection? At thirty-six, with women often comparing his likeness to Tom Cruise, he thought he might be married by now, more settled…

Well, if that plague book was right, it's moot, he contemplated.

Damon hated the idea of dying alone, even if he seldom let himself dwell on it for too long. He hated *being alone.* He knew that people thought he had it all, but for all his successes, the hollowness of the life he had made for himself was beginning to cast a pall over the glitz and glamor of the whole operation.

"THERE SHE IS!" Yasmina cried out as Liv arrived at the booth her friends had abandoned her for.

Yasmina stood to hug Liv, her tight black curls sticking to Liv's glistening cheek as they embraced. A fellow model of too many ethnicities to count who hailed from France, Yasmina had swiftly befriended Liv at one of her first photo shoots upon moving to Los Angeles. Yasmina had joined forces with Liv to walk off set together, following more than a few inappropriate remarks from the photographer's lecherous assistant. Soulful and sweet, a modern hippie who favored shrooms to alcohol; tonight she'd had a few too many cocktails and was wavering in her six-inch heels.

"These gentlemen invited us to sit with them!" shouted Marie, holding up a champagne flute and pointing out the three men in suits, sans tie. Curvy but not thick, and blonde—who knew what color her hair had been at birth—Marie wasn't a model but commanded plenty of male attention. And Liv couldn't understand how Marie was perpetually smiling, considering by day she was a harried ER nurse.

"We're just talking about crypto!" explained one of the men.

Liv couldn't help herself. "Of course you are!"

"Sit with us!" another demanded.

Liv knew sitting was a waste of time—her friends would table hop all night, getting twisted on champagne and teasing men until settling on someone hookup-worthy or going home complaining about the quality of men in "this town." Liv didn't judge her friends' antics, but if her body was her temple, she knew abusing it till two a.m. was an unhealthy prayer.

"I'm going girls," Liv said, tightening the vintage Chanel purse that had been hanging across her shoulders all night, "but this was sooo much fun!"

"Not yet!" whined Yasmina.

"We were supposed to go home *together*!" Marie added.

"I know, but you'll live," Liv chastened affectionately.

"We were just about to party…" added a Crypto Bro as he pulled out a silver bullet and indiscreetly poured lines of cocaine on the table.

Liv hated having to be polite to such an inebriated asshole. "Not for me, thanks. I'm going to the loo, then getting my phone."

"Ladies room!" called out Marie as she rose to her feet.

"We just ordered more Veuve…" complained a suit.

"We'll be right back," chirped Marie.

"Promise?"

"Absolutely!"

Liv looked to Yasmina, but she seemed content, accepting a rolled-up dollar bill from the suit. So Liv shook her head and put her arm through Marie's to lead her away.

"Fuckers could at least have the manners to stand," Liv grumbled.

Marie cracked up. "You are extremely antiquated."

"Maybe. But who needs men, anyway?"

"Um, me!"

DAMON SIPPED MINERAL WATER as he watched Jay turn off the monitors.

"Hold on," Damon interrupted, leaning in close to one of the monitors to study Yasmina, bent over the table seductively, the bill halfway up her nose. "Get security to table twelve."

Damon watched and frowned as Jay ordered as much into his headset. He knew perfectly well what happened in the bathrooms of his club and discreetly in the throng of the dance floor, but he couldn't afford the risk of having people pour it on his tables in the open. As he waited for security to appear in the frame, something else caught his attention. As Yasmina rose to dance with one of the men, another passed his hand suspiciously over two champagne flutes on the table.

"He's roofying them!"

Damon slammed his drink on the table and threw the office door open.

LIV AND MARIE RETURNED from the ladies' room just as Damon was pushing through the crowd to the suits' table.

"Hey…" Marie whispered to Liv. "That's Damon. He owns the club."

Damon's face showed calm wrath as he yanked the collar of the pill dropper. "Get the fuck out of my club!"

Pill Dropper rose defiantly. "What's your problem, man?"

"Nothing. You and your buddies just pay the bill and go, and I won't call the cops."

"You know who the fuck we are?" challenged the other suit.

Damon hazily recalled vetting the man and the word "father's billions" came to mind. "I don't give a shit how much money you have," he yelled. "Matter of fact, forget the bill. Your money's no good here."

"What's going on?" Marie asked with alarm.

Damon barely glanced her way. "This asshole slipped drugs in your drinks while you were in the bathroom."

"Bullshit," lied Pill Dropper. "And I'm not fucking leaving."

Jay and a bouncer were now coming up behind, but Damon didn't wait—he reared back and punched the man squarely in the jaw with his free hand. The man reeled, and suddenly his buddies were jumping in. Damon dodged fists as the bouncers took over, subduing the men and, after a struggle, binding zip ties to their wrists.

Liv felt the crowd, hungry for a spectacle, close in around them. Yasmina was laughing and Damon spun on her. "You need to go too."

"What? Why?"

"Because you're doing blow on the fucking table! All I need is to get closed down because you can't even party in the toilet stalls like every other idiot."

"Hey, don't pick on her because you're all spun up," Marie retorted.

"Fine." Damon waved at all three of the girls now. "You're all gone."

"Hold on," Liv objected, fighting to calm the situation. "Look, I really appreciate you letting us know these assholes spiked our drinks. That was amazing of you."

Damon blinked, adrenalin easing as the crypto trio was hauled off. "You're welcome. But I'm not losing my liquor license because of shit like this."

Liv nodded. "I understand."

Damon jutted his chin to a bouncer. "Get them their phones and call them Ubers—on the house. Make sure the guys don't leave till the cars are gone so they're not followed."

"But we were celebrating Olivia!" Yasmina couldn't help herself, clinging to Olivia for piteous effect.

Olivia shot her a look. "Yasmina. Leave now and we might be allowed back another night." She turned to Damon. "Right?"

Damon hesitated. He didn't need problematic women who couldn't take "no" for an answer harassing his staff, but they *had* nearly been drugged in his club. And, he had to admit he was caught somewhat off guard by this lithe woman soberly taking control of an escalating situation. Even the crowd was taking the cue and turning their attention away from the squabble.

"Absolutely," he answered.

Liv smiled at Damon. "Thank you. This was my first time here. And up until all of this, I was really enjoying it."

Damon finally got a good look at Liv. Sure, he noticed she had silken skin, naturally high-arched brows, and wide eyes that hovered somewhere between green and blue. But what impressed him was her graciousness. He was throwing her and her friends out, but she wasn't throwing a drunken fit.

"Olivia, is it? I'm Damon. Give me your phone ticket and my guys will make sure you all get home safe."

"Thank you," Olivia said as she fished out her phone check tag from her purse. "You're a decent human being."

Damon took it and handed it to a bouncer. "You got me on a good night."

"I got you?" she teasingly repeated.

He laughed at her wit. "Figure of speech."

"I know. Take care."

"You too."

The ladies started away, followed by a bouncer.

Olivia felt the urge to glance back over her shoulder to see if Damon was looking at her. *Don't do it, don't do it.*

So she did it.

And he was.

They shared a quick smile before the crowd crossed between them.

SETTLING BACK IN THE OFFICE, Damon sat beside Jay again, this time nursing a short glass of scotch to ease the hypervigilance he still felt.

He was pleased to see the people below had completely moved on from the skirmish. Damon opened High three years prior, and though it was an instant success, he still felt heavily protective of its reputation and his bottom dollar. Before High, Damon lived in Bali for a decade, starting as a surfing instructor and then promoting discos for tourists on the beach. By the time he was ready to return stateside, Damon had saved enough money to partner with a few silent investors and open High. His ample experience as a curator of the hottest parties propelled High into the success that helped him to pay cash for a phenomenal home in the Hollywood Hills. He'd also was invested his High profits in real estate and was slowly becoming what they called "on paper rich."

His secret, he'd once explained during a rare interview, was that his club was meant for people to "get high on life." The interviewer had burned Damon, leaving out the words "on life," so it was also his last interview. But he had to admit that even sordid press made the place more successful, to the point where he'd had to begin the online application process. People thought it was snobbish, but Damon had no choice. If he allowed just anybody in, his members wouldn't feel special.

Damon felt a buzzing in his pocket and took out his phone. Naturally, he allowed himself the privilege of a phone, though he followed the intent of the rule and never took pictures of guests.

He checked his messages—as always, there were too many to count. He tried to be a generous friend, but it annoyed him that those "friends" always seemed to want a last-minute table. He was acutely aware that not many of them would remain friends if he didn't have a nightclub where his buddies could meet the most beautiful women, or his female friends could find a rich husband.

He went to the club's Instagram page. The club followed zero people but had twenty thousand followers. Damon himself had no social media and only used this account to check profiles when people applied. He saw that it had been tagged in dozens of pictures. Damon scrolled through them to make sure no pictures from inside had slipped through the policy cracks—they hadn't. Then he blinked: High had been tagged in a picture by one OLIVIA "LIV" MATHERS.

Damon tapped the profile...

A million followers, he noted. *Impressive.*

And Liv's photos! *Jesus.* Seeing her in lingerie and bikinis reminded him he was a man.

He tapped on the story she'd tagged High in. It was a selfie of her and Marie, only slightly disheveled in the back of a car.

Somewhere special tonight, celebrating three years cancer-free! she captioned the story.

Damon's breath caught. *Celebrating three years cancer free?*

He suddenly felt like shit. This woman had come to celebrate something miraculous, and he'd kicked her out. Had he known this information, he certainly would have let her stay. He would have given her a private table and all the champagne she could drink. He'd have politely sat down and talked with her, gotten to know her.

He swallowed hard and returned his attention to his phone. Liv's next story popped up, clearly taken earlier in the day. Liv sat in a sterile gray chair, dressed in sweats, hair down and messy, while a blue-scrubbed Asian man pulled back a needle's plunger, filling it with blood. Hate needles, she'd written.

He was overcome with the desire to message her. He could invade her DMs, or even her email on her application. But what was he going to do? Write her and say, "Hey, I see you have cancer, sorry I kicked you out of my club!" And besides, Damon was proud of the fact that he'd never "slid" into a girl's direct messages. He'd never needed to—he met more women a night than most men do in a year. They slid into *his* inbox!

The story ended and Damon was once again faced with hundreds of pictures on Liv's profile. He felt a rush of shame, as if it were rude to take a second look at her in lingerie now that he knew she was a cancer survivor.

What a fucking night, he thought. *A girl with cancer, would-be date rapists... oh, and a fucking pandemic around the corner.*

Then Damon's thoughts were interrupted as his phone pinged with a message. The contact read ALYSSA.

My group is heading out. Should I go with them or...

Damon smiled at the "or."

I'm leaving, too. Come up to the office.

Already outside the door.

He pocketed the phone. "I'll see you tomorrow night, Jay."

Jay's face formed a knowing grin. "Who is she?"

Damon shrugged. "Not important."

"Man, I want your life."

"I'd rather be happily married like you."

Jacy chuckled as Damon turned and opened the door to find Alyssa, a soaring model with platinum blonde hair, standing expectantly.

"Hey, you," she purred.

Damon felt a stir in his loins if maybe not his soul. He wondered if he should go home alone, read a book, go to sleep before 4:00 a.m.? But the cavernous maw of his loneliness called to be fed.

It wasn't that he was a sex addict—he would eschew one-night stands in favor of a month or two with a woman where he did *try* to connect, but it only resulted in more heartbreak. Damon studied the beautiful, smiling creature waiting for him, and allowed himself to give in to the fantasy that maybe, with just one more fuck, she could be "the one."

He smiled back and said, "Hey, you."

"What a night," Marie slurred sleepily, resting her head on Liv's shoulder in the back of a black Mercedes with tinted windows. They'd dropped Yasmina off first; though she lived out of the way in Venice, Liv never let her girlfriends go home alone in an Uber when inebriated.

Liv didn't respond to Marie for a beat, her attention on her phone.

"Liv? What're you doing?" Marie prodded.

"Nothing—I posted something on Instagram. The account for High already watched it."

"So? They probably have a social media manager or something that keeps tabs on everything."

"Yeah, maybe…" Liv demurred.

Marie sat up straight, suddenly alert and sobered.

"Oh my God, Liv. Are you hoping it was Damon that watched it?"

Liv felt her face grow hot. "No! I mean, maybe. He was…interesting."

"Girl. Interesting doesn't even begin to cut it."

Liv shot a look at their driver in the rearview mirror. She assumed it was just an Uber Black that one of the bouncers called for them, but on the odd chance he worked for High, she elected caution.

"We're almost home," Liv whispered. "Let's wait."

"You're a fucking weirdo," Marie rested her head in Liv's lap. "But I love you."

The Mercedes completed its last turn up the winding road of Beachwood Canyon, passing the official designation where the neighborhood became North Hollywood, and came to a stop in front of Marie's house.

Although Marie's bungalow, purchased by her parents as an investment when housing prices were cheap following the '92 earthquake, would easily command two million dollars today, it was one of the smallest on the block, sandwiched between two puzzlingly dilapidated mansions. But because the home was small on its lot, it contained a modest guest house in the backyard—a studio apartment with an efficiency kitchen.

Liv considered finding the place when she'd moved to Los Angeles from Florida five years back a blessing, not just because it was so cute. How lucky that her landlord would also end up being her BFF.

"Right here, thanks," Marie said to the driver as it pulled to a stop, and they slid out.

Liv and Marie climbed the five steps to the front door, entered the living room and plopped on the couch for the evening debrief.

"Okay, wait," Marie said as she slipped off her heels. "What were we talking about?"

Liv held up her phone. "You said interesting doesn't begin to cut it. About Damon."

"Oh yeah!" Marie said groggily. "Well, he's got a bit of a reputation. I know a couple girls who have hooked up with him. Fell in puppy love, got excited about maybe getting to have a rich, handsome boyfriend, and then got dumped, *yada yada yada*," Marie waved her hand in the air for emphasis.

"Oh," Liv's heart sank a bit. "So you just mean he's a player?"

"Well, I don't know. He just seems to get around. But the *interesting* part is how little real information there is about him."

Liv raised an eyebrow. "What do you mean?"

"Okay, so like, guy's obviously loaded, right? And he runs the most successful nightclub in Los Angeles. And he's totally fine. So you think there'd be like, press on him, social media, *GQ*'s most eligible bachelor or whatever. But nothing. And he has these wild parties at this house in the hills but stays in his room all night like he was Leonardo in that *Gatsby* movie."

Marie paused thoughtfully before continuing, and Liv was surprised at her cogent train of thought through the champagne haze.

"Like. Look at my family," Marie continued. "If anyone wanted to know how a nurse my age owns a house on Laurel Canyon, all they'd have to do is Google my name, and they'd see my family is loaded. And then probably think I'm just some dumb trust fund baby. Which, like, I am a dumb trust fund baby, but I'm also a dumb trust fund baby who saves lives and shit."

Liv laughed at her friend's self-awareness. "Okay, okay. Boy's bad news. I won't give him a second thought."

"Good," Marie said. "Let's go to bed. But first, vitamins and water for everyone!"

Liv smiled at her best friend. Even if she was decidedly drunk tonight and *did* party quite hard when the opportunity was afforded to her, Marie was typically the mama bear of their friend group, doling out sage advice and love.

LIV CLOSED THE DOOR of her back house and looked around her room. Most of her friends, and especially Marie, kept their living spaces clean on the off chance they'd bring a man home at the end of the night, but Liv knew that she left the mess to ensure she wouldn't.

She collapsed on her bed and glanced at the window facing the rolling hills of the canyon, speckled with gorgeous homes she knew she could never afford. Taking up nearly the entire wall and encircled by smaller stained glass panes of green, blue, and red, the window was her favorite part of the apartment. At sunrise and even more at sunset, the panes created a near rainbow of colors. All of this made Liv feel like she lived in the early 1970s, a time of her favorite music and clothing. Although tonight she'd worn a tight black dress that one of her fashion labels had sent in exchange for a few tagged selfies, her closet was mainly filled with vintage wear that she loved to find in thrift stores.

Liv laid there, delaying the annoyance of having to wipe off her makeup. Despite Marie's warnings, she couldn't shake the thought of Damon. She so rarely found *anybody* interesting. Liv met both Marie and Yasmina not long before Christopher had broken her heart, and they both took any opportunity they could to tease her about her disinterest in men in the years since. *Maybe you're a raging lesbian and you just don't know it yet*, Yasmina had suggested more than once.

But it was all in good nature—Marie and Yasmina had more than proven their love for Liv. They'd been so supportive when Liv received her cancer diagnosis, even putting up with how Liv went MIA for months at a time, preferring to hide away like an injured animal. Her girls knew her well. They had her best interests at heart.

Liv buried her face in her pillow, the voice of reason and the voice of desire quibbling with each other in her head.

She sat up. She grabbed her phone.

She went to Instagram and typed High nightclub into the search bar.

She found High's profile, which was sparse, just blank spaces where pictures might usually be posted and a link to their website. Liv had already been to the site when she'd applied for entry, so she knew that was just a black page with instructions.

She switched to Google and typed in High nightclub owner Damon...Lautner. Google filled out his last name.

Then she stopped herself. Liv had always made it a habit not to Google men before she dated them. She wanted to get to know them in person. Hear their life stories from their mouths. And Marie had already told her she'd find nothing anyway, so why was she doing the deep dive?

Who am I, the nerdy schoolgirl staring at a yearbook quote from the popular boy?

She chastised herself as she put the phone away for the night. Even if it was technically morning.

THE CAVERNOUS BEDROOM WAS dark, lit only by lights twinkling through the window, a massive wall of glass seemingly without support. Beyond was a canyon overlooking all of Los Angeles.

Damon leaned over the edge of his bed, a massive thing fitted in crisp white sheets, and retrieved his crumpled T-shirt from the floor. He turned it right side out and pulled it over his head.

Fuck, that hurts, he sighed to himself as the T-shirt slid over the blemish on his otherwise handsome backside—a misshapen patch of pink in between his shoulder blades that still didn't quite match the tone of the rest of his back and a six-inch scar from his tailbone up.

"I've been meaning to ask you about that," Alyssa spoke gingerly, curled up beside him, hair mussed, idly scrolling through her phone as if to say she was interested, but not *too* interested.

Damon looked over his shoulder to study her. "Crashed a bike a few years ago. You hungry or anything?"

Alyssa shook her head and smiled politely.

Damon stifled a sigh and walked to his dresser to retrieve a blue glass hand pipe, its bowl already packed with a bit of weed. He retrieved his jeans from the floor and dug from their pocket a small yellow lighter. He lit the pipe and inhaled deeply.

"Is that for pain?" she asked.

He nodded and gestured the pipe at Alyssa. "You want?"

"No, thanks."

He sat the pipe back down on the dresser and crawled back into bed, planting a kiss on Alyssa's forehead.

"I'm gonna call a car," she said.

Damon leaned back against the headboard. "Really? I thought we could watch a movie or something. You could stay over if you want."

In truth, whatever fantasy Damon had briefly indulged in when he made the impulsive decision to leave High with Alyssa—that she might be *the one* if only they slept together just one more time—had been dissolved by once again finding a lack of connection in their sex. But even if this tryst wasn't going anywhere real, he really preferred not to spend the night alone with his own thoughts. And, his back hurt, or if it didn't quite *hurt* yet, he was sure it would soon. The distraction of some company—a warm body and a mindless movie—would have been welcome.

Alyssa stood up and began to gather her clothes. She turned to face him as she zipped up her dress. "I really do like your company, Damon. But let's be real. You're not the relationship type."

Damon squirmed a bit. He knew Alyssa was right. She might be a good-time-girl model, but she was keen enough to understand the situation. He knew he should just acknowledge the truth of her words, level with her, and part amicably. But he felt that familiar gnaw at his stomach—the panic of being left alone. He couldn't help himself.

"Yeah, maybe you're right. But if we just, I don't know, gave it a shot—I mean you've never even spent the night. Let me make you breakfast in the morning," he said, trying to keep his voice more casual than pleading.

But Alyssa narrowed her eyes. "Damon. I was trying to be nice but get real. I'm looking for a husband. You're fun, but I need someone ten years older and more stable. I'd be great second wife material. Pop out a child and be set for life."

Damon sighed and rubbed the back of his neck. He knew Alyssa's read was accurate, if annoyingly so. "Okay, let me at least call you a car—"

"Don't bother. I'm a big girl," she cut him off. Then, a bit more gently, "It was really nice getting to know you. I'm sure I'll see you around High at some point."

She leaned over the bed to kiss him on the cheek. Damon said nothing. Then she turned on her heel and walked out of his bedroom.

Damon heard her pad down his foyer in bare feet, knowing her heels were still clutched in one hand. Then he heard her close the front door, and the rattle of its frame seemed to echo through the cavernous mansion.

"Goddamnit," Damon murmured aloud. She'd left so fast he hadn't even had a chance to walk her out.

He knew he had embarrassed himself with that final plea. On some unconscious level, he knew that Alyssa would have been collateral damage in his constant need for company, the need to fill the void. After all, he'd tried many times over their dates to converse with her but found her uninterested in politics or current events. He'd mentioned the coming pandemic at one point as he'd driven them here to his home, and she'd looked at him like he was speaking Chinese.

Damon whipped open a drawer on his bedside table to retrieve a prescription bottle of Tylenol—six hundred milligrams each. He took three and hoped it would be enough to do the trick and not add any physical agony to the emotional turmoil he was already experiencing.

As he swallowed, a face formed in his thoughts.

Liv.

He found himself smiling. Besides her beauty, she intrigued him, and he wasn't sure why. Maybe it was her life experience? His own mother had died of cancer when he was a child, so there was *that*. And there was the way she'd handled the situation at the club.

Message her, idiot. So it's late. She'll see it in the morning.

He found his phone on the bedside table, glanced at the time. 3:40 a.m. He pulled up Liv's Instagram.

He tapped on the "Messages" icon on her profile.

Hey, Troublemaker, he typed out, It's Damon, from High obviously. Any chance I can take you to coffee tomorrow to apologize for bouncing you and your friends?

And then he hit "Send."

He groaned and massaged his temples. *Wow, Damon. You couldn't sound like any more of a fuckboy if you tried.*

2.

MORNING LIGHT SHOT RAYS of blue and red from the stained glass across Liv's bedroom as she read Damon's message with a mixture of giddiness and anxiety. She briefly wondered if someone were playing a trick on her—after all, was there really any way to know if it were actually Damon messaging from the club's account?

Liv wasn't sure how she would explain to Marie if she was meeting up with Damon after having promised she would let it go. And yet—what were the odds that she had fallen asleep agonizing over this stranger and woken up to a message supposedly from him? Surely, that was a bit of serendipity worth exploring.

It was only nearing 8:00 a.m., and Marie would surely still be asleep. Liv knew Marie had a twenty-four-hour shift the next day and would only emerge from her bedroom for sustenance before crawling back into bed. Liv could avoid having to answer questions.

She responded to the message, Hi, yeah, I think I deserve a coffee and maybe a scone, too, for that one. But how do I know this is Damon? This account is basically anonymous.

She was surprised when a response came almost immediately.

Call me, he wrote, followed by his number.

Suddenly, butterflies erupted in Liv's stomach, forcing her to pace the length of her studio and wring her hands. *Okay, okay, okay...*

Liv cleared her throat and uttered a quick vocal exercise, trying to shake the groggy morning from the sound of her voice. She called the number.

"Hey," Damon answered, making no effort to hide his own first-words-of-the-morning voice.

Liv's stomach flip-flopped at the gravel of his voice that made it easy to imagine him reclined in bed.

"Hi," Liv returned, and then laughed self-consciously.

"So...it's me, obviously. Coffee?"

Reason briefly took hold of Liv. "I mean, I've heard your voice for all of about five minutes. Can I really be sure it's you?"

Damon paused for a moment before returning gamely, "Well, I'm not sure where you live, but I was going to suggest Alfred Coffee if that's not too far from you. I haven't heard of many abductions taking place in broad daylight at Alfred in WeHo, so why don't you take a chance and come see? I'll leave now and sit on the patio so you can see me when you pull up. If you don't see me there, you can run."

Liv spoke before her brain could catch up. "Okay, I'm in North Hollywood, so I think I can make it there by…eleven thirty?"

"That's not too far for you?" Damon asked.

Liv held her phone to her ear with one shoulder as she began rummaging through her closet. "No…I can make it if I start getting ready now."

"Great," Damon said, and Liv was sure she could hear the smile in his voice. "I'll send you an Uber."

"What!" Liv squawked. "Don't be ridiculous. The Mercedes last night was enough. I know how to drive."

"Well, I won't fight you," Damon acquiesced. "I'll see you soon."

Liv hung up, froze for a beat, and then began the harried dash to ready herself.

DAMON IDLED A METAL chair on the patio of Alfred, a coffee shop made locally famous for no reason other than its great moniker and solid coffee.

Across from an empty chair at the small table, he made a sincere effort to appear nonchalant, but every few moments stole a glance up to see if Liv had yet turned the corner. Today was Saint Patrick's Day, so it was oddly festive with green ribbons and bows and young women carrying out green foamed lattes.

He spotted Liv walking up the street, and immediately the "cool" jig was up; he leapt from his seat and leaned over the patio's iron banister to greet her.

"Hey, troublemaker," he said as he gave her a quick hug over the rail.

"It's actually you," Liv laughed.

"Or maybe it's an elaborate disguise and this really is an abduction," Damon joked, then cringed at himself. "Come on in, let's hop in line. I haven't ordered yet."

Damon re-entered the coffee shop to meet Liv at the entrance, and they took their place as second in line.

"You first," Damon prompted as they arrived at the counter. "Whatever you want, obviously."

Liv bent slightly over the counter as to not compete with the voices of the busy shop. "Tall Americano with a splash of oat milk, please."

Damon did his damnedest not to admire the curve of her arched frame. He did, however, notice her outfit. Though she was every bit as gorgeous as he remembered her being in the dim light of High (and in the scantily clad images on her Instagram), her choice of garment was a far cry from the little black dress of the prior night or her bikini pictures. She wore waist-high pinstripe bellbottoms and a flowing beige blouse with a built-in neck scarf, looking more like a seventies babe than a bikini-model-influencer of 2020.

Realizing Liv and the barista were staring at *him*, he quickly rattled off, "Same."

"Do you always order an Americano?" Liv asked while Damon offered up his credit card.

"I'm unpredictable. Why do you ask?"

Liv pretended to be disappointed. "Would have been uncanny if we always got the same coffee."

Damon silently chastised himself for being honest and missing an opportunity for her to see him as having the same however small taste.

"Oh," said Liv. "And whatever *that* thing is," Liv added to the barista, pointing to a green flaky pastry in the baked goods window.

"Of course. For here?"

"Yup! Thank you so much," Liv said effusively.

"You wearing something green?" Damon asked Liv.

"What?"

"It's Saint Paddy's Day."

"Oh, that's right! As a matter of fact, I am."

Damon looked her over. "I don't see it."

"Just because you can't see it, doesn't mean it's not there."

He laughed. "True."

"And you?" she asked.

Damon thought a moment, then pulled out his wallet, and held up a green twenty-dollar bill. "There you go."

Liv laughed. "Fast thinking!"

Damon handed the barista the bill to pay. "Keep the change."

She handed them a number place card, and the two returned to the table Damon had left his sunglasses on.

"*So*, first of all," Liv said with mock indignation, "How have I already got the nickname of 'Troublemaker' when I was definitely the polar *opposite* of a troublemaker last night?"

Damon laughed. "You're right. I guess it doesn't make a ton of sense. I think I was just trying to be suave."

Liv arched an eyebrow at his candor. He certainly seemed more vulnerable and authentic than the bad boy that Marie had made him out to be. Either that, or he could put up one hell of a façade.

"Okay, to be fair, I guess I'm guilty by association. I'm really sorry about my friends. I promise they're not obnoxious—they were just cutting loose," she explained.

"No, I—" Damon paused, searching for the right words to not sound like a creep. "Listen, I mean, this is awkward, but I messaged you from the High account obviously, so of course I looked at your profile…"

"Sure, I would have looked at yours, too, if there was one to speak of," Liv quipped.

Damon laughed heartily, interrupted only by a barista who breezed past their table to set down two giant white mugs of coffee and collect their order placard.

"Yeah, I know, there's not a lot of me to stalk. But listen. I want to apologize for kicking you and your friends out when you were just trying to celebrate being cancer-free. Cancer is something I've been very close to in the past, and I was sorry to have learned about it—and I'm really sorry, and congratulations on your remission, and…shit."

Damon cursed himself at how flustered he sounded. He was typically a smooth social operator, but the presence of this woman seemed to completely disarm him of his typical competence.

But Liv was enjoying his struggle. She was even starting to wonder if Marie, typically an intuitive reader of personalities, was full of shit about Damon.

"It's okay, I appreciate the sentiment," she smiled. "And I'm sorry to hear that you know cancer well. It's honestly something I don't like to talk or think about too much. It's mostly in the past, anyway. I've had several cancer-free screens now. It's no big deal."

This surprised Damon. He thought of the story she had shared, needle in arm, showcasing her struggle to a million followers.

"Really?" he prodded. "You don't like to talk about it? I mean, I just thought…"

"Because of my Instagram? Yeah. I do post about it. But my online presence is very different from my real life."

"Of course. That's something I understand," Damon said earnestly. "But why broadcast something so personal to a million strangers if it's not something you talk about in real life?"

Damon had her there. But she did have an answer that was truthful—on the surface.

"I know what you mean. So obviously, I do make my living as an influencer. Typical," she rolled her eyes at herself, and Damon smiled at her self-awareness.

She went on, "So when I first started chemotherapy, started to lose my hair, the whole thing, I stopped posting for a little while. I started losing sponsors, which I sorely needed. I was getting emails about missed posting deadlines. Really stressful stuff while I was dealing with everything else. So I decided, to hell with it, I need to keep doing my job somehow. If I let the whole world see me half-naked, I might as well let them in on my struggles too."

"That sounds…really hard," Damon sympathized.

"I mean, it didn't feel great to feel so exposed online, but I'm glad I did it. Suddenly, I was getting a different kind of response—people messaging me who were going through the same struggles, sponsors who were more about wellness and self-help than just bikinis and lingerie…it was basically a good thing for my following in the end."

"Sounds like you ended up helping a lot of people."

Liv shrugged. "Yeah, you're right, and that does make me proud. But now that I'm in remission, my hair is back, and I can pose for normal photoshoots again, I'm pretty relieved to not have to share so much about my personal life anymore. I still post occasionally about the cancer to…I don't know, I guess, honor the people who started following me because of it, but I'm a pretty private person."

Liv grew suddenly self-conscious, having monologued much more than she would typically. Perhaps Damon's apparent nerves around her were putting her at ease.

But Damon nodded emphatically. "I'm private, too, so I get it."

Now Liv sat up straight, determined to uncover a piece of the mystery of Damon. "Okay, so, make *that* make sense," she demanded.

Damon sipped his latte and looked at her quizzically. "How do you mean?"

"Well, like I said last night, you've got this reputation…"

The word *reputation* stung Damon, and he felt himself clench in anticipation of whatever Liv was going to say next. "What do you mean by reputation?"

Liv laughed. "I'm sure it's not news to you. Marie—my friend—said you have these lavish parties, break a lot of hearts, you know...a bad boy."

"What's that quote? 'Whatever people think of me is none of my business,'" Damon deflected.

"Sure, and that's all fine and well. But if all that's true, and you're this notorious club-owning playboy, why aren't you on the cover of *GQ* or something?" Liv asked, quoting Marie.

"I'm a people person, that much is true," Damon spoke honestly. "But I find it best to fly under the radar. I'm loath to give interviews..."

Liv cut him off. "Oh yeah, like that *one* interview I read..."

Damon groaned. "God, that thing is going to haunt me for the rest of my life. That reporter did *not* quote what I said correctly. At all. What I actually said was—"

"Damon!" a feminine voice rang out from the street in front of the coffee shop.

Liv and Damon looked up in unison to see a girl with dirty blonde hair bounding down the street toward them, Tiffany-blue leash in hand and small white terrier in hot pursuit.

Damon laughed and called out, "Lindsey! You're up early. Didn't you close last night?"

Lindsey landed in front of them and removed an ear bud. Barely five feet tall, squat and curvy with a beautiful round face and a wide smile, she panted slightly as she spoke.

"I did close. But Coconut wouldn't let me sleep."

The small dog stuck her nose between the bars of the banister, and Liv leaned down in her seat to oblige the pup with a scratch.

"Too bad. Good to see you, though. Are you on tonight?" Damon asked casually.

"Uh-huh. But hey, I'm so sorry to like, interrupt your little daaate..." she glanced at Liv apologetically.

There was no malice in her phrasing of "little date"—her voice was sweet and honest, and she ended each phrase with an authentic Valley girl upspeak that made Liv feel unthreatened. This girl was clearly not one of Damon's alleged conquests.

"No problem," Damon sat back in his chair, the vulnerability that had been on display in Liv's presence giving way to his typical competence. "What's going on?"

"This is really awkward," Lindsey prefaced. "And I know this is like, probably, *totally* not the right place to ask this, but am I like, in trouble, or on probation, or *something*?"

Damon furrowed his brow. "No...not that I'm aware of. Why? Did something happen?"

Lindsey mopped a sweaty tendril from her forehead and bent down to pick up Coconut, who had begun to sniff an errant piece of scone on the ground.

"No, nothing happened, I don't think...but like, I haven't got my schedule for next week yet, and when I called Jay this morning to ask what was up, he said that *you* would let everyone know what's up. And I thought that was like, really bizarre, cause obviously you don't make the schedule, so I wondered if I was in trouble or something. I *did* serve those creeps at their table last night, but that was super early in the night, and they weren't like, drunk or anything..."

"Oh God, Lindsey, no. You're perfect," Damon interjected.

He leaned forward in his chair, his forearms resting on his thighs, fingers interlaced—confident, reassuring.

Liv couldn't help but enjoy a glimpse of the white knight she'd witnessed the night before, the one who landed a solid punch square in the jaw of one of the creeps Lindsey was referencing.

Damon went on. "Listen, there's just some things we need to sort out at the club for next week. Some nights are a bit up in the air. But nothing to worry about. You're fine, the club's fine, I just wanted to get involved in scheduling this week. You'll have your schedule by tomorrow night. You're good," he added for final measure.

Lindsey seemed confused. "But what about the quarantine?"

"Quarantine?" Liv asked.

"Yeah, Los Angeles just announced starting at nine tonight a complete lockdown of all businesses. We're not even supposed to leave our houses."

"Shit," Damon said as he pulled his phone out. On his screen was a citywide alert: "Los Angeles County announced curfew and lockdown..."

"Don't worry about tonight, Lindsey. Jay will contact everybody and cancel."

"Okay," she said. "I'm really sorry to have interrupted. I really couldn't help myself. I was really freaked!"

"Alright, Linds."

"Byeeeee," Lindsey called as she released Coconut back onto the ground and almost skipped away.

"One of my cocktail waitresses," Damon gestured apologetically after Lindsey as he sat up and turned his attention to Liv again.

"I figured," Liv said. "No problem. She was sweet."

"Yeah."

Damon put away his phone. "Well, since it might be a while before we get another chance to talk, might as well make the best of today..."

Liv nodded. "I hope it doesn't last long. But my roommate, Marie—one of the girls I was with at your club—she's a trauma nurse. She says they're already running out of beds in the hospital."

Damon nodded, trying to put the news out of his mind.

"That reminds me," he said, "I really admired how you handled last night. A lot of people would be hammered, or indignant about being thrown out...and you actually had *reason* to be indignant..."

Liv looked at the creases in his palm and briefly wished she could read them. She felt a twitch in her shoulder—the desire to reciprocate and take his hand—when a loud phone ring startled them both.

"Shit. Sorry," Damon reached into his pants pocket to silence the phone, but then registered the name on the screen.

"Shit," he said under his breath, almost aghast at the way the interruption.

"I'm so sorry, Liv," his eyes pleaded with hers for understanding. "This is so rude of me. I have to take this."

"It's okay..." Liv offered, feeling deflated herself, as Damon pressed the phone to his ear.

For the second time in minutes, Liv watched him furrow his brow. Her fingers absently fed her bites of the pastry, which kept her from looking like she was studying Damon.

"Mmm," is all he said to the caller on the other end of the line.

"Yeah," he said, a full minute of listening later.

"I was worried about that too. I'll meet you in thirty," he finished finally, and hung up the phone.

Damon looked at Liv with chagrin. "I'm so sorry, Liv," he said for the second time. "That was my main investor. If it wasn't an emergency, I wouldn't go, but it really is."

"Emergencies happen..." Liv said, but she was unable to conceal her disappointment.

"Truth is, I think we're going to have to close the club until this Covid thing clears up."

"Really?"

"I don't want to be all doom and gloom, but the truth is it's just a matter of time before everything shuts down and we're all wearing these…"

With that, Damon slid a white surgical mask from his pocket.

"Especially me," Liv answered. "I'm on a cocktail of drugs that keep me alive but kill my immune system. If I get a cold, it turns into pneumonia."

"I bet," Damon said with a shake of his head. "Anyway…"

Damon collected his book and stood up; Liv rose with him.

"Hey…" Damon said softly.

Liv looked at him.

He stepped toward her. "I'd really like to see you again."

"I would, too, if your *investor* permits," she allowed herself a bit of snark. It wasn't that she didn't believe him, but rather she couldn't let the first man to give her butterflies in five years get off of abandoning a date *that* easily.

"I promise," Damon leaned in. "If you give me a second chance, I'll never let an investor come between us again."

"I'll hold you to that," Liv said playfully.

He brushed her hair behind her shoulder to move in for a hug, only the second time they had touched since that quick moment at the shop entrance. Liv's breath caught for a moment with her head on his shoulder.

"Alright," she said as she pulled away,

He walked one way to his car, she the other to hers. And with that, Damon watched the second woman in twelve hours walk away from him. But this time, he felt…different. He actually *cared* about this one.

3.

"I'M SCARED TO DEATH," Liv admitted through one cough, then another, deeper one. She was lying on her bed in a T-shirt and sweats, her mother's sympathetic but ill-framed face staring back at her on FaceTime.

"I'm sure it's not Covid. You haven't even left the house since it began," replied Beth. Optimism was this fifty-eight-year-old's strong suit, even when a more grounded sense of reality might be more prudent. Widowed when Liv was six, Beth raised her daughter and kept food on the table by the skin of her teeth with a hodgepodge of working-class jobs (and a spending habit not always commensurate with her salary).

Beth drifted off Liv's screen—she was even less knowledgeable about technology than politics. All Liv could see now was the mosquito netting on the porch that defined the South Florida home she'd spent her first nineteen years in before going away to college.

"Mom, I can't see you." Liv couldn't disguise the frustration in her voice.

"Oh, these stupid rectangles. Sorry, I'll hold it this way."

Beth's forehead appeared on Liv's screen.

"Mom, you gotta move the camera b—" Liv's instruction was interrupted by a massive hacking cough that nearly sent her abdominals into spasms. She sat her own phone down to catch her breath.

"How would you have gotten Covid?" Liv heard her mother's voice through the speaker.

She picked her phone back up. "I'm not sure. I haven't left my apartment in three weeks. Marie strips down her PPE at the front door, and we're never in the same room together. I get my groceries delivered, and I wear a mask and gloves while I spray down the bags and boxes. I guess some germs could have lingered from Marie, but she's not sick…"

"Can you get tested?"

"My doctor says his office doesn't even have test kits yet. Marie's hospital has been testing people who come into the ER with respiratory problems, but there's none to spare, and she doesn't think I should risk going in. I can't believe how unprepared our country was for this thing."

"Well, I wouldn't worry so much. President Trump says it's no worse than a flu."

Liv wrinkled her nose with surprise. "*President Trump says*? Mom, the man's full of shit. Watch the news."

"Okay! Okay. Do you have a fever?" Beth changed the subject.

Liv sighed, too exhausted to interrogate further. "I don't think so."

"That's a good sign! See? Everything is going to be fine. You might even be making yourself sick with worry, doing all that extra stuff with the masks and the gloves and whatnot. What good are the masks anyway? You can still smell a fart through your underwear, can't you? So how would a little piece of fabric protect you from the China virus?"

Now Liv sat upright, alarm and disgust overriding her fatigue. "Seriously Mom, what the hell are you on about? You don't sound like you. Have you been watching Fox or something?"

"Relax, sweetie. I'm just saying. You gotta be able to see people smile! Not a lot of people are wearing masks around here."

Liv felt a pang in her heart. She had called her mother seeking comfort—but whatever *this* was made her feel even lonelier than she had before. Venom sprang from her mouth before she could stop it.

"Well, you had better hope that everyone gets on board, puts on their fucking masks, and does their best to stop this thing *soon*. Because I have no photoshoots right now. None. Nada. Zip. Just a few sponsorships for what little I can shoot by myself at home. And you know what that means for you?"

Beth was quiet.

"That means I won't be able to send your rent check soon if this goes on for much longer," Liv finished, already regretting the tirade she had unleashed on her mother. But she was stressed and didn't appreciate her mother not taking the situation she, and the world, was facing.

"Okay, honey," she relented quietly. "I just don't want you to worry yourself sick. Maybe you should come home for a little while? Maybe the isolation is getting to you."

Liv sighed, but her regret wasn't enough to make her apologize quite yet. Instead, she said, "Yeah, Mom. I'd like that. It's just not safe for me to take a plane right now. When it is, I will."

Liv hacked again.

"Okay, sweetie. Sounds like you should have some chamomile and get some rest," Beth said, the cheerfulness already returning to her voice.

That somehow annoyed Liv more, but she bit her tongue.

"Okay, Mom. Love you. Bye-bye."

"Bye, sweetheart."

Liv hung the call up quickly to spare her mother from having to hunt for the "End" button.

But Liv knew her mother was right about one thing: the isolation *was* getting to her. Even if Marie sometimes annoyed her by bursting through her door, Liv had come to miss it over several weeks of being unable to be in the same room with her. She could barely even speak on the phone with Yasmina, who had flown to France to be with her mother as soon as Los Angeles shut down. They tried to stay connected, but the ten-hour time difference made it nearly impossible.

Of course, Liv knew that many people were creating "social bubbles"— visiting with small groups of people that they trusted to keep each other safe. But to fight her breast cancer from returning, Liv took tamoxifen, an estrogen-moderating medication which also wreaked havoc on her immune system—she couldn't trust a "bubble." She had observed too many social media stories of friends in these supposed groups who had nonetheless come down with Covid. If one friend slipped, Liv could be looking at a death sentence: a trip to the ER, where she'd be put on ventilator, a device that only prolonged the inevitable. Marie always returned from work with harrowing stories of people on ventilators, who never lived long enough to have them removed, reports that she relayed over the phone from the other house.

Adding to Liv's anxiety was that her words to her mother about her income weren't just deployed to hurt Beth—Liv was already dipping deep into her savings account. Her saving grace was that she had always been a spendthrift, wary of becoming like her mother, who sometimes blew an entire week of diner tips on unnecessary clothes and jewelry.

As an influencer, Liv was gifted a lot of clothing, mainly casual yoga gear and sweats from companies like Alo. And, of course, she had drawers and drawers of lingerie and swimsuits, which, after posting, she was allowed to keep. But the companies only paid a couple hundred dollars for a post at most, chump change compared to her full professional photoshoots which commanded a couple thousand dollars at a time.

Liv rolled her eyes at the thought of her drawers and drawers of lingerie. *It's not like I have a man to wear them for.*

That, of course, made her think of Damon.

Liv's heart twinged a bit at the shit timing that occurred with the first man she had experienced an attraction to in years. After their encounter at Alfred, fraught with sexual tension, the consequences of the pandemic took hold swiftly. She and Damon texted a few times, but he'd seemed distracted; then she'd gotten sick. Liv couldn't even remember who'd texted who last.

She coughed as she looked at their text thread.

Hey Stranger, thinking about you.

Damon had. And she hadn't answered. That was over a week ago.

Now she felt sick and *guilty*.

She typed: I'm so sorry I ghosted you. Been sick. Might have covid.

Wouldn't blame him if he doesn't text back, Liv thought. *Maybe I'm one of those people who has to make do with being alone forever.*

Liv once hoped that she'd be married with kids by now while enjoying a successful singing career, but life had other plans. After graduating from Florida State at twenty-four with a degree in music composition, she'd moved to Los Angeles. It had been an ugly introduction, full of sleazy record producers trying to fuck her, and writing songs that she couldn't even get demos recorded for. But she held out hope, even meeting Christopher, who she thought was "The One."

And then, a small bump in her left breast was found while showering. At twenty-seven. Too young to have even attended a routine mammogram before—a colossal heap of terrible luck, landing Liv in the mere five percent of women diagnosed with breast cancer before the age of forty. A small lump in her throat grew to feel like a tennis ball as she thought of how Christopher had abandoned her during her fight to stay alive, and her eyes began to well over. She grabbed a tissue to wipe her face and blow her congested nose.

All her energy had to be redirected into the fight to stay alive, and her musical hopes withered along with her body. Chemo killed the cancer, but cancer killed her dreams. Emotionally drained after heartbreak from Christopher and the medical battle, Liv couldn't muster the enthusiasm to keep writing songs and subjecting herself to the music industry. All she could do was pour herself into her influencing brand. Modeling at least allowed her to travel and be somewhat creative in styling herself in the process of a shoot. And she was damn good at it. It gave her a sense of pride that kept her identity intact in the wake of all the tragedy.

And now, no influencing, no men.

But her reverie was interrupted by the sound of her phone ringing in her AirPods. She tapped one of the buds twice without bothering to look at her phone screen, assuming it was Beth. Mom often called moments after hanging up with one or two more annoying questions.

"What did you forget this time?" Liv sighed, her voice full of phlegm.

There was a pause. "Liv?" asked a male voice.

"Maybe. Who is this?" Liv began to dig through the sheets of her bed, trying to find her phone.

She found it just as he responded.

"It's Damon. Already deleted my number, huh?"

Liv's eyes vaulted with surprise. It was moments like these that made her believe in some of the spiritual woo-woo that many of her friends—particularly the Burning Man ones—subscribed to.

"Oh, hello!" she stumbled. "No, sorry, I didn't delete your number. I just answered on my AirPods without looking at the phone. It's, um, nice to hear from you!"

Liv tried to keep her breath even as her heart pounded.

On his side, Damon blinked as if he hadn't expected Liv to answer. "Um, how are you?"

Liv felt a cough coming up but pushed it back into her chest. "I'm okay. You?"

"You mean other than the fact that the world is falling apart? What's that saying? 'Other than that, how was the play, Mrs. Lincoln?'"

Liv's laugh mingled with a cough.

Damon's chuckle was shortened by worry. "Are you sick?"

Liv could hear the concern in his voice, and it felt good—it was the sort of sympathy she had been *hoping for* from her mother.

"Yeah, but I don't know if it's Covid. I haven't left the house in almost a month and have had zero visitors. Marie strips off her PPE at the front door and we're never in the same room together. How about you? How have you been holding up?"

"I'm healthy," Damon began. "But it's been rough. I was able to keep my employees on payroll for a month, but now the investors have insisted we furlough them. We're pretty sure it will be a year before we reopen."

"What makes you think it will last that long?" Liv's voice rose with alarm.

"Because that's what every epidemiologist that doesn't work for our president is yelling at the top of their lungs. This is just like the pandemic of 1918. That took *two* years for things to get back to normal."

"Wow, I'm so glad you called today," Liv teased, but the combination of the butterflies she felt, and her spiking economic anxiety made her feel queasy.

Damon laughed and Liv couldn't help but feel somewhat reassured by his low, masculine chortle.

"Listen, I can get you tested," Damon offered. "I have a concierge nurse service that will come to your house. They used to give IVs to people with hangovers, but now this is all they do."

"You can?" Liv said with surprise. She hadn't heard of anything like that, and the idea of putting her fear to rest sounded like manna from heaven. "How long does it take to get the results?"

"Twenty-four hours. They take your blood."

"How much does it cost?"

"A couple hundred, but don't worry, I'll pay for it."

"Why would you do that?"

"I'd like to help you out. I've been thinking of you, even though everything's been so chaotic. I'm sorry I sort of fell off."

Liv nodded. *Phew, he thinks he fell off.* "Yeah, I mean, I did too."

"I understand. Believe me, I'm taking this pandemic *very* seriously. I haven't left the house in weeks, either. I paid my maid six months' salary *not* to come to my house. And I've stocked up enough canned food and toilet paper to last through the apocalypse."

"So you're the one who's hoarding all the toilet paper!" Liv teased.

"Guilty as charged. If you need some of the good stuff, I'm your source," Damon said, then paused a moment.

Liv could feel the tension from the other end of the line: something left unsaid. She waited.

Damon drew a breath. "Seriously though, I was extremely disappointed to have cut our date short. But there's something I want to discuss with you. In person. I know that's difficult right now, but I'd like to see if we can make it work."

Liv was more than intrigued. Damon seemed sincere and direct. But they'd only met twice—what could he possibly want to discuss?

"It has to be in person?" she prodded.

"Let's put it this way. I think you'd be much more interested in what I have to propose if we met up first in person. Our third rendezvous."

Liv narrowed her eyes. "So mysterious. But how would we do that? I just told you—I haven't seen anyone in weeks; I have to be *extremely* careful."

Damon paused thoughtfully. "I have it all planned out: my nurse tests me after she sees you as soon as possible. Assuming we're healthy and you just have a run-of-the-mill cold, you come to my house when you're feeling better. We'll sit outside, very socially distant. Masked, of course."

Liv liked that he'd *planned it out*. She thought the rest aloud:

"Honestly, not much would make me comfortable going to a stranger's house alone for some mysterious offer. But I don't really have a backyard, and it's hard not to trust you after you acted like Superman at the club."

"So you'll come?"

Liv bit her bottom lip. *What's the option? Six months of isolation?* "Sure. Send me the nurse's info, and assuming the best, I'll come and meet you."

"Okay, sending the info. And I *am* paying for the test."

Liv heard tapping on the other end of the line. She would insist on paying her own way but knew that was a luxury she couldn't afford. "Thank you, Damon. Talk when we get our results?"

"Perfect."

Liv hung up and stood for a moment. *Did that really just happen?*

Then, a text came in: The nurse is named Allison. 3104632446.

Liv smiled as she typed, Are you always this kind? Or are you love bombing me like every other narcissist in LA?

LOL. If I was a narcissist would I admit to being one?

Good point, Liv admitted. But I'm warning you, I have a nose for weeding out players, fakes, and haters.

On my soul, I swear I'm different than every other man you've met.

We'll see... Liv typed with hope.

4.

Damon paced the empty dance floor of High. It was his third inspection of the establishment since it closed, but he slept fitfully at night with thoughts of flooding or an electrical fire with no one there to maintain the club.

He went through his mental checklist again. Ice machine? Drained, unplugged. Refrigerator? Empty, unplugged. Sound system? Unplugged. Roach and mouse traps set. Garnishes? Thrown away, not even an errant lemon twist kicked beneath a single booth.

But Damon knew that this repetitive inspection was a tool of procrastination to put off the phone call that he didn't want to make. He sighed deeply and began to ascend the winding staircase, carpeted in a deep red, to unlock and enter the security room. He sat down in the rolling chair that Jay typically occupied and massaged his temples. *Just do it*, he thought.

Damon pulled up Jay's number on his phone and hit "Call."

"Hey man, I was just thinking about you," Jay's deep voice answered almost immediately. Damon could hear the gleeful shriek of Jay's daughter in the background.

"Hey, Jay. How're you holding up?"

"Well, it's been good to spend so much time with Lyla. I think Sheila's about at her wit's end with daycare being closed, though. But we're doin' about as well as we can be. What's going on?"

Damon steadied himself. He prided himself on taking care of his employees, being a reliable and respectful boss in an industry full of less-than-desirable characters. He hated what he was about to do.

"Listen, Jay," he started. "I really wanted to keep you guys on payroll as long as possible…"

"Hey, man. Take a breath. I knew this was coming."

"Our accountant says we need to furlough everyone in two weeks if we're going to survive the length of this thing."

"Damon—I knew this was coming. There's those relief checks coming, there's unemployment, we're gonna be alright."

Damon's voice rose in frustration at the situation. "I know there's options—I just. Fuck, man. I know it's not as much as any of you were bringing in at the club."

"Damon, I'd much rather be able to come back to my job at High when this thing is all over than have the whole joint close forever. You do what you gotta—" Jay's sentence was interrupted by a peel of laughter from Lyla. "Lyla—no throwing balls in the house! We gotta go outside!"

Jay returned his attention to Damon's call: "I'm sorry man, I should probably go. Sheila's trying to take a nap. But like I said, no hard feelings here."

"Yeah, I should go too. I have a lot of calls to make. But wait, Jay?"

Damon made a snap decision.

"After those two weeks run out, you're all going to get an additional two months of payment. Not from the LLC. You all deserve it."

"Oh, you don't gotta do that, man…" Jay started, but his voice was a bit choked with emotion.

"I do, actually. I have to be able to sleep at night. Catch up soon, Jay."

"You're the man, Damon."

The two friends ended the call. Damon looked out the tinted window of the security room and at the dance floor below and wondered if everything he had built at High would come crashing down.

Damon knew that *he* would be okay—he had purchased his home outright, and had a diverse investment portfolio, that, even if the market suffered, would keep him afloat.

Still—although he did try to maintain professional distance at work for fear of being seen as untoward, his employees had become like a family to him. Damon had no siblings to speak of, his adopted parents were gone, his real family untraceable, so he took solace in caring for the people of High like they were his kin.

He put his head in his hands and thought of Jay, supporting his family on a single income. Or Shannon, his surly-but-efficient bartender. Or Lindsay. She was in a bad relationship that she couldn't quite shake free of and picked up more shifts than anyone else to stay away from home. He wondered what would become of her during quarantine.

His phone vibrated in his pocket. Taking it out made him smile, then he clicked on the speaker.

"Well?"

"I'm negative," Liv cheerfully reported.

"Hell yes!" Damon made no effort to hide his enthusiasm. He'd resisted the urge to contact her over the last thirty-six hours, even when he received the report from his concierge nurse that the appointment had been fulfilled. He didn't want Liv to feel pressured—negative or not.

"It was surreal," Liv reported. "The nurse came in a full hazmat suit and helmet. And I hate needles."

Damon laughed. He remembered that from the Instagram story but needed to claw back *some* of his cool persona after that schoolboy display of nerves at Alfred.

"And my cough is mostly gone today! Who knows what it was. I'm just so happy to not have Covid. I did probably make it worse by psyching myself out," Liv said.

"I'm a bit of a hypochondriac too," Damon answered. "I've gotten tested three times since this started, and I haven't even had symptoms."

"Okay, the suspense is killing me. Are you going to tell me why you called now?"

"In person."

Liv pretended to sigh. "Promise you're not going to lock me in a dungeon if I come meet you?"

"If I were going to kidnap you, I certainly wouldn't be above breaking a promise."

"Good point. Send me your address. I'll be there around four?"

Damon grinned. "I'll be waiting."

"But I'm warning you, I'm telling a very large male friend where I'm going, and if he doesn't get a call from me at an appointed time, he will bust down your door."

"If it would make you comfortable, we can push back our meeting, I'll get him tested, and he can come too."

"That would certainly put me at ease."

Damon sensed she was kidding but erred on the gentlemanly side. "Okay. Text me his contact."

"I was kidding. I don't have any large male friends. Come to think of it, I don't have any medium-sized male friends either."

He laughed. "Just wanted to err on the side of caution."

"Would you have really let me bring a friend?"

Damon shrugged. "If that's what you needed to feel safe."

"Well, the fact that you offered is a comfort. But I'm too intrigued to delay any more."

"Then you better get a move on. It's already two thirty."

"Practically out the door," Liv chirped.

BEYOND NERVOUS, Liv drove down the canyon west.

Everything about the situation was surreal—and not just the fact that she was making her way to Damon's house. First, it was rush hour on Wednesday, but the streets were virtually empty. Liv had seen videos of skateboarders cruising freely down the 101 but had yet to experience the eerie emptiness of the city for herself. She tried to keep track of any pedestrians she saw, but only clocked one in ten minutes.

She had the top down on her ionized baby blue 2008 convertible BMW, a thing now suffering with age and the particulars of the finicky make but chosen for style. As she passed a police cruiser driving the other way, she half expected him to spin around and pull her over. Curfew wasn't until nine that night, but Liv felt like she was stealing a little bit of happiness from a sick world.

She checked her makeup in the rearview mirror. When she'd dressed, she hadn't been sure how to present herself, something that Liv typically did not struggle with. And she wasn't sure what to make of the invite. Was this a date, or did he have some sort of business proposal? He'd certainly *seemed* more personal than professional. Liv sincerely doubted Damon was the sort of man to need an elaborate ruse to get women to come over, but she did wonder if whatever he had to "discuss" would be a whole lot of nothing. What could possibly warrant such mystery? Eventually, she'd settled on form-fitting high-waisted jeans and a vintage, silk, black and pink Prada top. An outfit versatile enough for whatever Damon had up his sleeve.

But now, nervous sweat began to soak the silk on her back, and she did *not* want to show up at Damon's door with a stained shirt. She leaned forward in her seat, letting the air dry her back as her GPS took her up Benedict Canyon in Beverly Hills.

"You have arrived at your destination," her phone announced as she slowed in front of a soft contemporary façade.

Modern but not impersonal, the home took up two lots and seemed to hover out and over the canyon point. The stucco was a glass-shaded gray held up by beams she couldn't spot.

Liv smiled. And she wasn't easily impressed, having attended parties at the homes of some of the wealthiest Angelenos.

Liv realized she was idling, then continued up the driveway lined by impeccably maintained hedges. She noted that there wasn't a gate and assumed there must be cameras watching—this jewel of a house had to have some sort of security. She wondered if Damon was watching her ogle the home.

As soon as she parked, the tall front doors of the house opened, and Damon stepped out.

"Hi there!" Liv waved, unable to conceal an ear-to-ear grin.

Damon looked particularly casual and quarantine-appropriate in gray sweatpants, an unironed white T-shirt and no shoes.

Liv felt a wave of self-consciousness about her own outfit. Then again, *always dress as if you have somewhere better to be.*

And even though Damon looked every bit as handsome in his comfy clothes as he did in his suit at High, Liv knew she didn't have the same luxury of comfort. A woman of her age and of her profession in Los Angeles had to pull out all the stops, all the time. She couldn't just go to the gym, she had to look hot in the gym. She had to dress up just to get groceries, for God's sake. Even that photo Damon had admired of her having her bloodwork done was carefully curated; a look that a man might perceive as "no makeup," a trained eye would recognize as a minimum of tinted moisturizer, a smear of blush, and mascara. And that "messy" hair in the photo? Dry-shampooed, oiled, and brushed.

"Welcome!" Damon called out. "I gotta say, I heard you before I saw you. Very cool car, though."

"Thanks," Liv said as she closed its door and patted the hood affectionately. "She, uh, needs some work…"

"Don't we all," Damon said as they made their way to the front door. He paused at the threshold. "Oh, sorry. If you'd rather go straight to the backyard, we can go around the side gate…"

"I think a quick little tour is in order…" Liv said, trying not to sound too eager.

"After you," Damon returned.

"Okay, let me just get this out of the way," Liv said as they entered the foyer, "this house is un-fucking-believable."

"Thank you!" Damon smiled but seemed uncomfortable; he hoped she wouldn't be too impressed by his money. "I'd been eyeing the lot for a while, and as soon as things were comfortable enough at High, I snagged it and started to work on it. But it's really too big for me, so I'm sure I'll sell it once the pandemic eases."

"I really love interior design," Liv said. "We lived in tract homes and mobile homes growing up, so I waste hours fantasy shopping for houses I'll never afford."

Damon blinked, unsure of how to respond to this glimpse into Liv's childhood. But he responded practically: "You never know. I bought and sold dozens of houses, each one just a little bigger than the one before, before I got to this level. And real estate's a great business. Look at my nightclub, closed for who knows how long. But people always buy houses. Especially in Los Angeles. Doesn't matter what the economy."

"Yeah…" Liv demurred, wondering what Damon would think if he knew how deeply she was dipping into her savings account and that she had to pay her mother's rent.

"Where's your place again?" Damon asked. "North Hollywood?"

"Yeah, up Laurel Canyon," Liv said, glad for the change in subject. "I live in Marie's back house; her parents bought the spot in the 90s. It's tiny, but if I squint, I can just make out the 'W' in the Hollywood sign."

She laughed at herself, glad as Damon joined in. "Just the 'W,' huh?" he teased.

Liv smiled. "I bet your view is better?"

"See for yourself?" Damon said, gesturing for her to walk ahead of him.

Liv paused a beat. "Okay, but don't forget my friend is standing by if he doesn't hear from me soon. Although I notice you don't have a gate, so I think I can flee without jumping a wall."

"That you can," Damon played along.

"But seriously," Liv said. "This house is a work of art. I'd think you'd want to keep it safe."

"It's safe enough, trust me. More alarms than a firehouse. And the lack of wall is purposeful. What's the point of building something beautiful if you hide it behind a wall?"

"Did you design it yourself?"

"I designed, built, and decorated it myself. Just had an architect for the plans. Even did some of the drywall and painting. Just to learn."

"A Renaissance man!"

"I don't know about that…" Damon's voice trailed off with humility as he watched Liv make her way through the living room.

She stared up unabashedly at the cavernous ceilings and ran her hand along the back of one of the giant sectional couches. She took it all in—the coffee tables dotted with Taschen books and walls of expensive art. Liv loved art, and in one glance recognized a Hockney, a Warhol, *and* a Banksy. It briefly occurred to her that they could just be prints, but each she passed was signed and numbered.

Finally, she was drawn to the forty-foot-high windows and pressed her forehead against one of them, taking in the skyline below.

"I'm sorry," she finally burst out, hoping she didn't sound like a gushing teenager. "But you have the most amazing taste. The house is beautiful but still warm, like a home."

"Thank you. Not bad for a spec house, huh?"

"You plan to sell *this*," Liv added. "I mean, I'm sure if you planned to flip it, you have a lot invested. But where do you go from here?!"

"Well, it's really too much for a single man," he said. "Sort of obnoxious, if you think about it."

"Maybe," Liv said. "Except for when you fill it with people from all those wild parties I've heard about."

Damon's neck grew a bit hot. "Yeah, well. Clearly not having many of *those* lately."

They arrived at the kitchen, complete with stainless steel double ovens, a warming drawer, and a nearly industrial fridge—designed for a chef of a far higher caliber than Liv.

"I could do some serious damage in this kitchen…" she said anyway. Liv's mother had passed on her love of cooking, but Liv rarely entertained. "Do you cook?"

"Nothing either of us would enjoy eating."

"You mind?" Liv asked, taking hold of the fridge door.

"Not at all."

"I once heard you can tell everything about a man by what he keeps in his fridge…"

Liv opened the polished double wide doors and looked surprised. She'd been to enough bachelors' kitchens to know that she'd probably find it littered with days-old Postmates containers, but Damon's fridge was filled and organized with fresh vegetables, fruit, and shelves lined with organic milk and juice bottles.

"So healthy," she muttered.

"I'm trying," Damon admitted. "Normally I order Postmates and pizza. I get home so late in the normal world. I'm just stocking up these days. I can, you know, *assemble* food, but not really cook."

"Oh, that's right. You're not only the reason for the toilet paper shortage, you're the reason I got about a *quarter* of the groceries I ordered yesterday!" Liv said playfully.

Damon laughed sheepishly.

Then Liv noticed a head-high glass wine fridge filled with bottles and pointed. "What about those? Just for show too? Or are you an alcoholic?" Her tone was still light.

He smiled while shaking his head. "Not my vice. But I do collect. You have to know your stuff when you're in my industry…"

"I love a good red at the end of the day. And white. And rosé."

"I've got it all for you, don't worry. You can take a look and pick out a bottle after the tour."

Liv smiled at the words *all for you.*

"Do you like to work out?" Damon asked as they moved on from the kitchen.

"Sure. I mean, I have to anyway, career and all, but I definitely have been very invested in my health since the C word. I start getting antsy if I go too many days without. And I gotta say, following YouTube yoga videos in my room has *not* been cutting it."

"Follow me."

Liv glanced toward the windows and that view. She caught a glimpse of water—a pool sparkling in the late afternoon light—and was eager to veer toward it, but dutifully went with Damon down a hallway.

There are so many doors, Liv marveled. She felt the urge to peer inside each one and discover what mysteries Damon kept.

He opened one door for her. "I personally hate working out, but a new house has to have a gym these days, so I went to town…"

Liv followed him into the gym and guffawed. It was huge, with every piece of equipment imaginable, even a Pilates reformer. One wall was mirrored from floor to ceiling with a ballet bar attached.

"What *don't* you have in this house?" Liv said in wonder. "A screening room? A recording studio?"

"Both, actually," Damon answered, trying not to sound boastful.

Liv perked up. "You have a recording studio?"

"A small one. I figured it would be a great selling tool in this town. I'll show it to you later."

"But you're not a musician?"

"No. I play guitar, but badly. What about you?"

"I can sing a little."

"Hm. What's a little?"

"Well, it's a long story, but that's why I came to Los Angeles."

"Really? But you gave it up?"

"Like I said, another time?"

Liv avoided Damon's eyes for the first time since they'd met. "I'm sorry, I didn't mean to pry."

Liv smiled to reassure him. "The question's not the problem. Hey, I really want to see your backyard. I'm a sucker for a good view. And we should probably, you know, stick to our original plan at some point."

Damon nodded. "Of course."

"Open," Damon said aloud as they approached a set of glass doors that slid aside, disappearing into the walls.

"Okay, that's ridiculous," Liv laughed as they stepped outside and walked along a pathway that cut right through the middle of a hundred-foot infinity pool. At the edge of the pool was a seating area, with a daybed that could comfortably fit six people, surrounding a firepit.

"Look at that..." Liv said in wonder as she stopped to take in the view of the city. To her left she could see the downtown Los Angeles skyscrapers—to her right, what seemed like the entirety of the Pacific Ocean. It was a clear day, and she could see all the way to Catalina Island.

"Yeah, this view is what sold me on building here," Damon said.

Liv fell silent and listened closely. With the city on lockdown, the air was unusually quiet, free of its ceaseless traffic noises. And she could actually hear birds chirping sweetly through the canyon that surrounded the house. She wondered if that, too, was a product of the pandemic, or if their coos always echoed through the hills over the noise pollution.

"You've built a paradise here, Damon."

Damon smiled—he liked how she'd said his name. Maybe she'd done so before in the last ten minutes, but he couldn't recall, and he wanted her to say it again.

Liv turned to face the house. She could see the second story had terraces and glass walls—bedrooms that faced this view, she presumed. She was dying to go up and see them, but certainly wasn't going to invite herself, particularly when she was the one who insisted they come outside. It also occurred to her that the fact that Damon wasn't in a hurry to show her a bedroom was a sign he was a gentleman. But her curiosity was growing, and she couldn't contain it any longer.

"Okay, so if you've brought me up here to sell me the house, I'm buying. Except I don't have twelve million dollars lying around. I'll need a month or two," she quipped.

Damon laughed. "Sit, please."

She sat on the day bed, and Damon remembered the bottle he promised her—a small distraction to stave off the possibility of rejection. "Hey, how about that glass of wine?"

"Thank you, but you don't have to go inside.'"

"You're right, I don't. I'll send you home with one of the collector bottles. But for now…"

Damon touched a cabinet built into the base of the firepit, revealing a hidden drawer replete with a wine fridge and glasses.

"Red, white, or rosé?"

"In the afternoon? Rosé."

Liv leaned back, resting on her hands behind her as Damon opened a bottle of rosé and poured two glasses.

He handed her a glass and she held it up to toast. "To?"

Damon considered a moment. "To us all getting through this damn pandemic with our sanity intact."

"Amen."

Liv sipped and then placed the glass down. "I have to tell you, coming up here already feels like a vacation. I've wanted to take a trip to Florida—that's where my mom is. But, like I said, a weak immune system with the drugs I take to keep the cancer at bay…it's just not even remotely a possibility right now."

"Well, at least you look healthy, that's for sure," Damon remarked, barely concealing his admiration.

Liv laughed graciously. "Yeah, I mean, I do my best. You said something about cancer being close to you in some way last time we met?"

Damon stiffened a little with the mention of that. He didn't like to talk about his family. But he *had* brought it up. Something inside him wanted to share—but not too much.

"Yes, my mother and father both. My mother when I was thirteen, and then my father when I was twenty. Throat and prostate. They were older. I was adopted…" Damon trailed off. "But I didn't bring you here to bore you with my family history."

"No, I'm genuinely interested. My father died when I was young too. Six. But that was a car accident. So, I know what it's like—kind of. Except the adopted part…" Now it was Liv's turn to fumble for words.

Damon sipped at his glass. "I'll save the details for another day. Hopefully. Now, down to brass tacks."

"Right. You said you had…a proposal?"

Damon nodded and set his glass down. He steeled himself and leaned forward so his elbows were on his knees—the same posture he took while listening to Lindsey's rambling monologue—all business. "It's going to sound a little strange, I think," he prefaced.

Liv laughed. "I read *and* saw *Fifty Shades*. If you have a basement filled with BDSM toys, it's not my thing, but I won't be offended."

Damon shook his head. "I thought of building one into the house as like, a novelty, a selling tool, but no, it's not my thing either."

"Okay…so…"

Damon smiled. He'd gone over how to tell Liv what he was thinking for days, but now that she was here and his chemical attraction to her was like a current in the air, he couldn't stop it from jolting him.

"I think this pandemic is going to make the next six months to a year very difficult. You know the club has been closed for weeks, so this house is going to be my sanctuary. And yeah, it's paradise, but the idea of spending the next year alone in here is really fucking daunting. And I know you're in a similar position."

Liv stared incredulously. She *thought* she knew where he was going with all of this, but she couldn't believe it.

Damon observed the shock on her face and dropped his attempt at composure.

"Listen, Liv… I've said it before, but I deeply regret the way this pandemic drove a wedge into our getting to know each other. I've been thinking about it for weeks if I'm being honest," he looked down and blushed.

Liv felt the urge to save him from his bashfulness with her own honesty. "I've been thinking about it for weeks too," she said guilelessly.

Damon grinned, spurred to go on. "So, here's what I'm thinking. And promise me you'll hear me out before you call me crazy."

"Can I *think* you're crazy?"

"Of course. I can't control what you think."

"Just don't say it?"

"Right."

"You have my word." Liv pretended to zip her mouth closed.

Damon laughed and said, "I need a roommate."

Liv squinted. His words confirmed what she thought he was going to say once he began, but she was still aghast. "You want *me* to be your roommate?"

Damon's nerves returned as quickly as they had been assuaged, and he spoke quickly, desperate to be understood—and not be thought of as a creep. "Let me explain. I've built this adult playground. But thanks to this damn pandemic, I have nobody to play in it with. And with every rational expert saying it's going to be at least a year before we get a vaccine and things return to normal, it feels like a jail. So, I thought, why don't I invite you to move in with me? I have a guest room—more like a suite, actually—upstairs. If you have a dog or a cat they can come, too. You can use the house like it's yours—the gym, the pool, the kitchen… and you'll be safe here. It's isolated, we can order whatever you need…"

Damon trailed off, starting to feel like a car salesman.

Liv looked at him askance. "Okay, but why me? I'm sure you have plenty of female friends who would love to live here with you. Come to think of it, you could probably have two women live with you!"

She didn't mean to sound dismissive of their connection, but Liv was enough at peace with being alone that she had to pry.

Damon laughed. "I could. But I'm not interested in having two women stay in my rooms. I'm interested in getting to know *you*."

"So you want *more* than just a roommate?"

Damon smiled. "Look, it would be dishonest of me to say I don't hope we might be more than roommates. But the truth of it is that I'd be okay if we remained friends. I'd never pressure you in any way. I just really want a friend to ride out the pandemic with."

Liv smiled as she looked at his beautiful house, his yard, the view… "Damon, this is great offer. I was just telling you I've been going stir crazy in my place…and living here would be like living in a hotel."

Damon waited. "I sense a 'but' coming."

"But moving in with you when we've only met twice…?"

"Crazy," they both said through laughter.

Damon stopped first. "Look, what better way to get to know each other than by full immersion? You'll find that I'm a complete gentleman, and you can always move out at any time…I just know that in the past month, I've never felt so lonely in my life, and I have to do something…crazy…before I lose my sanity."

"I'm getting pretty bored of myself," she said, secretly cursing herself. *Why can't I say I'm lonely? Lonely as hell.* "Most of my friends are creating these bubbles of four or five people, but I can't risk that, and I can't even be in the same room with Marie…"

"We could be a bubble of two," Damon offered. "Nothing is more important than your health."

Liv smiled but found it challenging to believe that a man this handsome, this devilishly charming, was this thoughtful. She felt anxiety well up—an anxiety she often felt when engaging with anyone new—romantic or professional.

"Damon, I'll be honest. I have a little issue with commitment. It scares the hell out of me."

"And you're feeling it now?"

She nodded.

"Well, guess what?" Damon said in a whisper. "That makes two of us."

Liv's nerves broke with a laugh. "You don't seem afraid of commitment, asking a stranger to move into his house."

"I do. I'm just hiding it really well. But somehow when I talk to you, I feel okay with it."

She smiled. "Feels good just to admit it."

"Right. So why don't give it a try?"

Liv inhaled and exhaled audibly. "Would you mind if I went home and thought about it?"

Damon brightened, happy that she would even consider as much. "Of course! Take as much time as you need."

She eyed him. "Unless you're interviewing other women?"

Damon's belly shook from laughter.

"What?!" Liv said. "I can't be the only woman you've considered for the position."

"It's not like I'm interviewing maids here," Damon playfully defended himself. "Yes, you're the first and only woman I've thought of inviting. And if you say no, I'll probably move to Bali, where I can be alone and surf to my heart's content."

"Why Bali?"

"Because the waves suck in Malibu. It's crowded and cold. And Bali is heaven on earth."

Liv nodded thoughtfully. "Just give me a few days before you start packing."

"Deal."

Realizing she had nothing else to say, Liv got to her feet.

Damon stood beside her. "One other thing?"

"Yeah?"

"I don't know your financial situation, but if it helps, I'd be glad to provide you with some kind of allowance. Since you won't be able to work for a while…"

Liv's head reared back. "You'd *pay* me to move in with you?"

"Sort of an allowance. So, when the pandemic is over, you'd be able to get back on your feet without worrying."

Liv felt her heart fall. Part of her understood Damon was being kind. But she couldn't help but find herself offended. Though Liv tried not to be judgmental about other girls' choices, she'd never been like those Los Angeles MAWs (model/actress/whatever) who became "Sugar Babies." Liv didn't take moral issue with it, but her pride was such that she'd rather live in a cheap studio and eat ramen than drive a Mercedes paid for by a man.

Her silence told Damon he might have made a mistake. "I'm sorry, I didn't mean to come off like Richard Gere in *Pretty Woman*. I'm not offering to pay you for sex."

"That's okay, I understand," Liv answered, but really wasn't sure she did. Although it might seem that Damon was too handsome to ever have to pay a woman for sex, Liv had run into enough emotionally stunted men in Los Angeles that had hookers on speed dial.

But seeing his discomfort, she decided to give him the benefit of the doubt… for now. But she made a mental note: *if* she came back, which wasn't a given, she'd ask him where this offer to give her an allowance came from. What wound led a man to think he needed to buy a woman's companionship?

"I appreciate the offer, I do," she went on. "But I'm not one of those girls."

Damon felt a bead of sweat form under his hair. "I really didn't… You think I'm an asshole now, don't you?"

"Either that or too kind. Not sure yet."

He laughed. "And you'll still think about roommating?"

"What a telling phrase. Room-mating."

"I didn't mean we'd be mating."

She smiled and shrugged. "I guess I'm the one with the dirty mind."

Liv held out a hand and Damon shook it.

"I'll call you," she said.

"I won't wax my surfboard yet," he answered.

DAMON CURSED HIMSELF as he stood in his driveway watching Liv's convertible disappear down the canyon.

Fucked that up, he ruminated. Things had been going so well until the last few minutes. He'd seen Liv's attraction to him. He could tell she would genuinely consider his offer, even if she ultimately chose to decline. But he had ruined it. She left so quickly he didn't even have the opportunity to give her the promised wine bottle.

Damon wasn't even sure *why* he'd offered her an allowance. He hadn't planned it, that's for sure. And he'd never given a woman a dime for sex. Maybe it was some fear that Nina's constant financial demands had pummeled into him? That if he didn't give a woman money, she was bound to leave?

Or perhaps he'd just summed up the situation wrong. He'd assumed at Liv's age, her modeling career was already struggling before the pandemic, and if he could make her life easier, he'd be proud to. But perhaps she was doing very well, and his offer was an insult to her career. And now he'd have to wait for her to call him—*if* she called him—and hope that offer didn't dissuade her from the idea of moving in.

And after today, Damon *wanted* Liv to move in with him more than ever. If this woman moved into his house, he knew he would fall for her.

The only question was *how hard*?

5.

LIV PACED THE LENGTH of her backhouse excitedly, waiting for Marie to get home and initiate their routine FaceTime call. She had texted Yasmina to make sure she could join at 8:00 a.m. her time in Paris; she needed all hands on deck for this one.

She knew she heard the front door of the main house open and close but tried to be patient and give respect to Marie's arduous sanitation routine. Finally, the familiar ring of FaceTime sounded from her screen, and Liv answered it excitedly.

There were dark circles under Marie's eyes, but she smiled at her friend, ever eager to support. "Hey," Marie said. "Let's patch in Yasmina before you tell us what the *hell* this gossip could possibly be."

Yasmina was added to the call, sitting on a pillow before a wooden coffee table with a small mug in both hands. "Good morning, you American swine," she said in her thickest French accent. The girls all giggled but Marie interrupted first. "Okay, let's get this show on the road. I want to drink wine and watch trash TV and turn my brain off."

Liv relayed the story of her day as concisely as she could, interrupted occasionally by squeals of delight from Yasmina and some chastising remarks from Marie: "You didn't even tell me where you were going! What if he was a serial killer? We would never even find your body!"

Yasmina was too impressed to offer any ribbing. She reiterated that Damon's house was famous, and slightly *infamous*. It showed how rarely Liv partied that she didn't know that Damon often hosted massive ragers before her friends had clued her in. Liv sometimes wondered if she'd have gotten farther in life if she socialized more, but she hated going to record label parties or film premieres. Most of her friends spent many weekends in Vegas, but she'd only gone once, and that was one time too many.

"You have to goooo," Yasmina whined. "That house is *sick*. It's something you'll regret forever if you don't."

"It's just so hard to believe. We've only met twice," Liv said. "The guy must be a player."

"Well, that's a given. But we're all in lockdown, so what do you have to lose? Certainly not your virginity."

Liv loved Yasmina's brazenness. But Marie had been silent, her brow furrowed thoughtfully.

"Liv…" she finally interjected. "I don't want to be, you know, an alarmist here. I really don't think he's something sinister, like a serial killer or whatever. But I do think… I don't know, it doesn't pass the smell test. It sounds like a guy who really can't stand to be alone, and I think it's weird he doesn't have any friends or family to invite instead of a woman he's met twice."

Liv felt her feet return to the ground. "Yeah, I mean, it has occurred to me…"

"I just think you should guard your heart. I'm not saying for sure don't do it. I'm just saying, think," Marie finished.

"Uggggggggh, you are *such* a buzzkill," Yasmina retorted.

"I mean, my whole day has been a buzzkill. And the one before that, and before that, and before that," Marie shot back.

"Okay, okay, Marie's right," Liv interjected. "What happens if I move in with him, and after a few weeks I just don't like him? Or we don't have anything in common and nothing to talk about? Or he decides he can't stand me?"

"It's impossible not to fall in love with you," Yasmina said.

"Ha! But won't it be awkward?"

"Probably very. But you can just move out."

"I do agree with Yaz there," Marie said. "If you go and decide it's a mistake, don't feel obligated to stay just because he's blessed you with the gift of his wealth. Just leave."

The three were quiet for a moment before Yasmina spoke, this time with conviction instead of girlish excitement. "You know what I think? I don't think you're afraid it will be awkward. I think you're afraid it *won't* be awkward, and you'll never want to leave."

"What?!"

"Mmm," Marie said thoughtfully. "Another point for Yasmina. You haven't even had a fling since before you got sick."

"That's not true!"

"Name one. And make out sessions don't count when you're thirty."

Liv thought but couldn't come up with a name. She'd dated guys for a week here or there, but she never really gave any of them a chance. And she knew why. So did Yasmina and Marie.

Marie went on. "Liv, it's been three years since Chris. Yes, he turned out to be the ultimate narcissist. But it's time you opened that massive heart of yours again."

Liv clenched her jaw shut. She abhorred talking about Christopher. She rarely allowed herself to even think about him. But she knew the girls were right.

They'd been together for two years when she got her diagnosis. *What kind of man breaks up with a woman two weeks into her first chemotherapy?* He'd claimed the stress was too much for him, but Liv was sure it was the first sign of her hair falling out that really turned him off.

Yasmina saw Liv look away to hide a tear-wipe. "Aw, honey, I'm sorry."

"Damn Covid. I wish I could just go out for a drink with Damon and get to know him. Like normal humans."

"There is no normal right now," Marie said.

"Let's think about the situation. A ridiculously handsome and successful man has asked you to move in with him. So, you barely know him. It's like God saw you sitting home alone and miserable and decided to throw you a bone. Now you can either take a risk, or you can spend the next four months or a year or whatever binging on Netflix. Alone. God, if I didn't have my mom and sister annoying me, I'd go crazy."

"I already am," Liv admitted. "But I don't know. I need to think about this more."

"Yes. Think about it," Marie agreed.

"Well, don't think on it too long. For all you know, he's got another girl lined up to ask if you refuse him," Yasmina quipped.

"He swore he didn't!"

"He's a man, Liv. If he doesn't now, he will soon."

Liv laughed, and then a thought came to her. "Maybe I'll make him an offer of my own…"

DAMON WAS VACUUMING THE marble kitchen floor when he noticed his phone blink on the counter.

For a moment, he wasn't sure if he even wanted to see who needed him. Damon liked his new routine of cleaning the house by himself. The home was over five thousand square feet, but the mechanical action satisfied an itch in his brain that only manual labor could resolve. It helped that he didn't make much of a mess—he wasn't exactly anal and didn't even grumble at drunken guests who spilled wine on his white couches. But then, he also hardly cooked, so apart from taking Postmates containers to the trash, dusting and doing laundry, vacuuming was the most time-consuming duty of being his own maid.

But that hesitation lasted all of two seconds when he glanced and saw Liv's name on the screen.

Damon suddenly felt like a teenager. Not only was Liv calling, but she was FaceTiming, which seemed like a good sign. *People rarely FaceTime you with bad news.*

"Hey!" Damon said as Liv's face appeared.

"Is that a vacuum I see?" she asked.

"This…" Damon said, pulling the thing up. "Is not just a vacuum. It's a Dyson!"

Liv laughed at his commercial voice. "That's a big house. Have you thought of getting a Roomba?"

"Yeah, those robots never work. Always get caught on rug edges."

"You know far too much about housecleaning products."

"Sad but true."

Liv grinned at their banter. "Sorry it's taken me so long to get back to you!" she said.

"Too long? It's been less than twenty-four hours!" Damon sat in a kitchen chair and rested his chin on the Dyson's handle.

"Well, I didn't want to leave you hanging. I don't get this whole Gen Z thing of ghosting and leaving people 'on read.'"

"So rude."

"*So* rude."

Damon rocked the handle back and forth in anticipation. "How was your night?"

"Oh, thrilling. I watched the first few episodes of *Tiger King*."

"So did I! I'm hooked."

"These people are absolutely nuts! But it's like crack. Not that I've ever tried crack, of course."

Damon snickered. "Neither have I, for the record."

"Come on, I'm sure you've tried every drug in the book, with all those parties I hear you throw up there."

"My wild days are behind me," Damon said. "Everything's on the up and up around here."

"Better be. I don't get invited to move in with men every day, you know."

"Well, for the record, I've only ever asked one woman to move in with me, and that was because we were getting married."

"Another long story for another time?" Liv guessed.

"Exactly."

A pregnant pause passed between them, and Liv broke into a wide smile watching Damon squirm.

"Okay, the curiosity is killing me," he finally said. "What did you decide?"

"Let me just start by saying how honored I am that you want to share your home with me," Liv began, grimacing at herself. *Too formal?*

"You're welcome. I hope you understand I gave it a lot of thought too. This wasn't just some spur of the moment thing. And honestly, if we hadn't got along so well again yesterday, I might have never actually gone through with asking you."

"Ha! You would have just played it off?"

"Mmhm. Let you think I was just a big old weirdo," Damon smiled winningly.

Liv appreciated the honesty. "We have been hitting it off, haven't we?"

"Yeah. I got the sense that we'd never run out of things to talk about."

"To that end—let's talk about something."

Damon cocked his head to the side. "Why do I get the feeling we're about to negotiate?"

Liv crossed her arms in mock weightiness. "Because we are."

"How's this?" Damon asked. "Whatever you want, I say yes."

"No! That's too easy."

Damon shrugged and crossed his arms back. "Okay, give me your best shot."

"Okay, here's what I'm thinking: I know that people agree to be roommates after knowing each other even less than you and I have. They meet on Craigslist for God's sake. But the difference is, we're obviously not talking about *just* being roomies, you know what I mean?"

"The whole room *mating* thing."

"Exactly. The stakes are much higher. So in my opinion, moving in with you so fast is a little, well, impulsive. And that's just not me. I'm a woman who thinks things through. I make pros and cons lists about what I'm going to wear to dinner!"

Damon laughed. "I hate lists."

"See? We don't even know each other. So here's my counter: I move in for a weekend."

"Just a weekend?" Damon's face fell.

"At *least* a weekend. Then on Monday, we sit down and discuss it again. And if we've had a nice weekend, I'll move in for month. If the month works, and the pandemic is still raging, I'm all in."

"That's very wise."

"I thought so!"

"I happily accept your counter," Damon said. "See, I told you I'd say yes to whatever you wanted."

Liv raised an eyebrow. "Be careful, a girl could get used to hearing that."

That didn't worry Damon at all. "Should we begin this Friday afternoon?"

Liv blinked. For all her pondering, she hadn't considered that today was a Wednesday. "I don't know. Waiting two days to join you in your beautiful home seems like a needless delay, don't you think?"

"I do. I was just trying to act more patient than I am. What time tomorrow should I expect you?"

Liv considered what she would need to prepare to be out of her home for the first time in months. "How about I surprise you? We certainly don't want things to get boring right off the bat, right?"

"Love it," Damon said. "But I'll make some lunch, just in case you find your way here before the sun goes down. Any dietary restrictions?"

"Nope, I eat everything."

"Well, that's a relief."

"Right? Can you imagine if I'd said I was vegan?"

"No, I'd be second guessing this whole thing."

They both smiled, each waiting for the other to end the call but neither wanting to.

"Guess I'll go back to vacuuming," Damon finally said. "Which reminds me, housework is my job, you don't have to lift a finger."

Liv shook her head, amused. "I do not understand why you're single."

DAMON HEARD LIV DRIVE up to his house before he saw her. It was noon the next day, and her ancient BMW rattled and sputtered up the canyon again.

Damon smiled and breathed a sigh of relief. He'd accomplished very little in the past twenty-four hours, anticipating her arrival, half expecting her to appear in the dead of night. And that anticipation was also marred by moments of wondering if she would show up at all.

Liv's convertible top was down, and as Damon approached, he could see she had just one suitcase in the backseat, a mid-sized Tumi overnight bag.

"I'm here!" Liv cried out as she put the car into park and turned it off.

"You're here!" Damon repeated as he opened her car door.

"Always the gentleman!"

"You bring it out in me," Damon said as he reached into the back to pull out her bag. As he did, the bottom of his white T-shirt pulled up from his worn blue jeans, revealing the coveted "v" where his obliques met his abdominal muscles. Liv caught herself staring, and then caught Damon catching her; she quickly looked away, tossing her keys into her purse.

"You saw me checking you out, didn't you?"

Damon grinned. "Maybe a little."

"Well, then," she said as she threw her purse over her shoulder. "It's only fair that I let you check me out."

With that, Liv playfully peeled her own top—a bright yellow yoga tank—up, just enough to show her own well-earned abs.

Damon laughed as she pulled the top back down. "Anybody ever tell you you're a character?"

"Everybody, all the time," Liv proudly answered. "Here, help me with the top?"

"Sure," Damon said. He gently put Liv's bag down, then walked to the other side of the car to help her replace the top from behind the back seat.

"Got an extra space in the garage, if you want?" Damon offered.

"She's good here for now," Liv answered, clicking on the remote again to lock the doors. "I might need to make a quick escape."

Liv gave a wry smile, but Damon sensed she wasn't entirely joking.

"THE ALARM CODE IS 2001," Damon said as he closed the front door behind them and pointed to a panel on the wall. "It's voice activated, so just say it and the alarm goes on or off depending on how you left it last."

Liv whistled. "Fancy. Inspired by the movie?"

"Yup. I'm a big sci-fi fan. Seen it?"

"No, I'm more of a rom-com person myself. You know: *When Harry Met Sally*, *Four Weddings and a Funeral*."

"Would you believe I haven't seen either of them?"

"You haven't seen *When Harry Met Sally*? That's a crime in my book."

"We are rectifying that this weekend."

"Rom-com weekend, it is. Hey, we can go right to the screening room, if you want?"

"Are you kidding? We haven't even finished the tour you started last time I was here. I have to admit, I've been wondering what's up *there* for two days!"

Liv looked up the long, curved stairwell.

"That's, right, I didn't show you the second floor, did I?"

"No, but I actually liked that you didn't."

"How so?"

Liv shrugged. "You weren't showing off. Refrained from showing me, you know, *where the action happens*. I thought it was a classy move on your part."

"I wouldn't say it was exactly a move," Damon replied. "But thank you."

"You're welcome," Liv answered. "Now show me the fucking upstairs!"

Damon laughed and waved a hand at the stairs. "After you."

"Admit it, you just want to watch my ass."

Damon chuckled. "Actually, I read that a man's supposed to walk behind a woman going up stairs, but in front of her going down, so that either way, he can catch her if she falls."

"I never thought about it that way."

"I heard it in some Jane Austen movie."

She laughed. "Now I feel like a bitch."

"Don't. I'm sure I'll still find a way to check out your ass."

Liv blushed a bit—despite the boldness of his proposal, it was, in many ways, the most sexually forward thing Damon had said to her. Behind her, Damon blushed even harder and made a concerted effort *not* to look at her behind.

As they reached the second floor, Liv whistled again. A long hallway stretched before her, beautifully lit by sunlight streaming in through dozens of glass windows set between doors. "My god, you have even views from your *hallway*."

Damon smiled. "There's six bedrooms. Your suite is at the far end there."

"I have a *suite*?"

"This way, madame."

They walked to the far side of the hallway and Damon opened the door. Liv stepped inside, opened her mouth to whistle again, but nothing came out. Around her was indeed a suite of the most expensive of hotels variety. The smell of new paint and fresh construction still clung to the air, cut only by a mild sandalwood fragrance. The "lounge" area of the room held a sectional couch and swiveling plush chairs, and a massive floor-to-ceiling window—the one she had spotted from the backyard and marveled over. The bed, a California King made up in a tasteful two-tone sheet and duvet set, was positioned against the far wall, so far it seemed like a jog away.

"What is this, a thousand square feet?" she asked.

"Give or take."

Liv shook her head, her eyes landing on a hallway that led to two massive walk-in closets. Liv moved through one, running a hand over its spotless empty shelves and into the bathroom.

"Jesus," she mumbled to Damon. "This isn't a bathroom, it's a day spa."

Damon chuckled as Liv took in the glass-walled shower large enough for four people with every sort of faucet.

"It's a steam room too," he explained. "Again, everything's voice activated. Try it."

Liv hesitated, then said aloud, "Shower, please."

She squealed with delight as water streamed from every faucet, steaming up the flat screen television in a corner, angled so someone could watch it while applying makeup at the double sink.

"Colder," Damon called out and the steam lowered.

Liv shook her head, then noticed the tub, circular with claw feet, only its jets and hardware pointing to its modernity.

"There's these brothers in Italy…" Damon said sheepishly. "They design tubs. It's a little out of place, but I can't get enough of them."

"A weekend here is starting to sound short," Liv said almost breathlessly.

Damon smiled at that. "Oh, and there's this in every room…" Aloud, he said, "Music. Beach House greatest hits."

"Space Song" began to play. Liv looked around but couldn't locate the hidden speaker.

"This really is insane."

Damon stepped into a closet and placed her bag down on a chair.

"Thank God there's no kitchen, gym, or pool in this room," Liv joked. "I'd never leave."

"Well…"

"What?"

Damon walked to the wall with the view. "Open doors," he said, and the glass doors slid aside to reveal a massive porch with its own dipping pool. "It's a hot tub, too, of course."

"Of course," Liv repeated, amazed. "And this isn't even the master suite."

Damon shrugged. "It's pretty much the same as this. I figured rich people rarely sleep together, so this takes the argument out of who gets what."

"That's sad but true."

Liv was dying to see where Damon slept, but he wasn't offering, and she didn't want to press.

"So why don't I let you get settled in?" Damon said. "I'm going to go take a dip in the pool. Where you're ready, come on down."

"Okay," Liv answered. "And Damon, thank you. Your home is even more incredible than I thought it was. I feel privileged you've invited me to spend time here with you. However long that may be."

"Thank you for trusting me," he said earnestly. "I know being in a stranger's house is a scary thing for a woman."

She grinned. "You make a woman feel safe."

Damon smiled humbly, then left the suite, closing the door behind him.

Liv stood there in the center of the suite, then pinched her arm.

6.

Liv wandered down the second-floor hallway. Most of the many doors were closed, and she didn't dare invade Damon's privacy by opening them, but one was slightly ajar. The room appeared to be Damon's home office, painted in tasteful earth tones and centered around a built-in bookshelf, stacked to the ceiling with books and even sporting a sliding ladder.

A nightclub owner who still reads!

Liv often chided herself that she ought to read more, and it was one of her New Year resolutions every year, but she was pretty sure she had ADD or ADHD. She'd managed to graduate from Florida State University but only just barely; if it weren't for the sketchy kids always stationed outside libraries peddling Adderall, she'd never have made it. But she liked books on tape when driving. Once in a while, especially after spotting an interesting book in the airport, she'd find the time and patience to sit, quiet her busy mind and read from the page. And when that happened, she found it so much more rewarding than listening to a book.

Liv tightened the wrap that she'd changed into. It covered a modest one-piece bathing suit, which she'd carefully chosen to spend time around Damon's pool. She knew it was impossible that Damon hadn't at least scrolled through *some* of her modeling photos on Instagram, in many of which she was extremely scantily clad. More than eighty percent of her Instagram followers were men, and Liv knew her audience. When she posted a lingerie or revealing bikini shot, her "likes" and "comments" shot through the roof. But if this was to be her first time lounging in the sun with Damon, she wanted to reveal a different side of herself— one not indebted to the leering eyes of men on Instagram.

He can work for that privilege, she thought, enjoying the idea that she might tantalize him.

Liv cheerfully trod downstairs and found that every one of the giant glass doors facing the backyard were slid into the walls, so it felt like the immense living room was one with the backyard.

She found Damon floating on his back in the narrow Olympic-size pool, palms up to the sky as if in praise of it, and took a seat on a chaise. It was sunny and cool, but not uncomfortable—the type of day that once brought tourists to SoCal—and the view was even more incredible than it had been on her first visit. To the south she could make out the outlines of Catalina Island, a tourist trap mainly, except for its famed scuba diving among kelp forests seventy miles off the coast.

"Hey, you!" Damon called out as he flipped to his stomach and swam to the edge of the pool.

Liv caught her first glimpse of Damon's marred back and tried not to stare at the angry red line up his spine. "Hi! Keep swimming, don't let me bother you."

"You bothering me is the whole reason I invited you here," Damon said as he climbed out of the pool and headed for a robe on a chaise lounge.

Liv bit her tongue as Damon shook droplets of water from his shaggy dark hair, the movement exuberant and debonair. He had an effortlessly impressive body—lithe and aristocratic, the sort of fitness attained through expensive adventure activities rather than any kind of disciplined commitment to the gym. *Even his scars seem to suit him.* But it was probably too early to inquire after their origin—*that's rude, right?*

Dried enough, Damon wrapped the plush white robe around him.

"Aw, I was kind of enjoying the show," Liv said with a teasing smile.

Damon laughed, his white teeth catching sunlight. "Even with my *wretched disfigurement?*" Damon asked, indicating his back and putting on a hoity English accent.

Damon was not self-conscious about the appearance of his scars—only in moments of darkness did they bring him an unbidden flash of shame. Otherwise, he tried to view them as a warning, a reminder of what horrors could come if he didn't keep himself in check. More than once while straining his neck over his shoulder to get a good look at the scars in the mirror, the pink blob took the shape of a small misshapen gremlin and whispered to him, *You are lucky. You got off easy.*

"Come on," Liv teased. "You know you're hot."

Damon did but liked hearing it from her. "Hot, am I?"

Liv rolled her eyes, not buying his modesty one bit. "Here," she said as she pulled off her wrap to reveal her black and gold vintage Chanel swimsuit. "You've probably seen all of me on Instagram anyway."

"Your pictures don't do you justice, Liv."

Liv smiled and sat back against the chaise. "It wasn't this nice and quiet before the pandemic, was it?"

"Pretty much. We're set back in the canyon."

"Where nobody can hear me scream."

Damon chuckled. "I'll allow you two more 'I'm afraid I've walked into a horror movie' jokes, how's that?"

She laughed. "That was my last one. Scout's honor."

"Thank you. And hey, for all I know, you're one of those girls who gets a guy so drunk he can't stand, then robs him blind. I'm taking a risk here too."

"Damn," Liv feigned guilt. "I *had* planned to slip a dozen pills into your drink tonight, then have five guys ransack the art collection, but I guess you're onto me."

Damon grinned, then snapped his fingers. "I'm such a terrible host. Can I get you something to drink or eat?"

"Would you judge me if I had some wine so early in the day?"

"Not at all. Rosé again? Or maybe champagne?"

"Well, since you're offering, why not the bubbly? Kick off our weekend with a toast?"

"Two champagnes coming up."

Damon summoned the wine drawer beneath the firepit, then deftly opened the bottle without so much as a pop.

"Well done!" Liv complimented.

"I tended bars long before I owned them."

"Them?" she asked as she accepted her glass.

"Only the one now, but I've had a few, less successful clubs before. I started out pouring drinks at a hellish tourist bar on the beach in Bali."

"I want to hear more about that, but hold on," Liv said, holding up her glass to toast. "To your brave invitation."

"And to getting to know each other."

Liv tipped her glass to him and sipped. "Something tells me this is going to be an interesting relationship."

"Interesting is good," Damon said as he sat on a chaise beside her. They sipped at their champagne quietly.

"It's funny," Liv softly spoke up. "I have a healthy amount of social anxiety. But with you, I feel at ease even saying nothing."

Damon paused thoughtfully. "Maybe the isolation of the pandemic is creating an expedited emotional intimacy between us, but I don't think so. I feel the same. It's like I've known you forever."

"Maybe in a past life?"

"I believe in them. No shortage of woo-woo spinning around in my head with all that time in Bali. Are you religious?"

Liv shook her head. "My mother tried to make me believe, but I'm sort of agnostic."

"Me too. If there's something up there, it's too unknowable, too complex to even try to describe it."

"Exactly. And I'm not judgmental. As long as someone doesn't tell me I'm going to hell for not believing what they do, we're good."

"Amen."

"Amen," Liv repeated.

Damon refilled her glass.

"That's going fast," Liv said with a laugh.

"I've stocked up almost as much champagne and wine as toilet paper," Damon joked. "And by the way, feel free to check your phone or your Instagram; I won't think it's rude. I know that's part of your job."

"I do need to post, but I usually do it in the mornings."

"Why mornings?"

"Algorithms. Nine to eleven a.m. is the peak time when my followers see my posts. Probably because most of them are horny men halfway across the world. They gawk at me after work."

Damon laughed, amused by her self-deprecation.

"I've been falling behind," Liv admitted. "With the world in lockdown, it feels insensitive to be posting shots of me in a bikini."

Her face fell a bit, and Damon wanted to avoid another misstep if the conversation turned to finances. "Do you like to cook?" he changed the subject.

"I love it, but I'm no Gordon Ramsey."

"Well, no pressure. I can't even follow a recipe, but I can hire a chef to make us meals and drop them off, if you'd like?"

"Damon, you are not hiring us a chef. Cooking is the least I can do to earn my keep here."

"Deal, but you have to let me be your sous-chef. Maybe I'll learn a trick or two."

"Sure, but you can just watch and keep the wine coming."

Damon laughed, but Liv groaned, "I'm starting to sound like an alcoholic."

"I'm sure they have virtual AA meetings," he teased.

"Ha! My family is half Irish, half Scottish. It takes me four glasses of anything to get my even tipsy."

"I'm the exact opposite," Damon answered. "Total lightweight."

"Do you have other vices? Get high?"

Damon attempted to hide a grimace. He wasn't ashamed of his past, but he wasn't sure that Liv's first day of arrival was the appropriate time to burden her with his demons either. "I do smoke pot, once in a while. I definitely went a little hard in the paint when I was younger. It comes with the territory when you're in my industry. But I've sworn off the hard stuff—besides, coke is just filthy now, even in Los Angeles. When your friend was sniffing lines, I was worried about more than my liquor license. I really want to avoid an ambulance outside of the club. It's only happened a couple of times."

"Yeah. I've got onto Yasmina about that before. Thankfully, she's with her mom and sister in France now, so hopefully that will chill her out a bit. What about other drugs, like psychedelics?"

"I've had my share—again, the whole Bali scene, but MDMA is more my thing if I want to, you know, feel connected to the universe and all that. I've only done it a handful of times, but each time it was like God reached down and made me open my heart. If you want me to fall in love with you, take MDMA with me. Oh, and I always test it, for safety," Damon finished.

Liv laughed. "Consider me warned!"

"Those commitment issues, huh? You show me yours and I'll show you mine..."

"On our first day together? Hell no!"

Damon laughed.

"But I do have one personal question," Liv went on.

Damon braced himself. "Oh?"

Liv sat up to face him. "What was with the offer to give me an allowance?"

Damon let out a hefty sigh—a strange brew of relief and chagrin. "I'm sorry I offered you money. I assure you, I'm not a sugar daddy, and I don't think of you as one of those girls."

"So...?"

"I guess I've been burned by some women in this town—or more specifically, in my club. Half of them are Russian hookers looking for a rich husband. I try to avoid them, but I was in a relationship a few years ago where a girl became very materialistic. Nothing was enough for her. I gave her whatever she asked for. But in the end, all I paid for was a broken heart."

"I'm sorry."

He shrugged. "I'm mostly over it. But it's more than that too. I really was just trying to be thoughtful of your position, but I'm sorry if it came out like I was propositioning you."

"Thank you," Liv said, sensing Damon's regret was sincere. "My love life hasn't been such a success story either. But give me some time to open up to you before I ruin an afternoon."

Damon laughed. "How do you do that?"

"What do you mean?"

"You always lighten things up at just the right moment."

"I don't know if it's a talent, or a bad habit, but…thank you."

"Welcome," Damon said and leaned back in the chaise, relaxation returning to him.

"Do you have speakers out here?" Liv asked as she joined his recline.

Damon raised an eyebrow playfully. "Do I have speakers out here?"

"Stupid question, huh?"

Damon called out, "Siri, play music."

From speakers, once again hidden from sight, came Siri's voice. "Of course, Damon. What would you like to play?"

Damon looked to Liv. "What do you like?"

"You'd hate my taste in music," she answered. "You choose."

"Okay." Damon thought a moment. "Siri, play a soft rock seventies playlist."

"Playing soft rock seventies."

Liv whipped to face Damon as Bread's "Make It With You" played on the hidden speakers, filling the backyard with its mellow guitar strings.

"How did you know?" Liv demanded.

Damon chortled a bit. "The vintage swimsuit? The bellbottoms the other day? I don't think it would take Sherlock to guess."

Liv smiled at the care he seemed to take in his observation of her. In just a few brief interactions, he seemed to already know that one of her favorite ways to fall asleep was to listen to seventies ballads, staring out her window at the lights of Los Angeles. Or that she wished she'd been born in 1960, so she could live in Laurel Canyon and listen to Joni Mitchel or Jackson Browne writing songs in the house they shared in the reaches of the canyon.

She looked over and noticed Damon had closed his eyes, so she did the same. And then Liv found herself feeling a little scared of this man—of his intuition, and of what this growing connection might promise.

Damon heard her take a deep breath and exhale slowly.

"Are you okay?" he asked.

She lied with a smile. "Just so relaxed for the first time in a month."

"Good," Damon said, closing his eyes again.

THE SUN WAS DIPPING below the mountains when Liv woke up on the chaise. She didn't remember falling asleep but had clearly got in a good two-hour nap outside.

I'm probably burnt to a crisp, she thought, then saw that she was shielded by a giant umbrella, no doubt moved by Damon while she slept.

Annnddd there he goes again, being thoughtful, Liv said to herself as she sat up and collected her day bag. Damon was nowhere to be seen and the music wasn't playing, so she took a moment to pull out her phone; the realization that she hadn't checked it in hours sending a jolt of worry through her body.

She checked her messages first. There were only a few—before lockdown, her phone was a constant source of texts about potential modeling gigs, but lately, it was completely dry but for some errant "likes" on old posts and a few friends checking in. Too relaxed to start bantering with her fingers, she chose only to answer one from her mother. She'd given her Damon's address and had promised to call her with a safety check hours ago.

Well??? Beth had written to her.

Liv typed back, Sorry, just woke from a nap. Everything great so far.

The text bubble lit up. You must feel safe there if you're napping.

Safe? Hell, I'm completely infatuated.

Her mother replied with a fireworks emoji.

Love you. I'll report back on Monday.

Beth sent "please" hands and pink hearts.

Liv's heart twinged and she regretted the terseness that surrounded some of their conversations of late. Liv and Beth always enjoyed a rare closeness after the death of her father, more sisters than mother and daughter. And, of course,

Beth had been there for Liv through her cancer fight. She moved to Los Angeles for the duration of her treatment, slept on hospital chairs, held her hand when she sobbed on the bathroom floor pulling out fistfuls of hair, and acted as her therapist when Christopher had fled.

Liv tried not to think about the fact that the family line would end with her. While her cancer was a convenient excuse, not technically in full remission until five years of clean tests, much of her hesitation came from the deep wound that Christopher inflicted.

Stop, Liv scolded herself. Here she was, a beautiful sunset unfolding, a handsome man waiting somewhere inside this dream home, and she was sorting through hatboxes of emotional baggage.

In an instant, Liv wiped all thoughts of cancer and Christopher out of her mind and rose to her feet. She was proud of her deft ability to free herself from negativity so quickly—it was the tool that brought her through her cancer, her father's death, Christopher, and a slew of other tiny tragedies dotting the landscape of her life. She tossed her phone back into her bag, slipped her wrap around her waist and headed into the house. As Liv moved through the living room, she heard the strum of an acoustic guitar—a song she didn't recognize. She followed the sounds down the hallway, past the kitchen, and found the door to the recording studio ajar.

Liv crept in. She'd been in recording studios before, mostly singing backup in the nicer ones, so she knew this studio was small by commercial standards. There was just a short soundboard, a few chairs, and a glass wall. In the booth on the other side of the glass she saw Damon sitting on a stool, strumming the guitar, the music playing on speakers.

He didn't see her at first, so Liv stood there a moment, admiring him. As he'd told her, Damon wasn't a great guitar player, solid at best, but he made a sweet sound.

Damon saw her, went flush, and clapped his hand over the strings.

"Don't stop!" Liv called out.

Damon laughed sheepishly, placed the guitar on a stand, and hurried through the booth door.

"Shit," he said as he glanced at the sound board. "I thought I turned off the speaker system. But I guess you heard that?"

"I like that song. What is it?"

"Nothing, just something to keep my fingers from losing their calluses."

Liv grinned at him. "Cut the modesty thing. Did you write that?"

"It doesn't even have a name!"

"You got lyrics?"

"No," he answered. "I really don't write songs. I just started playing a friend's guitar on the beach in Bali one day and liked it. But not enough to take it seriously."

Damon put his hands on his hips and looked away, seeming to Liv like an annoyed cowboy, so she backed off the subject. She couldn't exactly force him to talk about musical ambitions while hiding her own.

"Thank you for covering me with the umbrella," Liv said. "I'm fair skinned, so if you'd left me as I was, I'd need to soak in a bath of aloe all night."

"You really passed out."

"Yeah, I guess I've been so stressed lately, but how could I be stressed in paradise?"

"I'm a terrible napper. Can't quiet my mind enough."

"Have you tried meditating?"

"Even worse at that."

Liv laughed. "God, I couldn't survive without meditation. Do it every morning, rain or shine. There's lots of different ways to approach it. I'll teach you one day."

"Ah. Well, many gurus of Bali have tried, but maybe you'll be the one that does the trick. Rom-coms, meditating, we're just racking up things to do."

Liv felt the shiver of air-conditioning. "Mind if I go shower and put on some clothes?"

"Course not. Why don't I order dinner while you do that? Any requests?"

"For dinner?"

"We were so busy talking, we forgot lunch."

"True, but I'm not letting our first meal be takeout. Postmates is taking so long these days, everything comes cold. And I told you I love to cook."

Damon flipped a few switches on the soundboard and ushered Liv out. "Okay, then. What's for dinner?" he asked as he closed the studio door.

"You don't worry about that. Looked like your fridge was stocked, so I'll improvise. I'll make a dish like your song—without a name."

Damon laughed. "I'll open a bottle of wine and be your faithful sous-chef."

"Perfect. See you in the kitchen in ten."

"Ten minutes? That's all it takes you to get ready?"

"When dinner is on the line? Yes," Liv winked and headed out of the room, calling back, "Hope you're hungry, cowboy!"

"Cowboy?"

"It's an inside joke!"

"Inside with who?"

"Inside my head!"

7.

"Red or white?" Damon asked as he watched Liv mix sauce in a pan. They both stood barefoot in jeans and T-shirts, and Sinatra crooned low throughout the house.

"Either," she answered brightly.

Damon considered the bottles of wine on the counter in front of him. "Well, white goes better with fish, red with meat, but you won't tell me what you're making!"

"My mother always told me to keep men guessing. Otherwise, they get bored with you."

"I can't imagine being bored by you."

"And I bet no woman has ever broken up with you because they thought you were dull."

"Maybe not, but they find reasons."

"Like?"

Damon picked up a wine screw, pensive. "I'm a workaholic, for one. And with the amount of women I'm around, jealousy and insecurity usually come into play."

Liv studied Damon as she donned oven gloves. "Be honest, do you think you could spend the rest of your life with just one woman?"

"I don't know. But I'd like to try. I have tried before. I've spent thousands of dollars on therapy and think I'm right in that sweet spot where a woman could swoop in, and I'd be off the market for life."

"A man who commits to therapy! Vulnerability is so sexy."

"And you? A one-man woman?"

"Fuck yeah. When I'm in love, I like feeling like I'm owned. Fuck feminism."

Damon laughed as Liv opened the oven and carefully pulled out a porcelain dish containing a whole chicken, its skin brown and covered in herbs, surrounded by small potatoes and asparagus, and placed it on the stove top.

He inhaled deeply through his nose. "I've never smelled anything like that."

Liv smiled. "You obviously did some serious Instacart-ing before I got here, but as you said, you're not a cook, so we're missing some essentials."

Damon looked disappointed with himself. "Really? What didn't I get?"

"Oh, little things like salt and pepper."

Damon smacked his forehead. "Oops."

"Honestly, most people overuse salt because they don't know how to actually give a dish taste. And that's why I made the sauce. There's salt in chicken stock, and you had some in the pantry."

Liv whipped off her mitts to grab a knife and cooking fork. "I *should* let this sit for a few minutes," she went on. She cut into the top of the bird, sliced off a few inches of steaming white meat, dipped it into the sauce, and offered it to Damon. "Don't worry, the sauce will cool it enough, so you don't burn your tongue."

Damon let her feed him. She watched his eyes raise in wonder as he chewed it with a groan.

"You like?"

"Incredible."

"I'm calling it *Poulet Sans Nom.* Chicken with no name."

"Like my song! *Et la dame parle français*," he exclaimed, giving her an elegant little spin.

Liv smiled and shook her head. "I really don't understand why you're not married with little Damons running around here."

"And I don't understand how you made it to your thirties without a ring on your finger and children tugging at your apron."

"Having children when I'm not sure I'll make it to forty is pretty selfish, don't you think?"

Damon hesitated. This was the first time Liv had spoken of her illness with any indication of negativity or concern, and he didn't want to say the wrong thing. "I can understand why you'd feel that way."

"Yeah, my mother suggested I freeze my eggs, but I don't see any reason. Do *you* want kids?"

"I like children. I'm actually pretty good with them. But existentially, I wouldn't feel like my life was empty without my own."

"Sounds like a fancy way of saying no."

Damon laughed.

"Then I'm your girl. Can't have them after the cancer," the lie—well, mostly lie, slipped out before Liv's brain could catch up.

"You're my girl, huh?"

Liv's eyebrow arched. "Don't get cocky."

Damon smiled sheepishly.

"Oh, by the way," she said, an apology in the form of a subject change, "You don't have any aprons. I looked all over."

He nodded. "Tell you what, after dinner I'll give you my Amazon password and you can order everything you need for the kitchen."

"You mean everything *you* need," Liv corrected. "I might just be here for the weekend."

There I go again, she thought. She picked up the chicken with a dish towel and walked it to the dining table, set for two. Damon chose the bottle of white wine, opening it with the corkscrew as he joined her. "I say white will go best with *Poulet Sans Nom*."

"Agreed."

He poured two glasses as she drizzled the sauce gingerly across the meat.

Damon pulled her chair out. "Mademoiselle?"

"Merci, monsieur."

Liv sat, waited for Damon to do so, then raised a glass. "Let's see, we've already toasted to getting through the pandemic, and to my bravery in coming to this little shack of yours…"

That elicited a laugh from both.

"…Fuck it, let's just drink and eat," she finished unceremoniously.

They smiled and sipped in unison.

"That's amazing. I bet that bottle costs more than my monthly rent?"

"A gentleman never tells."

"You really are a gentleman, aren't you?" Liv reiterated.

It occurred to her that she should stop pointing to the chasm of economic disparity between them. In all her hemming and hawing about Damon's proposal, she had been careful to push a particular thought out of her mind—that staying with Damon might allow her to save a couple hundred dollars here and there, and thereby prolong her ability to help her mother. It wasn't among her chief reasons to join him, and she knew she ought not *count* on it, but the fact that the thought even arose made her feel like a hypocrite for chastising Damon about his allowance offer.

"You told me not to get cocky," Damon said. "But you sure are stroking my ego."

"Good point," Liv said as she put her fork down and leaned on her elbows. "Let's get to the good stuff then. How long have you been single?"

Damon took a sip of wine and decided to eschew dancing around the question—he knew what she was really asking about. "Her name was Nina. We met before I had all this. I was hosting parties on the beach in Bali. She was a surfer from Santa Cruz. After a while of building out my business model, I started to engage with some wealthy finance bros on wellness trips in Bali—started to put together investors for High. Things were going well. But the minute Nina and I landed at LAX, things changed. Things move faster in Los Angeles than Bali. And I felt the pressure of all the money from investors on the line. I tried to keep up…"

Damon squirmed in his seat. He had determined not to excavate his past for Liv today but couldn't skirt some of it.

"Popups for High were doing well, generating buzz, and the more I made, the more Nina asked for. Expensive purses, nicer cars—plural—a bigger house… This girl I'd met dancing on the beach in Bali turned out to have a hidden materialistic streak."

"Some people are just never satisfied. No matter what you give them, what you do for them, they're always looking for more," Liv offered gently.

Now Damon looked up into her earnest eyes and knew he'd have to come out with the whole story—or most of it.

"Well, she wasn't the only one out of control," he said stiffly.

"What do you mean?"

Damon swallowed. "I probably would have kept on showering her with whatever she asked for. But, like I said, I was trying to keep up—with the demands, with the lifestyle, and still trying to party the way I did in Bali…"

Liv waited patiently as he reached for the truth.

"We were doing a lot of cocaine. Like, an impressive amount. I was swinging between feeling invincible and like everything was coming up roses and being terrified it was all going to come crashing down on my head. In one of those invincible moments, Nina and I went for a ride on my Ducati. Just absolutely zooted. And we crashed. Badly."

"The scars?" Liv guessed.

"Exactly, yeah. I took a corner way too fast, clipped a guard rail at just the right angle, and then we flipped. I painted the road with a good chunk of my back. Still feel a lot of pain, every day. Luckily, Nina got flung off and landed in some brush. She was scraped up, ruined a few tattoos, but mostly scot-free, no concussion or anything."

"That's awful…" Liv furrowed her brow as she squared this story with the image of Damon that she had been piecing together.

"I don't deserve sympathy. That was completely on me, and I could have killed Nina. Or someone else."

"So she left you after that?"

Damon sighed and rubbed a hand across his chin, eyes fixed in a middle distance. "No…that's not what happened. When I got out of the hospital, it was a huge wake-up call for me. I knew I couldn't sustain my business's growth and keep partying like a fucking heathen. Even money aside, the guilt would have killed me if I ever did something like that again. But Nina wasn't ready to slow down, and I couldn't do it. Especially because I could tell immediately in the hospital that the opioids were going to be a slippery slope for me. They took away the pain *and* the stress. So I knew I needed a clean environment to get off of them as soon as possible."

"So then the marriage was off?" Liv asked gently.

"That never even made it as far as an engagement. It was always my intention, and I let that be known, but she always said she didn't believe in the institution. She called herself a 'free spirit.'"

"I hate when people call themselves that. It almost always means they can't handle responsibility. Let me guess, she was a Gemini?"

Damon looked impressed. "She was. But your read of that is…even more accurate than I care to admit."

"What do you mean?"

"She has a son."

Now Liv's eyes grew wide. "*Your* son?"

"No, not mine biologically. But I was in his life for six years. It was really hard to walk away. I'm still not sure it was the right decision."

"Is he…okay?"

"That's one thing I'll say for Nina. She's scrappy when it comes to Rand—in a good way. She could always pull it together well enough to be a mother to him.

At least better than bouncing around the foster care system. Believe me, I've had this debate with myself many times."

"Where is he now?"

"I ask but she keeps him from me out of spite. She shows up here every six months or so. Says she wants to work things out. I went for it a few times in the beginning, only to find that to Nina, *work things out* is code for *can I borrow a couple grand.*"

"Ouch. Did she ever get sober?"

Damon shrugged. "I can't be sure. Said she is, last time she texted. But it's not my circus anymore. I think it would be confusing for Rand if I breezed in and out of his life. It's not like I'm entitled to any parental rights."

Liv nodded thoughtfully, the new revelations settling with her *Poulet Sans Nom*. "It sounds like you made the best decision you could in the given circumstances. And part of it explains what happened the first afternoon I was here."

"You mean my offering to help you out financially?"

"Yeah. Forgive me if I sound like a dime-store shrink. But maybe deep down you're afraid that if you're not overly generous with a woman, she'll think *you're* not enough."

"That's what the expensive shrinks say too."

Liv laughed. "I'm a cheap one to all my friends. They give it back in kind though. Can I ask one more question?"

"Do I have choice?"

"It's a softball. Have you had any relationships since?"

"A couple. But they never had that feeling I remember having when I met Nina. Love at first sight. Twin flames. You know, magic," Damon interrupted himself for fear of making Liv self-conscious. "What about you? You're every bit the catch. Why are you single?"

Liv smiled, then noticed neither of them had eaten much. "I'm not avoiding the question. But what do you say we eat some, drink some more, then I'll answer any question you throw at me? Well, most."

"No hurry."

"Thank you. And thank you for sharing all that. Have you always been this vulnerable?"

Damon snorted. "No, I don't think I even understood words like vulnerability and intimacy until my heartbreak."

"We learn more from hardship than success," Liv said sagely.

"I'm living proof. But don't worry, I really have done the work and am in a good place."

Damon almost said *in a good place for a relationship*. Instead, he took a bite of the chicken and groaned with pleasure again.

Liv took her own bite but felt the familiar anxiety gnawing at her insides. *Fuck*, she thought, *I don't know if I can be that vulnerable with him. Or anyone.*

DAMON DRAPED A CASHMERE blanket around Liv's shoulders.

"Softest thing ever," she cooed as he came from behind the sectional by the pool and sat beside her. Their faces glowed from the firepit as embers sailed into the night.

Damon placed his bare feet on the pit ledge where another bottle of wine and their glasses sat. "Well, we've eaten all the nameless chicken, we've had our fill of wine, even though there's always more…" He swished the liquid in his glass. "… Are you going to tell me about *your* singlehood?"

Liv let her head fall back and looked up at the night sky. "Hey, you can actually see the stars tonight. With nobody driving, there's almost no smog. The silver lining to the pandemic."

"Don't change the subject."

Liv laughed and looked over at Damon. "That was pretty obvious, wasn't it?"

"More than obvious. I won't pressure you though. We've got nothing but time."

Liv took another sip of wine, thankful for its help in opening her emotional doors. She wanted to at least *attempt* to respond to Damon's honesty in kind.

"You're lucky I'm tipsy," she said. "I hate talking about myself."

"If it helps, I'm closer to outright drunk, so probably won't even remember what you tell me."

"Good! Then I'll make it up and keep my mystery."

They laughed together.

"Okay, here's the short story," Liv began with a sobering breath. "I was engaged to a man named Christopher, who I was sure was the love of my life. Then I was diagnosed with stage three breast cancer, and right in the beginning of my treatment, he broke off our engagement and moved to New York."

The brevity and weight of her story seemed to land like a bowling ball, so Damon took a few seconds. "You must have felt so abandoned."

"It devastated me," she admitted.

"Not that there's *any* excuse for leaving a woman when she's sick, but were you having problems before that?"

Liv squinted. This was a question she had agonized over before determining it unhealthy. She still didn't have a real answer.

"I didn't think so. I mean, our sex life was fine, we didn't argue. He'd seemed so supportive, all through my surgery and chemo. When I lost my hair, I went out and bought the most expensive wig and the sexiest lingerie. I turned being sick into an opportunity to make our sex life a little kinky. He said it turned him off and was gone a day later."

"What did? The effort?"

"I'm still not sure what he meant by that," Liv said quietly.

"I'm so sorry," was all Damon could find to say.

"Looking back, I can see he was the exact opposite of you," she continued. "He thought work was overrated. Believed in that 'work smarter, not harder' bullshit. Truth is, I was making almost much as him modeling swimsuits."

"What business was he in?"

Liv rolled her eyes. "He was a professional poker player. Think I missed *that* red flag entirely."

Liv took a sip to brace herself for what she was about to say. "Honestly, I think he looked at me and thought I was a losing bet."

"Because you got cancer?"

"Yeah. And he wasn't wrong for weighing the odds. Even though I get tested every three months and haven't had a trace of cancer show up in three years, technically I'm not in remission until it's been five years. I'm on a cocktail of hormone suppressing drugs because estrogen feeds cancer, so my immune system is basically shot. And if you ask the docs how long I have to live, they'll say it could be six months or sixteen years. But you know what they won't say? They won't say I could live sixty years. Any way you look at it, my time is limited."

She stared at him, and for a moment, her eyes grew hard, defensive. "Still think I'm a catch?"

A dare but Damon didn't blink.

"I think you're the bravest fucking woman I've ever met. So, the answer is a resounding yes."

Liv noticed his blue eyes were unblinking, and her own softened again.

Damon put his glass down. "Do you mind if I hold you?"

She laughed with nervous energy. "What?"

"I want to hold you."

"…Okay."

Damon gently lifted away the edge of the blanket that Liv clung to as protection. She slid closer to him while he put his arm around her shoulders, then let her head lay on his chest.

"Clearly I needed this," she admitted quietly, fighting back tears.

"*I* needed this. I haven't held anyone like this in years."

"Come on, you haven't had a woman in your arms by this fire before?"

"Not like this," he murmured.

Liv nestled up to him even closer. "You know what *I* really want to do?"

"What's that?"

"Jump in the pool!" she exclaimed, piercing the moment.

"But I have more questions!"

"Nope! Enough heavy talk for one night. The only question left is if I have the energy to go upstairs and get my suit."

She hastily untangled herself from the blanket and Damon's arms.

"Happy to go get it for you. I'll grab mine too," he offered, disguising the disappointment in his voice.

Liv seemed amused. "You know it's possible to be *too* much of a gentleman."

Damon laughed. "What do you mean?"

Liv shook her head and approached the edge of the pool. "Coming?"

Without waiting for an answer, she pulled off her T-shirt and let it fall. Then her bra dropped to the ground. Next came her jeans, and her lace-edged panties with them. Naked, silhouetted in blue and purple from the underwater sconces, Liv dove into the pool.

Damon guffawed for a moment. Then he stood, set his wine on the ground a foot from the pool, dragged his shirt over his head, and unbuttoned his jeans.

Liv came up to the surface but subtly turned to the side as Damon's jeans came down and he dove in behind her.

She trod water as he came up, facing her but keeping a few respectful feet between them.

"It's like a tropical ocean in here," Liv said softly. "I miss the Florida waters I grew up swimming in."

"When was the last time you were back there?"

"Almost a year. I need to see my mom, but my doctors don't want me to fly."

"How about we fly you there private?"

She shoved a palm of water at him. "Stop."

He pawed the droplets away from his chin. "Seriously."

"You're not kidding, are you?"

"Nope."

"You'd do that for a woman you just met."

"Only if she was you."

Liv ducked beneath the water and put a few more feet between them.

"I'm not letting you spend fifty grand or whatever to fly me to Florida. Especially after hearing about how some girl tried to clean you out."

"Maybe I'm crazy, but I trust you. I mean, you already turned down an allowance."

Liv closed the distance between them again, a dance.

God, I want to kiss her, Damon thought as she approached.

God, I want to kiss him, she silently echoed.

But she swam past Damon to the pool's edge and reached for the wine bottle.

"Getting drunk and naked on my first night here was not something I planned," she said as a slight stream of red dribbled down her chin. She offered him the bottle.

He swam to her and took a drink. Liv put her back to the edge and spread her arms along the stamped stone, her naked breasts under water to just above her nipples—an ending flourish to her chase-dance.

"Look at you," Liv said, studying his face in the pool light, his features angular and handsome, his hair wet and slicked back. "Here we are, completely naked, and you're not even trying to kiss me."

"And I'm not going to," Damon answered as she took the bottle from him. "Not yet anyway."

"Even if I want you to?"

"Even if you want me to."

"What if I try to kiss you?"

"I'll refuse."

Liv laughed out loud.

Damon demurred. "Okay, I'd probably stop breathing and drown."

"Why the hesitation?"

Damon smiled. He'd planned this weekend carefully. "It's simple really. I won't kiss you tonight, or tomorrow, or any time this weekend…"

"Are you asexual?" she asked with alarm.

"Not at all. I'm so turned on I can't explain it."

Liv couldn't help but glance down, where she could see the outlines of his erection under the colored water. "I see. So why not kiss me?"

"Because you've been burned, and I don't want you just for a night. I don't want you just for a weekend."

Liv stopped breathing for a few seconds. "Either you're trying to make me fall in love with you, or you're already in love with me."

Damon wondered if the wine was making him too forward. "Meeting you that night *did* make me feel something I haven't felt in a long time. But I know that we're two scarred people, so we have to take our time and explore this. And we're both a little drunk. When I kiss you, I want you sober. I never want you to think I took advantage of you in any way."

Liv took that in, staring at him. "I'm feeling dizzy," she whispered.

"I'll get a towel and help you to your room."

"You mean to my suite!" she exclaimed, too loudly now.

Damon offered a hand. Liv took it and allowed him to lead her to the steps. He got out of the pool, and she watched his ass with admiration as he wrapped a towel around his waist.

"I liked you naked better," she said woozily.

Damon laughed as he spread another towel out like wings.

Liv strode up the steps and into its embrace. Damon folded it around her, leaving one hand free to guide her inside with.

"What about our clothes?" Liv asked, looking back.

"I'll come back for them after you're safely in bed."

"In bed alone?"

"Uh huh, you can even lock the door."

"You realize this was a test, right?" she wagged a finger at him playfully. "Even drunk, I'm not easy."

"Then I'm glad I trusted my instincts."

"Oof!" Liv sighed as the bright lights of the living room hit her.

"I got ya."

Damon helped her to the stairs, then set her hand on the railing and let go so he could walk up behind her.

"You let go!" she whined.

"Temporarily."

Liv let go of the railing as they reached the top of the stairs. "I'm lost. Which way?"

"This way," Damon said, turning to the left and walking beside her.

"Can you make it from here?" he asked as he opened the door to her suite.

"I'm not that drunk, mister."

Damon laughed. "Okay, goodnight."

"Goodnight."

Liv closed the door.

She left it unlocked, turned, and collapsed on the massive bed. She discarded her towel on the floor and snuggled under the duvet and Egyptian cotton sheets. Her eyes slowly batted and closed.

8.

Liv looked for Damon as she trod downstairs, midday sunlight filling the house. She wore a white sundress, a bikini peeking out on her shoulders and neckline, and pink Prada sunglasses perched on her head.

Damon was nowhere to be seen, but Liv spotted a glass French press filled with coffee on the dining table, beside it a bowl of fresh cut fruit, a plate of croissants, and a glass of orange juice.

She sipped at the juice first, then let out a hungover sigh.

Real sugar, she noted as she saw the small dish beside the coffee mug. *None of this rat-killing aspartame.* She lifted a piece of mango from the bowl with her fingers and into her mouth, so fresh that she had no doubt it was organic.

Liv walked outside with a cup of coffee and two miniature croissants pinched between her fingers. Another perfect day made it hard to believe the world was in crisis.

"Good morning!" Damon said from behind her.

She turned and smiled. "I think it's afternoon?"

She hadn't even bothered to plug her dead phone in yet.

"Two p.m. to be exact."

"Holy shit, I never sleep this late."

Damon smiled. He didn't want to tell Liv that he'd set his alarm for six.

"I didn't dare wake you up," he said. "I want this to be vacation for you!"

"You're sweet. What did I miss?"

"Well, this morning the LA school system closed indefinitely."

"I'm going back to bed," she joked.

"Only good news for the rest of the day, promise."

Liv donned her sunglasses and took a seat on the lounge. "I was going to take some pictures and post something. Anything. Just so the world doesn't forget about me."

"I think you'd be doing the world a service by posting you in a bikini," Damon said as he sat opposite her. "Last night made me forget about the pandemic."

"I wasn't wearing a bikini."

Damon laughed.

"My view wasn't so bad either," Liv flirted.

Damon's smile spread into his flushing cheeks.

"Except for the scars," he returned modestly.

"Well, I've got a couple of my own," she said, and cupped both breasts in her hands to indicate her reconstruction.

"I didn't look at your breasts that closely."

"Liar."

Damon laughed. "Okay, okay, fine, I did, but I didn't see a scar."

"I want to write a book about my cancer experience one day," Liv said wistfully. "When I got my diagnosis, I studied my options like my life depended on it. I spent weeks on the phone with Blue Shield fighting for a halfway decent plastic surgeon and still had to pay for half of it. Got my reconstruction done in the same surgery they removed the cancerous tissue, which is rare. I want other women to know they have options like that."

"That would be a helpful book."

Liv picked up a croissant. "Who am I kidding? I don't have the patience to write a book."

"Let me hire a ghostwriter for you," Damon suggested.

"You're too generous. That Nina has no idea what she lost."

"To be fair, I bet if you ask her, she'll have a very different story of our relationship."

"Can I call her?"

Damon laughed. "Stick around. I'm sure she'll be knocking on the Bank of Damon soon."

Liv shook her head and stood, then slipped out of her sundress. This day, she wore a black bikini, one with much less fabric than yesterday's one-piece.

Damon felt his blood pressure rise as he stirred sugar into his own afternoon coffee.

"So, last night you mentioned mom's in Florida," he said to distract himself. "Did you end up three-thousand miles away because of modeling, or…"

"Singing," she answered.

"That's right. When are you going to sing for me?"

"*Never!*" she teased.

"What! Why?"

"Because. I'll have you know that I've shared more about my personal life in a day and a half than I do with most men after weeks of dating. I've already been singing for my supper."

"And why do you suppose that is?" he asked.

"Because I'm kidnapped here?"

"Seriously."

"Because you're a great listener," Liv shrugged.

"Well, don't you think I'd make a great audience then?"

Liv exhaled with an *ugh* in mock frustration.

"Okay. My failed musical career," she began. "Singing was all I wanted as a young girl. I was queen of the Jacksonville talent contests, then in some bands while I was in college. But when I moved to Los Angeles after college, I discovered I was a very small fish in the big pond. Girls out here start singing on Disney shows before they're out of training bras."

Damon chuckled. "It's a factory town."

"Well, this factory town ate me up and spit me out. I was lucky enough to find a manager, but all he wanted was to manage his way into my bed. The producers and record company execs were worse. One invited me to come sing for him at a studio, but when I got there, it was just the two of us in his office. At first, he just hit on me, then he made it clear I wasn't leaving the studio until I fucked him. He grabbed me, and I kicked him in the balls and fled."

Damon studied her as she stopped. "I can't believe you're so calm about this…"

"You have to understand what it's like to be a woman. If you haven't been assaulted, you're a statistical anomaly."

"Do you think that's changed since MeToo?"

"A little. But this was long before, and this asshole spread it around that I was difficult to work with. No other managers or agents would come near me. And any dream I had left was killed by my cancer. So I turned to modeling. And it's just creative enough."

"But still…you gave up a dream. That's a big thing to grieve."

"Life happens," Liv answered. "I don't have time for regrets or bucket lists."

Damon watched Liv sip coffee as if she had just commented on the weather. But maybe that was because she'd told it so many times, and this was the first time he'd heard it. Either way, he felt a rush of compassion. And the urge to *fix*.

"You could always record a song here…"

"No, I don't even sing in the shower anymore."

Liv gave him an appreciative smile and laid back in the sun.

Damon registered that the conversation was over and peeled off his shirt.

"No sunblock?" Liv asked, pretending she wasn't staring at Damon's chest.

"I'm good," he answered.

I bet you are, she thought.

THE REST OF THE AFTERNOON passed at the breakneck pace only exacted by bountiful conversation and the heady effects of the sun. Even when Liv and Damon left the backyard to walk side by side on treadmills in Damon's gym, the conversation rarely ceased. In the evening, Liv cooked simple penne with truffle oil and prosciutto, which they ate standing in the kitchen—a directive from Damon simply because "it tastes too good to waste time setting the table."

Later, they settled in his small but decked-out screening room and debated what to watch.

"Rom-com?" Damon offered as they settled on the couch with cashmere blankets pulled up to their chests.

"Do you mind if we watch *Tiger King*? I'm hooked."

"Me too. Those people are a danger to themselves."

Damon turned on Netflix, but huddled with her head on his shoulder, Liv soon noticed his breathing was slow and his eyes were closing.

"Are you falling asleep on me?" she said, sitting up and pausing the show.

"Of course not!" Damon lied, eyes suddenly wide open.

She laughed. "Want me to make you a cappuccino?"

"Then I'll never fall asleep. Why don't we try again tomorrow night…if you're still here, of course."

Liv felt a small jolt of remorse. It had been the equivalent of a weekend, and she still hadn't given any indication of her answer. "I promise, I'll let you know first thing in the morning. I just need the night to sleep on it."

"Understood."

Again, Damon walked behind her up the stairs and escorted her to her suite. At the door, Liv turned to face him.

"You're still not going to kiss me?" she challenged.

"Nope."

"But you want to?"

"Dying to."

"But don't you think it would be a good idea just to test it out? What if it's a bad kiss? What if it turns out all this chemistry falls apart the minute we get physical?"

"Not gonna happen."

"I like the way you smell."

"Pheromones don't lie," he answered.

"What if I *demand* a trial kiss?"

"Try me."

"And get rejected? Never."

"Good, because I would say no. I want a commitment."

Liv felt a churn of anxiety—the combination of having never wanted to kiss a man more and the decision that lay before her. She shrugged, playing cool. "Goodnight, I guess."

"Goodnight."

DAMON AND LIV LAID in their respective beds that night, the lights turned off, but both sleepless.

Liv wasn't playing coy—she truly hadn't decided if she was up for the commitment of moving in with Damon, even if temporarily for the unknowable length of a pandemic. If she were being honest with herself, she'd expected before to be going home in the morning. As tantalizing and dreamlike as the two days had been, the depth of their connection felt overwhelming. In her experience, things that got this hot this fast always fell apart swiftly and people—specifically *she*—got hurt.

In his own suite, the fear of the unknown racked Damon. They both knew they'd be more than roommates if Liv chose to stay, but he couldn't shake the feeling that his proposal would force Liv into a relationship she was not interested in. After all, they might have learned more about each other than most people learn in months of dating, but that was no guarantee that they were compatible in the long term.

No, Damon was going purely on instinct, and if Liv woke up feeling like everything was too much too soon, he'd have himself to blame. But the last few years had been a revolving door of hookups, one-night stands, and miniature almost-relationships, and where had they led? He knew he could back off and let Liv come and go as she pleased, but then all his passionate words and faux conviction might seem insincere.

But in the darkness, even his anxieties were drowned out by a crippling *want*.

And all of Liv's inner debate was shouted down by a similar intoxication.

Liv closed her eyes and ran through her memories of the past forty-eight hours until she came to a vision of Damon, naked and wet in the pool, treading water only five feet away from her.

Liv slipped her hands down to her belly, lowering them until her fingers found her folds below. She surprised herself with the growing puddle of wet she was met with. Liv rubbed herself in circular motions, and as she grew close to an orgasm, she slipped the fingers of her other hand inside, imagining they weren't her fingers at all.

Under his sheets, Damon was deep in the mirror image of her memory, remembering the contours of Liv's breasts as they bobbed on the water. No less surprised by how hard he felt in his hands, Damon tightened his grip, focusing his movements on the underside of his head, the pinpoint of his pleasure.

Damon and Liv closed their eyes and came at almost the exact same moment; him with a quiet groan, her with a muffled cry.

DAMON MOVED EGGS AROUND a pan, careful not to scrape the spatula too audibly. He wanted Liv to sleep as late as possible—anything to make her feel like living with him would be a permanent vacation. Or to prolong disappointment.

Finally, she bopped in, wearing sneakers and a tee.

"Good morning," Damon said, offering her an orange juice.

"Good morning," she returned, taking a sip.

"Sleep well?"

"Famously. You?"

"Good…" he drew a breath and resisted the urge to shake her by her shoulders and demand, *Out with it!*

Instead, he slid the eggs onto two plates.

"Oh, I'm not hungry yet. But when you're done, will you help me with my luggage?"

Damon's stomach fell through his ass. *She's leaving? Just like that?*

He faked a smile. "Breakfast can wait."

"You sure?"

"Of course."

She smiled evenly, giving nothing, confusing him even more. *What happened to make her want to flee like this?*

He wanted to ask her, but she was obviously in a rush, so he started out of the kitchen.

"Wait," Liv said, making him stop. "I want to say something."

"Okay..."

Liv stepped up to him. "Kiss me."

Damon blinked. "Kiss you?"

Liv rolled her eyes, put her hand around the back of his neck and pulled him toward her, into a deep kiss. The connection overtook Damon, and he let go of his thoughts.

Finally, Liv pulled back with a smile. "My bags are in the trunk of my car."

Damon shook his head like he had water in his ears, then it suddenly hit him, and he smiled. "You're staying, aren't you? Your bags are in the car because you packed for longer."

She smiled, enjoying her ruse. "I wanted to be prepared but didn't want you to know *how* prepared. Just in case I had to make a quick exit."

His arms around her waist, Damon chuckled. "You really do like to keep a man guessing, don't you?"

She smiled mischievously. "Did I scare you?"

"Nah," Damon lied.

"Liar. I'll have those eggs now."

Damon pulled out a chair at the island.

Liv sat, watching as he put two plates down.

"Damon..."

He looked to her. "Yes?"

"I want to say something else," Liv began in earnest. "I've joked around about my fear of commitment a few times, but you should know that it's a real thing. And the surest way to frighten me into leaving is to think of us as a relationship too quickly. So, let's hold off on all the 'moving in' talk. I came for the weekend, had a wonderful time, and I'm excited to stay, but I can't promise for how long. So let's just take it one day at a time, okay?"

Damon was more relieved than he thought he'd be—he knew that his own anxiety about relationships was somewhat on par with Liv's. And it also relieved whatever tumult he felt about the possibility of forcing her hand.

"Anybody ever tell you you're a wise young woman?" Damon asked.

"Rarely," she quipped. "My mother thinks I'm neurotic *and* naive."

"I can't wait to meet your mother," Damon said, then realized his faux pas. "One day, eventually, down the line…" he fumbled.

Liv laughed, thinking, *Who am I fooling? I can't wait for my* everyone *to meet this wonderful species of man.*

9.

SWEAT DRIPPED FROM LIV as she chased the tennis ball from one end of the court to the other. She wound up a double backhand and sent the ball flying toward Damon.

"Great shot!" he called out as he fumbled to return it.

Liv grunted as she sent the ball back down the line, just out of Damon's reach—he fell, his hands softening his landing.

"You let me win that point!" Liv complained as she headed for the net.

"Right, that's why I'm on my ass here."

"Don't fuck with me, Damon. You ever give me another point and it will be the last time we play."

Damon chuckled as he rose. "I think you have far too high of an opinion about me and my athleticism."

Liv balanced her racket against the bench and lifted her water bottle. Damon did the same, huffing for air.

Liv's initial assessment of the cut of Damon's body was accurate—he was blessed by genetics and an appetite for adventure rather than a disciplined commitment to his physique.

Not to mention the back thing, she thought as he stretched, and she briefly caught a shadow of pain pass over his face.

"Oh, I'm just competitive," Liv deflected. "If you had a billiards table, I would school you in pool too."

"Would you, now? I promise I'm better at pool than tennis."

"Ping pong too. I've embarrassed more than a few men playing."

"It's on!" Damon said, picking up his phone from the bench and texting deliberately.

"What are you doing?"

"Ordering us a billiards and ping pong table for the house."

"I would object to you spoiling me this way, but I have a feeling you'll ignore me. Everything I've asked for in the last week, you've gotten."

"I can't let you get bored of me this soon!"

Liv laughed—she couldn't possibly be bored with his generosity. If she merely mentioned she was hungry, food was delivered without him even asking what she was in the mood for, and it always satisfied her "spot." Damon seemed to have a sixth sense of how to please her. Just the other day, Liv had mentioned she might need more clothes from home, only to be surprised when a delivery showed up: boxes of clothes from Neiman Marcus and a Melrose boutique she'd mentioned to him in passing. Liv felt so spoiled that she thought before casually mentioning things she liked because, odds were, he'd buy them for her—and refuse to let her repay him.

Her infatuation with Damon grew daily, and they'd never had so much as a disagreement.

Not one.

"I think we should have a fight," Liv announced as they headed off the tennis court.

"Something bothering you?" Damon asked.

"No. I just have this theory that you don't know someone until you know how they fight, or more importantly, how they make up."

"Makes sense."

"See, you agree with everything I say!"

"Is it my fault I agree with you? Believe it or not, most people call me argumentative."

Liv laughed. "I don't know. I guess I'm afraid you have this whole other side of you that will come out one day. I mean...are you this agreeable with every woman you date?"

Damon whipped to face her as though he'd just caught her hand in a cookie jar. "You know that's first time you've said we're dating?"

Liv reached her arm through his and stopped to give him a kiss.

She felt his strong arms wrap around her, making her feel as safe as she felt desired.

What made Liv feel even safer was the fact that since their first kiss—a full week and a half ago—Damon hadn't pushed her to be *more* sexual. It clearly wasn't for lack of desire on either end; they necked and dry humped like teenagers constantly. On the couch, by the pool, in the pool, pressed up against counters and hallway walls. But each night, Damon would kiss her at her bedroom door and say, "Goodnight."

"Do you think it's strange we haven't made love yet?" she asked as Damon began to kiss her neck, making her shiver.

Damon calmed his own craving. "I'm dying for you. But I feel like a teenager again, and it's kind of fun."

She bit her own lip to keep from biting his neck. "Isn't it? But I'm getting a little curious. Is there something about you I should know? Like something wrong down there…"

Damon laughed, saving her from an embarrassing finish. "You won't be disappointed."

"Thank God! Okay, what about diseases?"

"Nope. Had a full panel the week before you came up here."

"Not very sexy talking about this," Liv bemoaned as they walked through the glass door into the gym. "But I'm healthy too. I was checked a year ago and haven't been with anyone since."

Damon raised a brow. "You haven't slept with anyone in a year?"

She waved her hand in the air. "Don't worry, I have no desire to guess how long it's been for you."

He answered with a grateful smile as Liv's phone was suddenly alight with rapid fire group texts.

In quick succession, Marie had texted the group:

Liv.

Immediately followed up by Yasmina agreeing:

Girl.

And then the two had "liked" each other's messages, for good measure.

Liv sighed and rolled her eyes. Her girls knew she was safe—they all shared locations with one another, mysterious proposals from wealthy men or not, and Liv had sent them a few quick check-ins to let them know that she was okay. But she hadn't exactly shared her level of infatuation, or that she had chosen to stay indefinitely.

"Marie and Yasmina?" Damon guessed.

"Exactly," Liv confirmed as she tapped back a quick response.

You're the ones who convinced me to come!! You can't complain if I'm MIA. She rounded out her text with a winking emoji.

Then Liv opened a thread with Marie alone:

I'm the worst, Liv typed. I need to call you.

Fuck yes you do!! Marie responded.

I need to stop by the house anyway. FaceTime when I get home tomorrow and have some privacy?

Ok... Marie came back with a smiley emoji. Let me know when you're close so I can sanitize the common areas and go to my room.

Liv finally looked up from her screen.

"Everything okay?" Damon prompted.

"Yeah... I just haven't really checked in with them, and of course they want details."

"Well, we can't leave the girls in the dark, can we?" Damon asked with mock gravity.

Liv laughed. "No, we really can't. But listen, this reminds me. I need to pick up some more stuff from the house. And before you offer, *no*, you can't order me more clothes."

"Okay, okay!" Damon conceded. "We can go right now; I just want to shower off really quick."

"Oh, I don't know that I'm in the mood to go today..." Liv looked away from Damon and his perennial eagerness to please.

"That's okay! How's tomorrow?"

"Listen, Damon," Liv soothed as she took his face in her hands. "I would rather die than let you see the current state of my room."

Liv tried not to cringe at the lie. There was another reason entirely—beyond a messy room or the desire to speak with Marie in private—that she wanted to go alone.

Damon responded with a laugh and removed one of her hands from his cheek to kiss its palm. "Of course. Sorry. You know how I am. Let's get cleaned up and *eat!*"

LIV PUSHED HER EGGS around the plate with her fork the next morning. Her lie—her *omission*—could surely be forgiven. It was such a private thing, after all, and she had signed no contract obligating her to share *every* intimate detail of her life with Damon.

Still, it didn't feel good, and that guilt was punctuated by Damon's cheerful disposition—he was even sunnier than typical, bolstered by the positive sign that she had decided to collect more clothes. He practically bounced in his barstool at the kitchen island.

"Don't stay away too long," he said as he drew her into a kiss and pulled her stool closer to him.

Liv's phone pinged, and she opened one eye just enough to see the notification on her phone:

Google Calendar: BIG C SCAN 2PM.

Liv pressed her lips harder against Damon's and didn't pull away until she was sure her screen had gone dark again.

"I'll be fast, but it might take a little time. I want to clean up a bit too. I'll probably be back at about five."

Damon watched Liv play with her food.

"Upset tummy this morning?" he guessed.

Liv almost shook her head, but then caught herself. The perfect opportunity had been presented to give herself cover if she felt sick the next day from her injections.

"Yeah, a little!" she lied. "I'll spare you the gory details. But I'm okay to go get my stuff, I'm sure."

"Good," he leaned over and kissed her on the forehead.

Liv swallowed a bite of egg hard and washed down the guilt with a swig of orange juice.

LIV FAILED TO CONNECT her house key to its hole three times before the cylinder finally clicked. The uncertainty of yet another cancer screening coupled with her guilt was not a combination playing well with her fine motor skills.

And she would have to speak to Marie, nerve-racking on two fronts. Although it was still too careless for Liv to spend any time with Marie in person, something about leaving her cozy back house vacant for an indefinite period of time, and amid so much turmoil, felt like a betrayal. And speaking her feelings about Damon out loud to another person would make them even more *real*.

As if on cue, Liv heard a window in the main house slide open, and she looked to see Marie's head poking out.

"You're here!" she called out.

"I'm here! I just walked in," Liv yelled back.

"FaceTime me so I can shut this thing and keep the air conditioning in. It's hot as balls!"

"Yes, nurse!"

SHE FINIFHED RELAYING THE basic events of the last few weeks with a deep sigh that didn't seem commensurate with the monologue Liv had performed for Marie. Liv had conveniently sidestepped any emotional content from her story, choosing instead to focus on the beauty of the house, warm nights in the pool, and, of course, the fact that she had chosen to stay indefinitely.

Her phone sat propped against her vanity so that Marie could see her as she rifled through her closet, choosing outfits and then discarding them just as quickly.

But Marie's eyes narrowed on the screen.

"What are you leaving out?" she asked.

"What do you mean?" Liv replied innocently.

"You want to stay, and that's not at all like you. So, it doesn't exactly sound to me like you're 'just having fun and want to prolong your decision a little,'" Marie said, quoting Liv's bookend to her story.

"No," Liv admitted. "It's starting to feel a lot more serious than that."

"This is wild. I mean, I know we talked about it, but I thought it would just be a way for you to have some fun *safely* in the middle of a pandemic fighting off cancer cells."

"I know. I haven't felt this way, ever. Even with Christopher. I'm kind of... really scared."

Liv held up a sheer white chiffon button-down and furrowed her brow at a sizable moth hole.

"Can you put the fucking clothes down for one minute and come look me in the eye?"

"Digital eye," Liv corrected, but turned away from her closet and sat at her vanity, chiffon top crumpled in one hand. "But you're right. I'm sorry."

"Thank you. And I mean, I think you should be, a little."

"Should be what?" Liv asked.

"Scared."

A moment of silence passed between them.

"Because it's so fast?"

"Yeah, Liv. Because it's so fast," Marie said gently.

"We haven't even had sex!" Liv blurted out.

"Fucking *what*?" Marie threw her arms up, knocking her phone over and disappearing briefly from the screen.

"Easy!" Liv chided.

"Sorry!" Marie righted her phone and returned to the frame. "But like, what is going on *there*? Do you think something's wrong with his ding-a-ling?"

"No! I know there's not!"

"How do you know there's not if you've never had sex?"

Now Liv flushed. "Well, I sort of, you know, saw the contours of it while we were skinny dipping and it looked like…one would expect. And I also asked him."

"You straight up asked him?" Molly guffawed. "So you guys have like, talked about the fact that you're not having sex? What's up with that?"

"Okay, okay. Listen. He refused to kiss me for the first three days. We're doing this…intimate dance of building tension and getting to know each other. We'll know when the time is right."

Marie let out a whistle of astonishment.

"It's like he wants everything to be perfect," Liv went on. "But not in an artificial or weird way. He wants everything to be perfect for *me*."

"Mmkay. So, if everything is all rosy and so intimate, *Beauty and the Beast*, blah blah blah, why didn't you ask him to come to your screening today?" Marie challenged.

"That's a silly question for *you* to ask. No one can wait in the visiting room right now."

It was a convenient excuse.

Marie rolled her eyes. "And that's a dumb answer for you to give me. It's a big deal this early on in your remission. He could have waited in the parking lot. Did you think he'd say no? *Did* he say no?"

"No! That's not it at all!"

"Then why!"

Liv tapped her screen to check the time and sighed again.

"Because…I'm scared shitless, Marie. He doesn't even know I have an appointment today."

"Now why wouldn't you—" Marie's next question was punctured by a sudden mournful sob from Liv's side of the screen.

Liv was just as shocked by her sudden outpour of emotion.

"Baby. What are you scared about?" Marie cooed tenderly.

Marie's immaculate bedside manner was an exacting tool, even through an iPhone.

The truth tumbled out of Liv.

"Because…"

Liv interrupted herself with three quick sobs.

"Because," she tried again, "what if I get sick again and he doesn't want me anymore and this whole fantasy was just that? A fantasy?"

"Oh, sweetheart…" Marie bent close to her screen.

"Or what if I don't even get sick again, but he suddenly really understands the odds of that happening, and he cuts his losses? He's a businessman, after all."

"Oh, honey. I'd wipe your tears if I could. You're ruining your mascara."

Liv snorted a small laugh at that.

"Liv. Listen to me. Forget everything I said before about being worried. You can't hold so much of yourself back for fear of being hurt again. No one picks up the pieces like you."

Another grateful chuckle came from Liv.

"But if you want a chance to see if something good *can* happen, you have to tell him everything. You have to take a chance."

Liv dabbed at her eyes with the chiffon top and sniffed thoughtfully.

"I know," she said finally.

"And look," Marie sat back in her seat as though to indicate the matter was settled, "you have to know I really mean that, 'cause I'm really not thrilled about the idea of you leaving me with a totally empty house for this thing."

Liv smiled. "I wondered when you were going to say something like that."

"Are you still going to pay rent?"

"Of course."

"Good. But I'm sorry, Bob the Monstera is going to have to be the sacrifice for your love. I'm not watering that finnicky thing anymore."

"Marie! He's been alive for six years!"

"I know. And who gave him to you?"

Liv groaned.

"Exactly. Sometimes old things need to die to make room for the new."

"You're right. Ugh."

Liv examined the chiffon top one more time and threw it in her waste basket.

LIV ROUNDED THE CORNER to the oncology center and tried to keep a brave face. The fact that it wasn't her first rodeo never made the experience more pleasant.

Two workers in painters' suits and masks stood in front of the entrance, just beginning to push rollers of white paint up the wall. Liv paused to read the splashy red graffiti, an unusual sight in this part of town.

"Who's Floyd?" Liv asked, pointing at the letters JUSTICE FOR FLOYD, only with the "D" half painted already.

One of the painters, a Black man, turned to face her and demonstrably rolled his eyes. The other just shook his head.

That was fucking weird, Liv thought as she entered the building.

"Welcome back, Liv!" chirped the receptionist as Liv approached. "It's going to be another successful day! I just know it."

"I hope so," Liv agreed, but wondered if no one had ever admonished the grandmotherly woman for her fortune telling. What if a patient's result wasn't "successful"?

"Pricha's already ready for you. She'll be right out."

Moments later, sitting at the blood drawing station with Pricha, Liv attempted to distract herself.

"Did Dr. Kehr make an enemy here or something?"

Pricha looked up from her syringe with concern. "I don't think so…why do you ask?"

"The graffiti on the wall outside—Justice for Floyd. Is there a wrongful death suit or something?"

Pricha looked surprised. "Oh! You haven't…do you read the news? That doesn't have anything to do with us."

Liv looked sheepish. "I haven't really been keeping up with the world. Covid news is too depressing, you know?"

"You're not on social media or anything?"

"Oh, I mean I am, I've just been off the grid. Who is Floyd?"

Pricha shook her head as she capped the second vial of Liv's blood and prepared a fresh needle.

"A Black man was killed by Minnesota cops a few days ago. One jabbed his knee into the man's neck until he died. A few others stood around. Someone took a video of it. It's all over everywhere. People are planning big protests. There've been a couple, even here, already. Obviously."

"That's awful. I hate this country."

"The video is really bad. I wouldn't recommend watching it, if you can help it."

Pricha inserted her next needle into Liv's arm, who stared at the wall and bit her lip, embarrassed of her own inner turmoil.

10.

DAMON PACED THE EXPANSE of his entire first floor, equal parts giddy and restless. He felt safe enough with Liv by now to trust that she wasn't using the excuse of gathering more clothes to cut and run, and he couldn't help but marvel at how well things were going. Where was the catch?

Unsure of what to do with his afternoon of solitude, he finally settled on browsing Postmates to order supplies in case Liv still felt ill when she got home. He'd already rush-ordered a billiards table from a local distributor as a surprise.

Pepto Bismol, pro-biotics, Pedialyte, ginger tea...okay, this is getting excessive.

Damon shut his laptop and picked at a thread on the couch. He wished he had more friends to talk to and wondered for a moment if Liv would find it unattractive that most of his friends had fallen off the radar now that he was no longer throwing parties.

It suddenly occurred to him that he hadn't even texted Jay in at least a week. He punched in Jay's number and hit "Dial."

"...Hey?" Jay answered, turning the word up like a question.

Damon was too enamored in his own world to really notice.

"Hey, guy! What's going on?" he asked cheerfully.

"Uh...you know. Same thing as last time we spoke. Getting run ragged by the kid. Playing Mr. Mom while Sheila works from home. What's up with you?"

"I dunno, just wanted to see how you are..." Damon wasn't sure how to launch into the story of Liv.

But Jay's response seemed laced with a strange suspicion. "Yeah? And that's all?"

Damon was somewhat taken aback. "I mean, yeah. I have stuff I'd like to share, but I wanted to hear about you too. Is...is everything okay?"

Jay blew air out through his teeth. "I'm sorry, man. I've just been getting calls from pretty much every white person I know telling me how sorry they are. It's starting to feel like a performance."

"Huh?" Damon realized as quickly as the syllable had left his mouth. "Oh! Jesus. I don't know if it's better or worse that *that* is not what I'm calling about at all. I'm…sorry? Fuck, man, I don't know what to say right now."

Jay let out an amused laugh. "It's all good, man. I'm glad to talk about something else for a while."

"I did see it on the news, I just haven't watched the video yet…"

"It's…pretty crazy."

"Yeah? Do you think it's going to be like Ferguson?"

"Man…I think it's going to be worse."

"Wow."

They were both quiet.

"I didn't mean to step on your toes though. It's okay. Tell me what you wanted to tell me," Jay said finally. "Are you climbing up the walls over there? The kid's driving me nuts, but I'm glad to have something to do."

"That's the thing…I'm not."

"What! I was sure you'd be going out of your mind without a party to throw. And I miss those private security checks too," Jay laughed.

"Well…I haven't exactly been alone."

"Aw, man. If you're calling to tell me you're having underground parties or something, I just can't do it. I need the money, and if it was just me, I would, but I have to worry about the kid…"

"No! No. *God* no. It's nothing like that. Do you remember that girl from the last week at High?"

"Which one?" Jay quipped.

"Ha. You know the one. Liv. The one I met for coffee the next day."

"Oh, yeah. I remember her."

"Well, she's kind of living here."

"Nooooooo," Jay groaned. "You caught another crazy one? A moocher?"

"No. I *asked* her to stay. For the pandemic, at least."

"Are you calling to tell me you're in *looooove*?" Jay teased.

"Well, we haven't used that word yet. We're taking it really slow. But she's great, Jay. I'm scared of fucking things up."

"How would you fuck things up? You're a great guy!"

"I'm glad you think so, but I don't exactly have the best track record with women—"

As he spoke the words, Damon's phone suddenly pinged with a text:

Damon. I called you twice. You know I wouldn't reach out if it wasn't important.

A volt of anxiety surged through Damon. *Speak of the devil and she shall appear.* Damon felt stupid for wondering what the catch was mere minutes ago. His past was the catch.

Jay went on about reasons why Damon was a great guy who should trust himself, but Damon couldn't pretend to engage happily now that Nina had reared her head again.

"Jay, I'm so sorry to cut you off, but something's just come up…"

"That's alright, man. I'll talk to you soon."

"And hey, don't worry about any secret parties. I'm going to send the whole staff something anyway."

"Damnit, Damon—"

But Damon hung up before Jay could finish his objection.

He knew he should open Nina's text thread and at least see what the present crisis was, but instead he procrastinated by opening his banking app.

He sent two thousand dollars to Jay and began to make his way down his list of employees until he maxed out his daily digital transfer limit.

He massaged his temples and opened Nina's thread, the one he hadn't answered in a year. He looked at the last several texts before the one that interrupted him.

Hey, how are you?

Are you going to answer me?

Why do you still do this, Damon? Please.

DAMON.

I told you I'm clean now.

And I'm not trying to get back together either.

I need something else.

Each text made Damon more furious. Despite the way her refusal to get clean had torn open his heart, he had supported Nina beyond any legal or moral expectations. But she kept coming back for more, holding him hostage through guilt. He could easily block her, but she'd just email him or find him on Instagram. And, as toxic as Nina was, Damon was deeply afraid that a day might come when she'd need him for something more than money. He wasn't sure what that need would be, what kind of trouble she'd get into, but knew he'd hate himself if he let his anger prevent him from being there for Rand.

The thought that Rand might have a problem that Damon could solve only amplified his anger—if it *were* something with Rand, it felt manipulative that Nina wouldn't just come out and text him the information. How difficult could it be to be transparent about her situation? "Rand needs money for basketball camp", "Rand needs a kidney", "I'm losing custody" —anything to illustrate what was going on.

Damon began to pace again.

It occurred to him that he'd probably be unable to hide his anxiety from Liv when she returned, and that thought gave him even *more* anxiety.

He knew three would be a crowd in his budding relationship with Liv.

Damon resolved to smoke a bowl to clear—or cloud—his head. All he had left in his bedroom armoire was some stale shake, but it would do in a pinch. He carried his pipe out to the backyard and packed it, thinking of Liv's picturesque form in the pool as he watched the ripples on its surface.

He was certain of one thing: Liv fit into his soul like no woman ever had before. And he couldn't uncouple that truth from how deeply he resented that his past could raze it all to the ground.

He took a pull from the bowl and furrowed his brow at the unsatisfying taste of the shake. It was only about 2:00 p.m., but he tapped on the firepit base to conjure the wine fridge and pulled a bottle of scotch from its dry drawer underneath.

An impulse overcame him that felt insane.

Damon set down the bottle, unopened, and stripped naked before retrieving it again and squatting on the paved bridge that divided the pool.

Then he lowered himself in with the bottle and leaned against the pool's edge in the same place that Liv had offered him her bottle of wine almost two weeks prior.

He closed his eyes and uncapped his scotch bottle, half submerged in the water, and began to tip it to his lips, but the visuals weren't right. The sun cast a garish red glow against the backs of his eyelids and ruined the memory. He covered his eyes with one hand to block out the sun and tried to submerge himself in the incantation of the night that he knew—even if he occasionally doubted himself—that Liv would stay.

By the time Damon felt prepared to extract himself from his imagination, he was at least tipsy, and it was only 4:00 p.m. He was loath to text Liv about her whereabouts and paint himself as controlling, but he was just as loath to explain why he was moderately inebriated quite so early.

In lieu of either, he scrawled a note with a Sharpie and page from a yellow legal pad:

"*Think I might have caught whatever bug you did. Maybe the sushi? Gone to bed. Organic chicken soup in the fridge, box of tummy aids should arrive by 7PM at the door. Ashamed not to kiss you tonight, but it's for the best. There's a surprise in the living room. XO.*"

LIV CHUGGED HER BMW into the driveway and paused before getting out of the car. She'd already removed the bandages from her left arm where the needles had gone, but now rubbed the skin where the faint imprint of the tape remained, hoping it wouldn't be noticeable.

She'd taken Marie's words to heart and knew she would have to come clean to Damon, but she was still woozy from her appointment and just wanted to sleep. She stooped to collect the Amazon box at the front door and opened it without thinking, discovering the stomach medicine with some guilt.

But her relief was swift when she discovered Damon's note.

Whatever suspicion might have arisen by Damon citing a stomach bug that Liv never actually had was choked out by the comfort that she could climb into bed and recover alone, like a wounded animal retreating from its pack.

But of course, she peeked into the living room first to find what she already knew would be there—a gorgeously crafted billiards table.

Liv smiled despite her exhaustion and trudged up the stairs.

BY THE TIME LIV descended those stairs the next morning, she sported a healthy glow and no indication of the day prior. She briefly wondered upon waking if the whole process of chemotherapy, radiation, and mastectomy might have been easier if she always slept in a plush king-sized bed with windows open to the canyons.

She smiled as she spotted Damon reading a book on the daybed in the backyard, in blue jeans and a heather gray T-shirt, bare feet crossed.

Liv aimed to please in a barely there yellow bikini sported beneath a sheer scarf wrapped around her waist; she'd even straightened her hair and applied a fair amount of makeup.

When Damon heard her footsteps and turned, his reaction didn't disappoint. "My God, you're beautiful today," he said as he laid the book down and stood.

She couldn't help but tease him. "Only today?"

"You're stunning every day," he said with conviction. "But after your stomach bug, I wasn't expecting you to come down looking like *this.*"

Damon kissed her lightly on the lips.

"I missed you last night," Liv murmured.

"I missed you too," he returned. "I'm feeling much better today. And it's a day for celebration!"

"Why's that?" Liv asked.

He took her by one hand and turned her gently to admire her outfit. "Because it can only be a good sign that you went to collect more clothes!"

She laughed. "Did you think I was making a grand escape?"

"Well, no. But I did peek in your room to make sure your stuff was still there. Just to be sure," he admitted sheepishly.

Now Liv laughed harder. "Why would I want to escape paradise?"

He shrugged.

"Well, it was a lot of work to put my room in order. Plus, it's a Friday—it'd be nice to feel like it's actually a weekend instead of this weird time warp."

Damon furrowed his brow in mock offense. "My house feels like a weird time warp?"

She smacked his arm playfully. "*No.* You know what I mean. No work, rising whenever we want. The days blend together."

"Then how should we celebrate and break up the days? I can cook for you for once?"

Liv ventured a brave suggestion. "Actually, I was wondering if we had something else to party with?"

Damon looked surprised. "What exactly did you have in mind?"

"Well, you said you like Molly. And I think it would be nice to stare at the pool and into your eyes and giggle."

Damon thought for a moment. "I should have it around here somewhere."

"Is it definitely safe?"

"It's pure, medical grade. I had it tested."

"How'd you get that?" Liv asked, then immediately felt silly. It was evident to her by now that Damon could get anything he wanted.

Damon shrugged. "I've been known to let a few doctors into the club."

"I've never done it before," Liv reminded him.

"You're safe with me. I promise, it's like being able to kiss your own heart. You know they use MDMA as an antidepressant, and now there are trials to see if it helps soldiers with PTSD."

"You had me at 'kissing your own heart!'"

11.

"I'm nervous," Liv admitted as she watched Damon parse the crystals onto a scale between their chaise lounges, then use a medicinal spoon to transfer them into clear plastic capsules. "Not that I have any reason to be. I've never had a bad trip with Ecstasy."

"When people have bad experiences with Ecstasy or Molly it's always for a reason," Damon explained. "They buy it at a rave from someone they don't know, so it's cut with speed or coke or Drano. Molly is supposed to be the pure version of MDMA, but it rarely is. So, they call it Ecstasy."

"Or they take it and dance till they drop of dehydration," Liv added. "I'm so careful I've never even had an Ecstasy hangover."

Damon placed one half-filled capsule next to a glass of orange juice on a tray. Beside a second glass was a cap with more crystals. "You get less because you're a good sixty pounds lighter than me."

"I'm so into this," Liv said as she took a pill from Damon. "But you have to promise me something tonight."

"Anything you want."

"You have to promise you won't tell me you love me."

Damon laughed.

"I'm serious, Damon! You know how Molly is. It makes everybody all lovey-dovey. And it's one thing telling complete strangers at a party that you love them. But we're living with each other here. If we're not careful what we say tonight, tomorrow could a complete emotional mess. We'll wonder if what we felt and said tonight was real."

"Actually, that's kind of brilliant," Damon answered. "More than one woman and I have used the L-word on Molly and regretted it the next morning."

"Exactly. You should definitely be sober when you tell someone you love them."

"It's a deal," Damon answered as they chased the pill with orange juice.

LIV FELT THE MOLLY hit her about forty minutes later lying on her back on a giant pink swan pool float. The sun was lowering, and the backyard and house's interior were lit only by candles.

Eyes closed, feeling the dip in her roll that produced perfect relaxation, Liv listened to Damon play guitar. He sat on a chaise, playing that tune she'd heard him play so often in the past few weeks. Except today, the melody felt like it was sinking through Liv's skin, raising the thin blond hairs on her forearms like antennas picking up the melody.

Damon heard Liv softly humming the song and smiled. He knew the Molly was kicking in for him, too, because everything in sight had turned a beautiful orange hue. He stopped strumming and reached out to try to touch the air and noticed his finger stirred the hue into a molecular swirl. Damon loved that Molly only gave him the softest visual hallucinations.

"Please keep playing," Liv whispered as she opened her eyes and smiled at him.

Damon happily began again.

Liv hummed with him and slid sensually off her swan to swim toward him, a siren approaching a hapless sailor. As she reached his knees, he could see water droplets on his tan legs sparkle like diamonds.

"I love your voice," Damon whispered.

His own seemed to reach right into her open heart. She wanted to tell him she loved his playing, she loved the way he looked at her, she loved…then caught herself and laughed.

Damon played a final chord and laid the guitar on the lounge behind him.

"I feel like I'm made of water," Liv sighed luxuriously.

Damon slid into the pool, letting himself lower under the surface, feeling the water tingle around him like a massage, and then came up facing her. "Whenever I take Molly, I wonder why I don't use it every weekend."

"It's pretty special."

"Reminds me I have places in my heart that are hidden away most of the time."

Liv wrapped her arms around his shoulders just above the water and Damon reached around her hips. Their lips slowly came together, tasting each other more than kissing.

"Need anything?" Damon asked. "Drink? Music?"

"Nope. Just you."

"I really like making you happy."

"I like making you happy."

Damon smiled and looked at his house—it seemed to be vibrating. "I was thinking of ordering a few things for us."

Liv smiled contentedly. "What else could you possibly buy for this place?"

"I don't know. I don't want you to get bored."

"Don't worry about me. I'm so happy, I feel guilty about the rest of the world."

Damon turned thoughtful but not troubled. "Do you miss work? Being creative?"

Liv felt like her face was molded into a perpetual smile. "I like that you understand that what I do is more than just getting half naked and posing. What about you, you *must* miss work?"

"I've been talking to my partners about tearing down the ceiling of the club."

"What? I know I'm high, but..."

They laughed together, and Damon explained, "The city is talking about letting open-air and courtyard restaurants open. Probably won't happen for a few months, but we'd start the work now."

"That's brilliant!"

Damon thought he detected hesitation in her tone. "But?"

Liv tried to pout but her face wouldn't allow it. "You wouldn't be here with me twenty-four hours a day."

"I'll work while you sleep."

"I bet you would."

Liv turned her head and watched the sun lowering, the orange hue turning a deep, pensive purple in her eyes. "You know, I wouldn't blame you if you didn't want this thing between us to be anything more than casual."

Damon felt a moment of fear arise, then get washed away by the roll. "Where did that come from?"

Liv's warm glow began to fade. "I'm just saying I understand—I can't even give a man a family."

"Liv..." Damon reached out and stroked her hairline, pushing her wet strands back.

She breathed deeply and looked at the sky, several shades of blue. "You'd be crazy to marry me. I could be gone in a few years. I lied to you about where I was yesterday."

The fear welled up again. "What do you mean?"

"It was more of an omission than a lie. I had a screening yesterday."

He tucked a tendril of wet hair tenderly behind her ear. "Why would you lie about that? Of course I know you have to get screenings."

"I just didn't want to remind you that starting something with me is a gamble. I'm not out of the woods yet. And I've been afraid that if you thought of me as a sick woman, this whole thing might come crashing down."

Damon noticed a tear shining like crystal drip down her cheek.

"Hey, look at me," he said softly.

She lowered her face to his, only inches apart, and Damon's smile made her do the same.

"Years, months, hours…" Damon whispered, "Whatever time you give me will be enough."

Liv's tears stopped and she rested her forehead on his shoulder.

"Besides," he said softly. "I told you I'm okay with not having children."

Liv sniffled back the rest of the phlegm in her throat and pulled her chin up enough to look at Damon. "But what about your complaints of a big empty house?"

"You're all the company I need. Besides…I don't know what kind of a real father I'd be."

"Because of Rand?"

"Yeah, that's part of it. And I don't know if I have the right genes for it. Or the right upbringing."

Liv drew her head back and floated before him, waiting, afraid to pry.

But Damon went on.

"My adopted mother died when I was pretty young. They were older—I told you that part. I always thought we were well off, and I guess we were, for a time… My dad lived sort of a playboy life after her death, and I sort of did, too, but in the teenager way. Didn't really apply myself in school, assumed I'd be taken care of with a trust fund or something. But that wasn't the case. My dad got drunk on my eighteenth birthday and told me we were living well beyond our means. So much money had been poured into helping my mother get better, and he gambled a lot of it away after that."

"That's terrible. What did you do?" Liv stroked his dark hair, her turn to comfort.

Damon shrugged a bit. "I did two years of college before I decided it wasn't for me and moved to Bali. My dad died pretty shortly after that, pancreatic cancer. In some ways it's the best thing he ever did for me. It wasn't much, but once I sold off all his assets and paid his debts and the leans on the house, I had enough to seed my first company."

"Have you ever tried to find your real parents?"

"I have—23andMe, private investigators, the whole nine yards. But they're gone. I was a fire station surrender. There're less than a hundred per year. We should start a club. Fire Station Babies of '88."

Liv wrapped her legs around his torso and bobbed against his chest in the pool. "You don't have to make jokes about it. I'm sure it still hurts."

He kissed the top of her head. "I know. But it's been a long time. And I'm just trying to provide context for why I'm not sure I'd be 'World's Greatest Dad.'"

"Then we're quite a pair. Can we go inside?" she murmured.

"Of course."

Liv took Damon by the hand and led him up the pool stairs. Damon noticed the orange glow of the sun melting into a sensual violet. He didn't know if minutes or hours had passed, but suddenly it was only night.

Damon lifted a towel from a chaise and wrapped it around Liv's back, using it to dry her. As Damon took one for himself, Liv began moving into the house, candlelight flickering on the walls and ceiling.

Damon stared at Liv and without a glance back, she let the towel fall. Then she untied the strings holding up her bikini top and let those drop too.

Damon felt pulled toward her like a magnet, so he followed, his own towel falling loose.

Liv reached the stairs and sensually used a finger to pry away her bikini bottom.

She glanced over her shoulder at Damon and saw his approach.

Even though he'd seen Liv naked before, she'd been obstructed by lapping water. Now, before him, she looked positively unreal.

She smiled at Damon, the house and pool behind him seemingly invisible. She offered her hand, and he took it, following her up the stairs.

Behind her, his eyes went to the bare skin on her back, the curves as it met her bottom.

At the last stair, she stopped, and they locked eyes.

"Do you know I've never seen your room?" Liv said dreamily.

"I wanted to invite you in every night," he admitted to her. "But I wanted you to ask. I wanted everything on your time."

"I'm ready," she cooed as she took Damon's hand and led him toward his room.

The door was ajar, so Liv slipped inside, her eyes widening, pupils large. Liv didn't even glance right or left—admiring the interior design was not on her mind now. She made a beeline for Damon's white sheeted and pillowed bed at the far end beside a glass wall looking towards the night.

When she turned to Damon, his shorts were already off. He moved toward her and rested his hands on either side of her thighs.

Liv felt her body quivering as Damon kissed her.

She felt his heartbeat quickening.

Damon let Liv fall gently atop the bed, then climbed above her, kissing her, enveloped in massive throw pillows.

Overwhelmed by his senses—smell, touch, taste, sound— Damon licked his way down her chest. He lapped at her breasts to taste her nipples and Liv gasped, winding her fingers into his hair and pushing him down her stomach. She felt him biting her stomach ever so lightly and gave him an encouraging moan. She pushed him further down below her navel.

Damon buried his face between her thighs, licking greedily at the taste— *just right.*

Liv felt Damon's tongue and fingers work their way through her folds and started to shake.

"Please, now…" she called out and pulled Damon up and into her, feeling him fill her insides completely, even places she didn't know could be touched.

Damon felt sucked into Liv and thrust back and forth, keeping himself from bursting, feeling her nails digging into his back, both of them making guttural sounds.

"I want all of you," Damon whispered.

Liv pulled him into her so tight he couldn't withdraw. With only the slightest of movements, they both orgasmed.

"More," Liv urged.

Damon didn't know if he was capable of coming again, but couldn't believe how hard he'd stayed inside her, so he began to move up and down on her. It was as if they'd never stopped.

Opening his eyes, he saw that Liv's were wide open, staring into his. Neither could look away. Or wanted to.

THEY DRIFTED in and out of sleep in his bed, limbs intertwined, unbothered by the crisp sunlight streaming in through window shades neither had thought to close, nor cared were open now.

Liv was the first to have a coherent thought. *Thank God I'm not hungover.* She knew she had Damon to thank more than God—he'd fed her before they'd taken the Molly and plied her with bottled water throughout the night; even during their sexual marathon, he'd occasionally beg that she let him get out of bed and come back with hydration.

Glancing around Damon's bedroom, an even larger but similarly decorated suite as her own, Liv indeed felt physically sober, but knew that her emotional sobriety was another story entirely.

To begin with, she kept returning her gaze to Damon's face. Yesterday he'd been one of the most handsome men she'd ever laid eyes on, but today he seemed like a work of art created by a Renaissance master. She couldn't keep her hands from reaching out and lightly fondling his cheeks, his nose, his eyebrows. And his lips…they called to her with such magic that as comfortable as she was lying in his arms, she was compelled to slide over and kiss him, even if it woke him.

Damon's mouth twisted into a smile before his eyelids darted open.

"I'm sorry," Liv whispered. "Go back to sleep."

"Back? I'm not sure we ever really slept."

She gave a proud laugh. "It's true. I've never had sex like this."

"Neither have I."

Liv opened her mouth to speak, then paused.

"What?" Damon asked.

"I don't know," she answered shyly. "Sometimes I wonder if you're just telling me what I want to hear. Or, in this case, if it's still the Molly speaking."

"The Molly wore off around two a.m.," Damon assured her. "And if you doubt my sincerity, just stick around. Eventually you'll have to believe I mean it."

Liv rolled atop him to pin his arms over his head and kiss him. She felt him getting hard again and laughed.

"I don't know how you don't run out of steam, but I might need a break. A little sore down there, you know?"

"Maybe I should kiss it and make it better?"

Liv groaned with anticipatory delight but pushed herself off him. "Seriously, I'll have lady issues, and we won't be able to fool around for a few days."

"Well, we wouldn't want that. How long a break are we talking about?"

"Just long enough to eat. And maybe ice it."

Damon laughed. "Why don't we take that break right here in bed? We'll order some food and talk. I'll promise to leave you alone."

"It's not you I'm worried about! No, I'm just gonna make my way to my bedroom and take a shower."

"Good luck!"

"You don't think I can do it?"

He caressed her arm with the knuckles of one hand. "I think you *can*. I'm just not going to make it easy for you…"

Damon smiled mischievously, the hand finding its way to Liv's breast.

"No, go away!"

Damon laughed and pulled his hand back, but Liv only shifted.

"We certainly made a mess of this bed, that's for sure," she said as she glanced at the sheets and pillows strewn about the floor. "But you know what I don't see around here?"

"What's that?"

"Condoms."

"We've both been tested. And you said you can't have children, right?"

"Yes, of course."

"So what are you worried about?"

Liv frowned as she tried to understand her own reaction. "Damon, are you sure you'd be okay without children? Because things are clearly getting serious here and I'd hate for you to wake up and feel cheated."

Damon nodded. "There is nothing about you that I don't like. Nothing I'm afraid of."

Liv looked down and saw that Damon was holding her hand in his. Though the mood had shifted from sexy too quickly for her liking, she couldn't help finding herself feeling even more drawn to Damon with every word he spoke.

"Okay, I'm gonna do it," she blurted out.

"Do what?"

"I'm gonna say it," she began, holding her breath. "I made us promise we'd avoid the word last night, but I heard it in my head the whole time we were making love. Because that's what we were doing. We weren't having sex, we weren't fucking. We were making love. At least I know I was making love. I'm in love with you. I love you, Damon."

Liv exhaled and stared at Damon, fraught with fear of rejection.

"I love you, too, Liv. I knew I was in love with you at first sight, at the club that night. I just never admitted it myself because you'd have thought I was insane."

"I would have! But I guess I've been in love with you almost as long. From that first weekend I spent here."

Damon felt his heart expand and was confident that Liv's beat for him as strongly. "Look at us fools, trying to pretend we can take it slow."

Liv laughed as she lay back down atop him. "I'm head over heels in love with you, Damon. You're the most attentive, caring, and thoughtful man I've ever met. No man has even come close to making me feel this safe. When I look at you, I can barely string a coherent thought together."

"Sounds about right," Damon said with flush cheeks. "Want to know what I love about you?"

"Only so I keep doing it!"

He paused thoughtfully. "I love how vulnerable you are. I love how adventurous you were for even considering an invitation to live with a complete stranger. I love how you share every thought that comes into your head, even if it's completely embarrassing. I love how in the moment you are. And how bravely you're facing..."

"Do not dare use the C-Word in this conversation," Liv interrupted him. "If you love me, it's without sympathy or pity. You love me for how fucking amazing I treat you."

"I was going to say, 'this fucking pandemic' but okay," he grinned.

Liv covered her face with her palms. "I feel so spoiled. All my friends are stuck at home and I'm living with the most kind and ridiculously sexy, generous man. I don't deserve this. I don't deserve you."

Damon kissed Liv's shoulder. "Who's to say who deserves good things? Life is a total crap shoot. We're just space dust spun into molecular patterns. And I, for one, am completely at peace knowing I spun into you one night and was smart enough to recognize a spark of lighting, and when the world started to collapse, took matters into my own hands so that we could have a chance at something together."

"You're a poet too! A guitar-playing poet!"

Damon laughed. "Do you know that every time you sing in the shower, I sit outside your door and listen?"

"You do?"

He smiled like a boy who'd just admitted to stealing candy.

"I'm in love with my stalker," Liv joked.

Damon took Liv's face in his hands and kissed her. She kissed him with equal fervor, and soon they were lowering into the bed, body parts connecting, breaths panting.

"What about that break?" Damon said through his gasps.

Liv answered by pulling him deep inside her—deeper, she knew, than she'd ever let a man go.

"BEING IN LOVE with you makes me realize I might have never been in love before," Liv said. "Does that make sense?"

She was on her side in bed, facing Damon, his arm outstretched under the pillow.

"Mm-hmm," Damon said. "I meant it when I told people I loved them before, but I didn't feel it this overwhelming. Now I understand why people call love a drug."

Liv laughed. "I hope you never need Liv Anonymous."

"Never."

Liv smiled as she slid towards him, as if the foot between her and Damon was too far. Three days had passed since they'd taken Molly, and they'd made forays out of his bedroom, but only for food or the occasional dip. And even then, they'd been unable to cook without Damon propping her up on the counter, unable to shower without pressing up against each other under the steam nozzles.

"There's usually a honeymoon period where you want to make love all the time, but this is ridiculous," Damon added, his hand caressing Liv's hip.

"Is that a complaint?" she teased, knowing the answer.

"Obviously not. But I do have a suggestion."

Liv concocted a British accent. "What is it, my love? How may I please you more?"

Damon chuckled. "Well, it's like this: the only time we're apart is when you're going to the bathroom or changing clothes in your room. But the minute you leave, I get anxious."

"That's so cute. So do I actually. What do you propose we do about it?"

"The toilet thing, I'll have to learn to live with. But I think you should move all your stuff into this room."

"Into your bedroom?"

"I want it to be *our* bedroom."

Liv gave a fake sigh. "You're so demanding. But okay, on one condition."

"Anything."

"You help me pack, so we're not apart for those twenty minutes."

Damon smiled, enjoying their loving one-upmanship. "Do you think we'd be this crazy in love if we weren't in lockdown?"

"I'm sure we would have met again somehow," Liv answered. "I never believed in soul mates and twin flames before. And I grew up with a looney mom who studies astrology, past lives, reads tarot and all that. She's gonna love that you made me a believer."

An idea worked its way into Damon's head. "Why don't we go to Florida and see your mom?"

"I wish. I do miss her. I've told you about how there's this distance between us of late…"

"Seriously, I'll fly us private and make sure the pilots are tested. I'm sure the doctors would say that's safe for you?"

Liv let out an exasperated breath. "Damon, you're the most generous human being on earth. But I'm not going to let you spend a fifty grand on a private plane for me."

"I wouldn't offer if I couldn't afford it."

"That's not the point. I'm not a spoiled child like your exes. I'll see my mom when it's safe to fly commercially."

"I respect that. But it's my money, so maybe I'll just rent the plane and leave an empty seat for you in case you change your mind last minute."

"You'd be that devious, wouldn't you?"

"You have no idea."

"Well, I hope you have a good time there, because I won't be on the plane."

"You'd be that stubborn, wouldn't you?"

"I would. And I want you to love this about me: I will not let you think I want you for your money in any way."

"What if I married you?"

"Then I'd fly private with you!" Liv answered cheerfully, then quickly added sternly, "But don't you dare propose. Love hasn't made us that stupid."

Damon laughed. "Okay. But I'm telling you, now my life will feel incomplete until I get you to Florida."

"Fuck, you're making me wet."

"Again?"

Liv answered by taking Damon's hand and pushing it down, under the sheets.

"Can't fake that," Damon said as he gently guided his fingers inside her and felt invitingly sublime, wet warmth.

12.

DAMON'S PHONE VIBRATED BESIDE the bed as Liv folded over the top sheet and plumped up the pillow.

Don't know why I'm even bothering to make the bed, she laughed to herself, then looked around for Damon, calling out, "Your phone is buzzing!"

"Ignore it, honey," he said as he carried in Liv's suitcases and headed toward the walk-in closet large enough for a family of four.

The buzz stopped.

Liv loved that Damon was rarely on his phone when she was around, and since that was basically *always*, she had noticed he rarely made calls or even checked his phone. Liv had been so inspired by this that she'd started going days without glancing at her own—days without checking messages and social media. At first, breaking that addiction had required discipline, but now she found it freeing. She was more in the moment, more present, less distracted. Now, instead of getting news from clickbait, Liv was aware of the outside world because Damon made a habit of watching the 6:30 p.m. NBC news.

Liv also loved that it came right before dinner, so their conversations often were spirited debates about current events and politics. It made her realize that before the pandemic, dinners with her friends were usually little more than talk about *The Kardashians* or Kanye's latest dramas. And Liv appreciated how Damon listened to her opinions. Even if ignoring real news had left her less knowledgeable about the history of most subjects, Damon never teased her. He had once joked that "good conversation is the best aphrodisiac," and Liv truly found herself turned on by their long talks.

Damon had also begun suggesting books for her to read, and without distractions, she'd started spending hours beside him by the pool, reading. This week, Liv was a third of the way through Hillary Clinton's memoir *What*

Happened. Perhaps her growing political awareness was widening the chasm she felt between herself and her mother, but she pushed the thought away.

The last few nights of news and conversation had been especially enlightening. Damon and Liv had watched the television in horror as footage was replayed of police in Minneapolis kneeling on the neck of George Floyd until he died. Thousands were marching in cities all over the country, "Black Lives Matter" their rallying cry.

Troubled by the recollection, Liv turned to Damon as he came from the closet. "Do you think there will be more Black Lives Matter marches in Los Angeles tonight?"

"I'd bet on it."

"I wish I could march."

"I'd go with you if you could," Damon answered. "But with your immune system, it's just not worth the risk. Not even masked. I know so many people who have it right now, it's ridiculous. It's bad out there. Hospitals are running out of beds and ventilators."

Liv folded her arms and stared out the glass wall toward the city. "I know. I'm still getting my dispatches from Marie. Such a lonely way to die."

"You're safe here," Damon said as he walked behind her and wrapped his arms around her.

"I know."

Damon's phone buzzed once more.

"It's been ringing off the hook," Liv told him.

"Really?"

Damon went to his phone with mounting trepidation. He scrolled through the texts, then clicked on a voicemail. As he listened to a message, Liv watched his countenance twist.

"Everything okay?" she asked as he hung up.

"Nothing for you to worry about."

"If it concerns you, I care."

After a second, Damon answered, aware that he could no longer avoid burdening Liv. "I've been ignoring Nina for a few months. Now she says it's important and that she's going to come up here this afternoon."

Liv sat up with some alarm. "How do you feel about that?"

"Somewhere between furious and fuming. I have to call her."

"You want privacy?"

Damon looked at Liv as if she'd suggested he cut off a finger as he dialed the phone. "Absolutely not. I want you to be a part of my life in every way."

Liv felt some relief that Damon had nothing to hide.

"What's going on?" Damon asked, voice low.

He listened, staring at Liv for moral support.

"Absolutely not," he told the person on the end of the line.

Then, after listening more, Damon grit his teeth. "Okay, but I'll have to send someone to get you tested first. And even if you're negative, we talk out back."

He listened, then seethed, "I don't care how careful you say you've been. Show up here this afternoon and I'll call the police. And you know I will. I've done it before."

Liv veiled her surprise at hearing that revelation.

"Okay, then," Damon said into the phone. "I'll have my nurse test you, and if you're negative, you can come over tomorrow at noon."

Damon hung up without a goodbye.

Liv moved toward him. "Are you okay?"

He opened his arms for her. "I will be."

"She wants money?"

"She says this is about something else, something she didn't want to talk about on the phone."

Liv bit her tongue, too respectful to push for an answer when Damon didn't seem to have one.

"Don't worry, I'll make sure it's safe for her to be here," Damon assured Liv. "And just to be careful, you should stay inside while we talk."

"I'll be fine if she's tested, and we're masked outside. It's more about me being there for emotional support, but I'll do whatever you want. Will Nina be upset if I'm here?"

"I couldn't give a shit what upsets her."

"Did you really call the police on her?"

"About a year ago. She was high as a kite, banging on the door for half an hour and screaming. She got arrested for drunk and disorderly."

"Wow, now I know why you don't answer her calls. But why don't you block her for once and for all?"

"I'd like to. But I'd hate it if something happened to Rand and I didn't know about it. There's something else too."

"What's that?"

"She's bringing him."

Liv was stunned into silence for a moment.

"How old is he now?" she asked.

"Fifteen. I met her when he was six, and left when he was twelve. He was just the sweetest boy."

"Did you make an effort to see him after you left?"

"Yeah, of course. But he was just too convenient of a tool for her to use to try to rope me back in. It got too manipulative…"

"That's terrible of her. You were his father figure for six years."

"I was more than a father *figure*. Rand didn't even know he had a biological dad. Nina once told him I named him in the hospital."

Liv accepted a cup of coffee he slid to her and took a seat on one of the barstools. "You said she was high the night she last came over?"

"Cocaine by night, Xanax by day."

"Jesus…"

"I wasn't perfect," Damon continued in earnest. "Obviously. I could have killed his mother on the back of a motorcycle. And I was emotionally immature in other ways, too. Like thinking that Nina and I would get happily married and play house when she expressed from the beginning that she wasn't the marrying type. But when it came to that boy, man, I was there… There would be weeks when I was the only parent. I even talked to a lawyer about getting custody but was told unless I could prove she was completely unfit or a danger to him, it was pointless. The only leverage I thought I had was money. Nina would promise me time with him but when I wrote her a check she just disappeared. I finally stopped trying to bribe her last year."

"So, she knows she has to bring him here first now?"

Damon sipped at his coffee, vexed. "I hope that's all it is. And honestly, if she does, I'll give her just about whatever she needs. Even after three years, when she said she was bringing him, my heart leaped."

Liv smiled, moved by the paternal side of Damon. "Why else would she be bringing him?"

"She said he was in trouble."

"Fifteen years old, living in Los Angeles with an addict mom…" Liv sighed. "I'd be surprised if he wasn't getting into things. But I'm sorry. I've never seen you look this worried."

Damon turned his stool to face Liv. "I'm sorry I haven't told you more about him."

"I understand. I haven't wanted to pry because I know it's painful for you."

"Thank you for understanding."

Damon pulled out his phone. "I'll arrange for them to get tested. And maybe I'll have the nurse also test her blood for drugs, while she's at it."

"Can you do that?"

"Legally, no. But I bet a grand will buy me a very cooperative nurse."

"Do it!"

"You think I should?"

"It's probably too much of an invasion of privacy. But I have to admit, it's kind of sexy that you're thinking about it."

Damon laughed. "You want me to be a criminal?"

"I guess not. But hearing it makes me feel like I'm on your team and we're in this together. It helps with the jealousy aspect too."

"That's exactly what I was afraid of. I never want you to feel jealous. You have no reason to be. I feel like I'm starting a whole new life here with you and I want to look forward. That's part of why I've been so tight-lipped with all of this."

"It is pretty overwhelming when you think about it, isn't it? How close we've become."

"Liv, I'm out of words to describe how much I love you."

"Those are words. Here's two more: kiss me."

They did so, each feeling a spark at a new opportunity to be united—on the same team.

LIV ANXIOUSLY WIPED the kitchen counters as Damon came downstairs the next afternoon. They both wore their usual jeans and T-shirts, their new pandemic uniforms, except Liv had covered her bare feet with sneakers, wore a spot of makeup, and had her hair tied back in a neat bun.

"Nervous?" Damon asked with a smile to reassure her that he wouldn't expect otherwise.

"No, I meet my boyfriend's estranged addict ex-girlfriend and their son every day."

"I'm sure she won't be high today. She knows I'd throw her out right away. And she said that she was in the program."

"Good for her," Liv answered, trying to sound supportive when her insides screamed, *fuck that bitch*. "But are you sure you want me around? Does she even know about me?"

"Yeah, I texted so she wouldn't flip out."

"And?"

"She wasn't thrilled that someone she doesn't know would be around. But I told her you weren't just anybody and that anything she had to say, I wanted you to hear."

Liv smiled and tossed the wipes into the trash as Damon came up to her with a hug. "I appreciate that," she said. "But promise me if you need me to step out, you'll give me a sign."

"What, like this?" Damon asked, tugging his ear.

Liv playfully slapped his shoulder. "I'm serious, Damon! I don't want to come in the way of you reconnecting with your son."

Damon smiled, appreciative of how Liv kept referring to Rand as "his son."

The doorbell chimed on Damon's phone.

"Meet you outside?" he asked Liv as he handed her a mask in an individually wrapped package, one of several he'd placed in a jar on the counter.

"N95s! I hear these things are impossible to find."

"I bought them from the nurse who tested us. You wouldn't believe how much I paid for them."

"Thank you," Liv said as she looped the strings of the mask behind her ears and headed outside.

Liv took a seat on the sectional near the firepit. She fidgeted with it, so nervous she thought she'd start sweating soon. Liv and Damon had been so careful with her health that this was the first person, besides her oncology team, that either of them had seen since she'd moved in.

She heard voices and turned to see Damon walking out beside a Black woman, stunningly beautiful even with a mask hiding her mouth. She wore stylish billowing pants that Liv speculated she probably bought in Bali and a Chanel purse over her shoulder. Liv blinked, wondering why Damon hadn't mentioned that his ex was Black, then felt guilty, realizing that even asking herself this was racist. *Why should Damon have told her?* On Damon's other side was a Black teenager in black camo pants and a black tee—Liv thought she detected a scowl, but couldn't see his mouth so she wasn't sure. But she *was* sure that she sensed all three of them were uncomfortable.

Only Damon's eyes lit up over his mask as he placed a hand on the teen's shoulder. "Rand, Nina, this is Liv."

Liv stood and held out her hand. "Nice to meet you."

Rand gave Liv a limp handshake and Nina didn't even raise her hand—just let out a curt, "Hi."

"Can I get anybody some coffee? Or a Coke?" Damon asked, looking at Rand for the second option.

"Coke's cool," Rand said without looking at Damon. Instead, he stared out over the expanse of the pool, eyes narrowed in what looked like resentment. Liv found herself wondering what Nina's home was like.

Nina ignored the question and tugged at her mask. "Can we take these off? You got us tested and we haven't left the house in more than a week."

Damon looked to Liv. "I think that's safe," she responded.

They all removed their masks. Now that Liv could see Nina's face, with her full lips and perfect skin, another twinge of jealousy shot its way through her body.

"Have a seat," Damon said while grabbing the drink from the outside fridge.

Rand sat on the sectional beside Nina, still glancing around the house.

"Dope fuckin' house," he finally spoke.

"Language!" his mom hissed.

Damon asked as he handed the boy a Coke bottle. "Do you remember much about me, Rand?"

Rand shrugged. "Sorry."

Liv saw disappointment in Damon's eyes. She felt bad for him, but he quickly waved the comment away, saying to the boy, "I'm sorry we haven't kept in touch."

"Whatever," the teen responded.

"The boy has no respect," Nina complained. "Fifteen and he's never in class, always getting high on something."

"Wonder where I get that from?" Rand grumbled.

"Don't you dare talk shit to me," Nina snapped. "I've been sober for almost a year, and if you keep it up, I'll send your ass to rehab."

But Rand didn't back down. "So what, you bring me here instead? What you think this man gonna do that you couldn't? I mean, what's he to me? You know what? I *do* remember him. I remember him doing a disappearing act. And some other stuff too," he said with a pointed look at Damon.

"I'm so sorry about that," Damon said.

Liv was impressed that Damon didn't add: *because your mother wouldn't let me.* Though he deserved to defend himself, he wasn't willing to poison the boy against his mother.

Nina broke the silence. "We all made mistakes. Damon did try, Rand. I just wasn't in the right place to see that."

The teen took a long sip of the Coke, looking like he couldn't care less whose fault it was.

"I'm just glad you're here now," Damon said. "Can you tell me a bit about what's going on here, now?"

"Do *you* want to tell him?" Nina looked at Rand.

"I don't know what you're talking about," Rand said moodily and kicked one of his sneakers at the stamped concrete.

"He's been stealing cars."

Damon raised a brow. "You stole a car?"

Rand shrugged it off. "That's not true. That's an exaggeration. It's not like I jacked one. I borrowed my mom's car."

"You didn't ask. And you don't even have a license!" his mother exclaimed.

"I'm halfway through my lessons. You drive with me. And I brought the car back in a couple hours."

"Because I called you and threatened your ass," Nina shot back. "And that's not the point. You could have been arrested! Or got in an accident and hurt someone."

"Well you wouldn't drive me and took away my phone so I couldn't call an Uber."

"Rand, you're too young to be marching in those protests."

"Wait a minute," Damon jumped in. "So he stole your car to go to a Black Lives Matter march?"

"Yeah. And it's not because he gives a damn. He just going because this girl goes. But she's seventeen."

"Why you make me sound like some horny little kid?" Rand whined.

"Because that's how you act."

Rand seethed.

"Look," Nina went on. "It doesn't feel good to be here right now. But we don't really have a community anymore. I've got my friends in NA, but there's not people I can call on to look after him. He needs a male influence in his life. Someone like you."

"I haven't always been the best..." Damon trailed off. He didn't want to appear to be making excuses not to help.

Now Nina gestured at the backyard. "I want him to have a positive influence—someone to look at and see why it's important to work hard and apply yourself."

"You make it sound like some corny 'Big Brothers and Sisters' program," Rand grumbled.

Nina ignored him. "I have my hands full here, Damon. He's running circles around me."

Now Damon interrupted her. "Rand, I'd love for you to stay with me and Liv for a few days."

"I'd *love* that!" Liv interjected, having held her tongue respectfully for several minutes now.

"I'm serious," Damon went on. "Let him stay here for a couple days. I'll talk to him about what's up and see if I can help."

"Thank you, Damon. Rand? What do you say, want a few days off from your bitch of a mother?"

"I guess," he answered without enthusiasm. "But I got nothing to do up here so can I get my phone back?"

"Okay, but you stay off Instagram and Snap. Understood?"

"Yeah sure," the boy said unconvincingly.

Damon looked confused. "Did something happen on Instagram?"

"Yeah, I had to delete his account because he was following nothing but women with no clothes on."

Rand looked ashamed. "That's not true. I have friends on there."

"Whatever," Nina said as she pulled the boy's phone out of her purse and handed it to him. "This is just so you can contact me. That's it. You download those apps again and I'll take it away for six months."

"Fine," the teen said as he turned on the phone. "I must have a hundred messages."

The boy stood and walked toward the pool to find a little privacy, eyes never leaving the phone.

"I'll run home and come back with some clothes," Nina said to Damon.

"Okay. And listen, I know we've had our stuff, but I really appreciate this. And you seem like you're doing well," Damon offered.

She nodded but sighed. "It's been hard. I did an outpatient rehab for three months, and I'm really grateful to be sober...but I'm scared the damage is done with Rand. He developed this damn rebellious shit and it's just getting worse. And he remembers a lot, Damon. It's scary how much he remembers."

"I'm glad you eventually figured it out," he said tersely.

Nina gave a knowing smile. "No, you're not. I was stupid not to follow your lead, I know. I just couldn't hear you telling me to get clean every day."

Liv fought back that jealousy again, sensing things were getting personal between Damon and Nina. "If you two want to talk, I can go make lunch."

"No, I'm going," Nina said, getting to her feet. "Thank you, Liv. I'm sorry we met under these conditions."

"Same," Liv answered.

"And watch your back with that one," Nina said, glancing at her son. "He's fifteen, mad at the whole world, and slippery as fuck."

"He'll be okay here," Damon said as he stood. "Let me show you the door."

"I can find the front door. I'll just drop his clothes on the porch when I come back up," Nina added. "In case he changes his mind."

Damon nodded. "Okay. I'll text you if I need anything."

"Please don't, I need a break," she joked. "Oh and take his phone before bed. Otherwise he'll be up all night with it."

"Okay," Damon answered.

Liv watched Nina head to the front door, then turned to find Damon, staring pensively at Rand.

"She was nothing like I expected," Liv said. "And she didn't ask for money."

"She will eventually."

"You still think her leaving him here is just a ploy?"

"I don't know. And I still don't care. When I opened the door and saw him, it was as if the last three years never happened. For me, anyway."

"It's amazing how much you love him."

The beginning of tears moistened Damon's eyes.

"Awe, honey," Liv whispered as she put her arms around him.

"I'm sorry," Damon said with a cracked throat. "I don't know why I'm crying. Joy, regret, hope, worry..."

"Damon, I think it's beautiful when a man can cry."

Damon inhaled to collect himself. "It's not too much drama for you?"

"Of course not. I'm so happy you get to spend time with Rand. And I want to get to know him too."

He pulled out of the hug with a smile. "You're too damn sweet."

"I guess I'm a pretty cool chick, huh?"

"Freezing."

Liv followed Damon's glance to Rand, sitting on the grass, tapping away at his phone.

"Now what?" Liv wondered aloud.

13.

LIV STOLE LOOKS OUTSIDE as she cooked dinner, where Damon and Rand hung out on rafts in the pool as the sun went down. Rand and Damon were locked in a battle of trying to stand on their respective rafts, succeeding for seconds at a time before flailing into the pool, to the great amusement of both.

The kid in everyone comes out in a pool, Liv mused. She was glad to have insisted she cook so Damon and the boy could have some time alone.

She spooned a bit of pasta into her mouth to test before calling out, "Dinner!"

Liv ladled the pasta onto plates, added an arrabbiata sauce she'd made from scratch, then sprinkled specks of Romano atop each.

Damon and Rand entered wrapped in plush robes as Liv carried the plates to the dining room table, already set with two wine glasses and a Coca Cola bottle.

"Can we eat, like, in our suits?" Rand asked.

"Of course! Sit!"

Damon smiled at her warm parental supervision and took a seat. He'd barely reached for his napkin before the boy was diving into the pasta.

Liv shared an amused look with Damon, then sat herself. "How is it, Rand?"

Mouth full, he gave a thumbs-up.

Liv, who'd never cooked for a child before, felt like she'd been awarded her first Michelin star.

Damon saw her delight and raised his glass. "To being reunited."

Liv toasted back. "To families, which come in all shapes and sizes."

Rand realized he was the only person without a glass, grabbed his Coke, tipped the edge toward them, and drank nearly the whole bottle in one gulp.

"I went easy on the spice," Liv said humbly to Damon as he tasted the dish.

"It's still…" he said, kissing his fingertips.

Liv smiled, then glanced at Rand, trying to approach him with as little pressure as possible. "So, Rand, where do you and your mother live?"

"In Venice. It's nothing like this place, but Mom likes being near the beach."

"I met your mother on the beach," Damon said. "Surfing in Bali."

"I know. She doesn't surf much anymore. She goes to a meeting like, every day. Sometimes two times a day. Now it's all on Zoom."

"I don't get out very often myself these days."

"My mom says you opened a club and didn't have time for her. But damn, look at this house. You got rich from just one club?"

"No, I also buy and sell real estate."

"That's smart. I mean, everything is closed up now. Think you'll open up again soon?"

Damon chose his words so he wouldn't frighten the boy with reality. "Things are going to be like this for a little bit more. They're working on a vaccine, but who knows when it will roll out."

"I ain't taking a shot. It's probably being made in the same lab the virus came from."

Liv and Damon exchanged surprised looks.

They had talked about Covid ad nauseam, and he'd always held a strong belief that the virus wasn't part of a governmental conspiracy.

"What?" Rand said defiantly at their shared look.

"I mean, we really don't know where the virus came from," Damon offered respectfully.

"Sure, but I don't trust a vaccine far as I can throw it."

"And why's that?" Damon asked.

"Psh. You ever hear of the Tuskegee Experiment?"

Damon nodded. "Ah."

But Liv looked at Rand with interest. "I haven't."

Rand scraped his plate with his fork to excavate the last of the arrabbiata sauce.

"Figures," he said with a shrug. "Not a lot of white folks have."

Liv stabbed a bit of pasta and waited respectfully for him to go on.

"The government wanted to study what happens when syphilis isn't cured. So, they take a bunch of black men from the ghetto, say they're giving them cures for the thing and they're gonna study the progress. Well, it was a lie. They didn't cure them. They just watched them go insane and die one by one."

"God," Liv said with horror.

"Yeah. And it wasn't a one-time thing neither. Went on for forty years."

"Truly horrific. But we're hoping—thinking—this vaccine is legitimate. It's important because Liv has a weakened immune system," Damon said diplomatically.

Rand nodded to Liv. "Sorry about that. What do *you* do?"

Liv was grateful for the change in subject, again feeling the heat of her relative ignorance of the world, but paused, recalling Nina's complaints about the boy's Instagram use. But there was no way around the truth. "Well, I'm a model and influencer."

"That's cool. How many followers you got?"

Liv started to feel uncomfortable; she didn't want Rand to go back to his mother and report that she was one of those women she hated him following. "I have a fair amount."

"You got a hundred thousand or something like that?"

"A little more," she dodged with modesty.

Rand rolled his eyes. "You know, I don't give a fuck if my mother thinks I'm a perv. Every teenager in the world follows hot girls."

Liv queried Damon with a look, and he said, "I agree with him. You have nothing to hide."

Liv sipped her wine. "Last time I checked it was just over a million."

Rand stopped chewing. "No shit. Can I see your 'gram?"

"I wouldn't want to piss off your mom."

"Probably smart. She'd chew both of our asses off."

Damon, who'd been watching this with some amusement, could tell that Liv didn't like her place on the hot seat, and changed the subject. "You really have a seventeen-year-old girlfriend?"

Rand blushed. "She don't call me that. She just teases me. But I follow her around like a stupid puppy dog."

Damon laughed. "I'm Liv's dog, man."

"No, you're not!" Liv objected, then turned back to Rand.

"What do you like about this girl?" Liv asked.

"Obviously, she's hot," the boy admitted. "But what gets me is that she's not like every other girl. She doesn't use filters on her pictures, and despite what my mom thinks, she's real. Her 'gram is all about social justice. She's why I stole my mom's car. Mom wouldn't let me go march."

"I'm sure she's just worried about your safety," Damon responded.

"No, she just doesn't get it. You guys had the sixties, but we have this. This is our chance to change things."

"We're not that old," Damon answered. "But I hear you. I can't say I know what it's like to be Black, but when I was out with you and your mother, I saw how people looked at us differently."

"Yeah, and the cops are the worst. The ones that killed George Floyd should get the electric chair."

Liv felt like she had little to contribute to a conversation about racial politics, but added, "It was horrible what they did to him."

Rand nodded as he polished off his Coke. "Can I have more pasta? Please."

"What a compliment!" Liv said as she stood and carried his plate to the kitchen. As she set more pasta and sauce in the bowl, she overheard Rand say to Damon, "Can I ask you a question?"

"Anything," Damon answered.

Rand crooked his head. "Before my mom got sober, she was always complaining that you didn't want to see me. She mellowed in the last year, but after all that, I don't know what's what about you."

Damon hid his surprise; the kid had said earlier that he didn't remember Damon, but now he was showing a different truth, one that probably held years of resentment and confusion over Damon's disappearance.

Damon put his fork down and looked Rand in the eye. "I don't want you more mad at your mother than you already are. As she said, she made some mistakes. And one of them was keeping me from you. But believe me, I never stopped trying to see you."

Rand nodded, his eyes showing a softer side of him. "Why do you think she's allowing it now?"

"Honestly? Because I think she's really upset by what's going on with you and realized you need a positive role model."

Rand let out a minor chuckle. "Like you're gonna show me how to be a strong Black man."

"Listen, I won't pretend I can just drop into your life and fix everything that you're feeling. But I can be a safe place where you can bring your problems. Maybe just having someone besides your mother to talk to will help you feel less confused, less angry."

In the kitchen, Liv paused, holding the plate, loath to interrupt their conversation.

"We'll see," Rand sighed, not wholly convinced.

On the silence, Liv carried the plate back to the table and set it before Rand.

"Thank you, Liv."

"You're welcome."

She sat and returned to her food.

"If you really want to help me…" Rand spoke up. "You'll take me to a protest tonight or tomorrow."

"And your mother would never let me see you again," Damon answered.

"Probably. But I'd know you cared as much as you say you do."

"I care about you, Rand. And I care about Black Lives Matter. Liv and I have been watching everything go down on the news every night. Why don't we do that after dinner?"

Rand sighed and said, "Sure."

But then he put his fork down, as if he'd suddenly lost his appetite. "Okay if I go chill in my room for a while?"

"Sure, I'll take you up there," Damon said, then stood and kissed Liv on the forehead. "I'll be down soon to help clean."

"Don't rush. I got it."

Liv watched Damon and Rand head toward the stairs, where a duffel bag of his clothes was waiting. Damon carried the bag up behind Rand, who had pulled his phone from his pocket and was checking it intently.

Liv thought back over the conversation. *Three years apart and now they have to pick up again.* She knew that her understanding was limited because she'd never and would never have a child of her own. *But maybe it's a blessing,* she pondered with sadness. *Even if I didn't have cancer, I'm not sure I could handle being a mother.*

IT WAS NEARLY MIDNIGHT as the three of them sat on the couch to watch the evening news, which Damon had taped so they wouldn't have to interrupt dinner.

While Liv had cleaned the kitchen, feeling content to be domestic, Damon had shown Rand around the house. The tour turned into a three-hour-long carnival—Damon teaching Rand how to play billiards and showing him a few chords on guitar in the studio, working out together in the gym, and a last dunk in the pool.

And now, sitting a few feet from Rand, Liv found it hard to believe he was the teenage timebomb his mother had described him as.

"Damn! That's the biggest ass TV I've ever seen," Rand said as the flat screen lowered from the ceiling.

"Just a few minutes of news, then we should all go to bed," Damon said as Lester Holt, the NBC anchor came on screen.

"It's so early!" Rand moaned.

Damon laughed and turned up the volume on the TV.

"Good evening, I'm Lester Holt. It's May thirty-first and yet again America is on edge as protests over the death of George Floyd spread through cities across the country."

The screen came alive with videos of protests, people chanting, "Black lives matter!" and "I can't breathe!"

Rand moved forward on the couch, attentive.

"Although most of the protests were peaceful, their messages were marred by looters who took the opportunity to break storefront glass and clean out stores in a matter of minutes."

"Dickheads fucking it up for the rest of us," Rand complained.

"Police, and in a few states, the National Guard, were under strict orders not to engage the protesters, but that became difficult as cars and a few buildings were set on fire."

Footage played of the fires and of police in riot gear standing toe to toe against protesters.

"See! I should be there!" Rand insisted.

Damon lowered the volume. "Rand, I think it's impressive that you want to join. But maybe you should wait till things calm down a bit and it's safer?"

"Easy for you to say," Rand mumbled.

"Because I'm White?"

Rand said nothing.

"Maybe you're right," Damon continued. "Maybe it's easy for me to sit back because my life is so comfortable. But you don't know what it's like to have people rely on you. If I go out there and march, even if everyone is wearing a mask, I could get Covid."

"Big whoop. Black people are killed and taken away from their families and shoved in prisons every day."

"It doesn't diminish your pain that thousands of people are dying every day, and we have to be especially careful in this house."

Rand chewed on that.

"Can I say something?" Liv asked.

"Of course," said Damon.

"Rand, what Damon is trying to say without actually saying it, is that I had cancer a few years ago, and have a weakened immune system because of the drugs I take for that. If I get Covid, I could die."

Rand blinked. "I didn't know that."

"I'll tell you what," Damon interjected. "If things calm down, I'll tell your mother she should take you to a march. I'm sure in a week or so things will be safer."

"A week or so?!"

"I'm trying to help," Damon insisted. "I guarantee fighting with your mom isn't going to get you there sooner."

"I guess," Rand answered with defeat.

Damon clicked off the television and stood. "Let's all go to sleep. Rand, I need your phone."

"Oh, man…"

"I'm sorry, your mom said you're not allowed to take the phone into your room at night."

Rand huffed as he pulled his phone from his pocket and begrudgingly placed it into Damon's hand.

"Goodnight, Rand," Liv said. "It was a really nice day."

"I guess."

Liv and Damon exchanged looks, accepting that this was as much a compliment as the teenager was capable of at the moment.

Damon stepped forward but stopped short of hugging the boy. Instead, he put one arm around Rand's shoulder. "Really means a lot to me that we're catching up."

Rand surprised him with a small smile. "Me too."

"You remember which room is yours?"

"I think I can find it in this maze, yeah."

"Sleep as late as you want," Damon added.

"Don't worry, I'm good at that."

Damon and Liv laughed as Rand shuffled to the stairs and headed up.

Liv stood and followed Damon into the kitchen where he plugged Rand's phone into an outlet.

"Ten bucks says he comes down in the middle of the night and finds it," Liv teased.

"Maybe. But what am I going to do, hide it? I'd rather he know I trust him a little, even if it means he goes to bed at three a.m."

Liv smiled, impressed. "Your parenting skills are off the chart. You're a great father figure. And you'd be a great dad."

Damon smiled to thank her. "Being a good boyfriend is enough for me."

Liv happily stepped into his arms.

"Of course, you know why he wants his phone, right?"

"Ha! When I was his age, all we had was dial-up Internet in the family room."

Liv hesitated. "Maybe I shouldn't tell you this…"

"Uh oh, what?"

She grimaced. "Earlier today, when you were inside, Rand and I were sitting on the couches outside, just on our phones. You came out and pulled him into the pool, so he left his phone on the couch near me. I glanced over and noticed he'd been on Instagram."

"He must have a fake account Nina doesn't know about."

"Gets worse—the profile he'd been checking out was none other than your girlfriend's."

"Oh, no. How did he find you?"

"He probably looked at who High follows. It's not hard—I'm one of what, twenty Livs on there?"

Damon rubbed his brow with exasperation. "Did he follow you?"

"I don't know. Want me to go through my new follows and guess which one is his fake account? Probably only had a handful yesterday."

"No, let's leave him his privacy. Unless it bothers you?"

"No, I just don't want Nina to flip her top."

"I got a hot girlfriend; can you blame him? I'll deal with Nina if it becomes an issue."

Damon pulled Liv into his arms. A foot taller than her, he kissed her forehead. "Thank you helping today."

"No," Liv said, closing her eyes. "Thank you for letting me be part of it."

"How was it for you?" Damon asked. "Meeting her, I mean."

"I admit I had a tinge of jealousy when she first arrived. She's very beautiful and exotic."

Damon didn't look eager to share the compliment, so Liv continued, "What about you? You can tell me if there are any lingering feelings. Love never completely disappears, I think."

Damon pursed his lips. "Honestly, the only thing I feel towards Nina is anger. I'm really glad she's doing better, for Rand's sake, but she's never even given me a real apology. It's going to take a while for that resentment to go away."

"I'm sorry, honey."

"Don't be. I wouldn't change a thing because it ultimately led me to you."

Liv answered with a blissful smile as Damon and she headed upstairs, turning out the lights behind them.

14.

LIV WATCHED DAMON TURN meat over on the grill the next afternoon, impressed with his talents. He'd chosen to cook burgers, hot dogs, and the few vegetables that he thought Rand might not reject. Liv began to set the table nearby, putting a Coke and a glass of ice where she thought Rand would sit.

"I wonder what time he came down for his phone?" Liv wondered aloud. They'd noticed the device wasn't connected to the charging cable when they'd gotten up a few hours earlier, laughed about it, and went on with the morning.

"I *don't* wonder what he used the phone for," Damon said with a teasing smile.

"Maybe I should kick off everyone who followed me yesterday and make my profile private?"

"Then he'll *know* we caught him and be embarrassed. You know what they say—the hardest thing to do is nothing."

Liv laughed as Damon checked his own phone. "It's almost two, I'm gonna wake him."

"I'll watch the grill," Liv said.

Damon set his grilling fork down and went inside. Liv happily took over the grill. She poked at a burger to check it, then looked out over the city—she was surprised to see the normally clear view speckled with at least seven helicopters, all toward downtown.

"Houston, we have a problem," Damon called out as he marched back with growing angst.

"He doesn't want to get up?"

"Worse, he already did."

"He's not in his bed?!"

"His bag is still in the room, but I didn't see his sneakers anywhere."

"Maybe he's in the studio or the gym?"

"I ran and checked."

"Jesus, he must have called for an Uber. Should we call his mother?"

"Not yet," Damon said, pausing to think. "I'll be right back."

"Where are you going?"

"Into the kitchen. I have a hunch."

"I'm coming."

Liv quickly turned the grill off and caught up to Damon in the kitchen. He went to a drawer and pulled it open.

"My Tesla keys are gone."

"Oh, no."

"He must have gone through every drawer until he found them."

Damon shut the drawer and hurried down the hall with Liv right behind. He opened the door to the garage, walked in and stopped.

His Tesla was gone. Only Liv's BMW remained.

"Oh my God," Liv gasped.

"*Now* we call his mother."

Damon pulled his phone from his pocket and dialed.

He glanced nervously at Liv and put the phone on speaker.

"Something must be fucked up for you to be calling me," Nina's voice greeted with angst.

"Rand took my car."

"I wish I could say I was shocked. When?"

"Sometime between one and ten a.m., when we woke up."

"Fuck. If we're lucky, he went to his girlfriend's house and not some late-night protest."

Damon had a thought. "Hang on, I can find the car's location on the Tesla app."

Damon navigated the app to the location page. "I don't know where *he* is, but the car is downtown, on Spring Street near City Hall."

"Answers that. With my luck he probably got arrested and is too embarrassed to call me."

"Where are you?" Damon asked.

"I'm up in Santa Barbara."

Damon chose not to ask why. "Stay there, I'm going to find him."

"I'm not just sitting here…"

"Okay, come to my house, Liv will be here. And please, wear a mask?"

"Fine. But you know the only reason I'm not pissed the fuck off at you is because he gave me the slip too."

"You warned me. See you in a couple hours."

He hung up. Damon glanced at Liv. "I hope he's okay."

"You want to take my car?"

Damon thought it through. "No, I should Uber so I can drive the Tesla home once I find him."

"I can drive you."

"Absolutely not. I know you—once you're there I know you'll want to get out of the car."

"I'll double mask."

"Liv, I appreciate that you want to help, but I would die before I let you near a protest. Who knows how many people are using masks?"

Liv knew he was right, so didn't argue.

"I'm calling a car and going to get my shoes," Damon said, heading back into the hallway. Liv followed him, only stopping as he ran up the stairs, two at a time.

Fucking cancer, she thought, frustratingly helpless.

A moment later, Damon came dodging down the stairs, sneakers untied, holding up more than two masks in hand. "Somehow I doubt he brought one…"

"Text me when you find him?"

"Of course. Car's only a minute away."

Damon kissed her cheek, and they walked to the front door. Outside, Damon put his arms around her. "Don't worry, everything will be okay."

"I believe you, but I'm still going to worry."

"I really love you, you know that?"

"I do. And I love you more."

"Not possible."

A black SUV pulled up the driveway.

"Wish me luck," Damon said as he donned one mask, then another atop it.

"You don't need luck. You're a superhero."

"Right," he laughed, muffled.

Damon waved at Liv as he opened the SUV door and climbed inside.

Arms crossed with unease, Liv waved back with one hand as the car drove away.

THE UBER SLOWED as it drove into the western edges of downtown. Damon noted the bumper-to-bumper traffic with some surprise, already spoiled by the typically clear pandemic streets. He sat in the back of the black SUV, refreshing his Tesla app over and over, but his car hadn't moved.

Then he spotted people parking their cars two or three deep, getting out and hustling towards City Hall.

"I don't think you can get in much farther. I'll get out here," Damon told the driver.

Damon hopped out as a police helicopter raced overhead. He could see it heading toward a patch in the sky where several more circled, news birds on the perimeter. Ominous gray smoke rose from below.

Sirens blared and Damon jumped toward the sidewalk to avoid police cars escorting firetrucks. Then he was carried along by the crowd. People of every color, most wore flimsy bandanas or surgical masks. Damon saw only a few N95s, like the black one he wore. He silently cursed how hard it was to breathe with the thing suctioned to his face, but knew it gave him so much more protection.

Damon checked the app again, and saw he was heading right toward his car, only a block away. He tucked the phone into his pocket and ran faster, slipping through the crowd which was slowing as it reached the heart of the protests.

The "*Black Lives Matter! Black Lives Matter!*" chants grew louder.

Damon spotted his parked car, easily recognizable by its blackened windows. The car lights went on as he approached, and he opened the front door. Nobody was in the Tesla, but the back seat was a mess of junk food wrappers and soda bottles.

Legs crossed and phone in hand, Liv sat watching the protests on Channel 11, the local news station. As night began to fall, things downtown were growing worse. The steps of City Hall were held by a line of National Guardsmen, the crowd of protesters looked to be thousands strong, and at least two old Crown Vic cruisers were aflame.

Liv checked her phone, but Damon hadn't messaged or called. She desperately wanted to check on him but knew he would let her know as soon as he found Rand.

Then it hit her: *Maybe I can help find him...*

Liv went to her Instagram. She tapped on her notifications tab and scrolled through them looking for who had followed her recently. She tapped on one or two with nondescript names.

Then one stuck out: a profile named DNAR2005. It took all of one beat to unscramble the anagram and figure out that 2005 was probably the teen's birth year.

She clicked on the profile, and it was obviously a new one because it had only about a dozen pictures. Looking closer, there he was: Rand hanging out with friends, tequila shots on the beach—teen stuff. But a few of the more recent photos were BLM related: a picture of George Floyd under the police officer's knee, and a completely black screen that just about everybody in America, including herself, had posted in support of the movement.

Liv tapped on Rand's stories; he had posted a selfie of himself the night before, no mask on, arm and fist in the air. The next one was a POV: running through a park, smoke from a gas grenade darkening the air, people around scuffling with police in riot gear.

He's right in the middle of it...

Liv tapped out a message: Damon, I found Rand's IG. He just posted a story from the park across the street from City Hall!

She stared at the screen, anxiously waiting to see if the ellipsis bubble would appear, but none came.

Damn felt his phone buzzing in his pocket as he approached City Hall. He couldn't see more than a few feet in front of him between the throng of bodies and colorful smoke arising around him. Amidst a cacophony of sirens and protestors' calls and helicopters, he heard an explosive burst, the sound of a gas grenade. The demonstration grew more and more militant in their chants of "No justice, no peace!"

Damon checked his phone while moving. He read Liv's message and immediately veered right, toward Grand Park, which he knew was a dozen acres spread from the Music Center to City Hall.

Sliding sideways amidst the protest, Damon saw the park ahead, separated from the steps of City Hall by one of four lanes. He could see police and National Guardsmen closing in on a crowd of protestors from four directions—the beginning of a kettle, a crowd control tactic that would allow no protesters, or bystanders, to exit. The kettle line was still too spread out compared to the size of the crowd to successfully prevent their movement yet, but several cops were firing rubber bullets at protestors' feet. Damon saw a protestor get hit in the face and go down, and he guessed it was only a matter of time before both sides lost control.

He saw Rand, seventy yards ahead of him, yelling "I can't breathe! I can't breathe!" with a fist in the air.

Damon tried to push his way to Rand but was slowed by a throng of demonstrators.

"Rand!" he called out but was drowned by noise.

In the blink of an eye, Damon looked toward the edge of the protestors and saw the kettle had been effectively closed on three sides. In response, the crowd pushed *hard* in the only remaining direction to go, and Damon felt himself pulled as if into a riptide. The pace of the throng quickened to a full run, and Damon had no choice but to stampede with them, losing sight of Rand completely.

Damon sucked hard for breath against his mask that had grown soggy with sweat, and stumble-ran as fast as he could, trying to zigzag toward the perimeter of the protestors, his only consolation being that Rand would have no other choice but to be running in the same direction as him.

Finally, about forty feet in front of him diagonally, he spotted what had to be the back of Rand's head and pursued. Rand was running with a group of young people down First Street and toward an alleyway.

"Rand!" Damon called over and over, but his voice was drowned out by the panic around him.

The crowd thinned out as they hit the alleyway and protesters scattered in multiple directions.

Damon finally caught up as Rand pounced on a chain link fence. The structure rattled with the force of Rand's weight, and he struggled to fit a sneaker into one of the holes to climb.

"Rand!" Damon called again.

Finally, Rand turned.

Rand's eyes widened. "What the fuck!"

Damon grabbed the back of Rand's shirt and pulled at him, but Rand broke free, ripping his shirt along the way.

"Rand!"

Rand scrambled over the fence and landed hard on the other side, skinning his palm on the cement as he braced his landing. "Fuck!"

"Stop!" Damon called out, but Rand took off.

Damon briefly considered his options, but there was nothing to do except scale the fence and try to pursue. As he braced his hands in two holes to begin his ascent, a group of ten more protesters came sprinting down the alley and hit the fence with great force, scrambling over Damon and climbing the fence with the agility of youth.

An errant sneaker kicked his face as a young man swung his leg over the top of the fence.

"Fuck!" Damon echoed Rand. He stepped off the fence to allow the rest of the group to finish their climb and looked both ways down the alley, seeing nothing but unnerved by their urgency.

When the last of the group was over the fence and sprinting, Damon threw himself onto it and scrambled over, noting which direction he saw the last protester turn.

He hit the ground only slightly more gracefully than Rand had, and felt the impact jar his knees before he took off running, praying he was headed in the right direction.

He turned the corner that Rand had, onto Temple Street, rounding it too swiftly to register that he had run straight into another kettle until he felt a rough hand on his shoulder.

Damon looked at the street in front of him to see rows of sixty or so protesters on their knees, hands on their heads, with five officers making their way down the lines and cuffing each one.

Rand kneeled at the front of the line, hands already behind his back and bound in the zip ties.

The hand that halted Damon belonged to a mustached LA police officer.

"Over there! On your knees, hands on your head!"

"Wait!" Damon pled. "I'm not—I'm not with them! I'm trying to get my son! He's just over there!"

"*On your knees!*" the officer barked.

In that moment, a group of three slight figures in black bloc burst through one of the two kettle lines and sprinted through the seated crowd, tossing three fireworks onto the sidewalks against the buildings as they ran.

The officer ordering Damon to his knees pursued, and the kettle line dispersed by half as a crowd of officers took off running after the kids in black bloc.

Several protestors, cuffed and uncuffed, took their cues and rose to their feet to run.

Rand rose to his feet as well, but paused and looked around, dazed.

Damon beelined for him and shoved his arm through one of Rand's.

Rand allowed him to and stumble-ran with Damon.

"*Move!*" Damon ordered, and Rand snapped out of it at the sound of his voice.

"The car is close," Rand said as they ran.

"I know. Follow me!"

All around them, the protesters scurried and at least a third were swiftly caught—peacefully and otherwise, but the miracle of chaos shrouded Damon and Rand as they ran until they could see Damon's Tesla. Damon felt one loop from his mask come loose from his ear but didn't dare slow his pace to fix it.

At the sight of the car, Damon released his hold on Rand, struggling to keep up with his hands cuffed. The Tesla beeped as they approached, and Damon swung his door open and reached over to open the passenger side.

"Go, go, go!" Damon urged as Rand ducked inside.

The two sat in stunned silence, chests heaving.

Liv opened the front door and Nina hustled in, wearing yoga pants and a mask.

"You hear anything?" Nina asked.

"Nothing yet," Liv answered, muffled by her N95. "But I found Rand's fake Instagram account and—"

"He has a fake account? How did you find it?"

"He followed me from it."

"Perfect."

Liv sensed the dig, but now was not the time to take anything personally. Her phone rang. She looked at the caller ID. "It's him."

She tapped the speaker on. "Are you okay?"

Damon's voice came out, "Yeah, and I have him in the car with me."

"Thank God," Nina said, sharing a relieved look with Liv.

"Can he hear me?" Nina called out as Liv handed her the phone.

"Yeah, you're on speaker. I can't give him the phone because he's wearing zip cuffs."

"He's cuffed? Why?"

"I'll explain when we're home," Damon said.

"Rand, you little *shit*!" Nina seethed.

"You were worried if I was okay for all of two seconds," Rand voiced.

"Don't even! I drove all the way down from Santa Barbara the minute Damon found you gone. And you stole his car!"

"Let's not argue," Damon interjected. "We'll be there in twenty minutes."

Nina bit her tongue and passed the phone back.

"Damon, are you okay too?" Liv asked.

"Yeah, but we got a little problem. My mask was pulled off."

"Shit."

"We're wearing them now, but you know what this means—I should isolate from you. I should do that regardless."

"Don't worry about that now. Just come home."

"See you soon."

Damon hung up and Liv forced a reassuring smile to Nina. "Well, he found him. That's something."

Nina nodded. "I don't know about you, but I could use a glass of wine or three."

"I thought you were sober?" Liv asked, regretting it immediately.

"Damon told you all about me, did he?"

"I'm sorry, it's none of my business."

Nina smiled to show Liv she wasn't offended. "It's true, I'm sober. From cocaine and pills. But you know how I got off drugs? By drinking more."

Nina laughed, but Liv wasn't sure if she was being sarcastic or not, so she just asked, "Red or white?"

"White," Nina said.

"You got it," Liv replied. She walked to the wine fridge and opened it, selected a bottle of sauvignon blanc by the cutest graphic on the label.

Nina peered over Liv's shoulder at the selection and whistled. "Must be nice playing house in a place like this for the pandemic."

Liv felt awkward and gave a small chuckle as she untwisted the cap of the bottle and grabbed two wine glasses. "Haha...yeah."

"But," Nina said, accepting her glass with a wry smile, "I don't know if I could stand to be around Damon while he's all cooped up. He must be like a caged tiger."

"Not really," Liv said evenly. "What do you mean?"

Liv perched on one of the barstools and Nina followed suit.

"You know him," Nina waved one hand. "Has to have people around all the time, constant attention, constant party, constant work, more, more, more."

"He's kind of said as much," Liv admitted. "But I really wouldn't know..."

Nina arched an eyebrow. "That's surprising. You know anything about attachment styles?"

"No. What is that?"

"It's, you know, the way we attach to people in a relationship. Comes from childhood. Avoidant attachment, anxious attachment. That's what Damon is.

Anxious attachment. From being an orphan, and then twice an orphan. He's got to have people around, so he doesn't go crazy."

Liv tried not to let her face fall as the worry that Damon might only be keeping her around to keep from "going crazy" crept in.

But Nina's own face fell visibly. "Rand's got that too. Anxious attachment. From me. We—I—fucked him up pretty bad. That's why he does shit like steal cars to follow girls around who won't give him the time of day."

"He's a great young man though. I mean that. Really smart, good at conversation. And from what Damon tells me and what I've seen, you've really turned things around. It's never too late," Liv spoke earnestly.

Nina put her head in her hands. "I hope so. It's one day at a time. But I can't leave him here in good conscience now. Not after this. I was really hoping this would help."

"Maybe we can work something out though. Have him do visits or something?"

Nina sighed. "Yeah. I'm just glad they're okay."

Damon and Rand entered through the garage door and walked down the hallway to the kitchen. While he pulled scissors from a drawer, Damon glanced outside and saw the women sitting at opposite sides of the sectional, wine in front of them, laughing like old friends.

Damon cut away Rand's plastic ties. "Think it's better your mom doesn't see you in these."

"You think?"

Damon tossed the plastic remains in the trash. "Come on."

He and Rand walked outside, the women rising.

"You little fucker…" Nina hissed while hugging her son.

Liv went to hug Damon, but he backed up a step. "I probably shouldn't be this close."

Her disappointment was palpable, but she knew he was right. "I'm just worried about you getting sick," he said.

Nina pulled her son to a seat on the couch. "Now tell me exactly what you did?"

"Can I have water first?"

"Right here," Liv answered, turning to the firepit drawer. She grabbed two and handed one to Rand, the other to Damon. But Damon placed it on the table and Liv knew it was intentional—after being exposed, Damon wasn't going to remove his mask around her, no matter how thirsty.

Rand slid his mask down and chugged the whole bottle, then held it in his hands, crackling it nervously.

"Okay, talk to me," Nina demanded.

Rand pulled his mask back up. "I told you I wanted to march. So, I borrowed Damon's car, picked up a couple friends and went downtown. Mom, you can't believe how powerful it was. Fifty years from now, they'll still be talking about today."

"And why were you cuffed?" Nina asked.

"Why? Because cops kill Black people."

Damon couldn't help but interject. "Rand, you stole a car. *Again*. How did that help to end police violence? You're *fifteen*. If you had been arrested and sent to juvie and your mother had to pay to drag you through the system, how would *that* have been social justice?"

The boy decided not to argue. "How did you find me?"

"My Tesla app told me where the car was parked," Damon answered.

"You don't need to cover for him, Damon," Nina said. "Liv found your fake Instagram. After I told you to delete the thing from your phone!"

"To be fair, I did find the Tesla before I knew about that…" Damon offered.

"What does that change?" Nina's voice rose.

Rand turned as red as his complexion would allow as his mother continued. "Baby, look, I applaud you wanting to be involved. And you're right, this is an important time. But you've broken every rule, so you've lost my trust."

"Well, how did you want me to go?"

"I don't know. Maybe if you had cleaned your act up, I would have taken you when things cooled down."

The boy laughed. "Right, and stand at the back of the crowd with a silly sign?"

"You're fifteen, Rand! You don't get to make choices that put you in danger. Forget the damn Instagram—if Damon and Liv hadn't found you, you might have had your head bashed in. And Damon is right! You think school sucks now? Think about juvy! See how many girlfriends you make in there!"

Seeing Rand lower his eyes, Nina lowered her tone. "You also screwed up the chance to get to know Damon again. I know it was my fault because I kept you out of his life. But I'm trying to make amends. He deserves to know you, and you him. But you're coming home today."

Rand wiped away a tear. "I'm sorry. I'm just so angry."

Damon understood the boy wasn't just talking about Black Lives Matter. "Rand, I know you're angry with me. For good reason. But I think you should go with your mom, and work things out at home. Then you're welcome back here any time."

Rand wiped his face with his T-shirt sleeve.

"Absolutely," Nina answered. "But first you show me you can follow some rules. And hey, I'll work on listening to you better, so I can help understand what's important to you."

"Thank you," Rand told his mother, then turned to Damon and Liv. "And thank you guys."

Touched, Liv smiled while Damon said, "You're welcome."

Damon shut the front door and turned to Liv, facing her without moving closer.

"How bad was it out there?" she asked.

"It was okay at first, then chaos."

"Rand's lucky you got there."

Damon nodded and leaned his back against the door. "You understand I have to isolate, right?"

"Can't you just wear a mask around me?"

"I wish. But I'd never forgive myself if I made you sick. I can't even be in the same room as you."

"Even if you don't have symptoms?"

"No. You know you can be asymptomatic for days. We can't treat this thing with hopeful thinking."

"Should we call your doctor?"

"He'll just tell me to do exactly what I was already going to do."

Liv closed her eyes and let out a long breath. "I'll move back into the other room."

"No, you stay in our room. I'll go into your old one."

"What is wrong with you?"

"What do you mean?"

"How can you be so concerned about *me* being comfortable?"

"It's called love."

Liv made a grumbling noise. "I'm going to FaceTime your ass night and day."

"I hope so. And we'll have a system: I'll text you when I come out to cook."

"Damon, you're not cooking. I'll be cook *and* maid."

"You'll be my maid, huh?"

He grinned and she knew what he was thinking. "Baby, you have no idea how domestic I can be. Although I don't know how I'll survive not touching you for a week."

"Ten days," Damon corrected with a smile.

Liv couldn't return it. "This is going to be torture."

15.

Determined to keep Damon's spirits optimistic while he was in quarantine, Liv put a plan into action.

That night, after moving a week's worth of clothes into her old bedroom, she cooked Damon's new favorite dish, *Poulet Sans Nom*. While cooking, Liv set up her phone on the kitchen counter so they could FaceTime.

Damon ate on his bed, phone propped on pillows.

"God forbid we aren't connected at the hip," he joked.

Liv failed at hiding her misery. "You know before this," she said, her food uneaten on the table, "we hadn't spent more than twenty minutes apart in three months."

And later, Liv made sure to climb into bed at the same time as Damon. She donned a revealing Honey Birdette lingerie ensemble she'd ordered a few weeks ago to save for a special occasion. This wasn't the first time she'd worn lingerie for him, but it was important to her that she start their ten days apart with a statement.

Liv darkened her room, told Damon to do the same, and they both lit candles to set the mood. She'd put her most erotic Spotify playlist on the speaker system that played throughout the house.

"How do we do this?" Damon asked as he held his phone, settling nude with the bed sheet covering just his lower torso.

"Have you never had FaceTime sex?" she asked as she climbed onto the bed in a robe, kneeling, setting her phone atop the headboard.

"Nope. Are you a pro at it?"

"Hardly! What kind of girl do you think I am?"

Her lascivious smile told Damon she wasn't really offended.

"Does this turn you on?" she asked, pulling the robe aside one shoulder, then the other, revealing the black push up bra.

"Holy God. I've never seen that on you before."

"Don't talk, baby," she whispered. "Unless it's to tell me what you like, what you want me to do for you."

He nodded and slipped his hand under the sheets.

"Let me see," she said, her tone turning guttural.

He pulled the sheets aside and she could see he was already hard. He obviously hadn't needed much stroking so she just continued, lightly, more to show her than please himself.

"How do you like this?" Liv asked, pulling the robe completely off to reveal the matching lace bottoms.

"You're so fucking beautiful," Damon whispered.

Liv turned so he could see her ass in the G-string, then posed in ways modeling had taught her were bound to turn a man on, turning her head back at the camera, pulling off her lace top off so he could see her breasts silhouetted in candlelight.

Damon stroked faster but steadily.

Liv turned and locked eyes on him, then peeled her panties off with one hand, barely lifting her body.

"Can I touch myself too?"

"Please."

She slipped two fingers into herself and moved them in and out, trying to match Damon's pace.

"I want to be there with you so bad," Liv said.

"You are here," Damon said, closing his eyes to imagine her atop him.

Damon tightened his grip on his cock. Liv pulled her fingers out and rubbed her clit back and forth, gasping as oxytocin spread throughout her body.

Damon was desperate to reach out for her; as if she'd read his mind, Liv used her left hand to cup one breast and softly caress her nipple, then squeezed both breasts together.

Damon's breath grew heavy. Liv put her fingers back inside herself, curling them to reach her G-spot.

"I'm cumming," Damon gasped.

"Me too."

They came together, Damon letting his head fall back onto a pillow, Liv closing her eyes and letting out a pleasured cry as she collapsed forward.

Damon stopped stroking, feeling his cum warming the skin on his stomach.

Liv took a few breaths and realized she'd dropped out of frame. She righted the phone and rolled onto her back, then held the screen up so she could see Damon above her.

Seeing Damon's glistened stomach, she managed to slow her breath. "That is so sexy."

Damon looked around for a towel but found none; usually right after they made love, Liv loved to jump and dance into the bathroom, coming back with a wet and warm towel.

"I'm sorry I'm not there to clean you up, baby," she said up to him. "Just lie here with me."

Damon smiled as Liv put the phone close to her face and said, "I wish I could hold you."

"I'm dying for you."

She relaxed; her head enveloped by the soft pillow. "Not a bad way to start the week off, is it?"

"You're more fun on FaceTime than most women are in real life."

"I'm just trying to find the silver lining in this."

"You found it alright. But I hope you can keep it up. You know I'm a morning person."

"Just watch me. Call me when you wake, no matter how early. I'll start your day off right."

Damon gazed at her through the screen. "I am the luckiest man alive."

"I'm the lucky one. And not just because you're amazing on FaceTime or in bed. But because you take care of me in so many other ways."

"I love taking care of you."

"I know. I love you, Damon."

"I love you more."

"Not possible."

Damon smiled, knowing there was no real way to compare or measure how much either of them loved the other. "Goodnight, Liv."

"Sleep well, baby."

They both put their fingers to their phones and reluctantly waited a beat before hitting "End."

THE COUGH WOKE LIV two mornings later.

That's all, a single cough. A dry hacking that she heard while walking toward the stairs to make breakfast for Damon.

She stopped mid-stair.

More coughs.

Liv closed her eyes. *Fuck.* Damon had Covid.

Phone already in hand, Liv texted, Are you up?

Her FaceTime rang—Damon lay in bed, bags under his eyes as if he'd been up all night. "You heard it, huh?" he asked.

"Just now. When did it start?"

"I just woke up with it."

"Do you have a fever?"

"Just took it. 102.6."

"Oh God. I'm so sorry," Liv said. "Is there anything I can do?"

"No. I'll have the nurse come and test me today, but I think it's pretty obvious I have it."

"The last couple of days you were fine. God was fucking with us!"

"For a woman who never prays, you sure do blame God for a lot of things."

Liv stared. "Nothing about this is funny, Damon."

"I'll be okay, honey."

"You better be. I'll bring you some hot tea with breakfast."

"I'll take just the tea for now. Not hungry yet."

"Starve a cold, feed a fever, honey."

"I think that saying was from the days before penicillin."

Liv didn't know how he could still be smart when he was sick. When she was ill, she liked to turn off her phone and hide from the world. "Are you going to call your doctor?"

"Already did. He said there's nothing I can do. He's sending over some cough syrup."

"Okay. I'm gonna do some research on holistic medicine."

"Don't bother, baby. Everything online is quackery. But I'm so glad I didn't let you come find Rand and that I isolated immediately."

"Part of me wishes we could be sick together."

"That would be romantic if you had a stronger immune system." He coughed a few times as if for emphasis. "I'm gonna try to go back to sleep. Wake me when the nurse arrives?"

"Okay. But text me if you need anything."

Damon hung up first, and Liv felt her phone hand tremble. Over the last few months, hundreds of thousands of people had died and cases were rising, among them even healthy young men. A few of her friends had posted about their miserable Covid experiences, and they'd come through it. But now that the man she loved was sick, it finally felt real. Frighteningly real.

God wouldn't take away the man I love, would he?

But then Liv thought of her own life and death battle. *Damn right, he would.*

LIV STOOD ARRANGING a Postmates delivery artfully on three plates and stopped when she heard the doorbell ring. She donned a mask and rushed to open the front door.

"Hello," said the woman behind a face shield, the rest of her covered by medical protective garb and gloves.

"Hi, he's this way," Liv said as she led the woman toward the stairs. This wasn't the same nurse as they'd seen before, and Liv knew she could have been less terse but put that aside. All she cared about now was Damon's health.

Liv knocked on Damon's door while opening it. Damon sat on the edge of the bed, double masked, in a ratty old T-shirt she liked to steal from his drawers.

"Come on in," Damon called out. "The nurse, I mean."

"Boo," Liv whined, then turned to the nurse. "If you don't mind, I'd like to ask you a few questions before you leave?"

"Of course."

Liv closed the door after her, then went back to preparing the plate for Damon. She spilled the rest of the Postmates bag onto the kitchen counter: a bottle of vitamin C, an over-the-counter asthma inhaler, zinc tablets, antihistamine nasal spray, and cough drops.

Liv was about to deliver the plates and supplies to Damon's door when the nurse descended the stairs and walked to the kitchen, keeping her distance on the far side. "You went to town at CVS…"

Liv wasn't in the mood to banter. "How's he doing?"

"He's got every symptom. I'd be shocked if he tested negative."

"It happened *so* fast."

"Covid is so unpredictable. Some people have it and never even know."

"Will he get worse?"

"Hopefully not too much. The main thing is that if he has trouble breathing, bring him to the ER immediately."

The thought of hospitals made Liv shudder. "I bought all this, and his doctor sent over a cough syrup, but maybe you've heard of something homeopathic?"

"I'm sorry, no. And whatever you do, don't listen to the guy with orange skin. The other day he said people should inject bleach."

"It would be funny if it weren't true."

The nurse checked her phone. "I'm sorry, I have people back-to-back."

"No problem," Liv said, staying a few feet ahead as she showed the nurse to the front door. "Is testing your full-time job now?"

"Yeah. I worked at a senior care facility before."

"I hear those have been hit really hard?"

"You wouldn't believe it. The place I worked in had to close."

Liv winced. She was pretty sure the nurse was offering careful wording to suggest that so many seniors died that the place had to close.

"I'll text Damon the results by midnight," said the nurse.

Liv looked surprised as she opened the door. "Oh, last time we were tested it took twenty-four hours for the results."

"The labs are constantly working on ways to shorten it. In a few months, we'll have at-home test kits."

"Seems crazy we don't have those already. It's been a few months."

"You'd think the most powerful country in the world would have made them and sent them out to every household by now."

"You're preaching to the choir," the nurse said.

Then she waved and headed outside to a silver Honda Accord, circa 1990. With its dents and duct taped bumper, the nurse's car made Liv's BMW look new.

A first responder and she can't even afford to fix her car, Liv thought. *America's priorities are fucked.*

16.

EXCEPT FOR THE CONSTANT COUGH coming from upstairs, Damon was frustratingly absent from Liv's life for the next week. She FaceTimed him often, but he seemed too weary to spend more than a minute on screen, so she resorted to only texting him to ask if he needed anything. He would answer eventually, telling her the fever and shakes kept him from sleeping much, and that even the syrup didn't help the unusually dry cough.

Liv went out of her mind trying to find ways to make Damon more comfortable. She left soup and all sorts of healthy foods outside his door, but he ate little. Liv suggested she could fill a bathtub with ice for his muscle soreness, but Damon said it hurt just getting up to walk. The only thing Damon asked of her was that she call Nina and check on Rand. Their conversation had been short; miraculously, Rand hadn't caught it.

At night, Liv kept her phone on the pillow in case Damon needed her, but he rarely did. And she understood Damon's behavior—she isolated the same way when she needed to heal. During chemotherapy, she'd spent months dodging friends, much to their chagrin.

One morning, Damon told her that he'd hallucinated the night before. Liv was curious about what he'd seen but didn't want to bother him with a barrage of questions. She just asked if he had any sleeping pills, and he did, but told her he was too afraid that if he forced himself to sleep, he might not wake up.

Damon talking about dying in his sleep terrified Liv, but she knew she couldn't share her feelings with him in this state. She'd just put on a good face in their all too brief FaceTimes and kept herself busy. But after months of being so connected to Damon, sleeping alone, eating alone, and working out alone fostered a loneliness she'd never known, typically so comfortable in her own company. Men she'd dated had complained that Liv's emotional shell was hard to crack, and she was always asking for "space." But now that she had a man she truly loved, space was the last thing she wanted.

One afternoon, a week after Damon had come down sick, Liv wandered aimlessly through the cavernous house. It was so quiet, and she'd run out of things to keep herself occupied. After a short text asking if Damon minded, which he hadn't, Liv went through Damon's closets and drawers throughout the house. With the exception of his bedroom, which she knew intimately by now, she wanted to find ways to be close to him, to know every obscure detail in his life.

She found nothing that truly surprised her but stumbled on a cabinet in his office that held dozens of framed pictures of Damon and Rand collecting dust. Liv worried that she'd also find pictures of Damon and Nina, but there were none, so she pulled out the frames, dusted them off and placed them on shelves throughout his office.

She FaceTimed Damon and showed him his shelves, and he thanked her. But of course, his coughing hadn't ceased and so the conversation ended quickly, but Liv felt appreciated. For the first time in her life, she was using time apart from a loved one to keep them close, bring them closer even. She wasn't running from fear of commitment, nor allowing Damon's own fear of showing vulnerability to come between them.

But alone in his bedroom, the smell of sweat and sickness beginning to cling to the air, Damon had another reason to fear dying in his sleep.

He hadn't mentioned to Liv that the cough syrup prescribed for him was the good stuff—codeine syrup. It was an innocent omission. Damon had weaned himself from the opioids after his crash with diligence and discipline, and rationalized that his chest hurt like hell, and that his problem was mainly uppers. Besides, Damon had read that staying active in isolation—doing calisthenics and forcing the lungs to expand—was helpful when fighting Covid if you were a healthy person to begin with. And Damon simply couldn't do more than a few sit-ups without collapsing in pain in his current state.

So, he ladled out the codeine on a spoon and forced himself to do thirty push-ups, thirty crunches, and thirty burpees when the pleasant opioid itch set in. When he finished, he laid back on the rug in his bedroom and felt himself sink into it, the codeine high and the endorphins from the exercise mixing to coax Damon into a dumb smile.

I have to be very, very careful with this, Damon thought as he stared at his ceiling and enjoyed the temporary quiet in his brain.

"Why didn't you tell me Damon was sick?" asked Beth that evening as Liv FaceTimed her from the couch, glass of wine untouched.

"We haven't really been talking much, Mom."

"Well the phone works two ways, baby. You didn't even tell me you were getting your scan until the results came."

"I know. I'm sorry, Mom."

"Anyway," Beth said, taking a second to correct her framing so that Liv could see she was alone at her kitchen table. "How's Damon feeling?"

"He's not getting better or worse. I'm not worried about him dying now, but it's so frustrating."

"How did it happen? I thought you were two were staying in the house?"

"It's a long story," Liv said. "Turns out, Damon has a sort of adopted fifteen-year-old son who was in the Black Lives Matter protests. He got into trouble and Damon went to help out, but his mask came off."

"Well, that doesn't surprise me one bit. Bunch of troublemakers," Beth stopped herself as she saw Liv's eyes narrow on the screen. She didn't want to alienate Liv during their first conversation in weeks. "But none of that matters right now. I'll pray for him."

"I'll take it."

Beth noted Liv's poor attempt at a smile.

"What else is going on, sweetie?" Beth asked.

"I don't have great news," Liv began, steadying herself. "I crunched some numbers today… Mom, I don't think I can keep helping you with rent for more than another month. There's just not enough brand deals that I can shoot at home alone to keep up."

For a split second, Beth's eyes got wide, and she looked like a panicked animal. Then she took a breath and calmed herself. "That's alright, sweetie. God will provide. I'll figure something out."

Liv bit her bottom lip. "I do have one idea…I just. Ugh. I wouldn't even know how to approach it with him, even though I know he'd be thrilled at the idea."

"What do you mean?" Beth prodded.

"I—I could move in here for good and stop paying rent at Marie's. She doesn't need my money. Hell, half the time she doesn't accept my Venmo. Then I could stop the bleeding and keep helping out."

Beth squealed with delight. "Honey! I'm so happy you've found a man you're comfortable doing that with!"

"Hold your horses, Mom. I didn't say I was totally comfortable with it. I'm scared as hell. I'm scared to commit."

"Of course you are. It's the first time you've been in love in years. I'm impressed you were finally able to open up and trust again."

"I didn't open up, Mom. He opened me."

"That's a nice sentiment but give yourself some credit."

Liv couldn't help but gush. "I'm serious—this whole thing came as a surprise. He's just the most caring, thoughtful man. He does everything right. We haven't had an argument since I've been here."

"Don't worry, you will. And when you do, that's when the real relationship starts. You don't know anybody deep down until you see how they handle conflict."

"You don't think it's too soon to move in *officially*?" Liv asked.

"Psh! Take a page out of your mother's book and throw caution to the wind! Live a little!"

Liv laughed at her mother's flippant remark.

"But seriously," Beth went on, "I've told you before, I don't think you've really taken a good look at yourself since the cancer. You never even went to therapy. So when something like this happens, it's hard for you to process. Have you talked with him much about your cancer?"

"He knows the basics."

"The basics? After four months in the same house, he should know the details."

"He knows more about it than any man I've ever been with."

"Good. Because if you have a future with him, he needs to know what goes on with you."

Liv grabbed a tissue from a box on the coffee table. "What if it scares him away, Mom? I mean the whole thing. The cancer, not being as rich as he is and asking to move in so I can help my mother pay the rent..."

"Maybe it will scare him. But from everything you've told me, he's nothing like Christopher. You have to take a chance."

Liv nodded. "You know what Damon told me? That he doesn't care how long I have to live. That he'll take whatever time I'll give him."

"That's beautiful."

"Thanks, Mom. It feels good to talk to you."

"I love you, honey."

"I love you, Mom."

"Let me know when he's better. I think it's time I meet Damon, even if it's on this stupid face thing."

Liv made a face. "Now that's a scary thought."

"Because I might not like him?"

"No, I know you'll love him, and he'll love you."

"So why's that scary?"

"Because then I have no excuse to run."

"Bingo. We call that 'fear of commitment.'"

"Oh shut up!" Liv teased. "Next call we talk about *your* love life, or lack thereof."

Beth's eyes widened, and she hastily said, "Bye!"

"See! I inherited my denial from you!"

Liv laughed as her mom fumbled with her phone, trying to find the button to end the call.

"Feeling human again," Damon exclaimed from bed the next morning, now eight days since the protests.

"That's the best news," Liv said with immense relief, still in bed herself.

Damon sat up. "The cough is still rough, but I slept the whole night, and the fever has broken."

"I'm too happy for words. When do you think you can come out?"

"CDC says I have to stay isolated until I test negative."

"I'm calling the nurse."

Liv sat up and scrolled through her phone log, inadvertently flashing her breasts to Damon.

"Wait! First, pull those sheets down more."

"Now I know you're feeling better..."

Liv grinned and pulled the top sheet down so her naked breasts were in frame.

Damon's desire was interrupted by a light but repetitive cough. "I'm not exactly up for real sexy time, but you have no idea how happy this makes me."

"Like hell I don't. I haven't touched myself all week."

"Saving if for me?"

"You get it all, lover."

A smile spread across Damon's scruffy face. "I'd like to get out of this room."

"Come outside today! I'll sit on the other side of the pool in a tiny bikini. Or nothing."

"You're killing me," he moaned impishly. "Actually, I was thinking I'd spend a few hours in my studio, playing guitar."

"Great! I'll camp out in the booth and just admire you."

"Sorry, but the same air circulates between the studio and the booth."

"But you'll be masked!"

"I'm not taking the slightest chance, baby. Trust me, you don't want this thing. Now I understand why your doctors are so worried—I'm in perfect health and I thought I was going to die a few times."

"I'll stay away from the whole studio," Liv carped. "But why the sudden inspiration to play guitar?"

"It's strange. The past few days were mostly a haze, but that melody I keep hearing turned into a song. I want to get it down before I forget it."

"That's amazing. And you said you hallucinated one night?"

"That was *not* amazing."

"How so?"

Damon looked troubled describing it. "I was sort of disassociated, inside my body, unable to move my limbs. All I could see was this thick black and red fog. It started to feel like a hellish nightmare I'd never wake up from. I tried to scream but I couldn't even open my mouth. Somehow I woke up and out of it."

"That's really scary. What do you think it means?

Damon paused to cough a few times and sipped from a glass of water on the bedside table. "I think it's pretty clear. I'm afraid to die."

Liv nodded but stayed quiet, thinking about the conversation she'd had with Nina, and wondering if a fear of mortality played into Damon's "anxious attachment" and need for company.

"Do you ever have nightmares like that?" Damon asked.

"No," she said, realizing she sounded curt. "But I rarely remember any dreams."

Damon raised an eyebrow, immediately clocking a tender spot. "Interesting."

Liv sighed at the recognition that Damon saw right through her and searched the ceiling for words. "Maybe it's selfish—I know that not everything is about me, or us, but I can't help but worry that maybe your nightmare is some kind of indication that you're…I don't know. Filling some kind of void with my presence, and I'll never be enough to fill that."

Damon furrowed his brow. "Sweetheart…where is this coming from?"

"Well, Nina said something that's sort of stuck with me."

Anger flashed across Damon's face. "Goddamnit."

She backtracked swiftly. "No, no, it's not like that. She wasn't saying anything nasty, or like, with the intent to hurt me…she just kind of *mused* that you have an 'anxious attachment style' and that you need constant stimulation. And now you're having nightmares…"

"Great. I'm being psychoanalyzed by my addict ex-girlfriend."

Liv waited.

It wasn't like Damon to be defensive.

"I'm just…feeling a little insecure," Liv admitted. "And I've been so worried about you. The last week has just been a lot."

Damon softened almost as quickly as his flash of temper had taken hold. "Liv—I can guarantee you that you're not the source of my existential dread. Being here with you over the last several months is the most stable—most fulfilled—I can ever remember feeling. But yeah, I'm afraid to die. I'm afraid I haven't accomplished enough. Haven't given enough. And even a broken clock is right twice a day; Nina's probably accurate when she says that I seek constant stimulation to fill the void. But I can promise you this: *you are enough.*"

Liv felt her eyes well with tears. "I really wish I could hold you right now."

"Me too, baby."

Now her face grew hot. "There's something else I'm feeling insecure about…"

"You can tell me anything, baby."

"I think…" Liv struggled with her words again, twisting her bedsheets into a knot in one fist. "Well, you know I promised I'd never take advantage of you, never ask you to provide for me…"

It was Damon's turn to wait.

"I think I need to move in."

Elation sat Damon up with such force that a cough racked his body before he could sputter out, "Am I hallucinating again?"

Liv looked sheepish. "No, I don't think so…"

"Liv, nothing would make me happier. Why would you be insecure about that?"

She thought for a moment. "It's not like it's not something that *I* want to do, because I do. But you know—my commitment problems. And I'd be lying if I said there wasn't a catalyst. I pay most of the mortgage on my mom's house. It's not much, but with no photoshoots…I can't keep paying rent on my empty apartment *and* her mortgage. So I hate that there's this extra baggage attached to a milestone like moving in."

"Baby. We don't always get to choose the way life interferes with us. The baggage doesn't bother me."

Of course, Liv knew that Damon would never say no to her, but still, she felt flooded with relief. "I can't thank you enough. And I want you to know this doesn't mean I'll be freeloading from now on. In fact, when I get my stuff from Marie's, I've got a whole professional lighting kit. I need to commit to making the at-home brand thing work. Who knows when Covid will be 'over.'"

"I've never considered you a freeloader, Liv. I would have died of malnourishment by now if you hadn't been plying me with food throughout this thing."

Liv laughed. "Okay, that much is probably true. Can we stop talking about existential dread now and get back to stuff like you asking to see me naked?"

Damon laughed and coughed harshly. "It's a deal."

"I'm sorry," Liv giggled. "I shouldn't make you laugh."

"It's okay. I'm actually hungry now too. Despite your best efforts, I think I lost ten pounds."

"You don't have ten to lose," she said as she scrambled to get out of bed. "Champagne and eggs coming up!"

No coughing for twenty-four hours! read Damon's text.

YAY! Liv instantly wrote back, sat at the dining table, remains of a pasta dish next to her computer. Come make love to me by the pool!

Waiting for the nurse to call.

Arrrghhhhh, Liv wrote.

Soon... Damon answered.

Liv sighed and went back to her computer. She was already making good on her promise to recommit to her brand, and now combed through smaller product placement offers she had overlooked throughout the last two years or so.

But it was difficult to focus. *The last two weeks have been so hard,* she admitted to herself. And she knew why: Liv, the loner, had become completely attached to another human being. And now, she was about to further secure that attachment by moving in with a man, for real.

Liv had never moved in with a man "officially" before. Even Christopher had moved into *her* apartment before fleeing.

When she logged into her Instagram to make a content creation schedule for herself, she felt twinges of guilt and concern at the realization that she had lost nearly fifty *thousand* followers in her social media absence. *You've been neglecting your livelihood, not talking to your friends…* She couldn't help but wonder if by fostering an attachment to Damon, she had gone the way of so many other women and given up parts of herself.

She chewed her bottom lip and considered that none of that was the fault of Damon—he hadn't restricted her communication or demanded that she stop working. She was simply growing complacent.

The best way out of this anxiety is to act, she told herself. And she knew the top of her priorities should be to come clean to Marie that she was going to have to vacate the back house.

She dialed the number before she could talk herself out of it.

"Well, well, well," Marie answered. "She's alive."

"I know. I suck. I'm sorry. Are you not working today?"

"Oh no, I am. In about half an hour. But getting a call from you these days is like getting a call from the president. I'm gonna make time."

Liv rested her forehead on the kitchen table and let the guilt course through her. "I was literally just thinking that I'm becoming one of those girls whose main hobby is her boyfriend."

Marie let out a lighthearted *tsk*, but said, "Hey, I mean, me and Yasmina encouraged this; we can't bitch too much about any unforeseen consequences."

Liv laughed. "Thank you. But seriously, I'll do better. I know you're still in the thick of it."

"You can say that again. But speaking of Yasmina…have you been watching her Insta stories?"

"I haven't been watching *anyone's* stories. I've lost fifty thousand followers."

"Damn, girl. You better pull it together. But go look."

Liv tapped her phone onto speaker mode so she could hear Marie and scroll Yasmina's page at the same time. She clicked on her circular avatar and was met with a series of videos—sleek, beautiful Parisians bathed in neon light, bodies grinding, pupils massive, and Yasmina in the thick of it.

An underground rave.

"Uggggh, Yasmina," Liv breathed.

"I know. She's got a lot of nerve. It's been like this for like…two weeks. I bitched at her a couple times, but she said she's going crazy in Paris, and she'll end up in the loony bin before she ends up on a respirator if she can't let loose."

"Yeah…I know it doesn't affect me personally, and she's like six thousand miles away, but it's…really disappointing."

"You gonna say something to her?" Marie prompted.

"I'm not sure. Maybe. I kind of have bigger fish to fry right at this second…"

"Oh?"

"Marie…I have to move out of the backhouse. I can only afford my mom's mortgage for another month or so, and I just can't justify continuing to sit on an empty apartment."

Liv could practically hear Marie's eyes roll in the back of her skull.

"Oh Jesus, Liv, how long have we known each other? Don't piss on my leg and tell me it's raining. You're moving because you're in looooove for the first time in forever."

"I don't want to be dishonest with you. I mean obviously that's part of it, but so is the financial strain."

"Girl, I know. I'm just giving you a hard time. I was pretty sure this call would come eventually. And three years is a pretty good run for a tenant, anyhow."

"You're not mad?" Liv's voice rose an octave with cautious hope.

"Liv, no. Of course not. You're not *obligated* to live with me. Besides, maybe I'll do something neat with the backhouse for myself. If I can ever get a break from work."

"You're my best friend, Marie."

"Ditto, kiddo."

17.

Spurred by the desire to be a good departing tenant to Marie, and to hopefully wrap up her move before Damon's tests came back, Liv rose at five the next morning to make the journey to North Hollywood and pack.

"Pack" used here very liberally.

Marie's backhouse was already furnished when Liv moved in, and most of her worldly possessions were her prized wardrobe and a generous heaping of accessories to style and direct the perfect shoot. So, it seemed silly to pack things away into boxes and label them accordingly when she'd only be driving thirty minutes away to unload them. Instead, Liv filled the backseat in her BMW until each square inch from floorboard to roof was loaded.

Liv had been so mired in the implications of what it *meant* to commit to moving in with a man that the wonder of suddenly being an official resident of a literal mansion did not register with her until she pulled back into Damon's—her—driveway late that afternoon.

She took in the façade and the stone address plaque—her address plaque, that she would need to forward her mail to—and couldn't help herself but give a giddy little jump. But she was calculated about what she pulled from the car to bring in with her. It wasn't time to play house yet.

It was time to work.

In the living room against the backdrop of the pool and Hollywood Hills through the floor-to-ceiling windows, Liv placed her phone on a tripod. Using a voice remote to control the shutter, Liv spent hours taking pictures of herself in several outfits, making subtle changes to her hair and makeup as she went so that she could use the content for longer. Then, she spent the early evening editing and tagging all the companies and designers, archiving enough posts for the next two weeks.

Within minutes of her first post, a seductive shot of her in a bikini that could only be worn in Miami, followers rewarded her with likes and comments, asking where she'd been. Liv was hit with a sense of pride, and yes, dopamine—not because she liked the popularity, but because it reminded her how much her career meant to her. She was pleased to feel her sense of identity rush back to her, unmarred by her new attachment. *How many people with stage three cancer, and a full mastectomy and reconstruction, support themselves by modeling?*

Liv shut the computer and glanced outside, where it was swiftly darkening.

She silently vowed to herself that no matter how much she loved Damon, she wouldn't lose herself in the relationship. *They say you really don't know a person until you've been together for six months. What if we start arguing and break up? If I don't keep up my career, I'll find myself abandoned and broke...*

Liv's thoughts were interrupted by warm hands covering her eyes from behind her.

"What?" she cried out. "You're negative!"

The hands dropped and she sat up and spun around to find Damon's smile unobscured by mask.

Liv screamed and jumped up, arms around him, mouth attaching to his.

Damon squeezed her. "I love you too!"

"I'm so happy I could cry!" Liv said, and indeed, tears of release and joy streamed from eyes.

"Aw, sweetheart," Damon said as he wiped her tears. "It's over, I'm okay."

"I know, I'm just so fucking relieved."

"We have some making up to do," Damon replied, then kissed her again.

Liv squealed. "Take me to bed or lose me forever!"

"What movie is that from?"

"*Top Gun!*"

"I hear there's a new one coming out."

"Shut up already."

Damon laughed as he swept her up into his arms.

"Don't ever be a hero again!" Liv playfully demanded as he carried her to *their* room.

"How is work going?" Damon asked as he sat down on the edge of the daybed, angled so that he blocked the sun from her face.

Liv looked up from the computer in her lap. "Good! Seems I still got it. I'm getting followers back way more quickly than I lost them."

"I noticed and am impressed."

Liv smiled and realized she was unaccustomed to a man who didn't complain when he wasn't the focus of her attentions.

"You don't mind me focusing on something besides you?" she asked.

"Not at all! I totally support your career."

"It's all about balance. I think I might have lost that in the last few months."

"Then I won't bother you."

"You're no bother."

Smiling, Damon stood. "When you're done, I need your help in the studio."

"Really?"

Liv looked intrigued—Damon had been spending almost all of his time away from her in the soundproofed studio, so she had no idea what he'd done with that melody.

"No rush," he said.

"Are you kidding? I'm dying to hear what you've been doing in there."

Liv closed the computer and slid it under a pillow for protection from the sun and stood.

"I'm so excited!"

She grabbed Damon's hand and pulled *him* toward the studio.

"Sit here," Damon said, pulling out a soft high back chair at the mix console.

Liv sat cross-legged, like an excited schoolgirl.

"Push this to talk and listen."

Damon pointed at a yellow button on the mixing board, then a red one with a piece of masking tape under it that read "RECORD" in Sharpie. "And this one when I tell you to."

"We're recording?"

"As long as I don't fuck it up," he chortled. "This may require several attempts, so just press the button again to stop, and again to start recording another take."

"What about all these other switches?"

"I've set all the levels."

"Got it. So excited!"

Damon kissed her forehead, then pushed through the door. Liv watched through the glass as he took a seat on a high stool and lifted his acoustic guitar from its stand.

He mouthed a few words, so Liv pressed the talk button. "What did you say?"

"I said I wrote this song for you."

Liv's heart skipped a beat. "You wrote a song for me?"

"I haven't written lyrics yet, but I was thinking when I'm done, you could sing it, and we'll record that together."

"Damon…I don't know what to say."

"That's a first," he joked, but could see Liv was truly touched. "Just listen to the song and see if it moves you. Hell, it's the first song I've ever written, and you'll probably hate it."

"Impossible."

"Promise me you'll be honest? I'd rather the truth than kindness."

"You have my word."

Damon gave her a thumbs-up, so Liv let go of the talk button and started to record.

Damon pulled a pick from between two strings and started to strum out a ballad.

Liv couldn't believe her ears.

Damon played a soft but beautiful melody that reminded her of the seventies songs they shared a love for. Not liking it was out of the question; Liv was moved to tears as she watched his right hand use the pick rhythmically, his left deftly changing chords without his eyes directing them.

He reached the bridge and noticed Liv wiping her eyes. Seeing her so stirred, he had to look away from her to keep his concentration.

Liv's love for the song grew with every chord change.

Damon closed his eyes as he finished the song on a high, optimistic note.

When he opened them, he saw Liv sitting there, tears winding from her cheeks to her jaw, her hand pressed to her heart.

Damon decided not to say anything through the speakers. Instead, he placed the guitar down and walked into the booth.

"I'm assuming you're not crying because you hate it?" he asked quietly, to match the vulnerable and intimate mood visibly enveloping her.

"Damon…it's so beautiful…"

He sat on the edge of the soundboard and reached out his hand to touch her face, wiping a tear with his thumb.

"Nobody has ever…" Liv whispered.

He asked, "Think you could write the lyrics?"

"Honestly, I don't think I could do it justice."

"Will you try?"

Liv blinked away the tears, her breath evening. "Damon, you have to understand… I knew my singing career wasn't going the way I wanted, and when I got sick, for me to walk away, I had to go cold turkey. Singing is like an addiction. If I even play around with it, I'm pulled back to it and feel so much sadness for failing…"

Damon bent close to her, intent on kissing her. "I understand."

Liv put her hands to his cheeks, holding him in the kiss.

Finally, Damon tenderly pulled her hands away and held them. Then he noted that the light above the recording switch was still bright.

"Oops," he said as he pressed it off. "I can't believe I finished it in one take. I must have played it a hundred times, and only finished this a couple times."

"Does it have a title?"

"Not yet. You give it one when you write the lyrics."

Liv laughed at Damon's insistence. "Anyway, I want to hear it again."

"I'd rather quit while I'm ahead."

"I don't mean record it. I just want to listen to you play."

Damon felt his own heart fill with gratification. "One more time. And you have to come in there with me."

"I'd love that. But I'm gonna need these…"

Liv clutched a tissue box at the far edge of the soundboard, and Damon smiled.

MAKING LOVE WITH DAMON that night, Liv heard his song in her head.

Though she'd made him play it dozens of times that day, then listened to the recording on her phone while cooking, and again while showering, Liv couldn't get it out of her head or heart.

And now, as the lovers moved in the ways they had countless times, the song became a soundtrack in her head, making each kiss, each touch, feel like their first.

They gazed unrelentingly into each other's eyes, tears of love and intimacy dripping onto each other's skin, mixing with beads of sweat.

18.

Side by side in the gym, Damon rode a Peloton bike in a virtual race through Italian streets, and Liv sprinted on the treadmill, earbuds in.

Damon coasted toward the finish line, stopped pedaling and grabbed a towel from the handlebars. Before wiping his own sweat away, he offered it to Liv.

She took it and pulled out her earbuds. "Thank you. You okay?"

Damon was visibly piqued.

"I'm fine. Just wish I were more like you. You're so dedicated."

"I'm dedicated to keeping cellulite off my ass."

"Can't argue with success."

"Oh, you like my ass?" Liv arched a knowing eyebrow.

"Why do you think I'm always trying to take a bite out of it?"

Liv laughed at Damon's tease.

"Someone's birthday is coming up, on July seventeenth," he said suddenly.

"How did you know that was my birthday?"

"Google, of course. Because you certainly didn't tell me!"

"I don't like to make big deal out of birthdays. They just mark my inevitable march toward Hell."

"If that's where you're headed, I'm right behind."

"Seriously, Damon, I don't want to celebrate it."

"Grinch."

She laughed and stepped off the treadmill.

"We don't have to celebrate it," Damon said. "But you're going to love my gift."

She mocked frustration. "I could pretend that I don't want you to spoil me, but you're so good at it that I'm curious."

Damon grinned—he'd been working on this surprise for a week. "Honey, how would you like to see your mother?"

Liv's mouth gaped open. "What were you thinking?"

"I thought we'd visit her. Spend a couple of weeks in Florida. Get a house on the beach near Jacksonville, just a drive for her."

"Kill me now. But you know my doctors won't let me fly."

"Not commercial. But I'm sure flying private would be okay."

Liv opened to her mouth to say something, but Damon quickly interjected, "And please don't tell me you won't let me give you this because it's expensive."

"We've talked about this before," Liv insisted. "It *is* too expensive."

"You haven't seen a member of your family in what, six months at least? And we've moved you out of your best friend's house. If I don't take heroic measures soon, people are going to start thinking I keep you locked in a dungeon."

She laughed at that.

"Please, Liv. Let me do this. I've already put most things in motion."

Liv took two bottled waters from the fridge and handed one to Damon. "I *have* been thinking about it ever since your initial offer. But I'd have to talk to my doctors. How do you think it would work?"

"My guy at NetJets said they'll test our pilots the day before and have them wear masks in flight. And it would be just you and me in the back of the plane."

"You got a guy, huh?"

Damon allowed the tease. "I found this beautiful house on a secluded beach."

"You don't have to sell me. I just need to check with Mom on dates. She's dying to meet you."

"Don't hate me, but she's already in."

"What? You asked my mother before me?"

"You gave me her cell in case of an emergency, so I called and introduced myself."

"Don't you have balls…"

Liv's wide smile told Damon that she wasn't unhappy.

"I'm having her tested the day before we arrive, and she's agreed to isolate a couple days before that. It will all be safe. So you can enjoy yourself."

"Damon, this is the most amazing, thoughtful gift you could give me. I used to visit my mother or fly her here every couple of months. Thank you, honey."

She kissed him, then licked her lips. "Mm, you taste good salty. We should work out more often. And what are we going to do for *your* birthday? When is it? Sorry, I know you mentioned it months ago but I don't have my phone."

"March tenth."

"Now I remember—right before we met! But how am I going to give you anything near as special as this?"

"All I want is you, Liv."

"You already have that."

"I don't know. My birthday is nine months away, and you're always telling me you're afraid of commitment."

"I am. This is just a casual thing. A long hookup," she teased, waving a hand in the air.

Damon laughed. "More like an addiction."

"But a healthy one."

Liv did her version of a quirky happy dance, singing, "We're going to Florida!"

DAMON'S ATTENTION TO DETAIL never ceased to amaze Liv and flying to Florida on a private plane was no exception—it was on full display as Damon drove Liv to the NetJet FBO at Santa Monica Airport. Naturally, Damon didn't want to risk Liv's health by exposing her to even a masked Uber driver.

Liv had only flown private once before, when a wealthy Beverly Hills surgeon who was chasing one Liv's girlfriends had taken them all to Vegas for a weekend, but it had been in a tiny Lear Jet, so cramped that she and two other people had shared the couch, and there wasn't even a bathroom.

But when Damon drove the Tesla up the tarmac, right next to the plane's wing, Liv realized this was a whole other way to travel. The Cessna Citation X was a long, sleek jet, and the red carpet before its stairs made Liv feel like a movie star. Two masked pilots, whom Damon had paid to isolate for five days, greeted them. No check-in lines, no TSA. Inside, the plane sported eight large seats, a kitchenette and a bathroom. The pilots disappeared into the cockpit and closed the door, so Damon and Liv removed their masks.

"Window or aisle?" Damon joked—each of the couplets of seats were both window and aisle seats.

"Normally I like the aisle so I can escape the idiots who hit on me easier."

"A beautiful woman like you can't even fly in peace?"

"Are you kidding? I'll wear the ugliest baggy sweats and a pull my hat down to here and I'll still get hit on." Liv plopped on a soft, gray leather seat.

"Normally the plane comes with a flight attendant," Damon said. "But I thought, why risk having someone else in the cabin if it's not absolutely necessary? But we do have food!"

Damon opened a cabinet and pulled out a tray of sandwiches and salads he'd ordered from Erewhon, Liv's favorite market in West Hollywood.

"I've run out of ways to thank you," Liv said as the plane pulled forward to taxi. Even this small movement gave her butterflies of excitement.

Damon set the food on a table between seats behind Liv, then sat next to her and reached across her to gather her seat belt.

"Oh man, I gotta wear one on a private plane?" Liv pretended to complain.

Damon laughed, clicked her in, then himself.

"Seriously though," Liv said. "This doesn't suck. I'm afraid to ask how much a trip in this thing costs."

"It's a treat, even for me."

The plane made a turn and started speeding up the runway.

Damon saw Liv's eyes go wide. "Are you afraid of flying?" he asked.

"Not at all. This is just so thrilling."

She took Damon's hand in her own and glanced out the window; the plane took to the air without a bump, Los Angeles appearing smaller and smaller beneath it.

The flight was five hours of heavenly relaxation. The jet was so quiet that as the sun disappeared in a maze of colors unmarred by smog or clouds, Liv, face plastered to the window, thought the feeling must be as close to being in space as anyone except an astronaut could get.

Liv dozed in and out in the dimly lit cabin, then woke to find her head on Damon's shoulder, a book in his lap. She glanced around the cabin.

"Are there cameras in here?" she whispered to him.

"Probably."

Liv thought a beat. "Have you ever joined the club?"

Damon smiled and put his book down. "No, you?"

She shook her head and stood in the ample room between rows, holding her hand out to him.

Damon took it and stood with her.

Liv led him down the aisle, glancing back at the cockpit like a nervous teen. She opened the bathroom door and slipped inside, pulling Damon in with her.

The room was tight for two, but Liv closed the door behind them, then pushed Damon down onto the cushion seat that covered the toilet.

Liv leaned toward Damon and kissed him sweetly, then harder. Damon's hands went toward her hips while she unbuckled his belt.

"Pull those down," Liv whispered.

As Damon did, she pulled her sweatpants down, panties with them, then turned so her back was to him.

Liv braced herself against the room's walls as she lowered herself down. She didn't need to look to know that Damon was already hard. Wet herself, she felt him glide up into her, his hands reaching under her top, cupping her breasts, pulling her back toward him.

She gasped.

Damon closed his eyes as he helped her slide up and down on him.

Damon slid his right hand from her top and grabbed the back of her hair, pulling her head back.

"Yeah," Liv said as she turned her face to him. "You fucking own me."

"I'm so fucking yours," Damon grunted as their lips and eyes met.

Liv felt her orgasm close, so she rode him faster. Damon sensed his own and moved his left hand to her folds, fingering her clit.

"Like that, yeah, faster," Liv cried as she felt Damon come inside her, the warmth of it spreading.

"Oh my God," Damon cried out as he closed his eyes, his body spasming.

He pulled Liv to a stop and laid his head on her back. Liv tried to calm her breathing and looked forward at the mirror above the polished satin wash basin beckoning her.

Liv didn't see a sexy couple who'd just fucked in an airplane's bathroom. She saw a woman sitting atop her lover, eyes filled with a passion few people would ever know.

THE PLANE LANDED at the Jacksonville Airport at 10:00 p.m. Liv and Damon disembarked, hand in hand, watching as handlers loaded their luggage into an SUV.

Under the tarmac lights, Liv noted another couple doing the same from a smaller Lear. The man was in his late fifties, the woman in her twenties, platinum hair and ruby-painted lips like an Eastern European runway model, towering over him in her knee-high boots.

Liv gave a polite wave, but the woman ignored her and jogged a beeline toward Damon, not tottering a centimeter in her heels.

"Damon!" Alyssa called.

What the fuck? Liv thought as she glanced at Damon, who was smiling back maybe one degree more friendly than she was comfortable with.

"Hey, Alyssa," Damon replied, but took a healthy step back to keep more than six feet of distance between them.

He couldn't help but note that all her aloofness from their final night spent together had evaporated completely. *I guess I did arrive in a bigger plane,* he thought cynically.

"What a crazy coincidence! What on earth are you doing here?"

Now Damon put an arm around Liv's shoulder and gave it a little squeeze. "Birthday trip for my girlfriend! Liv, this is Alyssa. Alyssa, my girlfriend, Liv."

Alyssa nodded, unfazed, and said, "Oh, how much fun! Damon really knows how to show a girl a good time."

Such a comment made Liv annoyed that she hadn't looked more fazed—gave a little pout or a flash of disappointment at Damon introducing her as *girlfriend*.

A man wearing a beige polo and white baseball cap appeared next to them. "Mr. Lautner? Your car keys."

"Thank you! I'm so sorry, Alyssa, but we've got a dinner date to make. I'm sure I'll see you around High when the world is right again."

"I'm sure I will!" Alyssa gave a curt wave and skipped back to the waiting older gentleman, who seemed to be scowling at Alyssa's neglect to introduce him.

Damon opened Liv's passenger door and shut it gently behind her. Liv watched Alyssa and silently laughed at herself for being so bitchy.

But doubt crept in as she watched Damon sign a few pieces of paperwork in front of the car. He *had* been a playboy, and before they got serious, occasionally admitted to doubting monogamy.

What if there hadn't been a lockdown? she wondered. Had Damon and her still met, would they have fallen in love so easily? Or would the ridiculous number of beautiful women he met in his nightclub have distracted him? And what would happen when lockdown was over? Would Damon return to his old ways? She chewed her bottom lip with worry.

But as Damon finally opened the SUV door and climbed into the seat, he didn't give the woman a second look. Liv suddenly wasn't even sure if the first look had been her imagination, a jealous fabrication.

You're being silly, Liv cursed herself. She wasn't going to let this moment ruin her birthday trip. And of course, she'd never really know what would have happened if there had been no pandemic, or what might happen once it ended. Time would tell. And in some odd way, Liv understood that her jealous insecurity was a good thing—it came with the territory of being so connected, so attached to another human being.

I guess the more you have, Liv thought, *the more you worry about losing it.*

THE CAR TURNED the corner onto Liv's street, and she was surprised by the realization that she hadn't yet thought to be embarrassed of her modest childhood home until that moment.

Damon had invited Beth to stay with them at the resort house but explained she seemed noncommittal for some reason.

"Maybe she just wants to give us privacy on vacation," he had mused. "So first stop, homemade dinner with Beth! Then we'll check out the resort house."

The row of tract houses had once been at least freshly painted and quaint, but now foliage overgrew most of them, roots waged war with the sidewalk, and a few yards were littered with abandoned car projects.

But when Liv and Damon opened their respective doors and the heavy, tropical air hit her face like a wet, warm towel, all she could think was *I'm home*.

Damon eagerly railed behind Liv as she practically danced up the walkway.

She arrived at the front door and began to knock "Shave and a Haircut," but barely landed the fourth knock when the door swung open.

"Mom..." Liv cried out as joyful tears sprouted.

Damon felt his heart swell with pride for having brought them together after so many months. Beth, still beautiful in her mid-fifties with arched brows and green eyes she shared with Liv, pulled herself away to look at Damon.

"Finally we meet!" Beth said as she hugged Damon, who set the luggage down to accommodate the great mama bear hug.

"About time!"

Liv beamed and wiped her tears. "The two people I love most in the same room."

"If that isn't a ringing endorsement for you, I don't know what is," Beth said to Damon, then ushered them forth into a modest entryway with chipped tiles. "So much love!"

"Okay, enough of the mutual adoration," Liv called out.

Damon indicated their luggage. "Where should I set these to be out of the way?"

He was already respectfully removing his shoes, though the state of the house clearly didn't warrant such a performance.

"Any old place is fine. Liv said you were a gentleman."

"Is that right?" Damon asked with a mischievous grin. "What else has she said about me?"

"What a daughter tells her mother, stays with her mother," Beth answered.

"Fair enough."

Damon bent over to tuck the luggage into a corner.

Liv glanced at Beth's eyeline. "Mom!"

"What?"

"You were checking out his ass."

Beth went beet red. "Who me?"

Liv broke out in a peel of laughter that was interrupted by a bellow.

"BeeEEEEth!"

The foreign male voice that called out somehow stretched the single syllable of "Beth" into at least three in an impressively grating way.

Liv looked aghast. "Who is *that*?"

"One second, pumpkin," Beth called out. "They just got here!"

"Well they won't be happy if you serve them cold slop on a plate!" the voice came, then erupted in laughter—funny joke.

"I was waiting for the right opportunity to tell you..." Beth started to Liv. "That's Wayne. He just moved in."

Liv looked to Damon, and they exchanged looks that said:

Did you know about this?

No!

"Like a roommate?" Liv asked Beth in a hushed tone.

"No...like a boyfriend."

Now Damon looked pained, torn between the desire to make a good impression and frustration that his carefully laid plans to ensure everyone was tested and safe for Liv were thrown asunder.

"Did he get tested as well?" Liv prodded.

"Well, no…but it's just one person and he's been alone here with me for weeks."

"*Mom!*" Liv hissed. "Damon spent all this money to make sure everything was safe. To protect *me*."

"Please, pumpkin. It's just a couple hours," Beth pleaded. "Can we all try to get along?"

Liv's skin felt hot at having to compromise her boundaries immediately upon walking in the door. She looked to Damon.

"We can do whatever you want, sweetheart," he said to her quietly, but his eyes were wide with concern.

"BETH! What is going on in there?" came the bellow again.

"Fine," Liv whispered. "But I need to sit six feet away from him. This is extremely not cool, Mom."

19.

Beth's table was beautifully spread with a perfectly cooked salmon, well-seasoned asparagus, and mashed Japanese sweet potatoes. Despite their initial hiccup, one thing was clear to Damon before even taking a bite: Liv had certainly acquired her culinary skills from Beth.

Wayne sat across the rectangular table at the opposite end from Liv, smilingly sizing up Damon while being sized up by him and Liv at the same time. In his early forties, but too physically haggard to be looked at like a younger man to Beth, Wayne sported a buzzcut that dissipated into an unskilled fade down the back of his neck and wraparound Oakley sunglasses that hung on his Washington Redskins T-shirt, a thing straining to contain his potbelly.

"Shall we?" Beth said as she reached out and took Liv's and Damon's hands in hers once Liv had finished.

Damon took his cue and outstretched his other hand to Wayne, who grasped it just a tad too firmly, and closed his eyes.

"Our God," Beth prayed. "Thank you for this wonderful food, even though I did all the cooking…"

Damon and Liv broke out in laughter. Beth gave them a good-natured glare, then closed her eyes again. "And, Lord, thank you for keeping us all healthy in this time of such great difficulty. Amen."

"Amen," everyone echoed.

"She always throws in something like that," Liv added.

"Why does prayer have to be solemn?" Beth asked. "You don't think God has a sense of humor?"

"Beth, I like your brand of religion," Damon complimented her.

Liv lifted tongs and served the table.

"Salmon's cold. Like I said it would be," Wayne grumbled.

Liv looked at him, fighting her contempt. "There's literal steam coming out of it."

"Oh, don't mind him, he's just a big ole grump when he's hungry," Beth dismissed, then eyed Damon with a welcoming smile. "Time for your third degree, young man."

"Mom…" Liv groaned.

"I'm an open book," Damon insisted. "What do you want to know?"

Beth eyed him with mock suspicion. "An open book, huh? In my experience *everybody* has secrets."

"I think I'd know his secrets by now," Liv countered.

"Well, you're all liberals to start," Wayne said as he stabbed a bite of salmon.

Liv grit her teeth. "First of all, being a liberal shouldn't be an insult. Second, how do you know what our politics are?"

"Liv told me about what happened at the march," Beth said to Damon. "You risked life and limb to help that kid get away from the mob."

"I wouldn't say my life was on the line…" Damon offered. "But Covid is nasty, I'm here to say."

"It's a good thing you were around to knock some sense into that boy," Wayne said.

The inherent racism in *that boy* made Damon bristle, but he let it go.

"And you got over Covid pretty easily, right?" Wayne went on. "I've had it, no biggie."

"For Liv it would be," Damon replied.

Beth jumped in. "I think it's heroic how careful you are around Liv. She went through absolute hell with her cancer."

Liv worked to keep her tone sweet. "Can we not talk about my cancer?"

Beth shot Damon a conspiratorial look. "Does she shut down when you use the C word too?"

"I'll plead the fifth on this one," Damon answered.

Liv leaned to kiss him. "Another reason I love him! He doesn't push for me to talk about *every little thing* that's gone on in my life."

"Then how do you really know each other?" Beth wondered aloud. "Aren't vulnerability and intimacy the keys to love?"

"Not everybody fancies themselves a shrink like you, Beth," Wayne said.

Beth grinned. "I do stick my nose into other people's business now and then."

"Stick away," Damon said. "My parents passed away when I was pretty young, so I don't mind mom questions every now and then."

"All dysfunction begins in childhood," said Beth.

"You can say that again," Wayne agreed with a nod. "That's why it's such a big problem that you *coastal elites*," he indicated Damon with his fork, "are indoctrinating our children."

Liv let her own fork fall to her plate. "I'm sorry—what is this? Do you have like, a list of all your Fox News talking points you're ticking off?"

Damon's eyebrows shot up. He'd never had the opportunity to hear Liv speak an unkind word to *anyone*.

"Can we just remain civil?" Beth asked. "This is a special night."

The table went silent as forks went to mouths. Now Beth directed her attention back to Damon. "Can I ask what happened to your family, Damon?"

"Sure. I was a fire station surrender and never have been able to track down my biological parents," Damon answered matter of fact. "My adopted parents both died of cancer within seven years of each other, Mom first, and then Dad when I was twenty."

Beth put her hand to her heart, a gesture Damon had also witnessed in Liv. "I'm so sorry. Do you have any siblings?"

"Nope. I'm an only child like Liv."

Beth smiled at her daughter. "I knew to quit while I was ahead."

Liv rolled her eyes.

"And you've got all that money," Beth prodded. "But you never married?"

"Jesus, Mom, you just met him."

"No, it's okay," Damon insisted. "I think Liv and I have a pretty similar story. We had a few disappointments which led to commitment issues. But look at us now—five months together night and day. I can't imagine life without her."

Liv smiled. "Killing me with love here."

"I want to know about *you two*," Damon said to Beth and Wayne.

"Ask away!" Beth chirped.

"How did you meet?" Damon asked.

Beth took a long sip of wine for bravery. "Promise neither of you will laugh at me?"

"I will absolutely laugh," Liv said.

Beth paused. "On a dating site called eHarmony."

"Oh, God, Mom…"

"Well now, I thought there was no way a man I met on a dating site would work out. But they ask you all these questions about yourself, so you know you're compatible. We started talking about five months ago, and the rest is history! I guess we're all on the same fast track."

"Well…" Liv started diplomatically. "You shouldn't be embarrassed. Everybody dates online now. I'm just shocked you never mentioned it to me in all these months."

"You've had a lot going on, and I wanted to make sure he was a keeper first."

Wayne cleared his throat pointedly and turned his gaze to Damon. The interruption caused Liv to trail off, which seemed to be his intention.

"So, Damon, I hear you own a real successful night club. Any idea when you'll reopen?"

"Afraid not."

Wayne grunted. "Too bad your idiot governor is wrecking small businesses everywhere with all the shutdowns. No wonder that state's such a shithole."

Liv again reared back in her seat, but Damon drew a breath in to diffuse. "Honestly, Wayne, even if it weren't mandated right now, I'd probably still keep High closed for the time being. A club with that many bodies in it—it wouldn't be safe for Liv to stay with me if I were in the thick of it most nights."

"She'd be fine. That's fearmongering, that's all it is. Sheep walking to the slaughter."

Liv suddenly stood from her seat. "Now I know where all this *bullshit* you've been spewing of late comes from, Mom!"

"Control your daughter, Beth," Wayne said gruffly.

"Hey!" Damon said and abruptly stood with Liv.

"Mom, look at me. I am your daughter. Who almost died of cancer. Who isn't out of the weeds yet. You watched me go through chemo, my mastectomy. How can you be with a man who has no fucking empathy for my health?"

"Sweetheart—please."

"No! We're leaving. Damon went through all this trouble to keep things safe for me, and you blatantly disrespected him for this…pig!"

"Oh, come on," Wayne said and smacked the table. "If you're too much of a snowflake to have an adult conversation, go ahead and go."

"Liv, no. Don't go. You've barely got here," Beth pled.

Damon looked to Liv for direction.

"Can you get our luggage," she pleaded with him.

"Of course," Damon said and, without a second look, put his napkin down and headed away from the table.

Liv bent down to put her arms around her mother. "I love you, Mom. But I can't be around this. Everything is so stressful, already. You can come around to the beach house *alone.*"

Beth nodded as she began to weep.

Liv began to walk out of the kitchen, then turned back on her heel to face Wayne. "And *fuck you.*"

20.

Liv and Damon Drove south along Florida Route 9, then east near Jensen Beach, crossing over Indian River Lagoon to Hutchinson Island wordlessly. Though Liv had grown up only an hour and a half north, and had spent many a weekend in Miami, two hours south, she'd never been to this less developed, marshy interlude before.

Finally, Damon spoke. "I'm so sorry, honey."

Liv stared out the passenger window. "I know. It's not your fault. I'm just embarrassed. And so, so angry."

Damon leaned over the console to wrap his arms around her at a stop sign. "I know, baby."

"I don't even want to think about her anymore," she said. "I want to try to enjoy our first vacation together."

"I'm sure we'll still have a good time."

Liv nodded. But something else was on her mind.

"Who was that girl at the airport?"

Damon raised an eyebrow at her sudden demand and gave a little laugh. "You're not *jealous* are you? I introduced you and let her know we were on vacation to celebrate you!"

"You've just never talked about her. Is she an ex?"

Sensing that this was not a moment to mock her, Damon dropped the mirth. "No. I would not call her an ex by any stretch of the imagination. We spent a few nights together, but she wasn't interesting. I never had any feelings for her."

Liv demurred at his honesty. "Another one of the gold diggers you told me about?"

"Psh, *yeah*! Did you see the stars in her eyes at the size of the plane? She probably would have acted like she didn't see me if it hadn't been for that."

Satisfied, Liv leaned back in her seat. "Okay. Jealous rage over."

"I'll take it as a compliment. Though I wouldn't exactly call it rage. Rage was you and Wayne."

"I came down pretty hard on him, huh?"

"Deservedly so."

Liv stared out the car window at darkness. "It's like Covid has caused a civil war."

"The divisions have always been there," Damon reasoned. "We just have a president who allows assholes like Wayne to finally show their true colors."

Liv nodded and curled up in the seat to sleep, her bare feet sliding across to lay gently on Damon's lap.

DAMON HAD NOT EXAGERATED when he'd described the island as "secluded." Even though it was night as they drove down an unlit road with sand from the dunes painting the blacktop edges, Liv could see only a few houses on the ocean side.

"Here we go," Damon said as they pulled up a short driveway to a one story, white wooden house with a tall angular roof and brown hurricane shutters hiding the windows.

"It's so lovely," Liv said as they climbed out of the vehicle.

Damon smiled and took in the sounds of waves crashing in the distance. "Let's go have a look around. I'll come back for the bags."

Liv felt the first bead of sweat forming on her forehead. "You do know that July in Florida can be miserably hot and humid?"

"I'll be in the water all day, anyway," predicted Damon.

"Pisces man!" Liv recalled with a smile.

Damon walked to the front door, checked an email on his phone, then punched in the security code. Liv followed him inside, and as soon as Damon flipped on a few lights, she gasped.

The house wasn't just lovely, it was heavenly and cozy in spite of its size, with classic Americana meets shabby chic furnishings.

"Wow, right out of *Architectural Digest*," mused Liv.

Damon laughed as they walked through the living room with high beamed ceilings and long white couches with cashmere blankets and pillows every few feet.

Liv checked out the wide kitchen, divided by an island of sandal wood and marbled top. Opening a cabinet, then the fridge, she saw that the house was fully stocked and suspected that was Damon's work.

"Let's see it together," Damon said, offering his hand, and together they walked down a long hallway. Damon opened one door and found a pleasant bedroom, but too small to be the master. "Was supposed to be for your mother..."

"Her whole house is only a little bigger."

"We're down the hallway," Damon said.

"I see you thought to put her on the other side of the house..."

Damon read her grin. "Yeah, I'd feel a little awkward."

"I know, I'm a screamer."

Damon laughed, then showed Liv to the north end of the hallway and opened the door. He touched a switch and the room lit up, along with Liv's face.

"It's huge," she said, drinking in every quaint detail: the king-sized bed, a desk facing the windows overlooking the ocean and sandy beach, lit up by a near-full moon.

"Look at this," Damon said as he opened the door to the bathroom.

Liv went to him to find a tub meant for two, a glass encased shower that could fit four, even a separate shower with sauna and steam heads.

"If I disappear, you'll find me in here," Liv told him.

They left the bathroom, and Damon opened the doors to a walk-in closet.

"Shall we unpack or have a glass of wine first?"

Liv cackled. "You know me too well. Wine first!"

"How about on the deck outside?"

"Sure."

Damon walked to the kitchen while Liv headed for the wall of glass doors that faced the beach. She found a switch and the deck outside lit up, revealing Adirondack chairs, an ancient bronze telescope on wooden legs, and a small pool, glowing blue in the night.

She opened a door and walked outside to take a seat; in the dark she could hear waves rolling in but could only see the small dunes fronting the deck.

Liv sat back, closed her eyes, and took a deep breath of the moist, salty air. *I'm home*, she thought to herself.

"Like it?" Damon asked as he sat beside her and offered her a glass of white.

Liv's face showed a calmness Damon had never seen before and was glad to find after the events of the evening. "I could live here for the rest of my life," she said.

"You wouldn't miss Los Angeles?"

"A lot, yeah. And living out of a city wouldn't help my career. But a girl can dream. You know, for the price of your home in LA, you could probably buy every house on the island."

"Hah. I could sell the house, the club… We'd live like hermits, making love on the beach all day."

Liv raised her glass. "To living like hermits!"

Damon grinned as they sipped; he knew, and he knew that Liv knew, that they'd probably get bored after six months on an island, but it was nice to enjoy the whim of fantasy.

THE GLARE OF SUNLIGHT made Liv cover her eyes as she woke. *Fuck, we forgot to close the blinds.* Damon wasn't in the bed or the room, and she couldn't hear him at all. She squinted at the giant bay windows, awed by the sight of the turquoise Atlantic Ocean lapping at the pearl white sand and saw Damon pop up to the surface.

She watched him dive under again, then pop up closer to shore. As he walked out of the ocean, she could see that he was completely naked.

"Oh my god!" she blurted out, then grinned mischievously as this wet Adonis of a man grabbed a towel from the beach and headed to the house, drying himself.

Damon arrived to find Liv waiting for him in a robe, a cup of coffee in either hand.

"How's the water?" she asked.

"Like Bali," he said, wrapping the towel around his waist. "And the sand is so soft. There are shells everywhere."

"We'll go shelling! Hey, what time is it?"

"Almost noon," Damon said.

"How is it you can always make me sleep in so late?"

Damon grinned. "It's a special talent, I guess."

THE DAYS LEADING TO Liv's birthday were right out of a film montage.

The two spent endless hours walking up and down the beach, hands locked together, collecting shells that spoke to them for some unfathomable reason, running and diving into the ocean, playing in the lolling waves.

Back at the house, they'd wash the shells off and lay them out on the dining room table to dry. Each day the shells took up more of the table, so they had every meal on the sandalwood table outside, under the sun or stars.

Liv's favorite routine of the vacation was after dinner when Damon would fill a pit he'd dug in the sand with driftwood and light a bonfire.

The picturesque days were marred only by the radio silence from Beth, but Liv could easily shove this from her mind by delighting in Damon's company.

On their third morning, Damon brought a set of two wooden paddles with hand straps attached from his luggage and set them on the kitchen island during breakfast.

"What are these?" Liv asked, turning them over with curiosity.

"Handplanes!" Damon said. "For bodysurfing."

"*Body*surfing?" Liv asked.

"Yeah, no board required. It's an ancient art. Founded in Tahiti if I remember correctly. You can do it without the handplanes, but they help to scoop water."

"So you just…ride a wave with your body?"

"Yup! It's been a while, but I used to love it."

"*This* I have to see."

And so the two marched down to the beach, and Liv watched as Damon caught a few small waves, pressing his feet against the walls of water, building back his confidence and shaking off a few small wipeouts before taking on more impressive ones gradually.

"You want me to show you?" Damon panted once he had his fill.

Liv laughed. "No. You look absolutely exhausted."

Damon put his hands on his knees and tried to catch his breath. "Like I said, it's been a while. But maybe if I keep at it here, I'll keep going when we get home."

Liv raised an eyebrow. "Just don't hurt yourself. Looks kind of dangerous."

He hugged her, still dripping wet, and she squealed at the soggy embrace. "Babe—I used to do much more dangerous stunts than bodysurfing."

EVERY EVENING BEFORE DINNER, Damon would sneak to the front door and collect boxes that FedEx or UPS had dropped off—Liv's birthday gifts. Damon would put them in a hall closet, then lock it and wrap the gifts himself. But of course, Liv wasn't fooled.

"Stop buying me things!" Liv playfully yelled at him one afternoon while he was on his laptop. This was after he'd asked her for her shoe size.

"Never!" he answered.

But Damon hoped the showering of gifts and baubles would be enough to make up for Beth's absence, if she chose to stay away.

On Liv's birthday, she woke to find wildflowers—red cardinals and purple milkweed—which Damon had collected from the sand dunes at dawn and placed in a vase by her side of the bed. She sat up and brought them to her nose. Her face lit up at the combined scent, one she knew she'd never forget.

Damon entered the room just as Liv had begun to stir.

"Good morning, birthday girl," he said as he climbed into bed and greeted her with a kiss on the forehead.

"Good morning," she cooed. "These are beautiful."

"There's pancakes for breakfast," he said. "And one more special surprise for the morning…get your robe on."

He prayed that it would be well-received.

As Liv walked down the long hall to the kitchen, she heard a tinkling of cutlery and plates being arranged—another presence in the kitchen.

"Mom!" Liv exclaimed, vitriol briefly forgotten in her surprise.

"Sweetheart," Beth rose to greet her. "I'm sorry, Liv. I should have said something. I shouldn't have let you go. But I want today to be all about you."

The two embraced, and Liv decided to accept the apology and leave it at that. Whatever axe there was to grind—and it was a substantial one to Liv—it could be put away for the day.

"It's a long drive here, Mom," Liv said. "Your car make it okay?"

Beth waved off the comment. "Of course. It was no bother."

The three sat to eat, and conversation flowed much more peacefully than it had on the night with Wayne. Damon pried Beth for stories of Liv as a child, and the two joined forces in playfully teasing Liv about embarrassing stories of yore, which Liv endured in good humor. In turn, Beth was eager to hear of the exotic adventures of this surfer orphan turned nightclub tycoon, and Liv was delighted by their easy rapport. And, most importantly, the subject of Wayne was avoided like the plague.

That evening, Damon showed Beth how to make *Poulet Sans Nom*, and she taught him how to properly bake a cake.

"I'm very handy around the house," Damon insisted truthfully. "Only three things scare me: electrical work, plumbing, and baking."

Basking in the pool, Liv heard their laughter, dried off, and came inside. "I want to be part of the fun!"

"Out!" Beth and Damon said in tandem.

Liv marched back outside with a "harumph," but was happier than ever. Not only had she found the man she loved, but that man and her mother had connected wonderfully, despite their tumultuous beginning.

That night, champagne flowing, surrounded by dozens of tall pink and white candles Damon had set around the outside table, they feted Liv. When Beth brought out the cake adorned by two lit candles—a three and one—Liv broke down in elated tears.

Then Damon brought out armloads of gift boxes.

"I've never seen a man wrap a gift before!" Beth pointed out.

"As if I needed another reason to love him," Liv boasted.

Damon handed her the gifts one by one in careful order. The first gift Liv unwrapped was a foot tall crystal jar with a few inches of sand at the bottom.

"So we can take our shells home," Damon explained.

Liv cupped her hand to her mouth. "We'll place it on my side of the bed there, too, so I can wake up and see them every morning."

Damon explained that the next gift was from her mother; inside, Liv found a sumptuous, leather-bound picture book. "You have to promise to fill it with pictures of you and Damon and send it back to me."

Damon's gifts for Liv kept coming: Balenciaga sneakers that Damon had heard Liv casually mention while scrolling through Instagram, Louboutin knee-high boots, her favorite Alo Yoga gear, a Taschen coffee table book about Florida's islands, and a stunningly beautiful rose gold Cartier Love Bracelet which Damon helped screw the ends together on her wrist.

Liv couldn't have stopped her tears from flowing if she'd wanted to. "This is too much, Damon."

"One last gift," Damon announced, standing from the table. "I'm doing the dishes and cleaning the kitchen."

"Who are you?" joked Beth.

Knowing that this thoughtfulness was not rare for Damon, Liv nevertheless smiled with gratitude. "Thank you. I love both of you."

Liv stood and went to embrace her mother, then moved to Damon, held his face in her hands and kissed him gently, then whispered to him, "You give good birthdays."

In bed that night, Beth lit a candle and said a silent prayer for her daughter. Then she settled into her bed and tried to ignore the faint sounds of lovemaking wafting down the hallway outside her door. By the hushed moans and giggled whispers, Beth knew Liv and Damon were *trying* to be quiet, but their sounds mixed with the ocean waves moving sand up the shore were beautiful to her, soothing her to sleep.

21.

"May I?" Beth asked Damon as she approached the Adirondack chairs with two coffee mugs in the morning.

He turned away from the view he was taking in, one of the last before they were to leave the next day. "Please! Good morning,"

Beth handed him a coffee and sat next to him. "Morning ended an hour ago."

Damon laughed. "True."

"Did you already take your morning swim?"

"I did. I wish I could do this every morning of my life."

"Why don't you?"

"Have you been to a beach in Los Angeles?"

"Actually, I haven't."

"Well, you're not missing anything. The water is freezing. It's a dirty secret tourists discover too late."

Beth laughed with her sip. "When I visit Liv, we're usually just going from one meal to another and talking. Or I make her let me take her shopping for her apartment. Well, her old apartment. She's lucky to be living with you during this damn pandemic."

"I'm the lucky one. The house is big and cold. Only when she's there does it feel like a home. We'll be sad to leave though. But Liv has her appointment coming up, and I still have things to manage, even when the club is closed."

"But you'll come back here again soon, right?"

"Absolutely. I can't tell you how happy I am here. And I'm so glad I could bring you and Liv together again."

"Your love for each other is beautiful."

Damon smiled, then had a thought. "You could always move to Los Angeles and stay with us?"

Beth almost laughed. "You'd want me living with you and Liv?"

"Absolutely. And if you ever needed your own space, I'd get you a house somewhere close by."

"I'm so touched. But the truth is, I have my life here. And Wayne..."

Damon said nothing, unsure of how to react to the mention of the elephant in the room.

But Beth plunged forward to another thought on her mind.

"Damon, I've wanted to talk to you about something. But I thought I should spend some time and see if you two were in as love as Liv said first."

"Sounds important..."

"It is. First, forgive me if I'm out line here. After all Liv's been through, I'm a little—okay, very—protective of her."

Damon smiled to reassure Beth. "You want to know what my intentions are?"

"Is that too old-fashioned of me?"

She winced and Damon put a hand atop hers, on the chair's arm.

"How's this for old-fashioned?" Damon said. "I want to spend the rest of my life with your daughter. I've even thinking of proposing, but knew I needed to meet you first."

Beth exhaled a loving breath. "Damon, that's so wonderful. Have you talked to her about marriage?"

"Not yet."

"Why not?"

Damon took a breath, feeling anxious to admit this out loud. "Liv told me early on that she's afraid of commitment, so I've been very careful to not pressure her."

"You understand why she's that way?"

"Sure. She doesn't like to talk about it, but I can't imagine how frightening it is not to know if you'll be alive for twenty months or twenty years."

Beth nodded, contemplative. "She doesn't even talk to me about it. But I know she's very afraid of getting cancer again and hurting people."

"Afraid of hurting *me*?"

"You, me, herself. Imagine the guilt she'd feel marrying you, knowing she might not be here for you. Knowing she'd leave behind a broken heart of tragic proportions."

"I understand, but I want to share whatever time she has left."

"Have you told her this?"

"Many times. But I guess that probably makes her even more scared."

Beth turned her body to face Damon. "And you're okay that you two will never have children?"

"Absolutely. She said she can't have children and that's fine with me."

"What do you mean, she *can't* have children?"

"Because of the medication she's on."

Beth looked uncomfortable for a moment, then finally said, "Oh, of course," quietly.

The conversation was interrupted by Liv sliding aside the glass door, her own coffee cup in hand.

"Morning, sleepyhead!" Beth greeted.

"Good morning," Liv said, kissing each of them on the cheek. "Telling secrets about me?"

Damon grinned. "Something like that. I even asked your mom to move in with us!"

Liv laughed. "I'd love that. But you'd need to find a new group of girls to play Gin Rummy with!"

"Maybe one day," Beth demurred. "But I'm sure there's some old broads in Beverly Hills who know how to play Gin Rummy."

The three laughed, interrupted only by Beth's phone buzzing on the table before her. She looked quickly at the screen, then returned it to the table, facedown. "I should be heading out soon. It's a long drive back."

"Okay..." Liv eyed the phone with suspicion. "But we're here all day, you know. You could stay for lunch."

Beth took Liv's face in her hands. "You know I don't like to drive in the evening, sweetheart. And you two should enjoy the last day of your vacation."

"I understand," Liv said, looking slightly dejected.

Damon and Beth exchanged a warm goodbye, then Damon lingered in the kitchen as Liv walked Beth to the front door to give them a bit of privacy.

He tried to busy himself but couldn't help but eavesdrop.

"Mom," Liv said in the foyer. "It means so much that you came. And I don't want to spoil that or seem ungrateful, but the other night was a wakeup call for you, right?"

"Oh, people disagree about politics, sweetheart. You're not the one sleeping with him, so why does it matter if you two had a little spat? It's a stressful time."

Liv couldn't help herself. "Because he's a *pig*, Mom, and he's rude! Politics aside, he doesn't treat *you* right. The way he acted says something about him as a person!"

"Please don't call the man I love a pig, Liv. I love him. If you respect me, you'll respect him."

"Respect? Mom, you're throwing your own self-respect away if you hang your hat on a man like him! You have to know deep down that there's a reason you hid his existence from me. Because you knew I wouldn't approve, and for good reason."

Now Beth's face flushed red. "Do you know how long it's been since I've been with someone? I'm not a super model like you. I'm in my sixties. Can't you just be *happy* for me?"

"*Mom!*" Liv's voice rose with frustration.

"I know what it is. You don't have any ability to commit, even to a man as wonderful as Damon, because you're carrying your damage around with you like a badge of honor. You can't understand my willingness to commit to a man, flaws and all."

Liv narrowed her eyes. "How could you even say that to me? I *live* with him, for the love of God!"

"Yeah, and you lie to him," Beth hissed. "You told him you *can't* have children, like that's a biological fact, when the truth is you just don't want them! I doubt *that* was some kind of miscommunication. You intentionally misled him."

The blood left Damon's face, and he cursed himself for listening in. He realized he had completely given up on feigning to look busy in the kitchen and began to crush gift wrap into tight little balls for the recycling.

"That," Liv said quietly, "is absolutely none of your business. I think you should leave before we spoil the night."

Beth shook her head sadly. "I think it's already spoiled. I wish you would trust me to make my own decisions."

Liv bit her tongue. "Goodbye, Mom. I love you. But you can be a real pain in the ass."

DAMON DRANK A LITTLE more wine than usual on their last day at the beach house. He had resolved not to trouble Liv further by sharing with her that he had overheard her secret, but the revelation weighed on him. He understood, perhaps, that lying about such a thing initially, when they had just met, would not be so unacceptable. After all, why should a near stranger be entitled to such intimate information? But it had come up several times now—what reason could she have for not setting the record straight?

On the morning of their departure, Damon resolved to get in one last bodysurfing session.

He rose at dawn, slipped the paddles onto his hands, and pressed out into the ocean. Over and over, he straightened his core and positioned himself to rise with the waves, his body sore from pushing himself to return to the skill level he once had.

But the strain of his muscles felt good and fighting the pressure of the water alleviated some of the pressure he felt in his own mind.

He knew he should wrap it up soon and head back to shore, and already his limbs felt shaky with exhaustion.

But he wanted to get *just one more big one.*

He spotted a wave begin to swell and scooped water furiously, angling himself against the crest.

He threw one arm forward—a final push—and felt the tear immediately.

His rotator cuff set ablaze with pain.

He tumbled with the wave, his balance ruined, and instinctively reached with his other hand to grab his shoulder, wiggling off one paddle and letting it fall away with the wave.

"*Fuck!*"

He swam awkwardly to shore with one arm, sputtering and barely keeping his head over the surface.

He collapsed on the shore and howled.

Liv rushed from the backyard, down the wooden steps and to the beach.

"Damon! What happened?"

Damon lay on his back in the sand, eyes shut tight, gripping his shoulder with one hand and sucking air in through his teeth.

"I think I tore my rotator cuff."

"Oh my god! Let's get you inside!"

Gingerly, Liv helped him up with his good arm, and Damon allowed her to, dejected.

They walked to the house, Damon squinting in pain. "Lost my goddamn hand planes. They were handmade."

Liv sat him on one of the couches in the living room and hurried to the freezer to find an ice pack, reemerging with only a bag of frozen peas.

"I told you to be careful," she said softly with concern as she pressed the peas to his shoulder.

"Can you go get my dopp kit out of the bathroom, please?" he asked.

Liv obliged, returning with the brown leather satchel. Damon opened it with his good arm and withdrew a bottle of hydrocodone, popping two.

Liv couldn't help but notice the label.

"You carry those with you?" she asked with surprise.

Damon blinked at the bottle in his hand, as though dumbfounded himself with the ease he had produced the pills in front of Liv. "Yeah, I guess I do…or maybe they were just in here from a long time ago."

Liv raised an eyebrow but said nothing. She knew he was too fastidious of a planner and packer to be unaware of the bottles in his dopp kit.

"Do we need to go to the hospital? Change our flight?"

Damon again winced with pain as he shifted the shoulder back and forth, testing its limits. "No. We're not going to the hospital, and I'm not quarantining all over again because of a torn rotator cuff. They'll just tell me to ice it and suck it up. I'll get some steroid shots back home."

"Okay…whatever you need, babe. I just want you to be okay."

"Yeah," Damon said and lowered himself flat on the couch. "I'm just glad we're already packed."

THE FLIGHT HOME was slightly bumpy due to headwinds. Liv held Damon's hand on his good side, but he read for the first two hours of the flight, immune to her chattiness, which he usually found captivatingly charming.

"That house was my version of heaven," got an "Mm hmm."

"Let's go through the pictures on our phones and figure out which ones to print and send to mom," received, "I'll let you do it," as Damon handed his phone to her without looking up from the page.

"I love this one of us!" brought on only a short glance and smile.

"Are you okay?" she finally asked him.

"Just tired," Damon said.

He closed his book, then reached back into his dopp kit to produce two more hydrocodone.

"Is that safe to do so soon?" Liv couldn't help but ask. "You just took a lot a couple hours ago…"

"I did," Damon said with a gruffness she was unaccustomed to. "And it still hasn't touched the pain."

He leaned his head back and closed his eyes, seeming to nap.

Liv bit her lip and wondered at his tolerance. Then she ran through the week in her mind and wondered at his distance. She knew he was in pain, but she'd seen him in pain before.

Don't overthink it. It's just a hiccup.

But after a silent car ride home, Liv grew concerned. As Damon insisted on carrying the heavy luggage upstairs with his good arm, grunting all the way, she poured herself a glass of wine and settled onto the couch.

"You probably shouldn't have wine with your medicine, but tea?" she called out as he descended the stairs.

"I'm okay."

"Another ice pack?"

"I can get it myself."

"Come sit with me, please?"

Damon nodded and sat beside her.

"I'm surprised that black cloud over your head hasn't started raining already," Liv said.

Damon looked at Liv's lighthearted smile. "I've been brooding pretty hard, huh?"

Liv took Damon's hand. "What's going on? If you're in that much pain, I don't want you to suffer—you should go to the hospital. Or call your concierge doctor. It's not too late at night…"

Damon took a beat to find an inoffensive way to say what was bothering him. "I overheard…something that upset me."

"You did? From who? Wayne? My mom?"

"Your mother."

Liv's heartbeat quickened with concern. "On a scale from one to ten—ten being furious—how upset are you?"

"About a four."

"What did you hear that upset you?"

"That you're physically capable of having children. You just don't want them."

Liv blinked. "So?"

"So you told me you *couldn't* have children because of the meds you're on. You lied to me."

"Damon… It was just a white lie. We had literally just met, and I didn't want to share every last detail about my body."

"I can understand that. But you couldn't you have clarified that any time in the last six months?"

Liv sighed. She knew he was right about the omission. "I'm sorry I lied. I just wanted to make sure you wouldn't try to change my mind one day."

"I'd never… Liv, I know you'd make a great mother, but I'd rather spend whatever time we have making you happy."

"Whatever time I have left…" Liv huffed with annoyance and stood.

"Liv, I don't think you understand the real problem I have with all this."

She crossed her arms. "What's the *real* problem?"

"Will you sit?" he asked.

"No! Tell me what I'm really doing wrong here."

"Okay, the real problem is that getting you to talk about any part of your cancer is like pulling teeth."

"So fucking what?"

Damon took a breath so only one of them was defensive. "Liv, I love you more than I've ever loved another human being. But I think you're in a little denial about a very important aspect of you, of our relationship…"

Fury turned Liv's face red. "Of course I'm in fucking denial, Damon! Do you think talking about death is going to make me happier? I spent months in therapy, and it didn't do shit. So what if pretending cancer doesn't exist makes me happy?"

Liv took a step one way, changed her mind, and took another step, then stopped, as if she was trapped.

Damon stood. "Liv, I don't want to fight. I'm not Chistropher. No matter what happens, no matter how scary things get, you can trust me."

Liv took a deep breath and forced herself to sit back down. "You're right, I'm sorry. You have a right to feel like I've been keeping a part of myself from you."

"Thank you," Damon said as he sat beside her, closer this time.

Liv felt the first tear trickle. "I'm afraid."

Damon reached out and caressed her cheek. "Of what?"

"Of dying. I feel guilty loving you when I know I'm going to leave. It's just a matter of time. And if I even think about how disappointed I am that I'll never have children, or could have them and leave them, I'll completely unravel… Just talking about it makes me hate myself for abandoning them."

Now tears dripped uncontrollably down Liv's face.

"Come here," Damon said, pulling Liv to him so she could bury her head against his chest.

"Honey…" Damon said quietly. "Nobody knows what will happen tomorrow. A *massive* percentage of people recover from breast cancer and lead happy, cancer-free lives until they die of natural causes. It's as if, even though you don't like talking about cancer, you're obsessed with death. You're stuck in it. You think because you had a setback in your singing career, you have to abandon it forever. You think because Christopher burned you, you'll never recover from your wounds. Whether we have children or don't, what's important *now* is that we love each other, and trust that whatever we go through, we go through it together. And the best way to do that is by being open and vulnerable with each other."

Liv pulled herself from his chest, but her eyes stared at his unflinchingly. "I'm afraid, Damon. I could have cancer spreading through my body right now and not even know it. Every few months, they take blood, and I shit in my pants for days waiting for the results."

"I know. I'm afraid too. That's okay if we have each other."

Liv wiped her tears away with her palms. "Like that imagery?"

Damon smiled. "Disgusting."

Liv located a laugh. "It actually feels good sharing how I feel with you."

"Because you realize you're not alone," Damon said. "I'll never let you be alone again."

"Promises, promises."

Damon took a breath. "You know what I told your mother?"

"No."

"Promise me you won't run out of the room?" Damon asked.

"Can I speed walk out of the room?"

Damon laughed. "That I wanted to marry you."

Liv's face looked like it had been split in half, one side delighted, the other frightened.

"Oh, Lord," Liv gasped.

"Don't worry, I'm not proposing yet."

"Yet. Baby, why would you want to waste a ring on such a neurotic woman?"

"You know the reason."

Liv did.

"I love you too. When were you thinking of asking such a crazy thing?"

"Haven't planned that far. But if it were up to me, tonight would work."

"Ha! Good thing I have to agree first. Which, to be clear, I'm not ready to do. Honestly, I'm not sure I'll ever be ready, and I need to know that you'll be okay with that?"

Damon didn't bat an eye. "Liv, I'll take you unmarried, married, it really makes no difference to me, as long as you're mine."

Liv flushed. "Although I *might* have had a few dreams of me in a white dress."

"Have you really?"

"No, I'm lying again."

Damon laughed. "You do realize we just had our first fight, right?"

"They say that couples who make up quickly, last longer."

Liv smiled and put both her arms around Damon's neck. "You know what I love about fighting?"

"I have a pretty good idea."

Liv climbed atop Damon and kissed him.

"Careful with my arm," he cautioned, letting it fall to the floor and out of the way.

As they fell together onto the cushions, Damon felt himself harden and unbuttoned his jeans, kicking his shoes off. Liv shivered eagerly as she slipped off her white cotton skirt, fingers taking her panties with them.

As soon as Damon pulled his black underwear down, Liv lifted her hips over his and went down, so wet that Damon slipped inside her without friction; she leaned down to lick his neck.

"You bit me!" Damon cried out.

Liv laughed. "It'll distract you from your shoulder."

Damon grabbed her hair and yanked her neck so he could bite her back.

"Harder!" Liv urged.

Damon ignored her command, pushed her off and spun her onto her stomach, entering her from behind.

"Do it!" Liv cried out.

Damon thrust a few times so hard that Liv cried out in pleasured pain. And though he knew that she liked it when he was forceful, he suddenly slowed down, sliding in and out of her. He leaned over her, close, and pushed her hair aside so he could lick the back of her neck.

Then he suddenly stopped, emitting hard breaths.

"What is it?" Liv asked, craning her neck around so she could see him.

"I will never hurt you, Liv."

"I know, baby. I know."

22.

TERROR GRIPPED LIV for the first time since she had lived in the company of Damon.

She had stirred in her sleep, and upon briefly fluttering her eyes open, she heard the bedroom door slowly open, hinges dragging in a labored squeak that belied their new construction. A tall shadow leaned into the door frame.

"*Damon!*" she screamed, and her hand smacked beside her to rouse him, but the bed was empty.

"Hi, baby. I'm so sorry," the shadow spoke, and Damon walked all the way into the bedroom.

"Jesus *Christ*, baby. You scared the shit out of me. What are you doing?"

Liv sat all the way up in bed and tried to slow her heart rate.

"I went to sleep in the guest room, but I forgot something."

Damon's frame disappeared briefly into the bathroom.

"Why are you sleeping in the guest room? Is everything okay?" Liv rubbed at her eyes.

"Yes, I'm fine. My shoulder's just really bugging me. I didn't want to keep you awake."

"You're not bothering me," Liv said, reaching for him.

"I'm just going to read for a while and see if I can't pass out."

He kissed her on the forehead.

"Okay…well what did you forget?"

Damon leaned over her body to grab a pillow from his side of the bed. "Tempur-Pedic pillow."

"Aren't they all Tempur-Pedic?" Liv asked.

"Yeah. But this one's firmer," he said, squishing the pillow on its sides to demonstrate.

"Okay," she said, turning back over. "I love you. Wake me up if you need anything."

"Love you too. Get some sleep."

Liv rested her head on the kitchen island as she waited for the blessed whir of the espresso machine to finish its business in the morning. She'd hardly got back to sleep after her fright the previous evening but didn't want to hover over Damon if he wanted to lick his wounds in peace.

He typically rose before her, and the fact that it was 10:00 a.m. and he still wasn't up—particularly with their body clocks still three hours ahead on Florida's time—made Liv resolve to *insist* that Damon call the concierge doctor immediately.

When the whirring stopped, Liv put each of her index fingers through the handles on the tiny cups, placed them on saucers, and carefully padded up the staircase, spilling only a drop or two.

She was about to call out to Damon to open the door for her when she reached the guest room but decided a kiss on the cheek would be a more welcome awakening if he wasn't feeling well, so she carefully set the saucers on the hardwood floors, reached for the handle, and turned.

She was so surprised to be met with resistance that when the knob didn't turn, she moved it the other way.

Locked.

Surprised, she stared at the closed door for a moment.

"Damon?" she called softly.

No response.

"Damon!" she called louder, pounding at the door.

"Come in," came his groggy voice.

"I can't come in, Damon; the door is locked."

She was met with silence for a moment, and then she heard the labored shuffling of feet, the click of the lock, and then another labored shuffling of feet.

She opened the door to find Damon already collapsed in bed again, facedown.

"Baby!" she said, then bent down to collect the saucers. "You must *really* be in pain. We're calling the doctor. Like, right now."

Damon didn't say anything. She put the saucers on the bedside table.

"How come you locked the door?" she asked.

"I didn't lock the door," he mumbled into the pillow.

"Well, somebody did. Baby, what is wrong?"

Damon rolled slightly so his face was no longer smothered. He heaved a steadying breath and spoke.

"I'm high, Liv. I'm not in good shape."

Even though he was cognizant enough to string together a sentence, Liv could detect a slight slur in his voice. She sat next to him on the opposite side of the bed.

"You poor thing," she cooed. "You were in that much pain? Give me your phone; I'll call the doctor. You took more hydrocodone?"

But Damon shook his head. Laboriously, he raised himself into a sitting position and leaned his back against the headboard. He dug one hand under the sheets, produced a prescription bottle, and handed it to Liv.

She turned it over to look at the label. *Oxycodone.* She held up the bottle. "What is this?"

"I already finished the hydrocodone," he said, his head lolling to one side against the headboard. "This is another bottle I had."

Liv felt cold. She stared at him for a moment, frozen in place at having been thrust into this new reality where Damon was no longer collected and capable. "Damon…what does that mean?"

"It means I have a problem. A bigger problem than a hurt shoulder. And we're gonna have to…" Damon slid back down the bed until his head was on the pillow again. "…talk about it at some point."

"Okay," Liv said. "But what about right now? What should I do for you right now?"

"Nothing," Damon mumbled. "Just…take the rest of the bottle and let me sleep."

"Damon," Liv's voice rose with concern. "You can't even keep your head up. Should I call someone? You're really fucking high."

He raised one finger in the air.

"And *you*, Livy, are *beautiful*. But tomorrow, I shall be sober, and you shall still be beautiful," he slurred even harder, bending the Churchill quote for his own purposes.

Liv sighed. She felt his forehead to make sure it wasn't hot, then put two fingers to the side of his neck. Satisfied his pulse was strong, she got off the bed, prescription bottle in hand, and did a quick hunt for any remaining bottles but found nothing.

Numb, she left the room and shut the door behind her. She sat on the top step of the stairs and pulled her phone from her robe pocket to text Marie.

How do you sober someone up from an opioid high?

Marie's response came almost immediately: Narcan. Why what's going on?

I don't think we're at the Narcan level.

Responsive?

Liv rubbed her eyes and felt a pang of regret for involving Marie.

She typed back: Yes, responsive. Talking. Breathing.

If it's not ER or Narcan level, then nothing. Time.

Liv groaned. How much time?

Depends. Maybe 4 hrs or so. What's going on? Are you ok?

I'm okay. I'll call you when I can.

Liv walked to their room and sat at the edge of their bed, cortisol tingling inside her stomach. She tried not to jump to conclusions. Damon was in a lot of pain. And that pain might have even been exacerbated by them making love on the couch the night before. Maybe he overdid it. Maybe he just grabbed that bottle of Oxycodone because it was convenient, and the Hydrocodone bottle was still intact somewhere.

But she knew that was wishful thinking.

Even if he was high as a kite, Damon was never one to be an alarmist. If he said he had a problem, he almost certainly did.

Liv knew she had just encountered a fresh new hurdle with Damon.

Liv DIDN'T CRY as she went about the business of her day, even though half her thoughts were a broken record: *This is it. This is the other shoe you were waiting on to drop. It wasn't cancer. It wasn't girls—like Alyssa. It wasn't not having children. It was this. And now I'm in too deep to want to leave.*

But if Liv was good at anything, it was moving through a crisis. She set up her lights. She took her photos, made "candid" videos, and planned out her product endorsements. She responded to comments. She made lunch. She sorted through which Florida pictures to have printed for her mother's photo album.

Finally, as she was folding her lighting setup into its case, Damon appeared in the living room doorway.

"Hi," he said sheepishly.

Liv finished zipping the case and looked up. "Hi. How are you feeling?"

"Sore, but not totally terrible…"

"Do you want to talk about what happened?" she asked evenly.

Damon crossed the length of the living room and sat next to her on the floor, knees up. He buried his face into his hands. "I'm so sorry, Liv."

Liv's stoicism began to collapse, and tears stung her eyes. "I'm not even entirely sure what you're sorry *about*. What is going on? Why did you have that bottle? How did you finish all the hydrocodone from yesterday?"

Damon lifted his face from his hands. "By an incredible feat of an exemplary liver?"

He stole a look at Liv with a weak smile, but she was in no mood to reciprocate his attempt at levity.

"I'm sorry," he went on. "I know this isn't the time for jokes. I know I scared you. I thought I had these impulses under control—but the cough syrup I had during Covid had codeine in it. It should have been a red flag to me when I specifically didn't tell you about it."

Liv sniffled, and Damon noticed her tears for the first time. He took his face in her hands. "I promise you, baby. This won't happen again."

"How do I know that?" she asked but didn't pull away from his touch. "I knew you struggled with this kind of thing—with cocaine, and then after your accident. But you said this morning that you have a *problem*. You said, *a bigger problem than a hurt shoulder.*"

Damon dropped his hands to his side and hung his head. "That's true, and I did say that. This is a wakeup call for me. I'm not going to let this fuck us up."

"So what do we do, then? I don't have any experience with this kind of thing."

Damon shook his head, thinking. "I'm not sure. I'll come up with a plan. Obviously, I'll give you the rest of my medicine. I do have a pretty impressive supply from the accident."

He searched her face, but her expression was far away. He felt anxiety creep through his body.

"Liv," he prompted. "What are you thinking?"

"I was just thinking that I really need you to be right, and for this to not become a thing. Because I'm in too deep to leave, and it scares me."

He put his arms around her. "I will."

She sobbed into his shoulder, a few deep heaves until she quieted.

"Okay," she said finally, pulling away from him and wicking away the running makeup under her eyes. "This isn't that big of a deal. We caught it early; we'll figure it out. I mean, I didn't even notice anything until yesterday. And you only had Covid, what, a month ago? Less? It's not like you've built up a tolerance or anything since then or will have to like, *withdraw*. This was just a hiccup."

Damon grimaced. "Yeah…"

Liv narrowed her eyes. "What are you not telling me? Has this been going on longer than that?"

"No!"

"Then what? Why did you make a face like that?"

"It's just…the amount. You know I don't half-ass anything."

"Okay…so how often were you doing drugs since it started?"

Damon's shoulders fell with shame. "Every day."

Liv's eyes widened. "Every *day*? Even in Florida? Even before your shoulder?"

"Yes."

"God *damnit*, Damon."

Now Liv rose to pace.

"You're mad," he said.

"*Yes, I'm mad.*"

She halted and turned to face him. "But let me be absolutely clear about *why* I'm mad. I'm not mad because you're struggling with this thing. Lots of people do. It's fixable, it doesn't make you like—a bad person or something. I'm mad because just last night, I got a whole ass lecture about the importance of honesty and trust, of communicating openly with you and giving you it all, the good, bad, and ugly. And you said that to me with a straight face, knowing full well that you've been popping pills every single day and lying to me about it!"

Suddenly Damon straightened his back, as though possessed by a new courage. He took a steadying breath and rose to face her eye to eye.

"Liv. You're right. I lied to cover my ass. I lied about why I had the pills before my brain even caught up to what I was doing. And even now, I'm lying. Lying by omission. And I don't want to."

Liv's eyes grew wide as a myriad of awful possibilities flashed through her mind. "What are you lying about?"

"I downplayed my struggle with the opiates after my accident. I made it sound like I recognized it was a slippery slope and was able to just stop. That's not the truth."

Liv sat back down on the couch and drew a breath. "Okay. I wasn't sure what you were going to say but that's…okay. Tell me more."

"I knew that the blow was a problem. I knew I didn't want to continue down that path, so I broke up with Nina, like I said. But opioids are insidious. I was in pain, so I was able to justify how much I was consuming. It went on like that for a couple months, until I nodded out in an investor meeting."

Liv gasped. "Nodded out?"

Damon sucked his teeth and nodded slowly, eyes far away in the memory. "Yeah. It was completely humiliating. Thankfully, I was able to cover my ass. Said that I had the flu and that I needed to check myself into the hospital. Well, I did check myself into the hospital, but not for the flu. I did two weeks of inpatient rehab."

Liv was silent as her head spun with the effort of processing this new information.

"So the truth is, I should have never hung onto those pills in the first place. I don't know what I was thinking. I don't know if I thought it made me stronger to keep them around and not take them, or if secretly I was saving them for a rainy day. I know better. There's no excuse..."

His sentence faded out as his voice began to choke.

He knelt beside her again and took both of her wrists in either hand gently.

"Liv...I swear to you. I will make this right."

She didn't respond.

"Are you going to leave me?" his voice was barely a whisper.

She looked away. "No. I just feel like I can't trust you right now. I want to help, but I'm confused, and hurt, and afraid."

"What are you going to do?" he asked.

"I don't know," she said again. "I need some time to think. But first, take me to your pills."

DAMON PROCEEDED WITH THE CEREMONY of turning his pill bottles over to Liv with such solemnity that it was difficult for her to hold on to her anger. But she knew she needed some time to process before embracing Damon with unbridled support and affection.

There were only four bottles left, but Liv felt satisfied that she had collected everything from Damon's remorseful attitude alone.

Afterwards, Damon retreated to his study to dig up old worksheets and resources from his time in rehab, and Liv expressed she needed some time to think.

She shut herself away in the guest room to call Marie and relay her story. Liv was surprised Marie did not become overly protective and pile onto Damon. Instead, she offered resources to Liv and explained some of what Liv had already gleaned from WebMD. Marie suggested Damon try the medications Suboxone and methadone, but Damon had already ruled out the standard medically assisted detoxes, since they helped but basically left you dependent on those.

"He's not going to feel *good*," Marie said, "but the good news is that opioid withdrawal won't kill him. Based on what you told me about his intake, he'll be in pain for a week or two."

Liv thanked her friend for her advice and support, but stared at the ceiling, restless. She felt more alone than she had in a very long time. She wished she could call Beth but couldn't stomach providing her an opportunity to say something like, *See, sweetheart, everyone has flaws.*

Liv's thoughts turned to Yasmina. She felt a wave of frustration that she was also unhappy with Yasmina at the moment, for the Instagram stories she had seen and Marie's reports. Still, she couldn't help but clock that it was 12:29 a.m.—9:29 a.m. in Paris. She found Yasmina's contact and hit "Call" on impulse.

"Oh my god! Hi!" came Yasmina's excited voice.

"Hi," Liv said weakly.

"Uh oh. Trouble in paradise?" Yasmina asked.

"Well, yeah. But I could ask you the same question."

Yasmina paused. "Uh, what are you talking about?"

"I guess I should say, *making* trouble in paradise," Liv didn't bother to hide the annoyance in her voice.

"I'm sorry, you're gonna have to spell it out for me. What's going on?"

Liv sighed. "I'm sorry—I have a lot going on right now. I just mean, I saw your Instagram story of the rave…"

"Ohhhh, that. Yeah, trust me I've already been reamed for that by plenty of people. It was definitely an error in judgment. Thankfully, I didn't get sick, and I wouldn't do that again."

"A one-time thing…?"

"Yeah, only happened once. I'm not trying to make excuses, I know it's really bad, but yeah."

Liv rolled her eyes. She had already had her fill of lies covering bad behavior for the day. "Marie said you've been posting stuff like that all the time."

"Huh?"

"I don't know, that's what she said."

Suddenly, Yasmina's voice rose with recognition. "Ohhhh. I know what she's talking about. Ugh, I love her, but Marie can be such a drama queen."

"Okay...so what is she talking about?"

"Not raves or parties or even a big group of people. I've joined this group, there's just three of us. Four, actually, including the guide. I've been doing ayahuasca ceremonies. Like, in the forest. Outdoors. I've done two so far."

"Ugh. Yasmina, you couldn't have possibly known this, but I've had my fill of talking about drugs for the day."

Of course, Yasmina asked what was going on, and Liv tried to make her story brief. Yasmina, of course, expressed her sympathy, but went on to clarify:

"Just so you know, ayahuasca is nothing like that. We do it in a controlled environment, with a spiritual leader well-versed in guiding people. It's really intense, but very, very healing. I've been sorting through a lot of generational trauma from my family. My dad leaving us, and before that, when my parents immigrated from Turkey to France. I don't want to sound like one of those people who like, takes mushrooms for the first time and is all, 'You have to try this man,' but you do really have to try this, Liv."

Liv sighed and pulled her covers up around her neck. Perhaps it was the relief of clearing the air with one of the people closest to her, but the events of the last weeks were finally starting to weigh down her eyelids.

"Actually," Yasmina went on, "Apparently it's highly effective in treating addiction. Maybe you and Damon should try."

"Maybe. I won't rule it out entirely. But I think we should, I don't know, get a little distance from one drug before experimenting with the next. Also, I'm finally getting tired."

"10-4 girlie. I'm really glad you gave me a call."

"I am too. Love you, Yaz."

"Love you, Liv."

When Liv hung up the phone, she briefly considered just falling asleep in the guest room, but the thought of it made her heart ache. She couldn't deny that whatever feelings of betrayal gnawed at her insides, the desire to support Damon was stronger.

Quietly, she padded down the hall to their room, where Damon lay in bed, eyes open, hands folded across his chest, staring at the ceiling. His face brightened when he saw her.

"I thought you might not come to bed tonight," he said.

"And stay away from you for two nights in a row?"

She climbed onto the bed and sat gingerly on his torso.

"Listen here," she said, bending playfully close to his face. "You're not getting rid of me this easily."

He laughed, relief flooding his face for the first time all day.

"Whatever it takes," she said, interrupting herself to kiss him on either cheek and then his forehead. "We're going to get through this. I love you."

23.

WHEN LIV DESCENDED the staircase in the morning, Damon was already in the kitchen, flipping an omelet. She noted he looked weary but wasn't surprised. The last week he'd barely slept, barely smiled. He rarely complained, but Liv knew he was knuckling through all types of body aches and pains.

"Hi," he said quietly.

Liv kissed him on the cheek. "Good morning. It was my turn to be the Amazon fairy this morning."

"Oh?" Damon asked.

"Yup. You've got bottles of folic acid, potassium, and iron on the way. I did some research. If you're going to stay sober, those are gonna help."

"I don't deserve you," he said earnestly as he plated the omelet and passed it to her. "For you."

"You eat already?"

"I'm too nauseous. Standard withdrawal diet."

She accepted the plate and sat at the kitchen island. "How are you feeling this morning?"

"Not great. I sweat a *lot* last night. I felt kind of bad that you were next to me in the swamp."

Liv laughed at that. "Okay, I'd be lying if I said I didn't notice you were pretty damp over there."

"Also," he went on, "I'm sore as shit. Even my back hurts way worse than it does typically."

Liv nodded. "Yeah, Marie said that was probably going to happen. You've been numbing your nervous system, so everything is coming back online and feels sharper than it probably did before."

"You told Marie?"

"I'm sorry. I know it's personal. I needed some support."

"I'm not mad!" he insisted. "I'm just...embarrassed."

"My friends wouldn't be my friends if they were judgmental."

"It's okay. I guess you need some support. I ordered some books myself, did some journaling…"

"Journaling?"

"Yeah. About my values, realigning myself with my ideas of the future…all of which include you, and none of which include being addicted."

Liv smiled. "That's good to know."

"Liv," he sat beside her. "I really can't forgive myself for finishing up your birthday trip with a scare like that. I need you to know that I'm committed to this, and I know I can't have *this* and go back to numbing myself. I want to be present for this. For us."

Liv smiled and kissed him again on the cheek. "You had better be, mister."

"I NEED TO TALK to you about something," Damon said a few evenings later when Liv emerged from the gym.

He was sitting in the living room, a copy of *In the Realm of Hungry Ghosts* by Gabor Maté, a book about the intersection between PTSD and addiction in his lap. He dog-eared a page and closed the book as Liv approached.

"Lay it on me," she said.

Damon sipped from his tea, which he'd been drinking instead of wine even at meals lately.

"The city has approved outdoor dining," he announced.

"Really?" asked Liv, unsure where this was going.

"Yeah. Listen, I'm not at all pointing to this as the main source of my fuck up, but as much as I love being on perpetual vacation with you…being idle is not really in alignment with my values. I'm a working animal."

"You want to open a whole other restaurant outdoors?"

"No," Damon clarified. "I talked to my contractor about removing the ceiling on the club and installing a massive skylight that can open, and close if it rains. Here, I'll pull up some initial drawings of what I'm thinking…"

Damon picked up his phone from the coffee table. Liv sat beside him; she was interested but also had a gnawing feeling of apprehension. She didn't want to shoot down his ideas, but it had hardly been three weeks since she found him high as a kite, and she couldn't imagine Damon returning to work so soon.

"I'd turn it into more of a high-end restaurant with secluded booths," Damon said as he handed the phone to her.

With her fingers, Liv zoomed in on the black and white hand-drawn pictures of the elaborate skylight. "Wow," she said, genuinely impressed.

"And obviously, I wouldn't do anything to risk your health," Damon added. "I'll only go to the club when the workers are gone and supervise the architect and contractors on Zoom."

Liv raised an eyebrow. "Damon, I don't want to be unsupportive, but…it's not only *my* health we have to worry about here."

"I know," Damon said quietly. "I've thought of that. But this would be different. It wouldn't be open that late. And Jay has accused me of being a helicopter parent to High before—this could be an opportunity for me to learn how to be a little more hands-off. I really think this would be good for me."

Liv smiled, allowing herself to share some of Damon's enthusiasm. "How long would it take before you open?"

"If there's no hold up, maybe as soon as ten weeks or so."

"Ugh. I don't know if I can take another week or whatever apart from you if you end up having to isolate again."

"Me neither. But I have to do something with the club. Keeping it closed is costing me close to half a hundred thousand dollars a month."

"Holy shit. Why so much?"

"The lease is a fortune. The loans we took to open the business have interest payments. And I've been supplementing the staff's pandemic relief whenever I can."

"You've been paying your workers this whole time?"

"As often as I can. They're like family to me."

"If I'd known, I'd have never let you fly me to Florida on a private plane."

"They're *like* a family to me. You are my family."

Liv couldn't hold at bay a small surge of jealousy. "Mm. And what about your regulars? Are they like a family to you?"

Damon thought for a moment. "Maybe a couple, yeah."

"Regulars like Alyssa?" she asked petulantly.

"Baby, no. You know better, don't you?"

Liv sighed. "I'm sorry. I do know better. I'm just nervous about this whole thing. If you need to go back to work for financial reasons and to feel good about yourself, I'll support you. But you have to prioritize staying off the pills above everything. If things get too stressful, if you get tempted…you have to talk to me."

"It's a deal."

As DAMON GOT BACK to work again with new resolve, life almost felt like it was returning to the normalcy of pre-pandemic days.

His sleep returned, so he'd go to bed early and would rise at dawn so he could go to the club and observe the work done the day before, which prompted Liv to begin rising even earlier to make breakfast for him. Then, she'd climb back into bed and wait for him to return an hour or two later. They'd begun to make love more regularly, and to Liv's surprise—a not unhappy one—Damon's libido was even stronger now than ever.

After some snuggling and coffee in bed, Damon would disappear into his office for a few hours to make calls and Zoom. Liv would tend to her posts, then cook lunch and dinner, enjoying domesticity in a way she'd never experienced. Even if Damon was a self-described workaholic, Liv never felt ignored; he involved her in creative decisions in a way that most men's egos didn't allow.

One night, with only a few weeks left of construction, Damon brought Liv to the club to see the progress. Since it was the first time they'd gone out in Los Angeles since March, Liv suggested they make it into a date night. Damon donned a black suit, and Liv a sexy black dress under a long, summer-thin emerald coat.

They arrived at the club after the workers had left. Liv carried a picnic basket with charcuterie, fromage, French bread, and champagne. Damon showed her in through the back door and turned on only a few lights to set the mood, but Liv was already entranced by the transformation before her. The dance floor was gone, replaced by more sleek leather booths set well apart from each other. A look at the roof revealed giant art deco windowpanes.

"Wow," Liv said as she looked up. "Can I see it open?"

"Of course. Be right back."

Damon kissed her, then hurried up the stairs to the office. Liv pulled a tablecloth from the basket and spread the food and wine atop a table.

She heard motors softy whir and looked up as the skylight slid aside, allowing moonlight to fill the room.

Liv's mouth gaped with awe as Damon returned. "Damon, it's beautiful. You've turned a nightclub into the most romantic restaurant in Los Angeles."

"I'm so glad you see it. Here…"

Damon helped Liv remove her coat, then stepped back to admire her. "*You're beautiful.*"

Liv did a turn. "Recognize it?"

"Of course. You wore that the night we met."

Liv smiled. "You know, this is the first time we've been to a restaurant together."

Damon got it. "It's our first date!"

She laughed and glanced around. "I wish I could be here when it opens."

"*We* won't be here," Damon corrected.

"That's sweet, Damon. But you have to be here for at least the opening!"

"Nope. Once this place has been inspected and approved, I'm washing my hands of it. Might even try to sell the place."

"For me?"

"Partly. But in truth, I'm tired of nightlife. I'd rather do more real estate and be home like a good husband."

Liv gave him a look.

"Don't worry. Just a figure of speech."

"Better be."

Damon laughed as Liv slid into the booth, then settled in beside her.

"I can't say I'm disappointed that you won't be coming here," Liv admitted.

"Oh?"

"I'd probably kill myself with jealousy if I weren't here with you."

"Oh. Duh," Damon said. "But are you actually worried if I went back to work like it used to be, I might have a hard time being faithful to you?"

"You did say that you had doubts about monogamy."

"That was months ago! Since you've come into my life, I can't imagine *ever* being with another woman."

"Are you sure? We've talked about a lot of things, but we haven't really ever had to talk about exclusivity."

"I didn't think it needed saying. Liv, I understand why you might want to talk about it, but my God, I was trying to talk you into marrying me a few weeks ago. And the only reason I haven't done so again is because I know you don't respond well to pressure."

"Ha, that's true."

Damon felt insecure now too. "Liv, tell me this isn't your way of saying that you're interested in having an open relationship?"

"No! God no! Damon, I get sick to my stomach at the mere thought of being with someone else."

"Phew," Damon said, visibly relaxed. "Honey, I assure you, the only reason I was a playboy for years was because I was searching under every rock for *you*."

Liv smiled. "That is so corny, but I love it."

"Seriously," Damon said. "You've shown me the power of being intimate and vulnerable. I'm so changed that if for some horrible reason, you broke up with me, I'd probably be celibate for the rest of my life."

"Oh, come on."

Damon smiled. "Slide over here…"

Liv shifted so she was right next to him. "Thank you for letting me vent my fears. I've never known a man who listens like you."

"Another thing I wasn't so good at before you."

"We bring out the best in each other, don't we?" Liv asked.

Damon smiled, then pulled her into a kiss. He reached into the picnic basket to retrieve the bottle of champagne and popped it deftly.

A flash of trepidation passed over Liv, and she asked, "Is it okay for you to drink while you stay sober from…you know, everything else?"

Damon laughed. "I understand why you would ask, but trust me, alcohol has never been my vice."

Liv was satisfied with that, particularly because she had never observed Damon *drunk* after spending every day with him for months.

"Okay," she said. "And no more skeletons hiding in the closet?"

"Not even a single femur," he said as he poured two glasses for them. "What about you?"

"Not a one."

They clinked their glasses together and shared another kiss. Liv savored it, then whispered to him, "Best first date ever."

24.

"GLOBAL WARMING IS REAL," moaned Liv, floating nude on a floatie in the pool.

"I read that it reached 121 degrees in the valley yesterday," Damon said as he glided up to her. "It's Africa hot."

Liv put her arms around his neck and let him float her around the shallow end. "Let's go there when the pandemic ends. I've never really traveled."

"We'll start in Europe," Damon said. "Eat croissants on the Champs Élysées, pasta in Venice, picnic at the Colosseum in Roma, then head south, stopping for spiced coffee in Morocco. We'll safari deep in the Serengeti, then keep going east; sushi in Tokyo…"

"Can we make our last stop Tahiti? I've seen pictures, and the water looks so blue."

"Maybe we won't come home? Buy a house over the lagoon in Bora Bora."

Liv let out a blissful sigh. She let her head fall back so her hair spread out to the sides just below the surface.

"Your hair is really blonde now," Damon said with a smile so Liv would know he meant it as a compliment.

"And long," she answered. "I haven't had it cut or colored since March."

"Me neither."

Liv laughed, but Damon had indeed been wearing his black hair in a ponytail more often these days.

She heard her phone ring with a short alert. "I'll be right back," she said, pulling away from him.

"You're *leaving* me?" he whined playfully.

Liv kissed him, then climbed out and gathered a towel.

"It's probably my medical app with my test results, I just want to check," she said as she picked her phone up from the chaise.

It was remarkable to Liv how little anxiety her last cancer screening had caused her. Of course, she was sure she could attribute some of that to the healing balm of time and distance from her battle, but she knew much of it was due to her newfound ability to discuss her fears openly with Damon. She had barely flinched when the needle went in and slept soundly in the few nights since her last appointment.

But there was no notification from her doctor's app. Instead, she saw she had a voicemail. She sat and listened to the message while Damon swam under the shimmering water.

Liv blinked, faintly worried, as she put the phone down, and wrapped the towel around herself, protectively tight.

Damon came up to the surface to see Liv's face. "Honey? What's going on?" he called out.

Liv felt her heart beating faster and tried to calm it with slow breaths.

"Liv?"

She couldn't look at Damon as he climbed out, wrapped a towel around himself and sat beside her.

"The doctor left a voice message."

"Baby, what did they say?"

"It's not what they said, it's what they didn't."

"What do you mean?"

"Well, usually, if I miss the call, the nurse will just leave a message that everything looks good. But this time it was the doctor. She said to call her."

"That doesn't mean she has bad news."

"I could hear it in her tone."

"Let's not read too far into it until you talk to her..."

"I'm sick again, Damon."

"Honey, you don't know that."

"You don't get it. This is how it fucking happens."

Damon put a hand on her knee. "I understand why you're scared. Let's just call her back."

Liv stood and paced the length of the pool, wringing her hands.

"Baby," Damon called out. "Please, sit. I'm right here. Let's not cause ourselves extra panic.

Liv nodded and returned to the chaise. She shakily picked up her phone and dialed from the message.

Damon rubbed her back tenderly as she spoke.

"Hi, Liv Mathers for Dr. Kehr," she said into the phone. "Yeah, I'll hold."

Damon whispered, "Is that her name, Dr. Care?"

"K-e-h-r."

"Still. Good name for a doctor."

Liv forced a smile, appreciating Damon's attempt to remain optimistic. "She's been my oncologist since day one."

A woman's voice came from the speaker in an even tone, "How are you feeling, Liv?"

"Is it bad news?"

The doctor paused only a moment. "Your white blood cell count is lower than we'd like, and we detected some abnormal cells."

"By abnormal you mean cancerous?"

"Yes."

Liv whipped her face toward Damon's. He looked calm, which calmed her not the least.

"But this could be something minor," Dr. Kehr's voice went on. "We might have caught it early and can just adjust your therapies. We should schedule a scan of your chest and lymph nodes."

"Do you think it's metastatic?"

"Not necessarily. We always check the lymph nodes first because *if* the cancer has spread, that's the first place it would go. Listen, I know this is scary, but let's get you in for the CT and a few more tests before we discuss treatment."

"Okay," Liv answered meekly.

"I'll have the scheduling nurse call you right away. Be strong, Liv."

"I'll try. Thank you."

Liv put the phone down, lifted the edge of a towel to wipe her face. "Three years. Three fucking years without cancer. God, I can't go through surgery and chemo again."

"Let's not get ahead of ourselves," Damon cautioned.

"Damon, I love you. But you have no idea what is about to happen. I do. And it's worse than anything you can imagine."

"Maybe. But whatever happens, I'll be here for you."

"Will you really?"

Damon sensed misdirected anger in her. "Honey, I'm not like the asshole."

"How do you know? You might feel differently after spending weeks watching me puke my guts out. Or when I lose my hair. And if the cancer has spread, who knows what they'll cut out of me. I could lose the tits you love so much. It could have spread to my brain. Wouldn't *that be fun?*"

"Baby, let's wait till we speak to the doctor..."

Liv stood from the chaise, threw her head back to the sky, and let out a deep, guttural *yell* to the heavens.

It echoed through the canyon.

Damon watched, only a little frightened.

Then Liv looked at him and actually *laughed.* "Okay. Enough fucking crying. This time I'm not going to let this take me down rabbit holes. I'm going to be a strong ass bitch."

Damon smiled and stood with her. "That's my girl."

But her resolve dissolved as quickly as it came as another thought occurred to her and she began to cry.

"All I want to do is call my mom. But I also *don't* want to call her," she said through sobs.

"I understand, sweetheart. I'm so sorry. You don't have to make that decision right this second. We don't have to do *anything* right this second. We can watch a movie, go for a walk..."

"No."

"Okay. Is there anything I can do?"

"No, not yet."

"Liv, I love you."

"I love you too."

She kissed him very briefly, then went inside with her phone.

Damon sat again and looked up at his house. In this moment, feeling helplessly worried, the home looked very small to him.

DAMON TRIED NOT TO SQUIRM as he sat beside Liv in a leather chair in the office, waiting for the doctor. His hand was interlaced with Liv's fingers, and he could feel her alternatively squeeze him, then let him go to wipe the sweat from her palm.

"Hello, Liv," Dr. Kehr said as she entered her office. Her short brown bob bounced around her face as she took a seat behind her desk. Behind her surgical mask, Damon could just make out the etches of crow's feet of a woman in her fifties.

"Hi. This is my boyfriend, Damon," Liv said, her own N95 covered with a pink bandana.

The doctor didn't offer a hand—nobody shook hands anymore. "Nice to meet you, Damon."

"Thank you," he said. "Liv said you saved her life a few years ago, so I'm already a fan."

"Liv saved her own life," the doctor answered. "She's quite a force."

Liv strained to smile, in no mood for pleasantries.

"My office arranged for you to be tested for Covid, right?" the doctor asked.

"Both of us," Liv answered. "And we've haven't left the house or seen anybody in weeks."

"Good. And I'm tested daily, so I think we can dispense with these..." the doctor said, removing her mask.

"Thank, God," Liv sighed as she and Damon removed their own and laid them in their laps.

"These new rapid tests are making a huge difference," the doctor said. "I'll see if I can sneak you some."

"Thank you," Damon answered.

"First off, how are you feeling?" the doctor asked Liv.

"Scared."

"That's natural," answered the doctor as she turned to her computer. "So. Your cancer has returned, but it's only in two lymph nodes on your left side."

Liv seemed surprised. "It's not in my breasts?"

"No, but as you know, since it started in your breast and spread, we still call it breast cancer."

Liv nodded. "This means I'm stage four now, right?"

"Technically, yes, because the cancer has metastasized. But the good news is that we found so little of it that you won't need any surgeries."

"That's a relief," Liv sighed for only a beat. "So, chemo and radiation?"

"We'll decide about radiation after the chemo. And since it's just in two nodes, we think we can attack it with a very short but strong dose of chemo. Three months, instead of the usual five."

"Red Devil?" Liv asked.

"Still the best we have."

Liv turned to Damon, who'd been listening intently. "You know what that is?" she asked.

"Yeah, a chemical called AL, which makes you pee red."

"Did his research," the doctor said. "I'm impressed."

"It's the nastiest shit," Liv said to Damon. "I'll be losing my hair quickly."

Damon smiled. "I have thing for bald women."

"Liar," Liv teased.

"Seriously, I can't wait to see you without hair. I might never let you grow it back."

"See why I love him?" Liv said to the doctor.

Dr. Kehr smiled. "Damon, do you have any experience with cancer?"

"A little. But I was pretty young, so I wasn't really a support system."

"Okay, well, I want you to know that I'm here if you have any questions. Here's my cell."

The doctor picked up a card from her desk holder and scribbled her number on the back.

"I appreciate that," Damon said as he took it.

"Told you she was the best," said Liv. "So when can I start?" she asked, turning back to the doctor.

"They'll call you. I'd like to get you in as soon as next week."

"And do I continue the hormone therapy?"

"Yes, but we'll adjust the dosage down, since we'll also be adding steroids and a few other meds."

"Ugh, the steroids…It's all coming back to me. Please tell me I don't have to get a port this time?"

Damon knew she was referring to a chemical port that was surgically attached to a chemo patient's chest so the infusions would go directly to the crucial arteries near the heart.

"That's up to you. Makes it easier for the nurses. But I think since it's a shortened course, you'll be okay without it."

"No port, please!" said Liv. "God, last time it made me feel like I had a gas cap in my chest. And you said three months this time?"

"Right, three weeks apart. So you'll have two weeks in between to get your strength back."

"Eh, this course is for amateurs."

Damon leaned forward in his seat. "Can I ask an administrative question?"

"Certainly."

"Does her insurance cover this? Because if there's any gaps, I'll take care of it."

"That's thoughtful, Damon," Liv answered. "But I'm sure Blue Shield will cover it like last time."

"Okay, but you'll let me know if there are any out-of-pocket costs?"

"Is he the best or what?" Liv cooed.

The doctor smiled, then turned more serious. "Liv, I know you've been through this before, but I want you to understand, chemo is different each time you take it. It could go smoothly, or you could have side effects that you didn't last time. And of course, this time we have to be super careful. As you know, chemo kills your immune system, so you do not want to get Covid during treatment."

"We're already hermits. Don't worry."

"Good. Then unless you have any more questions, we'll get started."

The doctor and Damon stood, but Liv took a beat to gather her purse. "I do have one more thing…"

"What's that?"

Liv glanced at Damon nervously, as if she wished he wasn't in the room to hear the answer but asked anyway.

"Well, now that I'm stage four, what does that do to my life expectancy?"

The doctor took a beat. "Assuming the treatment works, about thirty percent of patients with stage four metastatic breast cancer survive between five and ten years. But that could change, they're constantly working on new treatments."

Liv glanced toward Damon. Neither believed the doctor's qualifier. *Five to ten years* resounded through their heads as if they were connected by wires.

THE SILENCE IN THE CAR was like none that Damon had ever endured. He stole occasional looks at Liv, but she stared straight ahead through the windshield, at nothing really.

"Is there anything you want to talk about?" Damon finally asked.

"Nope."

Damon nodded and gripped the steering wheel.

After several minutes of silence, he inhaled sharply but bit his tongue.

Liv took notice.

"What?" she asked.

He knew he had to be extremely measured with any commentary.

"I was just wondering if you've decided to tell your mom or not."

"I'm not going to tell anybody. It's a short course, and I don't think her presence would be helpful to me after everything that was said between us."

Damon spoke with consideration. "I don't want to speak out of turn..." he started.

"But what?"

"But Marie and Yasmina were a huge part of your support system the first time around. And, to hear you tell it, your mom and the two of them were the *only* people you let in during that time. I just think...if you're not ready to receive support from your mom, why not let the other people who love you help you? Emotionally, at least."

"What would be the point?" Liv asked, her voice rising. "Marie has enough on her plate. She's literally an ER nurse. She doesn't need another sick patient. And what is Yasmina going to do? She's, what, five thousand miles away?"

"I understand they might not be able to physically hold your hand...but they could support you emotionally."

"I'll think about it," Liv said curtly.

"But it's your decision entirely. Obviously. I'm here to support you, no matter what. I want what you want."

"I *want* to be healthy and live to ninety-five."

She laughed with cynicism, then returned to her thousand-yard stare.

25.

L I V   W O R K E D   T O   D I S G U I S E   her despondency for the first forty-eight hours following the appointment with Dr. Kehr. The last thing she wanted to appear to Damon was *infirm*. She rose before him. She made breakfast, lunch, and dinner. She fulfilled her brand obligations with fervor, telling herself it would only be a matter of time before her skin took on a sickly pallor and her hair began to fall in chunks.

Liv was self-aware enough to know that with each picture she snapped, each meal she seasoned, and each forced smile she shot to Damon, her true aim was to give cover to her own frailty.

To stave off the fear that like Christopher, Damon would soon be gone.

She knew she had received every evidence to the contrary, but still alarm bells rang in her memory, and she felt yanked backwards in time.

On the third day since the appointment, Liv dutifully made breakfast, then announced she was going out to sit on the chaise and read a while.

She closed her eyes and slept. Her phone rang a few times, but the weight of her spirit made her arm so heavy that to lift the screen to her face seemed like an insurmountable task.

At dusk, she felt Damon peel a strand of her hair back from her face, plastered to her cheek with sweat and the spittle of sleep.

"Sweetheart," he said. "What are you hungry for?"

"I'll get it. I don't know. I'll get up."

"Okay," he said. "Have you thought at all about telling your friends what's up?"

"I've been too busy," she said groggily, and swung her legs off the chaise.

"Okay," Damon said tightly, and turned to leave.

But Liv noticed his tone.

"Wait," she called out, eager to please.

"Here, I'll Facetime Marie and Yasmina while you make dinner. Deal?"

Damon grinned with relief. "Deal."

Liv padded into the house after him and plopped on the living room couch while Damon began to pull out pots and pans. She sent a quick group text to see if her friends were available, and on their enthusiastic agreements, she started the calls.

"Hiii," Yasmina answered, a beach with balmy waves behind her in the background.

"Geez, where are *you*?" Liv asked as Marie joined the Facetime.

"I'm in beautiful Tulum!" she said gleefully, panning the camera around to show off the rest of the beach, a few vendors and two stray dogs sniffing at the bowl of fruit beside her.

Marie groaned in disapproval.

"It's not like that," Yasmina insisted. "I know you told on me to Liv."

"Yaz, I love you. It's just that you know I can't help but say something. I'm on the frontlines and you're traveling the world and going to raves."

"Okay, ladies…" Liv tried to mitigate, but Yasmina interrupted her.

"I understand why you'd think I'm just out here living it up and swapping germs with strangers, but that's not what's going on. I only went to that one rave in Paris, and yeah, that was a shitty thing for me to do. But I'm out here learning more about ayahuasca."

"Oh?" Liv raised an eyebrow. "You mentioned something about that before."

"Yeah. So like, I've done it a couple times now in Paris, but it's obviously harder to get. And I don't want to sound like one of *those* people—you know, like men who do mushrooms once and then experience the same amount of empathy that little girls have a for a crushed snail on the ground when they're like, four years old, but it really is life changing. It's made me realize I don't want to model or like, party in a shallow way anymore. I want to help people and learn more about this. And that's what I'm doing here. We meet in really small groups, it's all outside. I'm not like, partying."

"Okayyyy," Marie said. "I'll reserve judgment for now if it means you'll stop doing sketchy blow off of club tables."

"Ouch! But, heard. And thank you."

"And what's the update on you, Marie?" Liv asked.

Damon perked up his ears as he stirred a pinch of salt into boiling water. *She's stalling.*

"Honestly, it's been never-ending," sighed Marie. "We're all puckering our buttholes thinking that everything's going to go FUBAR again after the holidays. And we're still really short-staffed. People are dropping like flies. Just burned out."

"You need to get laid," Yasmina offered.

"I think I need a spa day more than a hook-up."

"Oooh, let me make you up a little spa care package and send it!" Liv said.

"I mean, that would be very cute, but you definitely don't have to. Then again, you *do* live in a mansion rent-free now, so I'd allow it," Marie said with a sly grin. "It's a done deal."

"Speaking of," Yasmina interjected. "How's life in *la chateau de Damon*?"

"Yes, spill all the tea," Marie agreed. "You've been so tight-lipped."

"Everything has been amazing. Damon pulled through that little hiccup really well, and it's just been day after day in paradise. I'm sure you guys have noticed I've been working again, and Damon's in the process of renovating High to be open-air. It should be open really soon! I thought I'd miss having him around, and you know, I *do*, but he's managed the work-life balance really well."

"Ahhh, that's so good to hear," Yasmina said. "So like, what else is going on with everyone?"

Damon stopped rolling meatballs to concentrate and listen.

Marie shrugged. "I dunno. Ordering more furniture when I can to fill out the guest house now that Liv is gone. I think I'm just going to leave it empty for a while. Hard to imagine finding a roommate as good as Liv. We're all like, probably too old to hop on Craigslist or something looking for a roommate."

"Psh. Speak for yourself. I have no idea what my living situation is going to be when I get back home. And everything is so cheap in Mexico, it stresses me out to think about paying two grand a month to live in LA again," Yasmina said. "And you, Liv?"

Liv glanced at Damon in the kitchen, now doing his best to look occupied as he slid the meatballs into an air fryer.

"Nothing much," she said casually. "My mom and I still haven't talked, which kind of sucks. Other than that, everything is okay!"

She saw Damon's shoulders raise and tighten in his white shirt.

"Oh yeah. That does really suck she decided to turn into a bitch right when she finally got to meet Damon. Especially cause she's always so great."

"Speaking *of*," Yasmina said mischievously. "Are you sure you didn't chain him up in a basement and steal his house? We still haven't met him!"

"And you never post him," Marie pointed out.

"Ugh, I know. I don't like that either. But you know, my brand and stuff. You know that seventy percent of my followers are thirsty old men who can't have their fantasy of me being single shattered. I will soon, though. Once I can establish some more wholesome brand deals."

"I get it," Yasmina said. "But is he like, around? We want to meet him!"

"Yeah! He's just making dinner. Babe, are you at a good stopping point?" she called out to Damon.

"Sure," Damon said shortly. He rinsed his hands and crossed into the living room.

"Hey, girls," he said with a weak smile as he pressed his face close to Liv's to appear in the frame.

"Oooh, you're just as handsome as Liv gushes," Marie teased.

"Do you remember us?" Yasmina asked. "I'm kind of hoping you were just so fixated on Liv that you don't…"

Damon allowed himself a small laugh. "Oh, I remember. But don't worry. You're not blacklisted at High or anything."

"That's a relief. Definitely woke up with a lot of hangxiety that next morning," Yasmina said.

"Hangxiety?"

"Hangover plus anxiety."

"I like how you make up words," Damon complimented.

Liv took pleasure seeing her lover and loved ones getting along.

"So tell us, what's up with you? And the High renovations?" Marie asked.

"It's not really a good time for me to chat," Damon sulked, then looked at Liv. "Meatballs are done in the fryer in a minute. Pasta and sauce are ready. Have at it. I've got some work to do."

Then, without offering a goodbye, he got up from the couch, walked to his library, and closed the door.

Liv followed him with her eyes.

"Goddamn," Yasmina said with a grimace. "What's up with him?"

"Yeah, Liv, he was kind of…"

"A dick," Yasmina finished for Marie.

Liv sighed and rubbed her eyes with her free hand. "He's really not, I swear."

"Are you sure? Are you like, *okay* over there?" Yasmina asked.

"Yes, I'm fine…he's just really stressed out with the renovations and things…" Liv began to lie, and then her voice trailed off.

The three were silent for a moment.

"Okay!" Liv suddenly cried as if throwing her hands up to the universe. "Okay."

"Okay *what*? What's going on?"

"Okay, the reason Damon is being a dick is because I specifically told him I was calling you guys to tell you something, and it was obvious that I wasn't going to. And he's annoyed with me."

"Oh my God, Liv, are you pregnant?" Marie gasped.

"No! Jesus, no. I wanted to keep this to myself, but I think Damon's being cold because I need a bigger support system. I mean it isn't fair for me to put this all on him…"

"Are you going to actually say what's going on?" Yasmina prodded, even as her heart sank.

"Yeah. I'm sorry. I'm sure you guessed. The Big C is back."

"Oh God, honey. No," Marie said, eyes brimming with sympathy.

"Yeah…"

"Why didn't you tell us?" Yasmina demanded.

Now Liv's voice began to crack, and she had to put her phone down for a moment. When she picked it back up, she whimpered, "I just don't want to be a burden to anyone. Especially not Damon, but obviously I had to tell him. And what is anyone even going to do? You're in Tulum, and you're in the ER in the middle of a pandemic."

"That doesn't matter!" Yasmina insisted. "How fucking pissed off would we be if we just randomly heard that you wound up dead?"

"Yaz!" Marie warned.

"Okay, I know, I don't want to scare you. You're obviously not going to die. But we can still support you emotionally. You have to let us in."

"Right," Marie nodded in agreement.

"Okay. I'm sorry. It's just a few rounds of chemo. No radiation at this point. I start in a week and a half. Should be a breeze," Liv said as her voice cracked again.

"It's going to be okay, baby," Marie soothed. "I know you're scared, even if you won't admit it."

"And we're here for you. In whatever way we can be," Yasmina said.

Liv sniffled. "Thank you, girls."

"You're welcome. And don't you forget it. Now, go fucking apologize to your boyfriend."

Liv's laughter pierced through your tears. "Okay, okay. I'm goin.'"

A WEEK LATER, Liv heard the sound of Damon's Tesla opening the garage door and furrowed her brow, puzzled. He'd only left for work an hour before, and she didn't expect him until the late afternoon.

She swung open the side door to greet him, but a familiar heel stepped out from the passenger door, its ankle clad in a permanent golden ankle bracelet.

"Oh my *God*," Liv squealed as she buried her face in Yasmina's bouncing kinks. "What are you doing here?"

"It's an ambush!" Yasmina cried.

"No, seriously, what are you doing here?" Liv asked breathlessly as Damon hauled her suitcase out of the trunk.

"I arranged the whole thing. Put my classes on hold, called Damon, came out the day after we talked. I've been quarantining in the Beverly Hills Hotel."

"Not a bad place to quarantine. But *you've* been keeping secrets!" Liv pointed at Damon in mock accusation.

"Yup!" Damon agreed proudly.

"Wait, how did you two even get in touch? Damon's not even on Instagram."

"I've been to this house, remember?" Yasmina said as Liv ushered them inside. "I got in touch with the dude that brought me, did a little flirting, then asked if he had Damon's number."

"Devious. But really, Yaz, I'm so touched. How long are you staying?"

"Long as you need me. This place looks *vaguely* familiar in the light of day and sobriety," Yasmina noted as she followed Liv.

Liv laughed. "I had almost forgotten that you've been here before. Come, I'll show you to your suite."

"My *suite*?"

"Yes! We'll put you in the one I stayed in for the first month or so."

"My suite," Yasmina echoed in a fake snob accent.

Damon chortled as he approached them.

"I'm going to show her the rest of the house first actually, okay?" Liv said to Damon. "I've got a feeling she doesn't remember much."

"Of course," Damon said as he began to lug the case up the stairs.

Liv slid her arm through her friend's and whispered, "Again, Yaz. It means so much you're helping me through this."

"What else would I do?" Yasmina said as she looked around the house. "Especially now that I see it's going to be a vacation."

"Some vacation. You know what the next week is going to be like."

"Yup. I get to have a slightly better seat for the action than I did last time, though. Does Damon know what he's in for?"

"I think so. And you can't believe what he's doing. He's been reading every book about cancer known to man. I mean, we've had a few conversations with my doctor this week, and he asks more questions than me!"

"Marry the man."

"Definitely the first time you've ever said something like *that* to me."

They walked past the kitchen and into the living room.

"Obviously the place has always been like *wow*, but something tells me you've been playing Suzy Homemaker in here," Yasmina commented.

Liv smiled—indeed, over months, Liv had added so much to the house—all of the culinary trappings they'd acquired in her first few weeks, but also flower-filled vases from the garden, coasters, even some art they'd bought together.

"I think I've turned it from a bachelor mansion into a home," she said, and pointed to the vase filled with shells from their Florida vacation. "From the Florida villa. Damon promised we'd go back for a month after my chemo is over. You're invited, of course."

"Invitation accepted!"

Liv let go of her arm as they walked outside. "How do you like the view? Does it hold up without the drugs?"

Yasmina looked out over the California vista. "Oh yeah. It's even better. I'll remember it this time."

"That's Catalina," Liv said, pointing out an island in the distance. "It used to be you never saw it, but with nobody driving, there's no smog anymore."

"Stunning. It's been *wild* being back in an empty LA. They say Covid's helping the environment better than any treaty could."

"All set up there," Damon said as he approached them. "Can we get you anything to drink, Yasmina?"

"No, thank you. Not gonna lie, I've been helping myself to the minibar at the Beverly Hills Hotel almost every night. Old habits die hard. Hope you don't mind?"

"That's why it's there."

Yasmina smiled her thanks, then turned her attention back to Liv. "So the first treatment is tomorrow?"

"Eight a.m.," Liv answered.

"And no visitors still, I assume?"

"The rules are worse now. Because of Covid you guys aren't even allowed in the building. No waiting room even."

"She can FaceTime!" Damon chimed in. "And we got her an iPad, loaded with movies and Netflix."

"Gonna be so fun!" Liv said with sarcasm. "Come on, I'll show you the suite." Liv grabbed her friend's hand again and led her inside.

Damon stayed back to let Liv and Yasmina catch up privately.

He took a seat on a chaise and leaned back, closing his eyes as the sun warmed his face. He was about to take out his phone, then changed his mind and left it in his pocket. He knew there would be a dozen messages waiting for him, especially since yesterday he had told his contractors that he'd be unreachable for the next week and hired Jay to keep an eye on things. They'd been curious to why, but Liv had asked Damon to keep her illness between them, Yasmina, and Marie for now.

Damon still wrestled with the feeling that Liv should share the bad news with her mother despite the distance between them, but then again, Liv wasn't sharing much with *him*. If Damon so much as asked her how she was feeling, she'd change the subject, and if he pressed or wanted to talk about his fears, Liv would shut down completely.

Damon had tried to be understanding—after all, it wasn't his place to tell Liv how to manage her emotions, and to her credit, the fury with which she had put up the façade of "everything is fine!" those first few days after the appointment had eased, but he still felt she was in denial. It impacted their conversations—they were suddenly having meals in silence, like some couple who had been married for fifty years and run out of subjects.

And though under the circumstances Damon would never complain, their lovemaking had come to a halt. He had tried to fill the emotional space between them by sleeping closer to Liv, but even then, he would wake in the middle of the night to find that she'd moved to the living room couch—something she'd never done before. For the first time since Liv had come to stay, Damon was feeling lonely. He was pretty sure he had prepared himself for the chemo treatment, but this worried him; if she shut down *before* she got sick, how would she treat him and their relationship during or after?

Damon loved Liv, and knew that she loved him, but he hoped that her hesitance to open up to him about her feelings was temporary.

26.

LIV WINCED AS THE IV needle was pressed into the vein of forearm.

"You okay?" the nurse asked.

"After all the needles this arm has seen, you'd think it wouldn't scare the crap out of me."

"It's a primal thing."

Liv tried to get a good look at the nurse, but she was in full hazmat gear, face shield, and like herself, double masked.

"I'm Judy. If there's anything you need, any discomfort, just press the button."

"Thank you, Judy," Liv said, peering with hate at the equipment she was attached to: the blood pressure and heart monitors, the slightly red fluid in the bag hanging above her. "What button?" she asked.

"This button," the nurse said with a grin. "Hey, Judy!" she called out.

Liv chuckled. She appreciated the nurse, as she had every nurse who had administered her chemo three years ago. They were a different breed, used to helping people fight death.

"I see you're all loaded up with entertainment," Judy said, glancing at the day bag which she, Damon, and Yasmina had prepared; inside was the iPad, brand new Beats headphones, and a few books.

Liv smiled and turned off her phone. She'd warned Damon and Yaz that she was going to leave her phone off as much as possible but would FaceTime if she changed her mind. Managing her anxiety during treatment was enough of a feat without jumping out of her skin each time her phone pinged. Liv understood that her behavior over the last week seemed cold to Damon, but she had to take care of herself in the only way she knew. Being strong and stoic had gotten her through a mastectomy and chemo three years ago. It was the only way she knew, and she wasn't going to change it this time around, even if it upset Damon or her close friends.

"Did you eat this morning?" asked the nurse.

"No, I fasted. I remember eating brought on the nausea last time."

"Oh, not your first rodeo?"

"Are you kidding? I'm a damn cowgirl. Last time I had removal, reconstruction, chemo, *and* radiation."

"So this should be a snap. I hope I'm here when you ring the bell."

Liv smiled, recalling how every patient rang a pink bell in the hallways to celebrate their final infusion. "See you in four hours," Liv said, reaching for her headphones.

The nurse switched on the IV; Liv felt the infusion warm her arteries, and her mouth drying with that metallic taste. She closed her eyes and squeezed anxiety from her chest.

Fuck you, cancer, Liv said to herself. *I beat you once; I'll beat you again.*

DAMON SAT IN HIS TESLA, watching the doors of the Cedars Sinai Cancer Center. It had been five hours since he'd walked Liv to those doors, and they'd been the longest five hours of his life. He had *planned* on going home and having lunch with Yasmina but had decided he didn't want to leave Liv there alone, even if he couldn't be inside with her.

His phone pinged in his lap. Damon quickly read the text: Done. Be right out.

Damon exhaled with relief, put the car in gear, and drove closer to the hospital doors. Just as he climbed from the car, Liv was wheeled out in a wheelchair by a hazmat-clad orderly, a bandage wrapped around her arm where the IV had gone.

"Are you okay?" he asked.

"Yeah. Ignore the wheelchair. It's hospital policy that they wheel me out."

"Oh, okay."

Damon helped her transfer from the wheelchair into the passenger seat.

"Thank you!" Liv called out to the orderly as Damon rounded the car and climbed in.

"Are *you* okay, is the question?" Liv asked Damon, pulling off her mask.

He pulled down his. "Other than being a nervous wreck…"

Liv laughed and gave him a quick kiss, then a hug. Damon held it for a good minute.

"How was it?" he asked quietly.

Liv leaned out of the embrace. "Can I tell you later? The nausea is never *supposed* to start until a few days later, but I think I psych myself out about it, and I'd like to get home as quickly as possible. For your car's sake."

Damon laughed and put the car in gear but noticed Liv's hands were curled up in a tight ball. He put his right hand over her left and headed home.

DAMON PARKED IN THE GARAGE, where Yasmina stood at the side door, waiting anxiously. Liv waited for him to run around and open her door, then suddenly felt intense pain in her stomach—she threw open her door, leaned out, and vomited a stream of Gatorade-orange liquid onto the ground.

"Get a towel!" Damon yelled to Yasmina, then pulled Liv's hair from her face.

Pained, face ashen, Liv managed a whisper. "I'm sorry."

"Don't apologize. I got you."

Liv heaved again—this time less came out, but the pain and nausea was so severe, she started to cry.

"I'm here," Damon assured her.

Liv looked up at him through wet eyes. "I love you so much."

"I love you…"

Damon started to cry too.

And just like that, Liv's stoicism disappeared. In that instant, she needed him more than she'd expected, and those walls she'd been putting up toppled.

"Here," Yasmina said, returning with a towel and a small trash can.

Damon took hold of the towel, kneeled, and wiped Liv's crying face.

"I don't remember it hurting like this," Liv moaned as she grabbed the trash can. She heaved into it in convulsions, but nothing but bile dripped out.

Damon glanced at Yasmina, who had her face cupped in her hands, unable to hide her own tears and sharing in their collective helplessness.

LIV SHIVERRED ATOP DAMON'S BED, trembling under a heap of blankets, the trash can on the ground a few feet from her closed eyes. Damon sat on the bed beside her, lovingly caressing her head until she finally closed her eyes.

Damon saw her breath and the shivering even out. He tucked her in, then stood and quietly trod to the door. It was open, and in the hallway he could see Yasmina sitting with her head against the wall, anguished.

"I think she's out," Damon whispered, "but I'm just going stay here and watch over her."

"I'll take over whenever you need."

Damon nodded. "I wish it was me, not her."

"Get in line."

"Should I call a doctor?"

"No. This is just the way it is."

Damon nodded, worry chiseled into his face.

IT WAS LIKE THIS for four days, with Liv rising only when she could handle cold soup or Pedialyte to hydrate her. Just the sight or smell of real food made her ill, and if she couldn't vomit, she'd dry heave, begging for relief.

Dr. Kehr checked in often, which Damon appreciated, but that was all the help she could provide. She'd prescribed an anti-nausea medication, but Liv couldn't keep it down long enough for it to help.

Damon gave Liv towel baths, then she graduated to actual ones. The chemo made Liv's throat unusually dry, so even a whisper hurt. Damon once tried to give her a massage, but the slightest touch pained her. And of course, she couldn't and didn't want to eat, and Damon was sure that Liv had lost ten pounds in just that week.

Liv was too uncomfortable to share the bed, so Damon slept on the couch in their room, waking up at the slightest groan or cough from her. The doctor had told him the worst thing that could happen on chemo was that Liv get a cold or flu, because it could easily turn into pneumonia, and she'd have to be hospitalized. Even talking, more like a harsh croak, was painful for her.

Thankfully, on the fifth day, while Damon was up early making coffee, he heard Liv's normal voice, soft and low.

"Can I have some of that?"

He looked up to find her walking down the stairs, in clean sweats, one hand holding the railing.

"She's back!" Damon called out. "How you feel?"

"Almost human. Just have chemo brain. It's like looking at life through a foggy lens. It'll pass."

"Anything I can do?"

"Just keep being an angel," Liv said. Then she ran her hand through her hair. "Look!"

Damon saw nothing in her hand. "Is it starting to fall out?"

"No! I'm just happy about that. But it will come eventually—I can already feel my scalp tingle."

Liv walked into Damon's arms. "I swear, I thought because I went through chemo already, I knew what to expect. But this time was harder than anything I remember."

"Yasmina said she didn't remember you being this sick either."

"God, I hope you didn't get on each other's nerves."

"Not at all. We're both playing on Team Liv. And there's enough square footage that we're kind of doing our own thing."

"I'll go let her know I'm among the living soon. But I'm still pretty wiped."

"Go and sit. I'll make some eggs if that sounds good?"

"I think I can hold eggs down."

Liv shuffled to the couch and sat on it gingerly, drawing her knees to her chest.

"The color's come back to your face," Damon pointed out as he opened the fridge and pulled out eggs.

"Don't get used it," Liv said. "In two weeks, we're back at it. And if my hair doesn't fall out by then, for sure it will after the next round."

"Hair's not much to give up to survive."

"Easy for you to say, you're a guy."

"I'll tell you what, when you go bald, I'll shave my head."

"You've been watching too many YouTube videos about how to support a woman through breast cancer."

Damon laughed. "Probably."

"And I like your hair, so what about that?"

"Can I clip it short?"

"Maybe."

"You're the boss."

"Ha, right."

Yasmina's voice came from the top of the stairs. "Welcome back to the land of the living!"

"Hey, Yaz…"

Yasmina reached the middle of the stairs and saw Liv try to stand. "Don't get up, I'm coming down."

Liv shifted back into the pillows. Yasmina came to her, leaned down, and kissed her on the forehead. "You look hot, babes."

"Thank you for helping Damon through this. I know it isn't pretty."

"I didn't do much. I'm feeling pretty useless, actually. The man's a rock, I'll tell you that."

"And I was afraid he'd run when the shit hit the fan."

"Over easy or scrambled?" Damon called out.

"The usual," Liv said.

"Over easy with a dash of salt, coming up. Yaz?"

"I'll make my own. *Je ne fais pas confiance aux Américains avec ma nourriture.*"

Damon laughed. "I understood enough of that to know to say, *putain.*"

Yasmina grinned at Liv. "That's *one* way I've been helping out around here. Fixing your boyfriend's atrocious French."

Liv smiled back and rested her head on her friend's shoulder. "As long as you're not going stir crazy."

"Are you kidding? Not hearing my sisters fight has been like heaven. Besides, if it doesn't work out with Damon, I say you, me, and Marie go in on a house like this and live there till we're ninety, being naughty little old ladies."

"Let's hope I make it to thirty-five."

Yasmina groaned. "I knew you were going to say that."

"Can't help it. I'd say it's gallows humor, but it's, you know, true."

Liv's prediction was spot on, as her hair started falling out within a week of her second treatment.

At first, she'd find a few strands on her pillow or between the sheets when she made the bed. Soon, clumps would fall from her scalp while showering, and she'd scramble to gather them up before they disappeared down the drain.

One evening, Damon came into the shower stall to find Liv naked, weeping as she kneeled to gather fallen blond strands from the tile. He got to his knees and helped her collect them.

"Do you want to make a wig of this?" he asked.

She shook the idea off. "I did that last time and hated it. Even though they mix it with other hair, I felt like I was wearing my cancer."

"You can donate it, too, right?"

She turned to him, crouched like a goblin, eyes puffy and red. "I know you're trying to help. But can you please go?"

"I'm sorry, I just—"

"Go!"

Damon nodded exited the bathroom and walked into his hallway with heavy steps. Yasmina stood at the top of the stairs with a night cap snifter in one hand.

"Uh oh," she remarked on his countenance.

"Yeah," he said weakly.

"Want to talk about it?"

"Maybe. I don't know. She just won't let me in, and she makes it seem like I'm being unhelpful. She won't make eye contact with me. Maybe I *am* being unhelpful."

He began to weep in spite of himself.

"*Fuck*," he growled, angerly wiping away his tears.

"Hey, it's okay. You can cry. I've been seeing lots of grown men cry lately. Sit," she instructed, indicating the top of the stairs.

He complied, and she joined him.

"Do you want me just to listen or do you want some advice?" she prompted.

"Please. The latter. Give me something."

"I know it seems counterintuitive but keep doing what you're doing. I know it hurts to offer help and have it rejected over and over. But Liv's like a rescue dog afraid to take the treat right now. You have to keep offering your hand. Let her reject you a hundred times. On the hundred and first, you'll have some progress."

"You don't think it would be best to just…withdraw? Let her have what she wants? Which is to be totally alone in this thing. I'm sure. This is Christopher baggage, you know."

Damon nodded. "Yeah. I know."

"And can you let me keep playing sage for a minute? Because this is very satisfying to me," Yasmina teased.

He snorted. "Sure. Hit me."

"When Liv went through this the last time, she white-knuckled it and gritted her teeth all the way through the ride, and when it was over, she stepped off the ride and never wanted to talk about it again. I think she's carried it with her all this time. Incorporating a little ceremony might be helpful. Maybe a spiritual thing, like an ayahuasca ceremony or something at the end of the chemo, something to look forward to and heal with, could be nice to bring up. And ceremony all the way through before that too. Some spiritual preparation before each chemo session, celebration after each. Ritual is really important."

"I get where you're coming from, but it sounds pretty woo-woo," Damon gave a half-hearted smile.

Yasmina raised an eyebrow. "I thought you were a Bali boy."

"Yeah, a Bali boy in the sense of taking tourist's money for a good time," Damon snorted again.

"Alright," Yasmina said knowingly. "Fair enough. But give it some thought. There's power in the woo-woo."

"I will. I appreciate your trying to help."

"One more thing. Do you think it would be good if I stayed with Marie for a while? We've been through three sessions so far. I'm starting to feel like an imposition."

"You're not an imposition!" Damon said earnestly. "I'm really glad you came."

"I mean, sure. But it's been a while since you and Liv have had real private time, and I'll be close if she wants me back. She might be more ready to open up to you if it's just the two of you against the world again."

Damon nodded thoughtfully. "Alright. You don't think Liv would be upset?"

"Are you kidding? It's not like she's opening up to me either. And again, I'll be close if you two change your mind. I'll just say I'm getting antsy all cooped up or something. She'll understand."

"Okay, Yasmina. Thank you again," Damon said, and gave her a quick hug.

In these days of quarantines and lockdowns, he thought it felt nice to be building a sense of community again.

THE NEXT TIME Damon caught Liv gathering up her hair was a week later, days after Yasmina's departure.

He had wondered why he'd never noticed the hair when he took out the bathroom trash, but now understood as he watched her stuff it into a plastic grocery bag, tie it tight, and bury it at the bottom of the can.

"Hey," he said from the doorway.

She about jumped out of her skin. "*Jesus.* Can you please stop doing that?"

"I'm not spying on you, Liv. I'm walking into my bathroom to take a leak."

"Okay. I'm sorry," she said as she closed the lid on the can.

Damon sat on the marble floor beside the can. "Can we talk for a minute?"

"Okay..." Liv sighed with trepidation, bracing herself.

She lowered herself from a crouching position down to sit in front of him.

"I know you're tired of suggestions, but can I please make a dumb suggestion? Please?"

"Alright. But just one."

"Okay. What if we wait until the hair is out to the point that you're ready to shave it, but save it all, and burn it, like some Viking funeral pyre."

Liv couldn't help but giggle. "Okay. I wanted to hate whatever you were about to say if it was about the cancer, but I actually love that idea."

"Yeah?" Damon asked excitedly, high-fiving Yasmina with both hands psychically. "What do you like about it?"

Liv shook her head thoughtfully. "I don't know. I like the idea of letting it go forever, instead of trying to wear it like a shitty toupee or donating it and knowing a stranger is wearing a part of my body, or knowing it was rotting in a landfill somewhere. When I was a little girl, my mom used to tell me there was magic in my hair."

Damon smiled. "You've never told me that."

"Yeah," she said sheepishly. "I guess that's why I'm always weird about when it falls out. So, let's do it. Let's be Vikings!"

"Okay," Damon said, affecting a strange brogue. "We the Norsemen of Cancer!"

Liv cracked up; her grief dismissed. She dug back through the trash can and handed the grocery bag to Damon. "Here, put it somewhere I don't see it."

Damon collected the hair from her hands and hid it in an Amazon box in the garage.

That became the ritual: she'd shed, he'd hide the hair.

And when her scalp started showing through the missing locks, they agreed it was time: they gathered in front of the mirror that ran from his sink to hers. She sat in a chair while Damon draped an old-fashioned barber's apron over her. As he clipped Liv's hair short and the pieces fell like leaves to the floor, she'd break into an occasional quick cry, and he'd stop to hold her and reassure her.

"Fuck this, let's go!" Liv would demand after a few sobs, bravely whisking away her tears.

When he was finished, Liv hated the results. Even with it shorn, she had bald spots.

"I swear, you look so beautiful," Damon said with sincerity. "You're an action star."

"Shave it, shave it all," Liv insisted.

Damon, who'd prepared for this moment by ordering a brand-new Wahl electric shaver, ran it over her head until her white scalp shone under the bathroom lights.

"I remember her," Liv sighed with resignation. "And don't tell me I look sexy bald."

"You look so sexy bald."

She glared at him, took the shaver, and ran it over her head, using her fingertips to find the last hairs standing.

"My turn," announced Damon.

"Please no, baby."

"I promise you'll thank me. In Bali, I kept my hair like this all the time. Girls loved it."

That made her laugh. "It's your hair."

Damon set the clipper length, then Liv went to work.

"Should we burn mine too?" Damon asked.

"Yup! So my hair doesn't go to Valhalla alone."

Liv clipped away until Damon looked like a marine recruit. She stepped back and admired him. "Damn, you do look sexy like this."

"Told ya."

She straddled Damon on the chair and kissed him. "Eh, stubble."

Damon helped her off, then looked down at the floor. "It looks like a stable with blond and black hay."

Liv laughed, stripped naked and stepped into the shower. "Coming?" she called out.

Damon pulled the apron off, then his clothes and joined her. And after they'd used their spongers to wipe the stubble from each other, they came together. Damon lifted her off her feet and made love to her under the sprays of water coming from every shower head.

It was if cutting away all their hair had shed the last of their emotional defenses. They felt more naked, more vulnerable, more exposed, yet closer than ever before.

THE HAIR BURNING CEREMONY came two weeks later.

Damon called it for sunset and hauled an empty metal trash can that he'd ordered on Amazon into the backyard. He filled the can with firewood and newspapers, then sauced it with Firestarter liquid; the flames were glorious against the darkening sky.

"Let's light this candle!" Liv called out as she came outside, carrying the cardboard box of hair, then broke into laughter. As a lark, Damon had also bought two Viking helmets and was wearing one, the other under his arm.

"Nobody has ever made me laugh like you do," Liv crowed as he put the helmet on her head, hairless, but tanned to match her skin. "Ouch."

Damon laughed. "You don't have to wear it."

"Thank you. But *you* look like a Viking god in it."

Damon removed her hat, and Liv opened the cardboard box. "Burn, baby, burn," she called out like Stud Cole.

Damon took out a handful of hair. "I think hair is really flammable, so just sort of sprinkle it in."

Liv grabbed the longest of pieces and together they let the hair fall into the fire. It crackled, but the flames remained level.

"God," Liv coughed, "It smells awful."

"Yeah…I did think of that. But I don't think the Norse gods will mind. They're used to burning whole villages."

"It took years to grow that back last time," she said wistfully as the smoke rose.

"It will grow again."

They both took handfuls and fed the shorter hair to the flames until Damon tossed the empty box into the fire. Liv smudged a stick of sage around the bin to try to mask the stench of burning hair to little effect, so they settled on a chaise to watch the last of the embers crackle into the dusk.

"Thank you for this, Damon. You've made losing my hair feel…meaningful. Powerful. I really do feel like a Norse god…er, goddess."

Damon drew her close and kissed her bald head. "Well, to be fair, I can't take all the credit. Yasmina said that adding some sort of way to mark the passage of time in your battle might be helpful."

Liv laughed. "She really is becoming a little shaman, isn't she? Who would have thought."

Damon paused thoughtfully. "Actually, she did suggest one more thing."

"What's that?"

"An ayahuasca ceremony. Something to look forward to."

Liv couldn't help but roll her eyes. "Oh yeah. She's been talking my ear off about ayahuasca."

Damon nodded. "Yeah, she's definitely gone all in. It's up to you, obviously, but I like that idea. It'd be another ritual. A ceremony. A celebration of how far you've come."

Liv thought for a moment. "Well, if it's half as powerful as this has been, I'm in. But not until chemo is over and I have a clear scan."

"It's a deal."

The last of the embers crackled out until only a whisp of smoke remained. Liv put her arms around Damon's waist and held him. "You make the worst of things special."

27.

"I FINALLY BELIEVE IN God!" Damon yelled to the heavens, overjoyed, champagne flute in hand, a black Armani tuxedo fit perfectly to his frame.

"And you call yourself agnostic!"

Liv beamed, smart her own evening wear—a tight black Prada dress and high Chanel heels Damon had bought her for just this occasion. She shifted her expertly installed dirty blond wig that made her look as if she'd never lost her hair. Although she preferred to walk around the house bald—especially since Damon fawned over her no less than when she'd had a full head—she wanted to make tonight special.

"I have faith in human beings again," Liv cried out.

Damon raised a glass. "To America for showing up."

They sipped and glanced at the television flashing images of a party in some ballroom. A chyron read: BIDEN ELECTED 46th PRESIDENT OF THE UNITED STATES.

"That's enough of this," Damon said as he used the remote to turn off the set; it had been running constantly since the night before, but only this evening did the coverage feel special enough to celebrate.

"I'm sure my mother and that neanderthal are crying in their beer," Liv sighed.

"I still don't get it," Damon answered. "How can such a sweet, caring woman believe Trump's lies?"

"I should have never gotten into it with her."

Fearful of dampening the mood, Damon shifted gears. "Siri, play Sinatra."

Damon wrapped his free arm around Liv's waist as "Old Blue Eyes" played on the speakers. "Dance with me."

Liv laid her head on his chest, and they danced in small, untrained circles.

"You know what's crazy?" Damon asked.

"What's crazy, baby?"

"Trump actually did one thing right. The vaccine is supposed to work unbelievably well, but he spent so much time pretending Covid didn't exist, nobody will remember his contribution."

"Not that it will help me. My doctors were nervous about me taking it before. Now that I'm stage four, I'll be lucky if I can come out of the house for another year."

"Hasn't been too bad being locked up with me, has it?"

"Honey, if it weren't for you I'd have shriveled up like an old lady or gone insane by now."

"Well, I'm not going out until you can go out."

"What about the restaurant?"

Damon broke into a broad smile.

"What's *that* smile?"

"I won't be needed at the club. I got an offer to sell it."

Liv took a step back from him. "I thought you were having soft openings in a couple weeks?"

"The restaurant's almost finished. But I'm approached once or twice a year by various investors. This time I think I'd like to cash out. Focus on you until you're well."

"And after that?"

"I don't know. It's a solid offer. Eventually Covid will get under control, and you'll be able to get out. Maybe we travel the world? Get married…"

Liv grinned. "You had to throw that in there."

"A boy can dream."

Liv sat on the couch and put her glass by a silver Tiffany tray of caviar, sour cream, and toast. "So your mind is made up?"

"No, I wanted to discuss it with you first."

"That's really thoughtful."

Damon joined her on the couch. "Well, what do you think?"

"I say you do whatever makes you happy. Would you be bored without a business?'

"Not if I'm with you. Honestly, I've hated every minute I've worked since I decided to redo the club."

"But you've always been a workaholic."

"I was. Now I'm a Livaholic."

Liv raised an eyebrow. "I suppose that's a good substitute for *other* things."

Damon smiled good-naturedly at the jab, so Liv went on. "You wouldn't be the first to retire early. And I love to travel. But what if *I* want to keep working?"

"No problem. We'll have the best photographers around the world shoot you in every exotic location."

"Oh my God! That's actually a great idea. I have to transition anyway. I'm not twenty-five anymore. I could be a travel and lifestyle influencer."

"The more we talk, the more I want to sell."

"Okay but don't be impulsive. Really think it through."

"Of course."

Damon dipped a toast end into caviar and handed it to Liv.

"Mmmm," she whimpered. "I can taste again."

Damon handed her a napkin. "Okay, I'm done thinking. I'm selling."

"This is the definition of impulsive, Damon."

"No, Liv. I've thought about this many times before we even met. And I know what's going to happen if I keep it. No restaurateur succeeds without being there night and day. It will be months before the vaccine is available, and all that time I'll have to come and go and risk bringing that fucking disease home. And if I do somehow keep healthy, I don't want spent the rest of our lives chained to a restaurant."

Liv took a sip of champagne without looking at him. "By the rest of our lives, you mean, the rest of *my* life."

"What?"

"You're worried about wasting whatever time I have left, right?"

"Liv, no…"

"It's okay, Damon. Let's just say it. I might die in six months or six years. But now that I'm stage four, the odds I survive past that have cut from, like, eighty-five percent to twenty-five."

Damon didn't flinch. "I know."

"With all your research, I'm sure you do. But, Damon, I don't want you making life and career decisions based on what time I might have left. That puts too much pressure on me."

"Liv, I swear, if we knew you were going to live fifty years, I'd still want to spend every waking moment with you. I've had enough of clubs, flipped enough houses…"

"I'm not. I'm not going to live fifty years. I can promise you that."

"I don't see how you can promise that. But it doesn't change a thing. I'll never find love like this again, and I want every minute of that you have left."

"You want every minute of me, huh?"

Damon saw that she was dubious. "I know you think you won't see forty, but I don't believe that. I think that as soon as this fucking pandemic is over, we're gonna travel the world. See the pyramids and safari in Africa. Drink wine in Italy and lounge in Saint Tropez. Do yoga in Indonesia and eat sushi in Tokyo."

She smiled. "These are beautiful fantasies, Damon. But I'm afraid I'll just disappoint you. Please stop talking about the future."

Liv stood but lingered, as if she couldn't figure out a direction.

Damon stood too. "Baby, I hear you. This has touched a nerve. I'm not pressuring you to marry me and even spend the rest of your life with me. I love and respect your independence. I'm just telling you how I feel, what I want. If you want something different, just say so."

Liv crossed her arms as if she could squeeze in the tears threatening to spring out. "I want the same thing, Damon. I'm just afraid I'll disappoint you."

"How would you do that?"

"Death is pretty disappointing."

Damon nodded. "Good line."

She rolled her eyes. "Oh, fuck off. You think you know just how to handle me, don't you?"

He smiled. "No, I am well aware that I'm the puppy on this walk."

She laughed. "I love you."

"Duh."

Liv sat back on the couch, Damon following her.

"Damon, sell the business if that makes you happy. Just promise that if you get sick of me or bored, you'll go back to work. I don't want to feel like I'm making you do anything. Whether I have a year or twenty, I just want it as normal as possible. I don't want to make stupid things like bucket lists or have a shotgun marriage on some mountaintop. I just want to live as happily as I can for as long as I can. If I had it my way, they'd never tell me the odds and I could just live in the moment. And of course, I'm crying again. I'm so tired of crying. The pain I can handle."

Liv laughed. Damon used one of the napkins from the tray to wipe her face.

"Okay, no bucket lists or shotgun marriages," Damon echoed. "And I'll think about selling the restaurant more. There's no hurry, I guess."

"Good. But thank you for consulting me. That was very respectful, even if I nearly ruined it with a melodramatic speech."

Damon laughed. "I like melodrama."

"I know. A few months ago, I caught you watching a Lifetime movie one night when you thought I was asleep."

"I'm in touch with my feminine side."

Liv laughed. "And I'm clearly in touch with my masculine. A.k.a., I can be a pain in the ass."

"Never. Life has thrown some hard shit at you. You've had to be really fucking strong. I love that about you."

"Love me when I'm puking all over the house?"

"Damn right."

"Good. Because my last round of chemo is next week."

"You get to ring the pink bell!"

"It's so silly, but I love ringing it."

"I love ringing *your bell*," Damon flirted.

She gave him a knowing grin. "I think it's about time we get back to ringing each other's bells."

"Thank God!" Damon yelled to the heavens and took the champagne out of both of their hands. Then he kissed Liv, pushing her down onto the couch.

"I'm sorry my libido took a vacation," she whispered between kisses.

"Abstinence makes you appreciate sex. Remember how we started out?"

Liv reached up and pulled his face toward hers again, her body writhing under his with anticipation.

Dr. Kehr pushed Liv's final Red Devil back a few days so she would actually have an appetite on Thanksgiving. The Monday after, Liv gleefully rang a pink bell to celebrate right before her last round of chemo, on the wall by the vacuum-sealed doors of the treatment room.

Liv quipped that it would make sense if they rang the bell *after* the infusion but understood that sometimes people were released from their IVs, climbed out of those comfy chairs, and promptly got sick. Damon, Yasmina, and Marie were thrilled to watch the event on their phones, Liv's held by Judy as several other nurses who'd tended to her applauded and popped champagne.

"You know what this means!" Yasmina half-whispered through the screen. "Ayahuasca time."

But of course, Judy, standing at Liv's side, heard her perfectly. "You just finished months of throwing up. Are you sure you're ready to do it again?"

Liv peeled with laughter. "Are you kidding? I'm a professional. What's a little more yack?"

28.

THOUGH SHE WAS INITIALLY trepidatious to assume the role of shaman for the purposes of their ceremony before her training had been completed, Yasmina gradually warmed to the idea until it fomented into an outright fervor. She had spent the previous few weeks preparing—ordering supplies, testing different tinctures, and consulting with her tutor in Mexico.

Now, arriving at Damon's house in a turquoise kaftan right before sunset, she moved with reverence and solemnity. In one hand, she carried a cooler of ingredients, and in the other, a tote bag of various spiritual aids—sage, four handmade clay cups for the ayahuasca, crystals, and candles.

Yasmina shooed Damon and Liv into the backyard, saying, "Go, be still and ready yourselves."

Liv couldn't help but giggle at her friend's transformation from party girl into witch doctor, but she'd already been impressed by Yasmina's instructions on how to take the experience to heart: they'd fasted all day, and for the last week they'd followed a "dieta" of no red meat, wine, or sexual interactions. On that last demand Damon and Liv might have cheated once or three times.

Liv and Damon congregated on the chaise lounges by the outdoor fireplace, where four plastic sick buckets had been arranged per Yasmina's request.

"Are you nervous?" Damon asked Liv as he lightly massaged her back.

"A little. I felt a lot more comfortable when we did the Molly because you were experienced with it. I can't believe the opportunity for something like this never came up when you were in Bali."

"It was around. But it wasn't as popular as it's becoming now. I've heard people are escaping Covid by spending weeks in indigenous camps in Costa Rica and Peru."

"And a healing medicine is okay if you're sober?"

Damon shrugged. "They say aya is nonaddictive, so…"

He leaned around Liv's neck to invite her into a deep kiss. "Hey, no funny stuff on ayahuasca!" Liv said with a laugh as her phone pinged.

"Marie's here!"

Damon drew a bracing breath. "Alright. Let's get this show on the road."

Marie, Damon, and Liv made nervous chatter over as Yasmina intermittently breezed in and out of the house, arranging her candles, a Tibetan singing bowl, mats for each of them, and finally, a small clay cauldron. When she exited the house for the final time, she had everybody gather together on their mats, then led them in meditation.

"I'd like to ask each of you to silently set an intention for this journey," Yasmina suggested. "In one way or another, each of you will be purged of something."

Yasmina watched the faces of her three friends as they closed their eyes, tiny contractions of muscle in each of their faces clueing her in as they sought their intention.

When six eyes again opened to peer at her with expectation, she went on. "Now I'd like you to spend a moment releasing that intention into the universe, with the knowledge that your intention may or may not be fulfilled. Mother Aya does not show us what we want. She shows us what we need. And like a mother, sometimes she knows what's best for us, even when we don't."

Yasmina collected her cauldron and began to fill each cup with a ruddy liquid, allotting herself only a half portion.

"It just looks like a thick tea," Liv remarked. "Like a red chai, or something."

Damon raised his cup to his lips and smacked them at the taste. "Bitter, but not the worst thing ever."

But Marie openly gagged as she drank. "Reminds me of shrooms. Remember that last time we took them? Burning Man two years ago?"

"That was fun," Liv remembered, sipping like it was hot tea.

"Aya isn't about fun," Yasmina reminded them. "It's about learning. So try not to talk. Focus on yourself, and if things feel dark, just trust the process."

Marie went to light cigarette—a habit she had only acquired in a bona fide way since the beginning of the pandemic—but Yasmina shot her a look. Away went the pack.

With melodic chanting music on the outdoor speakers, the four watched the sun begin its descent toward the palm trees in the distance.

"Do you think you mixed it right?" Liv asked after what seemed like half an hour.

But Marie snorted. "I've never done ayahuasca, but as a nurse, I can tell you that the second you start to ask, 'did we take enough,' that's when the trouble begins."

Marie's words were prophetic.

Moments later, Damon was the first to go—he crawled feverishly to his bowl and heaved violently, his back dipping then arching in an awkward spasm he might have been embarrassed by could he form a cogent thought. He moaned a ghostly sound between wretches.

Liv followed suit but with far more grace. After months of chemo, her abdominal muscles were accustomed to the motion, and she somehow managed a neat stream of bile into her bucket.

Marie watched them with a mixture of interest and concern, until she looked at Yasmina with the wild fear of a horse.

"Yaz..."

Yasmina knew exactly what that meant.

Wordlessly, she lifted Marie to her feet and steadied her as they hurried across the pool's bridge and back into the house.

"You're going to make it," Yasmina soothed as they reached the bathroom.

She yanked Marie's yoga pants down just in time as Marie sat on the toilet. Yasmina almost turned to go and afford her some privacy, but Marie's hand stayed clasped to hers, so she knelt and waited.

Had Marie had any of her typical wit about her, she might have said something like, "This is payback for all the times I've held your hair back in dive bar bathrooms," but the façade of all Marie's capable nature was already ripping apart at the seams. Pride and ego had left her without her even noticing.

In what was more inner vision than hallucination, she *saw* herself as an amalgamation of all her own patients over the course of six years—vulnerable, broken, grasping. Marie gripped Yasmina's hand so firmly that Yasmina briefly wondered if her fingers might fracture, but gritted her teeth, suddenly understanding that Marie's own hands had been gripped in such a way a hundred times over.

Finally, the spurts and gurgles ceased, and Yasmina handed Marie a wad of toilet paper, which somehow Marie's muscle memory helped her to use effectively.

Yasmina helped her walk back outside, and as the fresh air hit her face, Marie sat and began feverishly working an invisible IV drip for seconds at a time, then doubling over to grab her own hands and wail, then repeated the process.

But on the other side of the pool's bridge, another crisis of the ego was unfolding. While Liv rocked herself back and forth gently, eyes unfocused but turned toward the Los Angeles skyline, Damon lie writhing on his back on the smooth concrete beside the pool, eyes squeezed shut in agony.

As Yasmina approached, he rolled to his side and one hand accidentally grazed the surface of the pool, and Yasmina could see his instinct pass across his face—an animal's search for relief.

"Hey, hey, hey—" she grabbed him by his waist and thigh before he could manage to roll himself into the pool.

Damon tried to look into her eyes to plead with her, but her face morphed before him, vacillating between his memory of his adopted mother before cancer ravaged the structure of her face and some imagined fantasy of what his birth mother might have looked like.

Yasmina froze for a moment to allow him to stare and to give herself time to think. She briefly cursed herself for allowing the session to be conducted directly next to an open body of water, but her own mild dosage made her more inclined to trust Damon's instincts.

"Okay," she said. "But you can't go in like that. Like this."

Yasmina knelt beside his leg closest to the pool and lowered it in by the calf, then crossed behind him to take the other.

He seemed to get the idea well enough and scooted himself like a child to the edge, awkwardly lowering himself into the water until he was standing in it. He laid his head back and allowed himself to float, the weightlessness briefly soothing the agony he felt shooting up from his spine and poisoning each muscle.

Yasmina sat at the edge and watched him intently.

Behind them, a banshee's scream of glee and laughter.

Yasmina looked over her shoulder to see Liv, squealing with joy. Over and over, she howled laughter into the night sky, pausing only to wipe away ecstatic tears, hugging herself and rocking.

Yasmina sighed with relief. *After all Liv's been through, if anybody tonight deserved a good trip it was her.*

But just as suddenly, Liv vomited another neat stream of bile into her freshly cleaned bowl. She glanced around at the others, on journeys far more harrowing than her own. Liv was accustomed to her body revolting against her, and the purge felt almost cathartic. She seemed to float above the other three, and the affection she felt for each of them was life-affirming and sweet.

And then it hit her.

Her expectations and enthusiasm were sucked from her body as though through an industrial vacuum. She felt her body freeze for a moment as her thoughts began to warp and become impossible to untangle from a knot of stirring emotion.

And then, the pain.

Liv grabbed her breasts with both hands as explosions erupted in each, as if every nerve had sprouted from her skin and now lie outside of her body, exposed.

Almost as quickly as she could identify the pain in her breasts, the explosions seemed to communicate with each other and plan a rendezvous in the middle of her chest, the pain migrating into her heart.

She clutched her chest and looked at Yasmina in panic, a second of cogency allowing her to form the thought, *I hope she knows when to call 911.*

And then, darkness.

HOURS LATER, Damon, Liv, Marie, and Yasmina sat in silence on the chaises, wrapped in blankets and watching the flames of the fireplace.

"Damn," Marie said finally.

A chorus of agreement met her.

"Yeah."

LIV STIRRED THE NEXT AFTERNOON and woke to see Damon sat on the edge of the bed, eyes far away and contemplative.

She kissed his shoulder before resting her chin on it. "Morning, baby."

He turned his head to kiss her. "Hi."

"You okay?"

"I am. Are you okay?"

"Yeah. I thought I was going to get off way easier than you and Marie for the first hour or so, but then…wow."

Damon scooted back onto the bed to cross his legs and face her. "It definitely wasn't pleasant. But it was important."

"Can you describe yours at all?"

He nodded with resignation. "I can. It was a drug withdrawal. The worst of my life. My entire body felt like it was on fire. My back—I can't even describe it. I don't think it even hurt that badly when the accident first happened."

"That sounds terrible. But what was important about that?"

Damon hesitated. "I don't want to scare you."

But Liv laughed gamely. "How could you possibly scare *me*? I've been with you through one withdrawal—hopefully your last—and you've been by my side through months of grueling chemo."

She rubbed the fuzz of her bald head on his arm for emphasis.

Damon couldn't help but smile at the gesture. "It made me realize…I'm always going to have to be on the lookout for these demons. Whatever it is that makes me want to numb everything with pills, or cocaine, or whatever—it's a thing inside me that I have to make peace with. Acknowledge that it's there, all the time. It's like every time I run into a new vice, and then get over it, I think I have it licked. But there's always something else just around the corner. I have to be aware of it. Watch it."

He looked up at Liv for reassurance, then repeated himself: "I hope that doesn't scare you."

Liv took his hands. "It doesn't. I want to be there for you through it."

Damon let out a heavy exhale and squeezed her hands back. "There's something else too."

"What's that?"

"Well, I was in the pool for a while, and when I got out, the withdrawals stopped, and I was going through something different."

Again, he met her eyes for encouragement, and finding nothing but love, he continued. "This part might be hard to hear too. But listen to the whole thing and try not to get jealous."

Now Liv sucked air in.

"I saw…each and every woman I've ever had sex with. The good, the bad, and the barely memorable."

Liv raised both eyebrows. "Okay…"

"It wasn't like…reliving some kind of conquest or anything. But I can't lie and say it was all bad. It was like I was psychically waving hello to them. Or rather…goodbye. Because finally, I saw you, and the love we make, and the future I want to build with you. And it was like everyone that I met before you was just a stepping stone closer to your presence."

He hesitated before he went on. "Actually, that phrasing isn't quite right either, because it seems to be dehumanizing, and that's the last thing I felt about these women. They were all important in their own ways, and the wholeness and light of their existence isn't in any way diminished by the fact that your light for me just shines so much brighter."

Liv laughed in spite of herself. "I thought I was going to be *very* jealous for a minute, but that's…really beautiful."

"I don't need anyone but you, for the rest of my life. I want you for the rest of *your* life, and beyond."

Liv nodded at the caveat. She knew that Damon provided it because of the issue she always took with discussion of the future and time, and it was an elegant segue into her own experience.

"The rest of my life—that's what the beginning of my trip was all about. It was peaceful at first. Like the purge was about getting rid of the rest of my cancer. Or maybe more that I was getting rid of its hold on me. Even before this last round of chemo, it's like I had been carrying it with me, always. Like my life has been on pause, always waiting for the other shoe to drop."

"I've definitely noticed that, but wasn't sure how to bring it up," Damon agreed.

Liv went on. "And in some ways, that was its own grieving process. Grieving the last couple years of my life that I feel like I gave up on so much just waiting for the next piece of bad news. It's like I've just been waiting to die. Besides meeting you, of course."

Damon embraced her. "If that's what you've got out of this experience, it was all worth it."

Liv nodded. "And I saw you, and Marie, and Yasmina, and felt so much love, and I realized I've been withholding part of you from myself, a part that I can't even put words to. Whatever independence kept me going through my first round of chemo, I can put that burden down. I can lean on you."

"I'm so glad that was your epiphany, baby," he said and kissed her. "I have to say though, I'm surprised. You did *not* seem to be having a great time when I was starting to come around enough to be able to notice you."

Now Liv furrowed her brow. "Yeah…well all of that was the first part of my experience. That's the part where I actually understand what Mother Aya was trying to show me. But something changed. It was…violent. And I wish I could put words or meaning to it."

"Can you say what it felt like?"

Liv shook her head. "Not really. The pain was so intense, in my breasts first, which makes sense of course, but then in my heart and in my stomach, that my reasoning brain wasn't really present. It was all primal, animalistic. Just instinct and survival."

Damon kissed her forehead. "I wouldn't think on it too hard. Either it will be revealed in time, or a bad case of indigestion interrupted your spiritual journey."

Liv threw her head back and peeled with laughter. "I love you."

DAMON AND LIV JOINED Yasmina and Marie around the kitchen table for a light brunch that would be gentle after so much vomit—fresh fruit and a sparing portion of salmon.

Marie looked far away as she sipped her coffee.

"If you'd prefer to keep your experience to yourself," Yasmina said to the three, "you are encouraged to. But if you'd like to share anything, this is a safe place for that. You can also share with me privately later, and I'll be here to help you integrate your experience into your day-to-day whenever you need advisement."

It was evident the prompt was for Marie's benefit.

She shook herself from her reverie, set down her coffee mug, and stared at her hands in her lap. "I can't be a nurse anymore."

"*What*?" came Liv's shocked reply, but Yasmina nodded knowingly.

"Or I need to at least take a sabbatical. That's what the aya showed me. Working in the ER has never been easy, but this pandemic has just...compounded everything. Your best just isn't enough to stop the bleeding. The metaphorical bleeding. The whole system is so rotten."

A single tear escaped down her cheek, but her voice was steady as she went on. "I've known that I've been burned out for weeks now, in the back of my mind. But I keep pushing that knowledge away, because so many people have quit, and I don't want to let anyone down. But I can't help anymore when I'm sucked dry like this. I need to take a break."

Yasmina reached across the table to take her friend's hand. "I thought you might say something like that. It looked like you were working in an emergency room in your mind. You were acting out the motions. Do you remember that at all?"

Marie furrowed her brow. "Somewhat? But in an abstracted way."

"That's pretty common," Yasmina assured.

Liv jumped in. "The end of my journey was really abstract too. I can't make sense of it." She looked to Damon. "I'm jealous of him, he seems to have been shown all parts of his journey so clearly. But the second half of mine…I don't know, it was just pain. Maybe I'm not woo-woo enough to get it."

Yasmina shook her head fervently. "No, try not to cast that judgment on yourself. We all experience these things differently. And sometimes, there isn't language to describe what your body goes through. Thoughts, emotions, they're not just in your skull. We carry them in our bodies; we can be crippled by them. Maybe your body was just showing you something you're not able to understand intellectually yet."

"That's comforting. And I definitely got some direction out of the first part. That I need to file down this chip on my shoulder that cancer has given me. I'm not dead yet. It's time to live!" Liv threw her head back and let out a war cry.

"To *life!*" Damon called out, and the four toasted their coffee cups and erupted in laughter.

IN THE WEEKS that followed, Yasmina went back to Europe. Marie's dispatches from the frontlines became less weary, even as Covid numbers began to climb again as people gathered for the beginning of the holiday season. She had determined to stay in the ER through January as to not leave her comrades in the lurch ahead of the expected surge but having sight of the light at the end of the tunnel afforded her an energy in her step she had not felt in months. After January, she hoped to take an extended vacation, followed by another round of graduate school for psychotherapy.

"I can't believe I'm going to be a grad student again. Maybe the ayahuasca was just trying to tell me that I'm a masochist," she quipped whenever asked.

Damon found himself thinking twice each time a glass of wine was poured for dinner. Though alcohol was never his vice, his epiphany about the ever-present nature of his addictive tendencies stayed in the forefront of his mind, and he often found himself leaving his glass untouched all together.

He wondered privately if the utility of the ayahuasca trip was just psychosomatic—that he hadn't undergone some spiritual change but rather had assigned meaning to it that fomented a heightened awareness of any kind of substance.

Until he saw Liv in the living room early one morning, lying on her stomach on the floor, cocooned in a blanket and scribbling on a legal pad.

"You're up early this morning," he noted, giving her butt a light slap as he passed. "Working on a new content strategy?"

"No…" she said, her brow furrowed in concentration. "Some lyrics came to me last night, and I don't want to forget them."

Damon stopped in his tracks. He opened his mouth to press for more information but decided against calling too much attention to the change. Liv was writing lyrics to his music, and for the past few weeks they'd been happier, more in love than they'd ever thought possible.

Thank you, Mother Aya, he thought.

Then smiled and pulled the handle out from the espresso machine.

29.

With glowing skin and a fuzzy inch of hair growing under a cashmere beanie, Liv waited with Damon in Dr. Kehr's office. Terrible at hiding her nerves, Liv held onto Damon with one hand and tapped a frantic beat on her armchair with the other.

"I was really hoping this would stress me out less after the ayahuasca," she said wistfully to Damon. It had been a few weeks of healthy introspection for both of them, but a visit to the hospital had put a quick pause on that.

"I think it works in more subtle ways than that. It can't undo years' worth of conditioning to be nerve-racked in this kind of situation. It's not unreasonable of you," Damon said reassuringly.

Before Liv could respond, Dr. Kehr entered from a side door. "Good afternoon."

"Hi, Doctor," said Damon, while Liv studied her face for some indication of whether today was good or bad news.

The woman turned to wake up her computer. "Just a second while I pull up your scans."

Nothing, Liv thought. *The woman gives nothing.* Days ago, she'd undergone a full array of blood tests, CT, and MRI scans, and Liv couldn't quite remember if she'd had to come into the office for her first check-up after chemotherapy the first time around.

The doctor pulled off her mask. "They gave you a rapid test when you checked in, right?"

"And a PCR last night," Liv answered.

"You can remove yours if you feel comfortable."

"You're the doctor," answered Liv as she and Damon removed their masks.

It was the same dance they performed each time they all met; rechecking mask preferences had become a social norm as pedestrian as shaking hands.

"How are you feeling, Liv?"

"Relieved it's over, scared it didn't work."

Kehr pointed at a spot on the scan. "The chemo cleaned out your lymph nodes."

"That's great news!" Damon said, smiling at Liv.

Liv had questions to ask before smiling. "How were the blood tests?"

Dr. Kehr crossed her arms and sat back in her chair. "Unfortunately, your white blood cell count was lower than we'd like, so I added a few additional tests, including a tumor marker analysis, and those results came back this morning."

Liv froze. *Fuck. That's why she didn't call me earlier. That's why I can't remember having a meeting like this.*

"And?"

"I have a lot of information, so I need you to listen to everything before you react."

Liv shot Damon a panicked glance.

"The chemo worked, and your lymph nodes are clear," she repeated. "That's good news. But the markers in your bloodwork indicated that there was still cancer in your body."

Liv's hand shot up and cupped her mouth.

"The question was where. Naturally, I checked your breasts first, but they were clear, so I had my team scour your images."

Dr. Kehr brought up a different scan, but Liv squinted at it, unable to read it.

"This is a cross section of your heart…" the Doctor's voice began.

Liv didn't hear the rest. She felt disassociated as she was transported back to the grassy outer perimeter of the backyard, clutching her chest in feverish pain. *Mother Aya had been telling her she was sick.*

"Hold on," Damon said to the doctor, then squeezed Liv's hand. "Are you okay?"

Liv tried to nod but couldn't. She forced her eyes to focus. "I'm sorry, go on."

The doctor zoomed in on her computer and pointed at a tiny spot. "We found a mass about two centimeters wide inside this chamber of your heart."

"*Inside* my heart…" Liv noted more than asked. "How long do you think it's been there?"

"As you know, we take scans in between every infusion, but it wasn't even there six weeks ago, so it's growing very fast."

Liv tried to process this, tried to *feel* the thing in her heart as she had on the ayahuasca, but just felt fear.

Damon fought his, the businessman inside deftly choking out his emotions to take control. "Can it be surgically removed?"

"No, that chamber wall is too thin."

"Can she get a new heart? Just thinking out loud here."

"I'm afraid not. As long as chemo and radiation are available to her, the board wouldn't approve a transplant."

Damon nodded, feeling foolish for even suggesting it.

"How much of each treatment?" Liv asked.

"Six to nine months of chemo, and probably as many radiation treatments."

"Jesus, that much chemo…I mean, how do you even know it's malignant?"

"We'll biopsy it with a catheter, but between its shape and size, your bloodwork and history, it's almost a given. And, to be frank, I'd rather it be malignant."

"Why?" Damon demanded.

"Because chemo can shrink it. Otherwise, it would keep growing, and eventually block the blood flow completely. Without treatment, your heart would fail within a year."

Liv gave a curt laugh. "I bet I'm the first person to hope something in their heart is cancerous."

"This is very rare," the doctor admitted.

Damon saw reason to be optimistic. "Well, we know the drill. Back into chemo."

"It's not that simple," said the doctor.

"What do you mean?" asked Liv.

The doctor drew a deep breath and held Liv's gaze. "Liv, this matter is somewhat more sensitive. Would you mind if we asked Damon to step out for a moment?"

But Liv shook her head vehemently. "I would mind. Anything you have to tell me, I'd share with him."

Dr. Kehr nodded. "Okay. It is required of me to ask. We also found HCG hormones in your blood…"

Damon waited for the doctor to explain, but Liv understood and stopped breathing entirely.

"I'm pregnant?"

She shared a shaken look with Damon.

"It was a very small level. Even a home test could miss it. I'm guessing you conceived in the last two weeks."

"But how is that physically possible? I'm on the pill *and* an estrogen blocker."

"Your hormone therapy makes it difficult but not impossible to get pregnant. And chemo has been known to lower the effectiveness of birth control. But it's a little bit of a miracle."

"A miracle? I've been drowning it in chemo!" Liv's voice broke.

"Actually, it only takes forty-eight to seventy-two hours for the chemicals to pass through your organs. Naturally, you'd need an ultrasound and the standard tests, but right now there's no reason to think the baby isn't healthy. Many women are able to receive chemotherapy right up until the month of their due date."

"But it sure as shit wouldn't survive this next nine-month round of chemotherapy *and* radiation, would it?"

"I would strongly advise against carrying a baby through radiation. The baby probably wouldn't survive, and if it did, it would be severely physically and mentally disabled."

Liv leaned forward, hands clamped between her knees. "So basically, if I get treatment, the baby dies. If I don't, I die."

The horrible simplicity of that disturbed Damon. "I'm sorry, Doctor, but should we get a second opinion?"

"You're welcome to, of course. But believe me, with such a serious diagnosis, I've had the results looked at by several oncologists."

Damon nodded. "So what do *you* suggest we do?"

"Radiation, and continuation of your hormone therapy, would give you a fighting chance," the doctor said.

"At what?" Liv said with disbelief. "If the treatments work on my heart, what does this new diagnosis do to my life expectancy? Because *clearly* there were still some breast cancer cells hiding somewhere, and now they're spreading from one organ to another."

"I'm sorry. But you are correct. That's why we don't say you're officially in remission for five years."

Liv was losing patience and spoke slowly. "If I go through chemo and radiation, how long do I have to live?"

The doctor's dour face enraged Damon, although he knew she was merely the messenger.

"It's impossible to be exact, and we're developing new treatments every year," the doctor spoke in a stoic tone. "But with what we have now? Three to five years."

Liv's mouth gaped. "Three to five years? You want me to kill my baby just so I can a live a few more years?"

"Liv, if you don't have the treatments, the stress of pregnancy and childbirth on your heart might kill you before the baby is even born."

Damon watched Liv's frame begin to tremble and placed a hand on her shoulder, but she wiped it away.

"No! I know what you want me to do!" she hissed at him.

Hurt, Damon looked to the doctor for help.

"Liv, for now, I think the best thing you can do is go home, take a bit of time to reflect, and discuss it together. You don't have to make a decision today, or even this week, for that matter."

"Discuss what?" Liv burst into tears. "There's no good choice here! I have an abortion and go through treatment hell, only to buy me a few years. And then I'd probably get cancer somewhere else, so it's not like those years would be a party. How selfish is that? Or I can bring a child into the world who might never even know its mother. And that's *if* I don't drop dead before it's born!"

Liv put her wailing face into her hands. Damon began to reach for her but refrained. He glanced again at the doctor, but her professional composure had crumbled as well.

DAMON DROVE LIV HOME in silence once again. But now, he couldn't possibly begrudge her shutting down, even after so much progress. He had his own inner voices to contend with. *She's going to die sooner than I ever thought possible. Her instincts were right, mine were wrong, and I ignored her.*

He took a cue from her playbook and tried to ignore himself. Whatever fear he fought, he knew it could never compare with the cauldron of emotions Liv contended with.

"I'm sorry I snapped at you," she finally spoke in a cracked voice.

Damon gripped the steering wheel tighter. "I understand."

"I don't want my mother to know."

"About being sick or pregnant?"

"That I'm sick. I'll tell her I'm pregnant when I'm showing. If we ever speak again."

Damon ignored the fatalism. "When will you tell her you're sick? Don't you think it's time to reach out?"

"She'll find out when I die."

"Why wouldn't you tell her? The radio silence should end."

"Because if I'm going to spend the next year fighting to have this baby, I want it to be the best year of my life. I don't want her, or my friends, or anybody else worrying about me and pitying me. I want to be fucking happy."

She took a long beat then said, "I'm not going through radiation. I'm having this baby."

Damon did his best to navigate traffic as everything he understood about Liv warped into abstractions as difficult to set in order as in his ayahuasca trip. "Don't you think we should discuss that?"

"Why? I know what *you* want me to do. You want me to have an abortion."

Damon felt her icy tone. "I don't know if that's what I want," he answered evenly.

"Come on, Damon. You're always saying you want every last minute with me. And how often have you said you don't want children?"

Damon looked at her aghast. "*You* always say that you don't want children. You literally lied to me about it to disguise the fact that you just don't want to. You didn't even think there was a reason to freeze your eggs."

Liv shook off the accusation. "But the thought of having an abortion…"

"You don't believe in abortion?"

"Of course I believe in the right to choose. But not for me. Not like this. Why, have *you* had one?"

Damon didn't deny it.

Liv slapped the glove box. "So I'm not the only one who's kept stories that weren't immediately important to myself."

"Liv! You're deflecting! It's so obvious. That's not what we're talking about here!" Damon's voice rose and a second of objectivity passed over him as he realized this was quickly becoming their first shouting match.

"I'm not choosing to kill a baby just so I can have a few more years on this planet!" Liv yelled back.

"*Hang on!*" Damon shouted, then drew a breath. "Just hang on for a second. We are not enemies. The cancer is the enemy. I'm sorry I yelled."

Liv nodded and steadied herself. "Maybe it's hypocritical of me—maybe it'd be different if I had twenty years. But just to spend the next few years in chemo hell? I'd hate myself for killing it. And I'd probably end up hating you for making me do it."

"I wouldn't make you do anything. Liv, I appreciate your conviction. But shouldn't I have a say too? After all, I'm the one who will spend the next twenty years raising the baby."

"If you don't want the responsibility, my mother will. But I'd hope you'd think this child was a blessing."

"I'm sure I *could* if you gave me a chance. Right now, you're just steamrolling right over my feelings."

"Aw, I'm hurting poor Damon's feelings?" Liv spat, the venom returning to her voice as quickly as it had dissipated.

"Liv, I understand you were just told the worst news possible, but you're treating me like shit."

She laughed. "Come on, I'm doing you a favor. You always said you were afraid of commitment and monogamy. So now you can go back to your old ways. Re-open the club, travel the world like you want, date the hottest models in the world. Relive all those delicious experiences you remembered on the ayahuasca."

"What the hell are we even talking about right now, Liv? I was like that *before* I met you! Hell, every time I talk about closing the club you tell me not to. And God forbid I talk about marriage!"

"Yeah, you talk. But I sure as shit don't see a ring on my finger."

Liv laughed again bitterly. Damon shook his head in wonder.

"It's funny," Liv said humorlessly. "Part of me always wondered if the reason you invited me into this grand Covid experiment was because you knew I was going to die. It's so easy to commit when you know I come with an expiration date."

The dagger was exacting. Tears stung Damon's eyes as they pulled into the driveway. "This is insane," he whispered. "I don't know what to say."

"Let's just stop talking."

Damon said nothing. His heart pounded so loudly in his ears, he thought he might not have been able to hear her if she went on, anyway.

DAMON ENTERED HIS LIBRARY and closed its French doors hard enough that the glass windows rattled in their panes. As he uncorked the emerald bottle of scotch, it occurred to him vaguely that reaching for a substance in his moment of pain was absolutely addict behavior, but he couldn't be bothered to reflect on it. For her part, Liv had marched up to their room and locked the door. Knocks, texts, and FaceTime calls from him went unanswered.

Damon swilled the hundred-year-old whiskey like it was hooch, staring at the twelve-foot-high Christmas tree from his leather recliner. Delivered only yesterday, they hadn't had a chance to decorate it, and green twigs littered the floor.

Damon scoffed at the shabby picture it made, fitting of his emotions. He poured another ounce and tried to make sense of how Liv was acting. *Be patient,* he scolded himself. *After all, how can anyone understand what it's like to be handed a death notice?* Before today, Liv's death had always seemed like some far-off possibility, but now it had walked in through the front door.

Liv was right in one sense—he'd seen firsthand just how much courage it took for her to go through three months of chemo. And now, just when she was starting to recover, she would be right back at it, and contending with a dramatically more deadly foe. And he couldn't deny that Liv was right about what his choice would be: Damon loved her more than life itself, maybe even more than he would their baby. Unbidden, an image came to him of the fetus siphoning her life force, growing massive and grotesque as she withered away. He shook it off. *You're being morbid.*

Another image came to him—an infant girl with Liv's green eyes, swaddled in pink and bouncing on Damon's knee. This too he shook off.

He wanted her to fight. He wanted to champion her through the cancer, as he had for months. But he knew that if she made it *their* decision, not just hers, he'd support whatever choice she'd make. But how could he be sure what he wanted when Liv wouldn't even give him the opportunity to think about it?

His reverie was interrupted by a rhythmic banging on the steps as Liv lugged a giant suitcase downstairs.

"Where are you going?"

"To Marie's."

He rose. "Liv, please…"

"No! You had your chance to be supportive. Now I just want to be left alone."

He walked to her, but she pushed her bags around him, down the hallway to the garage.

"Honey, can we please talk about this first? Have you even told Marie and Yasmina what's going on?"

"I will when I'm ready!" she snapped. "But if you tell anyone a fucking thing before I get to it, you'll never even meet your child!"

Adrenaline poisoned Damon's veins as he followed her into the garage. She hit the wall switch and the doors rose. She used her keys to pop open the trunk but had trouble lifting the bag.

"Here," Damon said, coming to her aid. "Sweetheart, it's been months, the car might not even start…"

She didn't look at him as she got into the driver's seat. The engine turned over and rumbled to life, and she raised a haughty eyebrow at him before slamming the door closed.

Damon backed up as she reversed out of the garage, maneuvered a three point on the gravel, then sped out to the road and down the canyon.

Damon stood frozen, too shocked to move. *This is not happening.*

But it was. Liv was gone.

30.

"So, what's going on?" Marie demanded as she wrapped her friend in a tight hug. "You and Damon have a fight?"

"If it's okay, I'd really rather not talk about it yet," Liv answered tersely.

"Of course, whenever you're ready."

"We're just happy to have you back," Yasmina said as she carried in blankets and placed them on the couch beside her luggage. Since she was only days from returning to Paris, the moment Liv called and said she was coming to Marie's, Yasmina had insisted she stay in her old room again.

"And thank you guys for getting tested so fast for me," Liv said.

"Of course," said Marie. "Only took them nine months to get rapid tests. But it really feels like the world is starting to open up again."

Liv forced a smile, but it was obvious to both girls their friend was hurting.

"I'm really exhausted," Liv said. "Do you mind if I just lie down?"

"Of course, go. I'll let you know when dinner's up."

"I'm not hungry," Liv said as she pushed her suitcase past Marie and Yasmina and out the back door.

Yasmina and Marie exchanged a dismayed look.

"What. The. Hell?" Marie moaned.

"Do you think the doctor made a mistake? That the final round of chemo failed?" Yasmina asked.

"I don't know," Marie said. "Whatever it is, it's as bad as things get."

Marie and Yasmina waited three days. Three days of knocking on Liv's door and hearing their friend call out, "I'm okay." Three days of texts and calls not answered. Finally, as they were cooking one night, Marie turned to Yasmina and furrowed her brow.

"I'm not doing this Liv-going-AWOL shit anymore. I'm calling Damon."

"You don't want to give her a little time?"

"You know what she's like. I want to know. You stay here in case she comes back. I'm going to my car."

Damon picked up Marie's call the second it connected.

"Is she there?" he demanded breathlessly.

Marie pulled the lever to recline her driver's seat and covered her brow with one hand. "Yes. What the hell is going on? Did you do something?"

"No! Well, yes, kind of. But no. She told me she'd kill me if I told anyone before she could get to it. But this is getting ridiculous. You know she listed me as her emergency contact at her oncologist; they called me because Liv won't answer their calls..."

"Let me guess—the cancer is back?" Marie spoke grimly.

"It's worse than that..."

Damon gave her the bare facts about the diagnosis.

"I can't imagine what she's going through..." Marie began. "But it doesn't explain why she's *here* in a huff."

Now Damon's voice broke. "And she doesn't...she doesn't want treatment. She wants to have the baby."

Marie sucked air as Damon explained how Liv had walked out on him. When Marie composed herself, she didn't mince words. "I'm so sorry, Damon. What is she thinking? It's a crapshoot if the baby will even survive. We need to be aggressive about treatment if the tumor is growing this fast."

"I know." Damon's voice broke.

"I'll talk to her," Marie assured him.

"Thank you. I know she'll probably hate me even more for telling you. But even if she doesn't want help from me, she needs to talk to *someone*."

Marie nodded. "You did the right thing, Damon. And I'll do my best to make her understand that."

Damon fought tears of gratitude. "Let me know how it goes?"

Marie hesitated to nod. "I'll try but I can't promise anything. She's my closest friend, and she has to trust I'm not calling you behind her back."

"I understand. Thank you."

"Take care of yourself, Damon," Marie said as she hung up.

MARIE USED HER KEY to open the door to the back house. The lights were off, the curtains closed, and Liv lay in the fetal position in the dark.

She sat up and looked at Marie. "What?"

Marie sat on the edge of the bed. "Liv. I can't imagine what you're going through. But Damon hardly seems to be the enemy here. You've barely given him time to think. I thought you two were being more open with each other."

Liv slapped her hand on a pillow. "Mother*fucker*. He can't be trusted for thirty goddamn minutes."

"*No*," Marie said firmly. "We're not doing that right now. We're not going to shit on Damon for catching your friends up on something extremely serious going on when you've lost your damn mind. My house, my rules. We're going to talk about the real issue."

"We're not, actually. So, if it's your house, your rules, and that's a rule, am I not welcome to stay here?"

Marie ignored her petulance. "Liv, this is insane. What was your plan? To have a baby in my backyard? To go get prenatal care for a high-risk pregnancy in Bumfuck Nowhere, Florida? With your *mother*?"

"Why are you yelling at me right now?"

She hadn't been before, but now Marie raised her voice. "Because I'm fucking scared! Because I don't want you to do this! Because if you delay your treatment, and the baby might not even survive anyway, which there's a solid chance it won't, then you'll die and what will it all have been for? *Nothing*, Liv. Nothing."

Marie finished her tirade and choked back a sob.

But Liv was unfazed. She narrowed her eyes. "Like I asked before. Are you saying I'm not welcome to stay?"

Marie angrily wiped tears from her cheeks and got up from the bed.

"Of course you're fucking welcome to stay. Always," she managed, then slammed the door behind her.

Liv watched Marie cross to the main house through the window and retreated back inside of herself until the scene in front of her blurred as if through a film. Despite her resolve, she knew this was a nightmare.

She tried to parse her thoughts into some semblance of a plan—wills and power of attorney, obstetrics appointments…

She tossed the covers off as she tried to think, viscerally uncomfortable. This wasn't her home anymore, but she didn't want to think about her new home and the life she'd made with a man just twenty minutes north. The moment her doctor had said, "It's not that simple." Liv erected a wall around her heart so thick that logic couldn't penetrate. And love? Well—romantic love. She shoved that from her heart with the force that years of cancer had shown her.

Liv brought a hand to her stomach. She knew the baby was too small to feel, but still, she was sure she felt her energy sync with its tiny life force, enveloping it. Her hand balled into a protective fist. She had a purpose for the first time since her life had collapsed years ago. Nobody else mattered more; even Damon's slightest objections had infuriated her. It was as if the moral, unselfish man she'd fallen for had proven to be a fake, some mirage in a lonely desert. How could he even suggest what he did? Couldn't he feel her tiny energy, her growing spirit.

Her.

Liv smiled in the dark.

It's a her.

"So FAR, I have EVERY reason to think it's healthy," the OBGYN nurse said behind her mask and face shield as she ran the ultrasound wand over Liv's stomach.

"I knew it," Liv said, not boastfully, but with confidence.

The nurse pointed to a white pea-sized shape on the monitor, surrounded by a sack of black liquid. "Not much to see, right?"

Liv squinted but really couldn't be sure what she was looking at. A white bump, a tiny limb?

"But this is a good sign?" she asked.

"This is the best…"

The nurse hit a button and they could hear a swishing beat.

Liv gasped, but somehow felt empty. As hard as she tried to push Damon out of her mind, he sat on the outskirts, pleading to be let back in.

"Too soon to tell the sex if you're wondering," said the woman.

Liv held her breath to better hear the tiny thump.

The nurse raised her face shield slightly to display a bit more humanity. "Dr. Kehr explained your situation to me. My heart goes out to you."

"Thank you. And the other tests?"

The nurse knew that Liv referred to the blood tests that she'd come in for two days prior. "We could find nothing abnormal at all. We'll want to check again every few months, but right now the baby seems to be healthy."

Liv closed her eyes.

"Want a picture? the nurse asked.

"Of course!"

The OBGYN whipped off a printed picture and held it out. Liv took it and stared, unable to make anything human out of the image.

"I wish…" she said aloud. She stopped herself from finishing her sentence. *I wish Damon could see this.*

She fought back tears. Damon *could* see this. He could have been here, and she could have been preparing for the baby with him. All the preparations she was making alone in the back house, ordering books about childbirth, fantasy shopping online for baby clothes and cribs, learning about doulas and baby nurses, breast feeding timelines, and the best formulas in case she was too sick when the baby was born…all of this would be better shared with the man she loved.

But as she took the picture and left the hospital alone, her loneliness and heartbreak paled in comparison to the sense of purpose that flooded her veins with warmth. Damon's reaction to the baby was so ambivalent, even selfish in her eyes. But after waiting nearly a decade for the hammer of death to fall, this baby gave Liv purpose. She gently rubbed her stomach. *Why fight for a few more years to give to Damon, when the reason I was born is in here?* But the loneliness she felt in that moment did make it clear to her she needed to share her pain and purpose with *someone.*

Liv dialed Facetime as soon as she shut her car door.

"Sweetheart!"

Her mother's face told Liv that she'd made the right call. After all, Liv's own birth had given so much purpose to Beth. Whatever insanity and ignorance Beth had shown recently, she had never stopped showing her love and support. And if there was one thing she knew about her mother, it was that with her religious bent, Beth would never, *never* question Liv's decision to bring a child into this world. To Beth, abortion was an abomination.

Liv had heard her friends with children repeatedly say how having a child makes you understand and forgive your own parents. And suddenly she was overcome with cries of forgiveness. Of sadness. Of fear. Of need.

Her mother started to cry with her. "Liv, honey, what is it?"

31.

DAMON WATCHED RAND fiddle with the focus of a new Lyrica camera, trying out which lenses to best capture the wide canyon backdrop of Damon's yard.

"It's a very thoughtful Christmas gift, Damon," Nina noted, sitting a safe six feet away from him in his backyard. "He hasn't even looked at his phone for ten minutes!"

Damon laughed. "Well, with his interest in what's going on the world around him, I thought maybe he could observe the next BLM marches from a distance."

"Black Lives Matter seems like ancient history already. Maybe because Trump losing let us feel like we'd won a battle."

Damon laughed. "Not that he's making the transition easy."

"You know Rand hasn't missed a day of school since we last visited," Nina remarked, sitting on the outdoor sectional with Damon. "Well, Zoom school, that is."

"That's great news," Damon answered. "I'm really thankful you called."

She laughed. "Two visits now, and I haven't asked you for a dime."

"I know! You told me not even to put something under the tree for you!"

"I'm doing okay. Found a gig doing online marketing. Was either that or OnlyFans, like all my girlfriends."

Damon worked his unshaven, tired face into a smile. "I'm glad you're doing well. And of course, if Rand needs anything, just tell me."

"Thank you," she answered, taking a sip from a Diet Coke can. "Honestly, once I stopped spending everything I had on blow and Xannies, my financial worries disappeared."

"Funny how that happens."

Nina put the can down and leaned forward, her elbows on her knees. "Where is Liv?"

Damon's expression contorted in angst.

"What's going on, Damon? I can still read your face."

Damon inhaled. "She swore me to secrecy, but if I don't talk about it with someone, I'll lose it. And I suppose I've already fucked that up, anyhow."

"For better or worse, you know I keep secrets."

Damon knew Nina had kept secrets all right, from the drugs she took to the men she cheated on him with, but those dramas were far from his mind since he met Liv.

"The short version? Liv's cancer returned and spread, but she's pregnant and getting radiation would kill the child. Oh, and she's not speaking to me."

Nina's face dropped with her heart. "Damon...I am so sorry."

Damon held back tears. "She wants to have the baby, even if it means she'll die soon after."

"That's a horrible choice to make," Nina sighed. "What do you want her to do?"

"Honestly, I'd rather she give it up and live for another few years. But of course I'll support her if that's what she decides. The problem is, because we've agreed so many times that kids weren't in our future, she doesn't believe me."

"Well, that's not fair of her. She changed her mind, why can't you?"

Damon shook his head. "When it comes to communicating her feelings about cancer, she always shuts down. I thought we were past that. But this time, she's not just shutting down, she's barred up the whole door."

"That has to be hard."

Damon nodded and glanced at Rand, momentarily distracted from his camera and texting furiously. He wished himself a child again, with child problems.

"You know, Damon, with your looks and charm and success, it took me years to believe that me and Rand were the most important people in your life. Women are hardwired to be insecure. I know that was part of the reason I blew up our relationship so many times—it was easier than waiting for you to fuck up and hurt me."

"Well, I did fuck up. I almost killed you on the back of a motorcycle. But I've grown."

"Have you ever heard the saying, there's a difference between what you feel and what is real? It might be hard for you, but Liv has to be more afraid than either of us could imagine. Any threat—real or imaginary—to what she thinks she wants, this baby, she's gonna respond to. So, *you're* going to have to do more than what's required to prove to her you'll support her decision."

"I'd do anything to prove it."

"Okay, then maybe take her cue and stop trying to talk to her."

"Huh?"

"She's made it clear she doesn't want to talk to you right now. Respect the space she's asking for."

Damon groaned and put his head in his hands. "I've been trying that for weeks. I can just feel her pulling away even more."

"Okay, so actions are worth a thousand words. Show her."

Damon shrugged his shoulders "I do have an idea. It's sort of a version of the romantic grand gesture in movies."

"You mean, like running to the airport and stopping the woman before she gets on a flight."

"Something like that."

"Why don't you run it by me?"

"You wouldn't mind?"

"Of course not. I'm so relieved we can talk like this, as friends."

Damon smiled. "Who'd have thought I'd be asking you advice about women?"

"Covid has changed everything, hasn't it?"

32.

"HALT," MARIE DEMANDED AS she pulled the string on the floor lamp beside her, illuminating herself and Yasmina on the couch.

Liv about jumped out of her skin. "Oh my *god*," she said, closing the front door behind her. "Why were you two sitting in the dark? What is this, an intervention? Sorry I'm late for curfew, Mom and Dad."

Marie looked to Yasmina. "I'm Daddy, by the way," she joked.

"Very funny," Yasmina said. "But we're not here to make jokes. We're here with rules of engagement."

Liv dumped her purse on the floor and took a weary seat in the armchair across from Yasmina and Liv. "I'm not going to negotiate on this one," she said.

"We know," Marie and Yasmina said in unison.

"Rule number one," Yasmina began. "You're not allowed to shut us out on this one, if you want to stay in this house."

"Girls, I won't be—"

"No," Yasmina said sharply. "I have the talking stick right now. Rule number two, we will love and support you, whatever you decide to do because you're our best friend. And we would be aunt—"

Marie shot Yasmina a withering look. In their strategizing session, they agreed to be supportive, but Marie demanded no romanticizing of the pregnancy. *Yet.*

"Rule number three," Marie interjected. "If you choose to do this, you are *not* getting prenatal care in Florida. And you'll let me oversee all of your doctor's recommendations."

"Rule number four," Liv said. "No one is going to try to talk me out of this. My mind is made up. And I can do it with or without you."

Liv's eyes welled with tears. "But I'd really prefer to do it with you."

At that, both Yasmina and Marie stood from the couch to embrace Liv. She wept there in their huddle, tears of fear and heartbreak and happiness, and gratitude for the support of her friends, even if it was less than perfect.

Liv pulled her head back from the group. "But you might take back your offer to have me stay in the house when I drop this bomb on you."

"Oh boy."

"My mother will be here in a few days."

"Oh *Jesus*," Marie slapped her forehead. "We have a whole damn sitcom on our hands."

Liv glanced at Beth's famous cheesecake, nearly finished in the old brick oven of Marie's kitchen. Liv's belly had not yet begun to show enough for anyone to notice, but she instinctively smoothed a loving hand over her stomach, then pulled off her apron.

Marie rounded the kitchen corner warbling "White Christmas" along with Bing Crosby and moved to pull open the oven.

"Wait!" Liv stopped her. "Beth is *extremely* particular about the crust."

"Wouldn't want to interfere with Beth's kitchen," Marie teased.

"Where is my mom, anyway?"

"In your room, Facetiming with *Wayne*."

Liv rolled her eyes, sharing Marie's distaste for the man. Mother and daughter had avoided any conversation about that divisive figure, but each night, Beth slunk away to speak with him, like a teenager hiding a sweetheart.

And despite his intrusions, and the initial apprehension of everyone involved about packing four women with big personalities into the old Hollywood bungalow, the last few weeks had passed as idyllically as possible, given the circumstances. Beth's unrelenting cheeriness about the baby had ground down Marie and Yasmina's resolve in short order, and soon, all the women were aflame with baby fever, tittering over tiny clothes and gadgets and arguing about gender predictions. In fact, the idea of the baby became a rallying force among the women, as though Liv's love for the thing alone could vanquish the cancer inside her.

Now, on Christmas Eve, the four were united in joy. A modest Christmas tree in Marie's living room stood completely dwarfed by a mountain of presents from and for each of them, especially the baby. Marie had decided to stay home for the holidays and avoid the cold patrician gaze of her family, but she relished the pomp and circumstance of Western Christmas. With the waft from the oven sweetening the air, Liv could go through the motions of domestic bliss, even as her heart stung for want of Damon.

Liv shook off the latest pang. She could hide it from her friends but not herself.

"I'll go get Mom," Liv said as she made for the back door.

"Liv, wait…" she said quietly. "I hate to bring it up. But I have to ask. Still nothing from Damon?"

"No," Liv lied.

In truth, she'd received a spattering of requests to talk via text and voicemail, but she left these unanswered.

"But I'm glad," she lied again. "I don't want to see him and give him another opportunity to try to talk me out of this."

That last bit was the truth.

"I understand," Marie said solemnly. "I'm sorry I asked."

"It's okay."

Liv crossed the backyard and moved to turn the doorknob but stopped when she heard Wayne's voice on speakerphone through the open window. She couldn't help but eavesdrop.

"Please, try to understand, baby," Beth pled with him in a broken voice.

"What is there to understand?" he asked. "This isn't what I signed up for. She's a grown woman. I need you. I'm here on Christmas Eve eating a goddamn TV dinner!"

"She's my only daughter."

"And I'm the only man who loves you at your age! And size."

Now Liv swung open the door, wrathful.

Beth waved her away, but Liv crossed the small bedroom in two strides and tried to seize the phone from Beth's hand.

Beth clicked "End" on the call with uncommon dexterity.

"Mom," Liv said quietly. She wrapped her arms around her mother, cradling her as she began to sniffle like a child.

Beside them on the bed, Beth's phone began to buzz again.

"Don't answer that," Liv said.

Beth buried her head in her hands. "He's just stressed," she offered.

"That's not stress. Mom, how can you let him talk to you like that?"

"He loves me."

Liv shook her head. "That's not love."

"I don't want to be alone, Liv. I'm not as strong as you are. Having this baby all by yourself. Sticking to your guns," she said and cupped her daughter's face in her palm. "I admire you so much. I did one thing right. The best thing I ever did."

Liv placed her own hand on the back of her mother's.

"You are as strong as I am, Mom. Where do you think I got it from?"

Beth shook her head and stared at the headboard. "I have no idea."

33.

DAMON KNOCKED ON MARIE's back house door on the rare chilly—for Los Angeles—afternoon of January sixth. Christmas and New Year's had come and gone, and the only reason Damon knew that Liv was still in town was by driving passed Marie's house to see her car parked outside.

Nobody came to the door, so Damon glanced at the Ring camera doorbell.

"Please, Liv. I know you can see me on your phone."

Indeed, inside the living room, Liv sat against the couch, staring at Damon's visage on the Ring app. She'd managed to avoid his calls and texts and informed her mother and Marie and Yasmina not to respond to his check-ins to them. But here he was, at her doorstep, carrying some sort of soft briefcase. She noticed his hair was growing faster than hers but remembering why he'd cut it just brought pangs of guilt to her heart. Damon certainly had responded to her chemo better than Christopher. And her anger at his initial hesitation about having the baby had eased *some*… She understood in an intellectual way that she might have pushed him away out of fear he would try to convince her not to have the baby. But emotionally, she was still so confused and afraid to let him in enough to actually have what he deserved—a conversation—because she was so convinced it would only end in even worse confrontation and heartbreak.

But she just couldn't trust herself or him. So, she closed her eyes and muted the call.

Outside, however, Damon was resolute.

He walked around to the front of the main house. He raised a hand to knock on the door, but it swung open before his fist could connect.

In the doorway stood Marie and Beth.

"Beth, Marie. Please. I need to speak with her."

"She's hiding," Marie volunteered, a note of apology in her voice.

But Beth was fiercer. "I'm sorry, Damon. She doesn't want to see you. She's having my grandbaby, and she won't be convinced otherwise."

Damon cleared his throat and made no attempt to hide his look beyond their shoulders, searching for a sign of where she might be.

"Fine," he said loudly, projecting for an unseen Liv. "Liv, I'm just going to talk here."

He sat a black briefcase at his feet and opened his phone to refer to his Notes app as he spoke.

"You don't have to come out, but I hope you'll listen and finally believe that I love you more than life itself. And that not only do I support your decision completely, but I will be the best father to our child that you can dream of. Long after you have left, I will be our boy or girl's protector. I will teach them everything you want them to learn, so that they will know and love you as I do."

Damon took a breath and reached into his jacket. "First of all, our baby will not be born to a single, unwed mother."

He took out a black velvet box and held it high in the air, over the heads of Marie and Beth, who stood agape. "Can you guess what this is?" he called out into the foyer.

Damon opened the box and pulled out a platinum ring with a classic cut diamond, then got to one knee. "Liv, will you please marry me?"

There was no answer, and Damon's voice began to shake with anxiety. Marie and Beth exchanged shocked looks.

He stood and put the ring back in the box. "I'll hold onto that until you're ready to talk to me," he said, somewhat more quietly.

Then he leaned down, opened the briefcase, and pulled out a thick set of documents. "Next, to show you how little going back to work means to me, these are the executed copies of my sale of the club."

Damon found the signature page and held it again above his hand. "See the signatures?" he acknowledged Beth and Marie. "For the next year and beyond, I have nothing to distract me from our child's birth or from being a full-time dad."

Damon thought he could hear a stirring in the kitchen, but no one came, so he put the papers back into the briefcase and produced another set held together by clips. "Now, if that's not enough to show you my dedication, consider this: it's the transfer deed to my house, which I managed to find a buyer to pay in cash with a fifteen-day escrow. They even bought the furniture, so I'll be moving out in the next two days."

"Damon, this is too much," Marie whispered as a pit of dread opened in her stomach for this man before her who had well and truly risked it all.

Damon raised his voice again. "I suppose you're wondering what kind of father I'd be if we had no place to live, huh? Well, check your phone. I'm sending you a picture of the new house I bought for us. Where I think we should have our baby. Where I'd like to raise the baby with your mother's help..."

Damon glanced to Beth, who was nodding up and down quickly.

Damon pushed send on a message already cued up.

He opened his mouth to go on but realized he had come to the end of his list. That was it.

He'd pulled out all the stops.

He had nothing left to offer, and she still hadn't come.

Damon's heart fell through his ass.

Then he heard a scream from inside.

"Oh my *God*!"

Damon's smile spread from ear to ear as Liv pushed through the middle of her bodyguards.

In sweatpants, red-cheeked and breathless, she turned her phone screen to face Damon.

Filling the screen was the Florida beach house they'd rented for Liv's birthday.

"You bought this?" Liv asked, searching Damon's face.

He nodded. "For us. For you and the baby, if you still think I don't want it. It's fully paid for and in your name, so you could never speak to me again and you and the baby will always have a place to live. I also set up a trust, so, again, if you want to do this alone, our baby will never have to worry about money."

Liv started to cry through breaths. "Damon, I can't believe you did this. Any of this."

"Well, they say actions speak louder than words. And you weren't listening anyway, so I had to show you. And it only scratches the surface of how much I love you, support you, and love the child we'll have together."

Liv wiped her nose with her sweatshirt sleeve. "Sorry."

"Here," Damon said, handing her a white handkerchief from his pocket.

She laughed. "Smart to have this handy."

"It was actually for me; in case you sent me away."

"Can I just say something for one second?" Marie interjected.

Three faces turned to her.

"Oh my *fucking* God!" she squealed.

"Language!" admonished Beth.

"Can we—can we get some privacy for a second?" Liv asked the women, who nodded and scampered away like schoolgirls.

"Damon," she went on. "Do you know what I've been doing since I got back here?"

"Other than getting your car booted?"

Liv smirked. "Have you been stalking us?"

"Only occasionally."

"Well, I can't blame you. I've been locked up in here, cursing myself for pushing you away. Honestly, if it weren't for this baby, and the girls being completely in my business, I would have killed myself with sleeping pills."

The thought made Damon grim. "Does that mean yes?"

"To which part?"

"Well, let's start with this," he said, pulling out the ring box again. "Will you marry me?"

Liv moved closer to Damon to kiss him, both of their eyes closing as they connected.

"Till death do us part," she said as she drew back to breathe.

"Longer, much longer."

Damon removed the ring and placed it on her finger. "How does it fit?"

"Like it was made for my finger. How did you do that?"

Damon blushed. "Lucky guess. But I do have two other sizes in my briefcase. Just in case."

Liv laughed and held the hand with the ring to her heart. "I can't believe you sold the club!"

"I told you I was ready. I just didn't want to make the decision unless you signed off."

I do! I do! Liv thought, but knew she owed him an apology before anything. "Damon, I am so sorry I didn't give you the chance to make this decision with me. If you treated me the way I treated you, I'd never forgive you."

"It's been a rough month," Damon admitted. "But nothing like what you must be going through."

Liv shook her head. "I've missed you. But honestly, having this baby has been a blessing. I feel like I have something to live for, even if it's not as long as what I might have."

"We still have a fight ahead of us," Damon pointed out.

"But it's us now. Us is always stronger than me."

Damon ran a hand through her hair, now a stylish pixie cut. "And your mother, apparently."

Liv laughed at herself. "And I thought I could drive my lemon to Florida."

"Speaking of, we'd better fly to Florida quickly, because I won't have a place to live here tomorrow."

"I'm going to miss your house."

"Not a place for a child. Or you while pregnant. We need somewhere with less stairs and near your mother."

"How did you know the owners of the beach house would sell?"

"They weren't enthusiastic until they saw my offer."

Liv laughed. "You certainly spend your money on important things."

"I spend it on you. And the baby. The only things that matter to me in this world."

"That's all I wanted to hear."

Damon kissed her, then went to pick her up. "Should we indulge the girls with a romantic display?"

Liv giggled ferociously as Damon carried her into the living room and dipped her down into a kiss, which Marie and Beth applauded while squealing.

ALONE IN BED, with Liv gone at Damon's for a final night in their house, Beth bit her lip and stared at the ceiling. She felt overwhelmed with joy for the luck of her daughter, and her only dark cloud was the contrast of Damon's behavior against that of her own significant other.

Beth mouthed a prayer at the ceiling for strength.

Then she took her phone, and sent a simple, two-word text to Wayne:

It's over.

34.

The speed at which Liv and Damon packed for the move was astonishing. Beth, seeking to distract herself from worry about what state her home might be in from the aftermath of a wrathful Wayne, volunteered to organize and pack Liv's belongings that were at Marie's house.

Damon had dozens of large boxes delivered to Marie's and to his house. It only took half of the first day for Liv and him to pack her clothes, made easier by her desire to forgo bringing anything else of sentimental value; dishes and blankets, even art and photographs that lined the wall, stayed. She wanted the next year to be the beginning of something beautiful, a fresh start.

They arranged for Liv's car to be picked up by a charity they'd donated it to in the next few days, and, in the interest of expediency, Damon sold his Tesla at a ridiculously low price. He assured Liv he had a new car waiting for them at the Florida house—"something more appropriate for a family" was all he'd say.

Damon's clothes fit into even less boxes; that night, the only things of value left to pack were his guitar and the jar of seashells.

"We'll return the shells to where they belong!" Liv said as they had—what else—*Poulet Sans Nom* outside. The house lights were off and only the firepit and stars lit the balmy night sky.

"That's a nice thought," Damon agreed.

"Don't pack the guitar yet," Liv suggested.

Damon saw her trying to conceal a sly grin. "What's going on?"

"I want to use the recording studio one more time. It's probably the last time I'll ever be in one."

Damon was astonished. "What do you want to record?"

"You'll see."

She headed down the hall, Damon beside her, guitar out of its case.

When they entered the studio, Damon went into the recording booth. Liv remembered how to prepare the mixing board to record, then surprised Damon by joining him in the booth.

"We're recording together?" he asked as he quickly got her a chair so she could face him and adjusted the microphone between them.

Liv smiled and the waterworks began.

"What's wrong, baby?"

"Nothing. I'm just so in love with you. Even when I pushed you away, you were all I thought about. I kept listening to the song you wrote for me over and over…and the lyrics started coming to me."

"No!"

Liv burst out in nervous laughter. "You have to promise to tell me if you hate it, and to *never* let anyone else hear it without my permission."

"Of course. You want me to read them first?"

"Nope. Just play and I'll sing. And don't stop, even if one of us flubs something. I barely have the courage to do it once."

"It's your song," Damon said, strumming and tuning his strings some.

"I think I might have made it the baby's song. That's the title. 'Baby's Song.'"

Damon covered his mouth with his left hand.

"Keep it together for me, okay? So I don't lose it," Liv pled as she opened her phone to a note where the lyrics were typed out.

"I'll do my best."

Damon started to play the melody, softly so he could hear Liv's voice—melodic and honey sweet.

"*Two were born for one,*

One is born for two.

Three become like one,

A lifetime left to do."

Damon played without looking at his hands, gazing instead at Liv's face, made soft by the dim, orange studio light.

"*Our child who may not know me,*

Forgive the time I could not give you.

Your father will tell you all I did see,

All I hope for you, all I knew."

Liv stared at Damon as he played, ignoring her notes as if she'd sung this a hundred times.

"Love creates while life fades,
Giving meaning to every kiss.
Giving reason for your days,
Never forgetting this.
Two were born for one, one is born for two."

Damon's couldn't hold his tears in as he played a light solo.

Liv smiled at him as she finished her last verse, then began weeping. "Is it okay?"

"It's beautiful. And I thought you were holed up in your apartment, too angry to think about me."

"No, just to talk to you."

Damon put the guitar down, got up and walked to her. He drew her head to his chest, right over his heart. "I'm sorry."

"I'm sorrier," she answered.

"Not possible."

THEY CALLED IT A "going away" party despite the fact that it was only a party of five. At sunset on their final night, Beth, Yasmina, Marie, Liv, and Damon gathered in the backyard of his house.

"Couldn't you have offered a thirty-day escrow?" Liv teased Damon as they walked to the front door to greet their guests.

"It was a grand gesture, what can I say?"

"The most romantic ever. And I feel amazing being off the hormone meds, even if I'm dying. I feel stronger than I have in years."

Damon didn't balk at her morbid language this time. He was learning to accept Liv's changing moods, shutting down, then laughing about everything as a pattern he should love, not just tolerate.

"That's irony for you," he answered as he opened the door.

"Liv!" screamed Yasmina as she and Marie rushed inside, into a three-way hug with her.

Beth followed close behind, carrying a boxed cake.

"Come in, please," said Damon, ushering them toward the living room, where champagne and caviar was set up on the dining table.

Marie couldn't help but quip sardonically, "I can't believe you're trading this for a beach house in *Florida.*"

"I'm sure it's not a shack, Marie," said Yasmina.

"It's heaven on earth," Liv answered. "Maybe you'll come visit?"

"Absolutely!" Damon added as he poured champagne into crystal flutes.

Damon handed them each a glass and held up his. "To the future. I'd say 2021 has to be better than 2020, but meeting Liv was a silver lining that made it the best year of my life."

"Cheers," they said, sipping.

As the girls launched into chattering, Damon put down his glass and looked at the house that had been his home for years, and a temple for him and Liv during the pandemic. That was far from over, but with people starting to get vaccines and death rates falling, he was no longer worried that Covid meant the end of civilization. Millions around the world had died, but the dire predictions in those books he'd read a year ago had been managed by quarantines and masks. Politicians would debate their efficacy until they turned blue; in the end, there was no doubt that science had won.

It was hard for Damon not to be sentimental about leaving this house, but he understood that beyond the times he'd spent here with Liv, it had for many years been a playground of sorts. Before finding Liv, he buried his fear of being alone in throwing parties and bringing home women who, like the house, were beautiful, but more for play than love. He'd grown out of his extended childhood and Damon was happy to be moving on to a new, more adult and responsible place.

He thought of a conversation he'd had when helping Liv pack. Overwhelmed with nostalgia and sentiment, she had explained that she too had used it as a cave to hide in. As Damon had feared being alone, she'd feared opening up and trusting other people.

Damon didn't know what the next year would look like. The doctors believed Liv would live long enough to have their baby, but the time she would have to share the joys of motherhood was less certain. How would Damon deal with the tragic loss that was certain to come? And how long would it be before he was raising their child on his own?

The answers were mysteries to him, and he'd have to accept living with uncertainty, fear, and heartbreak. Because he loved that woman more than he ever thought was possible.

35.

THOUGH LIV'S EARS BUZZED from the constant cacophony of jigsaw sawing and hammering, she smiled as she made a grilled cheese sandwich in the kitchen.

She turned off the stovetop, flipped the sandwich onto a plate, picked up a glass of iced tea from beside the pitcher, then carried the lot through the beach house. The house hadn't changed much since they'd arrived a few weeks ago, or even from how it had been when they'd first come here. But the difference was obvious as she walked into the smallest of the three bedrooms which Damon was renovating himself.

"What do you think?" Damon asked as Liv hand-fed him a bite of sandwich.

She glanced around: the tacky wallpaper had been stripped bare, the walls sanded, and Damon was in the middle of building a dresser with a flat top for changing diapers.

"I think the carpenter look is sexy on you."

He laughed as he looked down at his dirty overalls, gloved hands caked in sawdust. "I'll be painting in a few days, so we'd better decide if we want masculine or feminine colors."

Liv put the sandwich plate down and helped him sip the iced tea. "I already told you; I think it's a girl. But we should cover our bases with neutral—everything white with light gray accents."

"We're in no rush. I can always hold off until June. I read the fifth month is when they can tell us the baby's sex."

"Will you hate me if I don't find out?"

"Of course not, but you're not curious?"

"I'm dying to know if I'm right!"

Damon frowned at the use of the word "dying."

"Sorry, no pun intended," Liv said. "But seriously, it will give me just another thing to fight for. I want that moment where the baby comes out and is handed to you, and you tell me if it's a boy or girl."

"Love the way you think. By the way, I found a nurse. She's supposed to a home birth genius, and she says she can order all the equipment to monitor the stress on your heart."

"Thank you, honey. And you're okay with my mother moving in for the last few months?"

"Of course. But I wish you'd stop saying things like 'last few months.'"

"I'm sorry, I'll be more careful with my words. I guess I'm just at peace with the inevitable."

Damon took his gloves off. "You want the truth? Liv, your doctors said you might not even live to see the baby born. The last trimester is going to put that much stress on your heart. So don't be at peace with death. Chemo or not, I need you to fight death with every breath."

Liv's face softened. "I will. I will."

BETH STRODE ALONG THE SAND, Liv in the center with Damon on her other side. They'd all agreed she would spend a week at the house every month until the last one or two, then she'd move in for as long as Liv needed her. Or as long as Damon and their baby needed her.

But today was a perfect one, with nothing to worry about. The beach was isolated, the waves lapping gently. Damon and Liv wore bathing suits and as soon as their skin warmed, they would jump into the ocean and swim like playful children.

Damon wore shorts with deep pockets, and as they walked, he would empty a few shells from the jar onto the sand.

And Liv was in a hopeful mood; a few days prior, they'd driven down to Jacksonville, where an OBYGN had given her an ultrasound and some genetic testing—the baby's sex was still a mystery, but it was healthy. Liv could only hope that the birth would be as smooth.

AFTER BETH WENT HOME, one evening, the fire at its peak, the sound of small waves gently lapping on the sand, Damon and Liv sat on the Adirondack chairs.

They stared contently into the dark, dotted with stars so many of which could only be seen this far away from a city.

"Guess it's time we make our marriage official," Liv said quietly.

Damon smiled, pleased, and thought out loud.

"Can't exactly have a big wedding. Between our friends being on the West Coast, and the jab still months away from being available to us."

"I don't even need a wedding," Liv said. "I just want the legal stuff done, so the baby and me will have your name."

Damon bobbed his head. "I'll have my lawyers file and send us the papers to sign."

"Thank you."

Liv turned pensive.

"Something else you want?" Damon asked.

"Mm hmm. But you're not gonna like talking about it."

"I'm ready."

"First, when I go, you'll keep contact with Marie and Yasmina."

Damon took a sharp breath to hold in his emotions. Neither of them liked conversations about the hereafter of things, but when parceled out, it could be done without being morose.

"Don't worry," he answered. "I love both of them and will make sure they're always a part of our family."

"Thank you. Now here's the big one: whatever happens, I don't want to die in a hospital."

Damon squinted, indicating he wanted more information.

"I'm saying that no matter how sick I get," Liv continued, "the only reason to take me to a hospital is if the baby is in danger. And even then, I want a first DNR."

Damon nodded through his reluctance. "If that's what you want. But why? They could make you more comfortable..."

Liv looked up at the almost full moon, choking up. "I don't want to die hooked up to machines and make you have to decide how long to keep me from going. I want to die here, in your arms. I want you to lift me out of bed, carry me out onto the sand and hold me. I want the last things I see to be my baby's face and your face. I want to feel you kissing me as I go."

Damon dropped his tearful face and stared at the sand.

"And I want to know that you'll be okay," Liv continued. "You can mourn for a few months, six tops."

Damon had to laugh; he loved how Liv could lighten a conversation on a dime.

She went on in the same tone. "By then I'm sure you'll be vaccinated, so I want you to move somewhere. Keep this place for weekends. Miami would be great. Mom's close but not too close. My God—you, a single dad—talk about eligible bachelors!"

Damon rubbed his eyes, as if thinking that far into his own future was torture.

"And that song of ours," Liv added. "Only you and the baby get to listen to it. Not even my mother. It's just for us, so don't go getting some stupid idea of trying to release it. I don't want my career resurrected after I'm dead. So cliché."

Damon chuckled. "I was thinking about sending it to a few record producers."

"See! I know you too well. You're so thoughtful I've learned to be careful what I ask for."

"I promise. Only me and…"

He paused, making Liv curious. "What?"

"Well, I guess we should talk about names."

"Right. Do you have any ideas?"

"Not a clue. But I bet you have them already picked out."

Liv grinned. "I like Dylan for a boy. Sort of a hybrid between Liv and Damon."

"I like that! And if he's a she?"

"Actually, Dylan still works."

"You're right! That was easy."

"For you maybe. I've been driving myself crazy over names for weeks. Oh! And when Dylan's old enough, I want the two of you to go to all the places you wanted to take me. Europe, Africa, Asia, South America…"

"I get the picture. There will be no part of the world Dylan doesn't see."

Liv smiled, then turned contemplative again. "Dylan should know her or his brother, Rand."

Damon understood her fear. "Don't worry, Liv. Our child will have a family."

"Lastly, you have to promise not to cry when I'm dying in your arms."

"Considering I'm barely holding it together now, I'm not sure I can promise that."

"You'd turn down a dying woman's last wish?"

Damon took a deep breath to fortify himself. "The last thing you see will be me and your child smiling at you."

"Thank you. Okay, talk over. Let's go make love. I'm going to need a lot of that before I get fat and ugly."

"I got news for you," Damon said, "I'm among the men who find a pregnant woman sexy."

"Prove it…"

Liv took Damon by the hand and pulled him off the chair and into the house.

36.

"CAN YOU BELIEVE that it's been a year since we met?' Liv asked as she walked the line where the water had last come up to the sand.

"Only days before the pandemic hit," Damon added, strolling beside her with his hand in hers.

"You knew we'd be more than just roommates, didn't you?" she teased for the hundredth time.

"I hoped. But I never expected we'd fall in love, and that you'd change me from a cold-hearted player into a sniveling poet."

"You don't snivel! You're a romantic poet."

Damon laughed as he turned so Liv was silhouetted against the morning sun. "Hey, I think you're showing!"

"Really?"

Liv pulled her silk sundress against her midriff. "I have a bump!"

She gleefully ran into Damon's arms.

"Can you feel Dylan kick?" Damon asked.

"They say I won't for another month, but I swear I feel something going on in there."

"What does it feel like?"

Liv searched for the perfect description. "Like someone is dancing inside me."

"And you call me the poet!"

She laughed. "I'm no poet. But being with you has changed me, too, you know."

"How's that?"

"I was so cynical and closed off when I met you. I swear, for the first month I just wanted you for the sex."

"Oh, come on."

"Okay, so your no-sex rule definitely contributed to that. And I was afraid of being alone too. I'd just given up on men and was waiting to die."

Damon laughed, then leaned down to collect a shell and slid it into his shorts pocket.

"You know, we were supposed to be putting the shells back on the beach," Liv said. "But every time I walk by our jar, there's even more inside than the day before."

"What can I say, I'm a jar-half-full kind of guy."

Liv smiled as if she had no care in the world. "Here, this one's beautiful."

She bent down and picked out a shell, polished blue with white specks, sparkling from water and sun.

Damon put it in his pocket, then reached out and took Liv by the hand.

"I love you," Liv said.

"I love you more," Damon answered.

Liv smiled. "Not possible."

Hands tethered, they strolled along the sand. For miles ahead of them the beach was just rolling dunes, the few sparsely developed houses behind them fading away. For Liv and Damon, the last year had been one of love and illness. But together, they had stripped away the masks they'd worn, over their faces and their hearts, and all they felt was love.

THE END.